Caught in the Rain

With a swift movement, Tobin lifted her into his arms. "I'll get you through the mud and to the back porch."

"Thank you, Mr. McMurray," she whispered, leaning her cheek against his shoulder, feeling the warmth of his body through wet clothes.

A moment later they were back in the rain. His arms held her tightly as he ran for the house. Circling her arms around his neck, she did what she'd done when they'd been riding, she hung on tightly.

When they reached the porch, he set her down gently and put a blanket around her shoulders.

Liberty snuggled into it, laughing. "Thanks," she said, looking up at him. "But you're dripping wet also."

She circled her arms once more around him, enclosing him within the blanket.

For a moment he stood still, letting the heat from their bodies blend. Then he lowered his mouth to hers and his hands closed over the sides of her ribs and pulled her hard against him.

Praise for the "Queen of Texas Romance" *

"Packs a powerful emotional punch . . . [Thomas's] latest Western historical romance highlights the author's talent for creating genuinely real characters . . . Exceptional."

—*Booklist*

*Midwest Book Review

continued . . .

TEXAS PRINCESS

JODI THOMAS

BERKLEY BOOKS, NEW YORK

THE BERKLEY PUBLISHING GROUP
Published by the Penguin Group
Penguin Group (USA) Inc.
375 Hudson Street, New York, New York 10014, USA
Penguin Group (Canada), 90 Eglinton Avenue East, Suite 700, Toronto, Ontario M4P 2Y3, Canada
(a division of Pearson Penguin Canada Inc.)
Penguin Books Ltd., 80 Strand, London WC2R 0RL, England
Penguin Group Ireland, 25 St. Stephen's Green, Dublin 2, Ireland (a division of Penguin Books Ltd.)
Penguin Group (Australia), 250 Camberwell Road, Camberwell, Victoria 3124, Australia
(a division of Pearson Australia Group Pty. Ltd.)
Penguin Books India Pvt. Ltd., 11 Community Centre, Panchsheel Park, New Delhi—110 017, India
Penguin Group (NZ), 67 Apollo Drive, Rosedale, North Shore 0632, New Zealand
(a division of Pearson New Zealand Ltd.)
Penguin Books (South Africa) (Pty.) Ltd., 24 Sturdee Avenue, Rosebank, Johannesburg 2196,
South Africa

Penguin Books Ltd., Registered Offices: 80 Strand, London WC2R 0RL, England

This is a work of fiction. Names, characters, places, and incidents either are the product of the author's imagination or are used fictitiously, and any resemblance to actual persons, living or dead, business establishments, events, or locales is entirely coincidental.

TEXAS PRINCESS

A Berkley Book / published by arrangement with the author

PRINTING HISTORY
Berkley edition / November 2007

Copyright © 2007 by Jodi Koumalats.
Excerpt from *Twisted Creek* by Jodi Thomas copyright © 2008 by Jodi Koumalats.
Cover illustration by Jim Griffin.
Cover handlettering by Ron Zinn.
Cover design by George Long.

ISBN: 978-0-425-21825-9

BERKLEY®
Berkley Books are published by The Berkley Publishing Group,
a division of Penguin Group (USA) Inc.,
375 Hudson Street, New York, New York 10014.
BERKLEY® is a registered trademark of Penguin Group (USA) Inc.
The "B" design is a trademark belonging to Penguin Group (USA) Inc.

PRINTED IN THE UNITED STATES OF AMERICA

10 9 8 7 6 5 4 3 2 1

CHAPTER 1

Whispering Mountain Ranch
Texas Hill Country
September 1855

TOBIN MCMURRAY WALKED OUT OF THE BARN JUST as first light promised dawn. He rolled his tired shoulders. The imaginary weight he had carried for three days remained. Sunrise wouldn't change what he had to do; nothing would.

His sister, Sage, stepped onto the wide back porch of the family's ranch house and stared at him. He knew she was waiting for an answer. He could see the hope in her brown eyes, along with tears she wouldn't let fall. Almost nineteen, he thought, and she still believed in miracles. At twenty-five, Tobin wasn't sure he ever had.

He moved toward the house knowing they only had one chance left to save Glory, and in order to do so he'd have to complete the journey he hated most in this world.

He hadn't reached the porch when she asked, "Any change?"

Tobin didn't want to see hope fade in those eyes that always reminded him of their mother. He'd made her leave the barn stall at midnight, but she didn't look like she'd slept. "I can't even get Glory to stand," he said as he stepped beside his little sister and circled her shoulders with one arm. "I'll ride into town when it gets full light, but if the medicine's not at Elmo's place, we'll have to put her down."

Huge tears bubbled onto her cheeks. "Oh, Tobin, you can't. Glory's the first horse I ever rode. She's so smart, I swear she knew how green I was from the first day she saw me. Remember how she used to bow down a little so I could reach the stirrup."

He held Sage as she silently cried. "I know," he whispered, "but I can't stand to see her in so much pain."

They moved into the kitchen and drank Martha's strong morning coffee. The housekeeper made breakfast, but Tobin couldn't eat. He'd dreaded this day since they'd found Glory lying in the dirt of the corral three mornings ago. Glory had been his mother's horse until Autumn McMurray died giving birth to Sage. Tobin and his brothers had kept the mare gentle until Sage grew old enough to ride; then Glory had been Sage's favorite. The McMurrays raised horses. Others were faster, stronger, but when Sage wanted to outrun her worries by galloping over their land, she always saddled Glory.

Tobin had a true gift with horses, but he couldn't stop an animal from aging and he seriously doubted any medicine his brother Travis sent from Austin would help. Glory had been sickly last winter, and Tobin had seen it in the mare's eyes again this fall, felt it when he stroked her neck . . . her spirit was fading, and as his Apache grandfather would say, "It was time for her to run across new land."

But the medicine Travis said he mailed was one last thing to try, and Tobin would attempt even the impossible to keep his little sister from crying. She'd already shed enough tears.

By the time the sun crested Whispering Mountain, Tobin rode the back way through the hills toward town. Normally, if he'd been riding anywhere else, he would have stayed on the dirt and grass, making it easier on the animal, but this trail was different from any other. Since his father first learned of the path crisscrossing through the hills behind his ranch, Andrew McMurray had taught his sons to ride on the rocks, leaving no trace.

Tobin smiled. He'd been six when his father was killed fighting for Texas's independence, but he could still hear his words. "Protect each other. Trust no outsiders. Hold the ranch. Never let your guard down. Never!" So, today, even in a hurry, he followed orders from a man almost twenty years dead. He covered his tracks and left no sign along the secret entrance to their huge ranch.

At the top of the last hill, before he started descending, he hesitated and turned back for one final look. For as long as he could remember, he'd hated the thought of leaving his land. Even the short trips he sometimes took to deliver horses were painful. This is where his heart lay. He planned to live and die right here. Whispering Mountain was where he belonged. He'd learned that hard lesson when he'd defended the ranch with his life.

Tobin turned his mount and moved on. He told himself he'd long ago lost the fear of people who weren't family. He just didn't like them, didn't want to have anything to do with them. He'd deal with the folks he had to, like Elmo at the trading post, but no stranger would ever get close. If he had his way, Tobin would burn the bridge again at the main entrance as they did when Andrew died . . . only he'd never rebuild it.

As Tobin emerged from the trees that grew at the bottom of the last hill, he looked up in surprise. In the months since he'd ridden to the small settlement around Elmo Anderson's trading post, the community had doubled in size. Elmo's store looked shabby next to all the new wood frames going up. Sage said a stage station was being built and a church, but she forgot to mention the other half-dozen buildings in various phases of completion.

He rode on, hearing the bustle of a growing population even before he could make out faces. Men swarmed like ants over skeletons of wood, while the tapping of hammers played a tuneless melody.

As he slowed his horse and moved in between the lumber piled up along the road, Tobin noticed not all the changes were good. One man had pitched his tent beside his half-finished building and planted a sign that promised a free first drink to all comers. As Tobin passed, he heard a woman's loud laugh and guessed liquor wasn't the only thing sold in the tent.

Mrs. Dickerson, the schoolteacher, had a small sign in front of her place saying she took in respectable female boarders. A few other signs wanted carpentry help. The town was definitely growing but not necessarily improving.

Tying his horse to the back of Elmo's Trading Post, he entered the old store that had served the area for almost twenty-five years. Barrel-chested Elmo greeted him with a nod and motioned for Tobin to step into the area he called his post office. In reality, it wasn't much more than a desk behind a waist-high counter with thin bars separating the space from the rest of Elmo's cluttered stockpile of goods. Atop the desk in the makeshift post office were huge boxes marked Incoming, Outgoing North, and Outgoing South. No mail went east or west from here. If someone wanted to send a letter to New York or California, the letter first went south to Austin.

Looking over the counter toward the trading post, Tobin studied the people. The early morning crowd surprised him. There had to be ten or twelve strangers milling around and several more crowded in the corner where Elmo kept a pot of coffee boiling.

Tobin forced himself not to back against the far wall. People didn't mean trouble, he reminded himself as he had a thousand times since he was six. They were just going about their business same as him. He turned back to the mail.

The incoming box was packed. Tobin began to shuffle through the letters and boxes, having no idea what size post Travis would have shipped from Austin.

Elmo leaned his head around the corner. "You need any help, McMurray? I'm busier than a two-headed snake in a rat's nest."

"No, I'll find it," Tobin answered.

Elmo raised an eyebrow. "Martha didn't happen to send a list with you, did she, boy?"

At six feet, Tobin hadn't considered himself a boy in years, but he was the youngest of the McMurray brothers so he guessed the store owner thought of him as younger. "She didn't." Tobin saw no need to explain further. He'd learned that the more he answered, the more the older man talked.

Elmo disappeared as he called back. "You might check that crate over by the door, McMurray."

Tobin glanced at the open crate. Though it was addressed to Whispering Mountain Ranch, someone had pried two boards up. Tobin wasn't surprised. Elmo's curiosity would someday get him killed, but not over horse medicine.

He pulled the thin bottle from the mass of straw. The crate would be hard to carry home, but the bottle would fit nicely in his coat pocket for the ride. He smiled, guessing Travis's wife had been the one to pack the medicine so carefully. Rainey had a way of taking care of details.

Just as he slipped the bottle inside his coat, he heard someone yell, "So you're the youngest McMurray."

Tobin fought the urge to hurry. Instead, he faced the men crowding along the other side of the counter. They stared at him through the thin bars as if he were an animal on display for their amusement.

The one who'd addressed him was maybe a year or two older than Tobin. He stood several inches shorter, with his shoulders rounded, but he easily outweighed Tobin by twenty pounds. The stump of a man smiled when he saw he had Tobin's attention. "You're the one they say has horse blood in ya."

The other men with him laughed.

"They say you don't talk to nobody but horses." The stout man laughed. "Heard tell you was shot when you was a boy. Fell beside your dead horse and the blood mixed."

A redheaded man on the stranger's left joined in. "That's right, Willie. This is the one. I've heard folks say he can talk to a horse as plain as you and I is talking right now."

Elmo stepped in front of Tobin, holding up his hands. "Now why don't you fellows finish your coffee and get back to work. There ain't nothing wrong with this man. He's just quiet, that's all. Likes to be left alone. There ain't no crime in that."

Tobin took a step backward, toward the door.

The stump man shrugged. "We don't mean nothin'," he mumbled. "We was just being friendly. Tell me, McMurray, is it true you was shot that day in the heart and lived?"

Another man laughed and mumbled, "I hear tell McMurrays ain't got hearts."

Tobin reached the back door. He wasn't running, he was avoiding a fight over nothing. There were already enough reasons in this world to fight without fools inventing new ones.

He remembered once when he'd been about twelve . . . he hadn't run. The ranch hands they'd hired to help build new fences surrounded him one hot afternoon. He'd fought hard, but they'd stripped him to the waist so they could see the scar where he'd been shot in the heart.

When his oldest brother, Teagen, then eighteen, found out what they'd done, he'd fired them all and claimed the ranch would do without fences before McMurrays ever asked for help from the likes of them again.

That summer, Tobin had joined his older brothers in the habit of always wearing a gun. No one would ever force him to do what he didn't want to do again. They'd hired two Apache men to help a month later, and the brothers had worked from sunup to full dark until the fences were in place. The McMurrays rationed their help after that, using men only in the spring, and all three brothers kept the habit of traveling armed.

Tobin slipped from the back door of Elmo's and walked to his horse, glad that he hadn't had to pull his sidearm. He brushed the chest pocket of his coat, making sure the bottle was safe, then stepped into the saddle. He was ready to get back to the hills and away from the stench of too many people.

As he rounded the trading post, he found the cowhands waiting for him. Like hungry coyotes, they scurried off the porch and blocked his way. He counted five on the ground, one on the porch.

The redhead fired a round from his rifle, and the bay Tobin rode danced with panic while the horses close to the porch bolted and galloped away.

"So, tell me," the stout man yelled. "If you got the blood of a horse in you, maybe you got the brains as well?"

Tobin leaned forward, whispering into the bay's ear to calm her. He watched the men spread out, but he still didn't go for his gun. He'd practiced with his brothers and knew he was both fast and accurate, but six-to-one odds would never be good.

The stout man grew braver. "You won't mind if we have a look to see where that bullet went into your chest. Would you, McMurray?"

Tobin bent low across his horse. He had no intention of talking with these men or of stripping like a curiosity for them. "Stand back," he ordered.

The man laughed. "Ain't you all the bossy one now. I heard about how high and mighty you McMurrays all think you are. Just 'cause you own your own hunk of Texas don't make you special."

The stump nodded toward the man on the porch. His friend raised the rifle aimed at Tobin. "Unless you want another bullet hole in that chest, you'll cooperate. It ain't nothing personal. I just got a bet on whether you was really shot as a boy."

Tobin saw no need for further conversation. He leaned closer and whispered into his mount's ear, then gave the animal her head.

The bay bolted through the cowhands as if they were no more than rain. He passed the stout man so fast the cowhand didn't have time to jump out of the way. Tobin saw the man spin and tumble into the steps with a hard thud as a shot rang out from the porch.

Tobin was well away when he felt something thick and warm soaking his shirt. For a moment he thought he'd been shot again. But there was no pain and Tobin would never forget the agony of a bullet firing through him. He pushed harder not daring to slow until he reached cover.

Memories poured into his mind like lava . . . He'd hurt so badly nineteen years ago that even breathing made him fight screams. The bullet must have passed through him, a hair's width from his heart. His horse died beside him that day, with Tobin too injured to help. The men who'd shot them both kept circling, kept firing. He'd gripped his rifle, feeling their bullets hit the horse he hid behind. Blindly, he raised and fired, reloaded, fired again, and again, until finally he heard his brothers calling his name.

Tobin shoved the memory aside. He'd been so young, a lifetime ago, but he still remembered every detail of the day he'd been ambushed. At six he'd almost died.

He pushed harder toward home. Well within the trees, he glanced back to make sure he wasn't followed, then finally pulled the reins. Sliding his fingers into his coat Tobin felt glass cut a thin line along his thumb. He pulled out what remained of the medicine bottle. Glory's last hope.

When he reached the shelter of the rocks, he climbed down near a stream and washed off the medicine. He'd rather face the cowhands again than go back and tell Sage he'd broken the bottle. She'd give up.

He could tell her the mail wasn't there, but she'd find out the truth soon enough. Unlike him, she liked going into town, and on most trips it seemed she talked to everyone she saw.

Climbing back on the bay, he decided there was only one thing left to do. Like his Apache grandfather once told him. "When the truth only brings sorrow, wrap it in the comfort of a lie."

Now all he had to do was think of one before he made it back to Whispering Mountain.

CHAPTER 2

THE NOON SUN BURNED DOWN AS TOBIN RODE INTO the McMurray ranch house yard still trying to think of how he'd explain to his sister about breaking the medicine bottle. If he told the truth, she'd never understand why he ran from a fight, plus she'd be so angry she'd probably ride to town and take on the cowhands on behalf of her brother. He might not want to fight, but none of his siblings shared his hesitance.

He noticed the wagon he'd pulled up near the back porch was gone, telling him that Sage and Martha had carried lunch over to the men working on Travis and Rainey's little cabin in the trees.

When his brother married a few months ago, everyone thought the new bride and groom would stay in Travis's room when they were home from Austin. But the newly-weds' first visit convinced Travis that having them stay in his small room was a bad idea. Between his wife's walking in on Tobin almost nude and Teagen's complaining about the noises after midnight, there was no doubt the couple needed a place of their own.

Travis picked a spot in a clearing surrounded by pecan trees and well out of hearing distance of the main house. They slept on the ground for three nights before Travis decided exactly where he wanted his new home. Rainey drew up the plans, and he started building. A week later he was called back to Austin to help with a trial, but he sent a couple men to get the job done as fast as possible.

The workers were well trained and no trouble. They slept in a tent beside the construction. The only problem seemed to be that Travis promised meals, and they had a habit of eating three times a day. The bunkhouse cook, who came every spring to cook for any hands, had retired to Galveston, leaving Martha and Sage to prepare meals for any men working on the ranch. Martha swore she'd have the grassland to the site worn to dirt by the time the men finished Travis and Rainey's house, even though she only delivered their three meals once a day.

Tobin looked in the direction of the clearing but couldn't see the wagon returning. He jumped from his horse and headed straight for the barn.

Glory lay in her stall, just as she'd been when he left. Her pale yellow-brown mane blended with straw. It seemed as if she were vanishing a little more every time he saw her.

"Hey, pretty palomino." Tobin whispered the greeting he'd used for her all his life. "You want to stand up and say hello?"

Her ears twitched, but she didn't move.

He slid his hand along her sleek neck. The handkerchief he'd used to bandage his thumb was now soaked in blood, but Tobin hardly noticed the wound. If Glory didn't move soon, he knew she'd be dead.

"Come on, pretty girl, stand up for me." He rubbed his hand down her long nose wishing he had just a little of the medicine left.

When his hand crossed the end of her nose, she snorted and opened her eyes.

Tobin smiled. "Morning." He moved his fingers over her

once more, and she snorted again when she breathed in his bloody bandage.

He unwrapped his hand and let her smell the fresh blood.

Glory huffed her disapproval.

He gripped her head, making her smell again as a few crimson drops splattered over her.

She jerked away, but he kept his hand against her nose. "You hate that smell, don't you, pretty girl?" If he couldn't get her to react to kind words, maybe it was time to make her mad. He released his hold, but kept his bloody hand close so if she breathed in, she'd be smelling blood.

For a second, he swore he saw anger in her wild eyes. He offered no words to calm her as he usually did.

She pulled back, raising her head and mane out of the straw. A moment later Glory stood on all four legs and jerked her head out of his reach.

Tobin laughed. "It's all right, pretty girl. You don't have to smell that anymore." He wrapped his thumb, then lifted her water bucket with his unharmed hand. "How about we start with a little water for breakfast?"

She smelled the water, hesitated, then drank. The water splashed across the end of her nose washing away Tobin's blood.

He'd just fed her oats when he heard Sage. "Tobin!" she called as she strode into the barn. "I'm so glad you—" She walked around the end of the stall and froze. "Oh, Tobin, it worked. It worked."

Tobin nodded as Sage took over the care of her horse. He stepped back and watched as his little sister babied the big animal as though they were best friends. He felt like he'd tried everything to make Glory better, but he hadn't tried anger.

"The medicine's all gone." He stayed with the truth.

"It doesn't matter," Sage answered as she began brushing Glory down. "She's better. That's what counts."

Shrugging, he walked toward the house. He'd never understand females, even the four-legged kind. That's one reason he never planned to marry. If he had to live with a woman, be around one all the time, his brain would probably explode from trying to figure her out. People in general confused him, but women seemed to have their own brand of mystery.

Once, several years back, when Sage had been running around yelling at them and crying over nothing, Teagen had demanded to know what was wrong with her. Martha shook her head and, after wishing they had a parent to talk to, said that Sage had gotten Eve's Curse. The brothers sat on the porch for an hour trying to figure out what Eve's Curse was and hoping it wasn't catching. They finally elected Tobin to go back in the kitchen and ask Martha more about the strange disease. He'd barely got the first question out when she thumped him on the head with her flour-covered wooden spoon. End of discussion.

Martha now met him at the back door as his steps creaked across the porch. Tobin couldn't keep from smiling at the old housekeeper. To learn anything from her always came with the threat of brain damage.

She didn't bother to return his smile. "About time you got here. Sage jumped from the wagon before I could stop to run check on that old horse. I had to carry all the pots in by myself, and I'm no spring chicken."

Before he could apologize, she caught sight of his hand. "Lord, boy, what have you done?"

He raised one eyebrow. That was the second time he'd been called a boy today, and it was starting to irritate him. He didn't answer the housekeeper as she unwrapped his thumb and pulled him toward the sink. From the day she'd arrived on the ranch, Tobin always had the impression Martha hated all men, and boys were simply shorter versions.

Teagen hired her to take care of baby Sage and run the house. Their parents were both dead and the three boys had been fighting off rustlers for two months when Martha showed up with everything she owned in a pillowcase. She took one look at Tobin and declared that he was the dirtiest living thing she'd ever encountered. Martha bullied and bribed them all until they "cleaned up" enough to come inside. At one point Tobin claimed he'd rather live with the horses than follow her rules, but like his older brothers, the smell of home cooking eventually changed his mind.

In all those years, the only crack in her attitude toward the McMurray boys came when one of them was hurt. Then she was worse than any mother hen with a single chick.

"Soak that hand while I get the medicine box. I'll not have you getting that cut infected."

Tobin didn't argue. He followed orders. Within minutes she'd doctored his thumb, wrapped it tight to hold the sliced skin together, and served him a piece of pie—all the while keeping up a running lecture on how he should be more careful.

The housekeeper had carried his handkerchief and a towel out to soak in cold water when Sage walked into the kitchen. She took one look at her brother and said, "You're hurt?"

He kept his injured hand beneath the table. "What makes you say that?"

Sage smiled. "Martha wouldn't be cutting you a slice of the pie she baked for supper unless you were injured. I know her bedside manner. Doctor, lecture, feed sweets."

Tobin took his hand out from beneath the table. "I broke the bottle Travis sent from Austin and sliced my thumb open picking up the glass."

"Is it bad? I could take a look."

"No." Tobin returned to the pie. "It's nothing. Time I eat all the pie, it'll probably be well."

Sage laughed. "You'd better save big brother a piece. He's over at the building site and heading this way. It seems Teagen had some trouble with the senator down near Victoria who was buying his spoiled daughter a new horse. He'll probably tell you all about it when he gets in, but I'd better warn you, his mood is dark."

"He only has two colors of moods—dark and black."

Sage agreed as she grabbed a few carrots for Glory from the vegetable bin and hurried out the back door.

Tobin didn't have long to wait to hear the details of his brother's trip to deliver one of their finest horses to a rich senator's ranch east of Austin. Within ten minutes Teagen sat across from him complaining as he finished off the rest of the pie.

"You should have gone, Tobin. I told you that from the first. You handle an animal better. You would have showed the horse off to his best advantage."

"But we both knew you'd be better dealing with a senator." Tobin echoed what he'd said over a week ago when his brother left.

Teagen nodded. "Maybe with the senator, but not with that daughter of his. She's the devil's little sister, I swear. She took one look at one of our best three-year-olds and said the animal would never do."

"Give any reason?"

Teagen downed coffee before answering in a low voice, "She said the horse looked dull-witted."

"What?" Tobin rocked forward in his chair, making the front two legs slam into the kitchen's polished floor. "She said one of our horses looked stupid?"

Teagen nodded, pleased at his brother's reaction. "Exactly. I told her we don't raise stupid horses, but once in a while we made the mistake of selling one to someone who isn't too bright."

Tobin laughed. "What'd the kid say?"

"She ordered me off the ranch. I was five miles gone when her father caught up to me."

"Did you straighten him out about our horses?" Tobin couldn't get over the fact that someone would have the nerve to call one of the McMurray horses dull-witted. They were the finest horses raised in Texas, maybe in the South.

Teagen shook his head. "The senator is a man who likes to give his only child the best. He offered to pay us double if we'd bring another horse for her. He said she's a little high strung. 'A princess,' he said. If you ask me, spoiled rotten is more the word."

"You said no?" Tobin didn't even want to think about letting such a girl ride one of his horses.

"I did," Teagen answered. "The senator offered to pay triple."

Tobin frowned. Above all, his oldest brother was a businessman. He loved horses, but not in the same way Tobin did. For Tobin they were like family; for Teagen they were the family livelihood. "What did you say?" Tobin finally asked.

Teagen shrugged in silent apology. "I said you'd bring another."

Tobin shot out of his chair. "No." He accidentally bumped his thumb against the table and swore.

His brother raised his hands. "I stopped by Travis's place in Austin, and we talked about this. The senator would be a good friend to have. Travis said the man's running for re-election and if he wins there's a good chance he'd be one of the most powerful men in the Senate."

When Tobin didn't say anything, Teagen added, "He'd be an important friend to have if Travis ever decides to run for office. You can't blame the senator for wanting the best for his daughter. We could use the money and we are in the business of raising horses to sell."

Before Tobin could think of a comeback to his brother's logic, Sage wandered into the kitchen. She poured herself a cup of coffee and turned to her brothers. The fact that they were both a head taller and double her weight never seemed to frighten her when she wanted to join an argument. "I have the answer."

Both men looked at her. Since she'd turned eighteen last year, the brothers all agreed that she would have an equal vote in the running of the ranch.

Sage smiled. "Send her Sunny."

"Sunny?" Tobin frowned. "Sunny is the orneriest horse we have on the place."

Teagen laughed. "Or the smartest."

"He's a beautiful animal." Sage sat at the table.

Tobin agreed. The palomino was one of the finest-looking horses they had and a great-great-grandson of Glory.

But Tobin had wasted hours trying to train the animal. Sunny didn't have a mean bone in his body, but he had a mind of his own. More than once the horse left Tobin to walk back to the barn. When any rider turned him toward home, he'd better have a firm grip on the reins.

"He can run," Sage added.

"Toward home," Tobin mumbled. He'd never had a horse who showed no interest in leaving the corral and went full out to get back each night. Tobin grinned when it crossed his mind that he and the animal might have one thing in common.

"He has a good sense of direction." Sage laughed trying to turn Tobin's comment into a strength. "And he's independent."

"A kind way to say he doesn't do well as part of a team."

Teagen stood. "Sunny, it is. You can start in the morning, Tobin."

Tobin didn't argue. He knew they were right. If Sunny had been a mare, they could have kept her to breed, but too many males caused trouble. The spoiled senator's daughter could find nothing wrong with the fine horse, and she'd probably only ride now and then. What did it matter if her horse was barn-soured? As long as she didn't get off the animal and leave him untied, Sunny might be just what she wanted.

By nightfall, Tobin had packed and checked on Glory. The old girl was still standing, looking stronger than hours ago. It appeared she planned to be around a little longer. Sage helped him brush her down then they walked back to the house.

The air had cooled reminding them it was early fall. Tobin put his arm around his little sister who'd forgotten her jacket as always. He'd been taking care of her all her life. When their mother lay dying just after giving birth, she'd ordered him to take Sage to the porch. He'd picked her up and wrapped her as best as he could in a blanket. He'd known that moment that he'd be near whenever she needed him.

"You'd better marry a fat man who can keep you warm," he teased.

"Maybe I should go up and sleep on Whispering Mountain so I can dream my future?"

They both glanced at the dark outline of the tallest point on the ranch. Their father had dreamed his future when he'd been seventeen. He'd dreamed his death and spent the next twelve years preparing for his sons to take over. Andrew McMurray had ridden away to fight for Texas and left his three sons to defend the ranch. That year Tobin had lost both his parents, but he'd never felt alone. He had his brothers and Sage. He had Whispering Mountain.

When they reached the porch, Tobin took one last look. "I'll never climb that mountain to dream. I know my future. I plan on staying right here until I die."

"What about marriage and a family?"

"No marriage. No kids. That life is not for me." He didn't want to tell even Sage that he didn't need to climb the mountain to see his future. The same nightmare had haunted his sleep since he'd been shot at six years old. He dreamed of being covered in blood and feeling himself letting out one last breath. Years ago he'd sworn to himself that he'd never do what his father had done—marry and leave children to face the world alone. When he died, there would be no widow, no orphans to mourn him.

"Well, I'm going to marry, and when I do, that will leave you and Teagen alone in this big, old house with only Martha to tell you what to do."

"Got anyone in mind for my future brother-in-law?"

She moved toward the door. "As a matter of fact I do, but I'm not ready to tell any of you." She disappeared before he could ask more.

Tobin smiled. They'd all seen the way she'd kissed the young ranger in Austin good-bye months ago. Several letters had come for her from him. Any man brave enough to kiss Sage in front of her three big brothers just might be a match for her.

An emptiness filled Tobin's chest. He'd spent most of his

life alone or in the company of his family. He knew little or nothing about things like flirting or falling in love and had no plans on learning.

Then, when he took that last breath as he visualized doing in his dream when the nightmare visited, he'd do it without any regrets.

CHAPTER 3

LIBERTY MAYFIELD DARTED THROUGH THE SHADOWS behind her massive three-story home and ran toward the barn. The tiny rocks along the path jabbed into her feet, but she didn't slow. Satin shoes might be perfect for dancing, but not for running and tonight she wished she could run until dawn. Maybe then, she would outrun her own foolishness.

Feeling unsure, or even stupid was one thing, but knowing that she'd made the biggest mistake of her life was quite another. Her father had warned her to tread softly, but, as always, she rushed in at full speed. She'd agreed to marry Captain Samuel Buchanan without knowing what kind of man lay beneath his crisp uniform. She'd seen his true colors tonight, and the one glimpse had chilled her heart.

Liberty slipped into the barn and moved silently toward the last stall. If anyone came looking for her, she had no intention of allowing them to find her. In the blackness of an empty stall not even her pale blue ball gown would be seen.

Just as she swung the gate closed, she heard footsteps.

"Liberty!" Samuel shouted. "Liberty! I know you're in here. I saw you leave the garden."

He sounded angry. As angry as he'd been at one of his men earlier.

She closed her eyes wondering if she could take a blow like the soldier had without breaking bone. No, she reasoned, Samuel wouldn't hit her across the face. He wasn't fool enough to draw her father's wrath . . . but once they were married she'd be alone with this man she realized she barely knew. Her father would go back to Washington and his campaign, leaving her with a new husband. She'd have no one to call friend in all of Texas.

Samuel's promises of marrying her and taking her back to Washington were empty. Once she agreed to the engagement, his plans had shifted almost daily. First, he'd said they might have to stay at his present post longer than expected. Then her father had explained to them both all the advantages of Samuel taking command of a frontier post. Samuel had agreed, forgetting any promise he'd made to her in favor of his career.

Tonight, she'd not only realized the kind of man she was marrying, but just how alone she would be once the wedding happened.

"Liberty! Get out here. We're not playing this game." He sounded impatient.

She didn't answer.

"Come out," he said more slowly. "Once I explain my actions, you'll see reason."

She wiped her mouth, wishing she could rub off the taste of his kiss. He'd never been so bold before. His kisses had always been polite, almost cold. But tonight he'd been drinking, celebrating their upcoming wedding. After he'd disciplined his man, he noticed her watching from the shadows of the veranda and grabbed her as if she were his prize after battle. His kiss, his embrace, had been nothing short of an assault.

She could hear him moving about the barn, kicking things out of his path. "Come out, pet," he said in a voice she hardly recognized as his. "I'm sorry if I shocked you, but I'm a soldier and I'm used to taking charge. Once you're my wife you'll get used to it. Even your father admits you need a little taming."

Samuel turned up a lantern somewhere and light sliced through the slats in the stall gate. The normally empty barn came alive with sounds of horses being stabled because of the party that night. Several of the guests planned to stay through to the wedding four days away, leaving Liberty little time to speak to her father alone.

She mumbled an oath. There would be no wedding. Not if she could stop it. Samuel shifted from being formal one moment to violent the next and she could never live with such a man. She'd loved the facade of him, a handsome army officer on his way up, but Liberty knew now that she'd never known or loved the man.

"Come out, pet, I'm tired of this game." His voice held an edge.

Glancing back for an escape route, Liberty froze in surprise. A man, sitting up from his bedroll, watched her as he dug his hand through straight, chestnut brown hair. She opened her mouth to scream, then suddenly realized that the man outside the stall posed far more of a threat than the one she'd obviously awakened.

She nodded slightly toward him, her finger on her lips.

The stranger nodded back in understanding.

Liberty returned to watching her fiancé move angrily from stall to stall. It wouldn't be long before he reached her. If he found her here, with another man, there was no telling what he might do. She closed her eyes as a shiver chilled her all the way to her heart. If he found her alone, he might carry out his whispered promise from minutes ago.

She could still feel his words against her ear. He'd grabbed her, kissing her hard before he'd said in a voice so low she wasn't sure he knew he was passing along his thoughts. "Don't ever question anything I do, Liberty, or you will be sorry." His fingers had bit cruelly into her arms before he shoved her away. She knew, in that instant, she'd just seen Samuel's true self.

Liberty heard the slam of the gate three stalls down. The

stranger behind her stood. He was taller than Samuel but she guessed he wouldn't have a chance. The captain was looking for a fight and this man was at the wrong place at the wrong time, thanks to her.

Her father had mentioned something about a man bringing in another horse tonight for her to consider. Looking at the stranger's face, she recognized a younger version of the rancher who'd tried to sell her father a paint. The silent man didn't appear as cold or hard as the man she guessed was his older brother, but he'd still leave just as disappointed. She had no intention of riding or even buying a horse. That was Samuel's plan, not hers.

"Your name?" she whispered.

"Tobin McMurray," he answered as the gate two stalls down slammed.

"Stay here." She met his stare and was surprised at the kindness she saw there. He hadn't said any more, but she knew he was worried—not about himself, but about her.

She stepped out of the stall. "You're looking for me, Samuel?" she said in a bored voice.

The captain looked first one direction, then another. When he was satisfied they were alone, he said, "You ran out before I had time to finish our kiss. With only four days to our marriage bed, don't you think it's about time you warmed up?"

She took a step backward, hating herself for being a coward. "I think we are quite finished, Samuel." She wanted to add that she'd never warm to him, but fear held her tongue.

He smiled, that perfect smile he always made as if posing for a painting. "Now, Liberty, I know you're upset over the threats your father is getting, but I assure you nothing will happen to him the day of our wedding. If it takes every man in my command to guard him, the senator will be safe."

The worry over her father had been in the back of every thought since her father received a death threat three days ago, but that had nothing to do with what she was about to say. Lifting her chin slightly, she faced him. "I think we should postpone the wedding." He'd been the one who wanted it from the beginning and she'd been the fool who'd gone along with it.

"I will not hear of it." He said the words slowly, each one a nail into the coffin of her freedom. "You agreed to this wedding, then even begged that it be so extravagant. Neither your father nor I plan to let you change your mind."

He took another stride toward her.

She stepped back, guessing she had three or four more feet before she hit the barn wall.

He moved forward again as if playing a game with a child.

Liberty straightened preparing for yet another argument. Behind Samuel, she noticed the stranger she'd awakened slip from the stall and move silently across the barn. At least he was smart enough to escape. She wasn't sure she'd be so lucky.

She'd felt it coming for days in subtle words and looks. Now, she couldn't believe she'd first thought it was endearing when Samuel became possessive. He'd ordered for her in restaurants without asking her and claimed he knew her better than she knew herself. Then, a few days ago, he'd told someone what she thought, as though she were a mute standing next to him. And earlier tonight when she'd wanted to dance a new dance, he'd said he wouldn't allow it as if she were a child who wouldn't dare disobey.

He'd been perfect when he'd courted her, paying her all the attention her father never had time to show her. But since their engagement the earth had been shifting until suddenly Liberty had nowhere to stand.

Liberty took her last step backward. Maybe some of this was her fault. She'd been so caught up in marrying the handsome captain she hadn't taken the time to get to know him. Then, when he'd proposed, she'd gone along with whatever he wanted thinking it would make things easier. Only somehow his take-charge manner had twisted into arrogance. It felt almost as if he would be owning her, not wedding her.

Her father had played his part too, giving her everything she wanted except his time. He'd agreed with Samuel, happily moving the wedding up so that he could get back to his campaign.

"Samuel," she began, trying not to notice the hardness in his face. "I've been thinking about what you said."

He stopped, interested. She noticed Tobin silently lift the gate at the far side of the barn and lead out a horse. The animal nuzzled him playfully, but any noise they made blended in with that of other animals in the barn.

"I know you're angry that I refuse to learn to ride."

"You will learn to ride," he answered calmly. "I insist on it."

She wanted to yell that she didn't care one hair what he insisted on, but now wasn't the time. "That's why I came to the barn." She stumbled slightly over her lie, but he didn't seem to notice.

He raised an eyebrow and she hurried on. "I wanted to see if the new horse had arrived." What she wanted to do was kick him and run, but she wasn't sure what would happen in the darkness if he caught her between the house and the barn. Inside, she'd be safe—her father would protect her. But not here and definitely not alone with Samuel. Her arms still ached from where he'd gripped her and the memory of the blow he'd landed on one of his men still haunted her thoughts. She'd play along until she could pick her battlefield and then she'd end this between them no matter how few days were left until the wedding.

"Oh," she said as if surprised. "There's the horse now."

Samuel stared at her a moment longer as if suspecting a trick, then turned slowly.

He held his surprise well as Tobin moved closer with a beautiful horse in tow.

"Thank you, Mr. McMurray, for bringing him out." Liberty ran past Samuel. "I hoped to show him to the captain."

As she neared the horse, she caught Tobin's stare and prayed he would play along with this game as far as she wanted to go.

The animal bobbed his head causing the bridle to rattle.

Liberty jumped back a few steps.

Samuel let out an exasperated sigh. "My bride-to-be is afraid of horses. Hell of a curse for a cavalryman's wife. I plan to remedy her problem as soon as possible."

Tobin didn't answer the captain, but his grip tightened slightly on the reins. She caught his slight nod and moved forward once more.

"I'm thinking of taking this one." Liberty managed to reach out and *almost* touch the horse.

"You will take this one," Samuel corrected. "He's a fine horse and we've no time to look further. You'll be on his back tomorrow."

Liberty shook her head, but Samuel had turned to Tobin. "There'll be extra in the sale if you can teach her to ride. I've got my hands full right now or I'd take on the task myself."

When Tobin didn't answer, the captain pushed. "You can teach her to ride, can't you?"

She felt insulted for Tobin McMurray. The captain was talking down to him as if he were slow-witted. But Tobin only nodded.

"Good." Samuel turned back to Liberty. "Come along, dear, we should be getting back to the ball." He offered his hand. "I'm sure there is no party without your presence."

She thought of the darkness between the barn and the house and answered, "I want to stay here and get to know my horse. I'll be along in a few minutes."

He seemed bored with her. "Fine. Suit yourself." She felt like a toy he'd grown tired of playing with. "I need to talk to your father anyway." He marched toward the door, then turned. "I'll see you before I leave tonight. My men are setting up our camp between the house and the creek." He looked her up and down as if inspecting one of the troops. "Don't get anything on that dress. It wouldn't do to have my future wife appear less than perfect."

She saluted. "Yes sir."

Before, he'd told her he thought her salutes charming; now, he looked irritated. Without another word, he turned and left.

Liberty closed her eyes and took a deep breath, stretching her arms out as she tried to rid herself of tension. When she looked up, Tobin was staring at her.

"What are you looking at?" Her words came fast and angry, more at herself than this stranger. She wouldn't be surprised if he said, "A coward," and he'd be right.

"Your dress," he answered simply.

His words surprised her. "What did you say?" Maybe he wasn't as smart as she gave him credit for being. Maybe the captain had been right to talk to him as if he were simple.

McMurray shrugged. "I've never seen so many frills on a woman, and so much skin exposed at the same time."

Liberty looked down at her low-cut-gown. It was daring, but not by Paris standards. "You must not only sleep in a barn, Mr. McMurray, you must have been born in one as well. There is nothing wrong with my dress and I'll thank you to stop looking or even referring to my skin."

He didn't have the decency to be embarrassed.

She pulled the thin shawl that hung at her elbows. "There, is that better? Am I modest enough for the barn now?"

He smiled, an easy smile that was catching. "Oh, I wasn't complaining, miss, just observing."

She wasn't sure whether she should be insulted or flattered. Most men were respectful around her because of her father's power. This one didn't seem to know, or care, that he was talking to a senator's daughter.

"Well, stop observing my state of dress and introduce me to this horse. I have no intention of riding, but I owe you a look at him for what you did for me tonight." She almost expected him to ask what he'd done and was surprised when he didn't.

"Give me your hand," he said in a low voice she decided she liked.

She offered her hand. He closed his large rough hands around it. "The horse is named Sunny because he's the color of the sunrise along Galveston Harbor. He's smart." Tobin moved his fingers slowly over her arm to her elbow. "I have an Apache grandfather who believes a horse makes up his mind if he likes people by smell." He grinned as his fingers closed gently around her hand. "Sunny will like you better if you smell like me."

Liberty couldn't figure out if he was telling the truth or lying. Part of her didn't care. The warmth of his touch had eased her nerves. Without another word, he cupped her hand in his and stretched it toward the horse.

The animal nuzzled against her fingers. She would have pulled away, but Tobin's hand, just behind hers, made her feel safe. She could feel the nearness of his body standing only an inch away, backing her up in case she panicked. The warmth of him surrounded her. She sensed no threat from this quiet man. He was big, strong, yet there was a gentleness about him.

He laced her hand in his and stroked the horse's neck. The stiff hair of the mane tickled across her fingers as Tobin guided her. The strength of his arm brushed against hers as he slowly taught her how to say hello to a horse. The powerful animal didn't seem nearly as frightening with Tobin so close. Even the nightmares Liberty had experienced since her mother's death seemed distant with him near.

The horse shifted. Liberty bumped against the wall of Tobin's chest. His free hand touched her waist, steadying her.

Liberty closed her eyes. She knew she should move away. It wasn't proper to be pressed against a man she hardly knew. She could feel his heart beating. His breath whispered across her bare shoulder.

"You're all right." His words were far more a statement than a question.

Embarrassed, she straightened and took one step away. "I'm fine," she answered as if he'd asked.

Turning, she saw his eyes. Beautiful blue eyes that said it all without him having to say a word. He hadn't been advancing or trying to seduce her. He'd had no plan to be so close. He was as shocked as she was by what had just happened.

Whatever Tobin McMurray was, he was not a man who touched women often or without care. Her nearness had affected him as deeply as his had surprised her.

Liberty fought to recover. "I'll tell my father about the horse," she managed as she almost ran from the barn.

Halfway back to the house, she slowed to breathe. In the midnight blackness, she tried to slow her heart for she was sure it would out pound any music. What had just happened? She was twenty years old and nothing had ever made her feel so . . . Men had stolen kisses, they'd held her too tightly while dancing or accidentally touched a part of her body while helping her into a carriage . . . but nothing like tonight. She felt like she'd been asleep and he'd awakened her with the brush of his hand.

CHAPTER 4

TOBIN PUT THE HORSE IN THE FIRST STALL AND WENT back to his bedroll, but sleep didn't bother to visit. The stormy day, green-eyed woman he'd just met—just touched— haunted him. Her eyes reminded him of a late summer rain when the land turns greener than green beneath cloudy skies. Her body was long and lean like a colt's just before he learns to run. Her black hair, piled high with a wide ribbon running through it, was the most beautiful mane he'd ever seen.

He may have spent most of his life on the ranch, but he knew how rare a beauty she must be.

Staring up at the rafter, Tobin decided a week on the road with little sleep must have turned his brain to straw. When did he ever bother to notice a woman's eyes? And what kind of man compares a lovely woman's hair to a mane. She figured in his life in only one way—the sale of a horse. What did he care if some rich spoiled beauty fought with her fiancé? If she had a problem with the captain, she could always run to her powerful father. She didn't need him to protect her. But something in the man's countenance toward her rankled Tobin. He wanted to protect her.

Tobin needed to forget about Miss Liberty Mayfield and he planned to, even if he could still feel the softness of her skin against the tips of his fingers.

He swore and covered his face with his hat. Sleep was hard to find, even on a good night; tonight bordered on impossible.

It would take the Grand Canyon to hold all he didn't know about women. Especially this one. This beautiful one was sophisticated. Something he was not and never would be. He knew his family owned one of the finest ranches in Texas, but they'd never played the society game. To her, he was no more than a cowhand who'd brought a horse that she had no intention of riding. Whispering Mountain was a working ranch. From what he'd seen when he rode onto the Mayfield spread, all the senator's land was for show. Even the stable boy had said the Mayfield family was rarely in residence.

Like counting sheep, Tobin listed just how different Liberty was from him. He didn't even know how to dance, and she owned at least one ball gown just for that purpose. Her father was probably one of the richest men in the state, with plans, some say, to go all the way to the White House. Tobin worked a family ranch and never planned even to see Washington, D.C. She was all fire and fight. He'd seen it in her eyes when she'd looked at the man she called Captain. Tobin avoided arguments even with his little sister.

They were no match, he knew that, but then why had he touched her and held her against him like he had some kind of right. Why had the feel of her branded itself into his flesh, his thought, as if the nearness of her were a promise unfulfilled.

If she hadn't pulled away, he probably would have kissed her.

Tobin swore again and mumbled. "She's afraid of horses. What kind of woman fears horses?" Then, just for good measure, he answered his own question, "Not any woman I'd ever want."

"Mr. McMurray?" an Irish flavored voice came from the other side of his stall. "Mr. McMurray, ye in here?"

Tobin stood, brushing hay off as he walked to the stall gate. "I'm here," he answered, wondering what anyone would want with him this time of night.

A wiry man in his fifties stood in the center of the barn. His dark red hair had turned white at the temples, but his smile was genuine. "Pleased to meet ye, Mr. McMurray. Dermot is me name. I hope ye found all ye needed to make ye and that gorgeous horse, I seen in the first stall, comfortable. The senator told me to be on the lookout for ye, but I got busy with all the carriages coming and going."

Tobin offered his hand, deciding he liked the Irishman.

Dermot didn't seem to notice Tobin hadn't said a word. He continued, "Worked for the senator, I have, since I stepped off the boat in New York. Finer man never lived. Me and the missus come with him every year when he sails down to Texas. The senator may be all spit and polish in the city, but his roots plant themselves in the West."

Tobin nodded agreement even though he'd never met the senator.

Dermot lifted a lantern. "I met your brother Teagen when he came a few weeks ago, and your other brother, Travis, once when he was a Texas Ranger." The Irishman came closer. "Ye don't look like him, but I see the kin in your build. Ranger Travis McMurray saved the senator's and me hide back in 'forty-eight, and we'll never forget it. Far as me own judgment, his kin is family. Have ye had supper?"

Tobin shook his head answering the last question. He'd thought of riding the six miles into town for a meal, but in truth, he needed sleep more.

"Well, we can take care of that in straight order. Me Anna's in charge of the kitchen and busy as she is with the party, she'll still have something on the back of the stove for supper. How about we go over and have a meal? I've been so busy I haven't had time to sit down meself for a bite."

Tobin needed sleep, but he didn't want to seem impolite.

They moved toward the house as Dermot continued, "Tonight starts the parties that will last the rest of the week, right up to the wedding. We've got a house full of important

people, not that 'tis anything new. Hisself loves his dinner
meetings and Miss Liberty loves her parties. Back in Washington, D.C., we sometimes go a week or more having parties every night."

They entered a large kitchen with half a dozen servants in
white uniforms moving about. While Tobin was being introduced, he couldn't help but grin wondering how Martha
would react if he brought one of these uniforms home. Their
housekeeper at Whispering Mountain had worn blue dresses
with white aprons since the day she arrived. When a dress
wore out, she simply ordered more yards of blue material.

He saw huge trays of tiny little bits of food and was thankful when Dermot's wife, Anna, offered him a bowl of stew.
They ate at a side table off the main path. Dermot liked to
brag about all the places he'd been with the senator, but he
seemed a nice enough fellow. His wife ran the kitchen and he
managed the carriage house in Washington and the barn here.

Halfway through the meal Tobin got in a question. "What
happened to the senator's wife? I met the daughter when she
came to the barn to see the horse I brought in."

Dermot shook his head. "Ye might have met Miss Liberty, but I don't think she came to the barn to see a horse.
The lass has been afraid of them since she was a wee one
and her mother got thrown. The senator's lady hit her head
and died instantly, 'tis said. Hisself blamed her death on a
storm that spooked her horse. Little Liberty blamed it on the
horse. She screamed so bad every time she saw that horse
that the senator had me sell the animal."

Dermot scratched his long bushy sideburns. "If Miss Liberty was in the barn tonight, the lass was running from
something. The little princess flies like the wind when she's
frightened and 'tis no telling which way she'll go. When she
was a child I sometimes found her up in the loft crying her
little eyes out over something. But when I asked her what
had upset her, she'd storm around, claiming nothing was
bothering her. Anna used to find her curled up in the attic,
her whole body shaking as she cried. But Miss Liberty
would open up to no one. Got that from her father. He holds

his feelings close to his chest." He shook his head. "Life . . . 'tisn't easy on that lass."

Tobin looked around him at all the silver and crystal. He had a rough time believing Liberty had a hard life. He bet she hadn't gone a day without food, and all these people were hired to wait on her every need.

The memory of her hand in his walked over his mind so strong he could almost feel the softness of her palm. Not a callous on it.

He fought down any comment. She might have them fooled, but he had a hard time believing this "little princess," as Dermot called her, suffered any problems. She probably hadn't done a day's work in her life.

Tobin accepted a slice of pie from a pretty maid whose smile hinted that she'd be willing to offer more. He turned his attention back to Dermot and asked the first question that came to mind. "Isn't it a little strange that she'd go to the barn if she was upset, what with her fear of horses?"

The Irishman shook his head. "Most of the time I keep the horses in the corral. The barn is empty. Even just after the accident that killed her mother, her father made the lass go with him to the barn. I made a point of bolting any stall in use." Dermot looked up from his food. "Senator Mayfield weren't trying to be cruel to her. He's just a man who struggles with the meaning of fear. He never backed down from a fight in his life, not when he's in the Senate or in his younger days when he was fighting pirates along the gulf. He even rode with Sam Houston at San Jacinto in 'thirty-six and he would have been with Zack Taylor at the border in 'forty-seven if he coulda. But by then, his battles were at the Capitol."

Tobin thought of asking how such a brave man would sire such a frightened child, but he decided to eat his pie instead.

Dermot talked about all that was going on, mentioned several important people who would be coming in for the wedding, and ended by telling how Captain Buchanan's troops were adding extra guards because, as usual, the senator was getting threats. Senator Mayfield's insistence on improving relationships with Mexico was not popular with many Texans.

Tobin politely listened to Dermot complain about the mule-headed leaders who wanted to slow progress, but while he understood the senator's reasoning, he also remembered. He'd only been a boy, but the stories of the Alamo and Goliad were branded in his memory. Memories of how Santa Anna's army had attacked the Alamo mission, outnumbering the Texans twenty to one. Rumors of how, after the Alamo fell, the Texans' bodies were dismembered and burned. At Goliad, it had been worse. Those men, many from southern states, had surrendered, most believing they would be allowed to lay down their weapons and leave. But they'd faced a firing squad instead.

Tobin's jaw tightened. His father had been one who died. Oh, yes, he understood the men in Texas who didn't want to trade with Mexico, but he couldn't condone them threatening the life of the senator for disagreeing with them. That very act went against everything his father had fought and died for.

"How long will ye be staying?" Dermot broke into Tobin's thoughts.

"A day or two. I thought I'd show Miss Liberty how to handle her new horse."

Dermot shook her head. "She won't ride. I'd bet on it, but ye can try."

Surprisingly, Tobin wanted to. He couldn't figure out if he just wanted to show off his horse, or if he wanted to see the lady one more time. The fact that he wanted to linger near anyone other than family forced him to his feet. He thanked Anna for the meal and headed back to the barn.

In the shadows at the side of the house, he paused watching the dancers at the ball. Music drifted out to him as he stared at a sight unlike he'd ever seen. They all looked like china dolls twirling across marble, no more real or related to his life than the shadow of a rainbow.

Just as he turned to go, he caught a glimpse of Liberty, circling the floor so gracefully she could have been gliding on ice. Tobin couldn't help but stare. Her pale blue dress looked like it was made of a cloud whirling at her feet and her black hair danced over her shoulders as she turned slightly in the arms of a soldier in full dress uniform. The picture they made was like something out of a dream.

When the man turned slightly, Tobin recognized the captain. Looking closer, Tobin thought he saw a hardness in Buchanan's grip, imprisoning, not holding, her. As the couple moved, Tobin saw Liberty's face and all the beauty of the scene vanished. Her beautiful green eyes held the edge of panic as she stared out as if she were in prison.

Tobin took a step toward the window, then remembered where he was. He couldn't enter her world. He couldn't save her. He could only watch. The fences that held her in were the barriers that kept him out.

As the dance ended, he turned away and walked toward the barn. He needed to get out of this place as soon as possible. He'd not stand by and watch her again. She was surrounded by strong men who could save her; she wasn't likely to turn to a man she'd just met tonight.

He swung open the door to the stall where he'd spread his bedroll and almost collided with a stranger dressed in black.

"What . . ." Tobin took a step backward and rested his right hand on the handle of his holstered Colt.

Whoever the man was, he certainly wasn't an outlaw. The gold chain on his watch shone in the dark, as did the diamond tie tack at his throat. Even for his age, he had a military bearing.

"McMurray?" The man huffed the word as if impatient with being kept waiting.

"That's right," Tobin answered. "Who's asking?"

The man nodded once as if in recognition and said calmly, "A man who might need your help."

Tobin glanced at his bedroll figuring he could probably forget sleep tonight. Somehow he'd picked a spot busier than a train platform to spread his blankets.

"I'll know your name first." Tobin hadn't removed his hand from his gun, but he sensed that he was in no danger.

"Mayfield," the man said then waited a moment as if letting his name register. "Senator James Mayfield. Your brother

Travis saved my life a few years back. We were on the road together several days and he told me of his brothers and of your ranch. I also talked with your other brother, Teagen, less than two weeks ago."

Tobin saw no point to question the senator's word.

Mayfield hesitated, then added one more McMurray to his list of friends. "I rode with your father near Goliad. He turned west toward the mission and I rode east hoping to catch up with Sam Houston's men. Your father thought the battle would be won at Goliad, but I feared we'd need more men and a soldier like Houston to lead us before we faced Santa Anna's army."

Again Tobin didn't question.

"Your father was a good man, son. One of the best I've ever known. You and your brothers are cut from the same cloth."

Tobin didn't know what to say, but he did lower his hand from the Colt.

The senator's shoulders relaxed. "Teagen said you'd be the one who could help me."

Tobin doubted he could do anything Travis or Teagen couldn't, but the old man had him interested.

"Walk with me," the senator whispered as he moved out of the stall. "I don't want anyone accidentally overhearing what I've got to say."

They strolled as far as the fence line where the moon shone almost as bright as a gas lamp. With no trees within a hundred yards it was unlikely anyone would be close, but when Mayfield turned to Tobin he lowered his voice once more.

"I believe there are men who mean to see me dead."

Tobin removed his hat. "I've heard that's not unusual, Senator."

The old man laughed. "You're right, it's not. But of late, the threat is so close I can almost smell it, taste it on the tip of my tongue." His laugh bore no humor. "Maybe I'm turning into an old woman as I age, but I feel I need to take care.

Not for me—I've always been able to defend myself—but for my daughter. A blind man could see that if she were hurt or killed, I'd be crushed, unable to go on with my duties. I treasure her dearly."

"How can I be of service?"

The senator smiled and offered Tobin a cigar as if they were simply talking of the weather. "I need two favors tomorrow. Neither of which I'd like you to discuss with anyone," he said as he lit his cigar. "First, no matter how she fights, you've got to teach her to ride. I can't go back to Washington and leave her out here without knowing that she could handle a horse if she needs to. A lady in the cities can do without such a skill, but not out here. Her life might depend on it one day."

"I'll try," Tobin answered.

"I'll see that you get the chance. I'll talk to her if I have to, even threaten her if I must, but she *will* learn."

"And the second favor?" Tobin asked, thinking that the first might prove impossible.

The senator took a long pull of his cigar then let the smoke out slowly. "If the danger I fear coming tomorrow proves real and I need the second favor, you have to promise me you'll act immediately."

"All right," Tobin answered. How could he not help if Mayfield or Liberty were in danger? "What do you want me to do?"

The senator looked straight at Tobin so there would be no misunderstanding, no doubt of how serious he was. "If there is an attempt on my life tomorrow, I want you to kidnap my daughter and ride like hell is chasing you toward that mountain ranch your brothers told me about. It just might be the only place in this state where I'd know she would be safe. Captain Buchanan and his men will worry about me. They don't have the men or time to protect her. And, if I'm in danger, the last thing I want is her with me."

A hundred questions came to mind, but Tobin just stared at the senator. The sounds of the night were around them, blending with only a whisper of music coming from the house.

Finally, Tobin said, "All right." The other questions didn't matter. He'd do what the senator asked.

"I'll have your word, McMurray. You'll keep her there until I come after her."

"You have it, sir," Tobin answered.

They walked back and shook hands in the darkness between the barn and the house. When Tobin lay back on his bedroll wide awake an hour later he'd figured out a few things.

One, the senator hadn't asked the favor lightly. It must have taken months to plan and check out the McMurrays. He already knew and trusted Travis, but buying a horse had given him the chance to meet the other McMurrays. If Liberty's life were in danger, the senator would look for a fortress and Whispering Mountain was just that.

Two, Mayfield had no intention of telling his daughter in advance. Maybe if he said anything about her being in danger it might upset her too much, or she'd want to call off the wedding.

No, Tobin reconsidered. The old man wasn't worried about upsetting her; after all, he wanted Tobin to kidnap her. Surely that would upset the fair Liberty. But, for some reason only the senator knew, Liberty wasn't in on her father's plan.

Third, Mayfield didn't trust Captain Buchanan's ability to guard him. Tobin had learned earlier that the captain's men were the guards. Maybe Liberty hadn't said a word to her father about the problems with her fiancé, but the senator wasn't blind.

Tobin swore, wishing he was back on the ranch. This trip confirmed his belief that people in general were to be avoided. The lives around him were more complicated than the plot of a novel.

A tapping sound rattled the stall door and for the third time since sunset, Tobin reached for his Colt.

"Mister," a female whispered. "Mister, are you awake?"

Tobin sat up. "Yes." Around this place no one must ever sleep.

The door slipped open just enough for the top half of a woman's body to enter. The pretty redheaded maid from the kitchen smiled down at him. "I was just wondering," she said with a slow smile, "if you need anything to make yourself more comfortable tonight?"

"What's your name?" Tobin asked.

"Stella," she answered. "And you are Tobin McMurray. I asked."

"Nice to meet you, Stella." Tobin didn't want to hurt her feelings. "I don't need anything. Thank you, but I'll look forward to seeing you tomorrow if I'm welcome back in the kitchen."

She grinned. "You are. I'll make you hot buttermilk biscuits myself. Everyone says they are the best in Texas."

Her eyes raked his body and Tobin had the feeling he wasn't the first visitor she made biscuits for.

"I'll look forward to it. Good night, Stella."

She hesitated a moment, then disappeared.

Tobin smiled, thinking he'd look forward to a hot breakfast tomorrow, but it would be green eyes that filled his thoughts tonight, not buttermilk biscuits.

CHAPTER 5

WHEN LIBERTY RETURNED TO THE DANCE, SHE'D tried to skirt past all the people wanting to give her their best wishes and find her father. Somehow, she had to make him see reason. If she couldn't talk him into calling off the wedding, at least she'd get him to postpone it. He might be neglectful at times, but face to face he'd never been able to tell her no.

Finally, she found him in his study, staring out the window and deep in thought.

"Father," she said as she walked into his outstretched arm. His embrace was indifferent as it often was when she'd disturbed his thoughts.

"Princess," he whispered, hardly looking at her. "Having fun?"

"I need to talk to you," she said. "I have a problem."

"Can it wait until morning? I need to set a plan in motion before it's too late."

Liberty guessed it would be a waste of time to tell him how unhappy she was about the wedding. "Of course, until morning." She tried not to think of the hundred conversations he'd postponed over the years and never found the time for. Oh, he loved her, she'd never doubted that. Whenever matters of state gave him a minute to remember he was more than a senator, he always looked around for her.

Hugging him tightly, she whispered, "Good night, Father."

"Good night, dear," he mumbled. "Enjoy the rest of the party."

At the door, Liberty turned back for one last glance at him. For the first time in her life she might have to solve a problem without him. Her father had handpicked the captain, saying Samuel would grow into a fine officer in time. She remembered how the senator introduced them six months ago, bragging that Samuel was on his way up in the world and Liberty would be lucky to win his favor. Once, when the senator wasn't aware she stood near, he'd said Buchanan was the son he wished he'd had.

It wasn't likely her father would see her side and call off the wedding. She sometimes felt as if the marriage had been set in a smoke-filled room before she had even entered, and the bargain wasn't hers to change.

Liberty straightened as she marched down the hallway, not knowing if she was strong enough to fight them both. For the most part, she thought of herself as more the mouse type. She'd never crossed her father—not over anything important. And the captain was used to taking charge.

Long, powerful fingers closed around her arm. Liberty let out a small cry as Samuel moved up beside her.

"There you are. Come with me, Liberty. There are people I want you to meet." His smile was polite, professional and cold.

She followed aware that he'd ordered and not asked. They seemed to be beyond small talk. Straightening her gown, Liberty took a deep breath telling herself Samuel had a great deal on his mind. It was his job to keep her father safe. Trouble brewed on the border. He'd just accepted a new post he had to report to after the wedding. Captain Samuel Buchanan no longer had the time or energy to court her and the cracks in his polished manner were showing.

But none of these excuses made any difference. Samuel was not the man for her. She knew it all the way to her core. He was handsome, had high goals, and had been chosen by her father, but he was not the man for her.

Like a boy showing off his prize, Captain Buchanan circled the ballroom. After he'd introduced her to everyone he thought important, he insisted on dancing.

As she followed his steps on the floor, she wondered how she'd gotten herself to such a hopeless place in her life. She'd been spoiled and pampered since birth. The only child of two only children. The motherless daughter of a powerful man. The beauty every man wanted to court. But now . . . where had it gotten her? Engaged to a man who probably knew to the penny how much money she had in her trust fund, and already considered her to be his property. Her father was too worried about something else to care.

Unwilling to make a scene, she sat next to Samuel for a late supper. Her fiancé talked about their wedding and his plans immediately after. "We'll have our honeymoon on the road to my new post," he'd said as if she would have no objection. "I want to get there as soon as possible, and I know your father will want to get back to Washington. Once he's back it will only be a short time before he misses you and I'll be transferred."

Liberty nibbled on her meal as he changed the subject to horses. "I know that fellow in the barn probably has no idea how to act around a lady like you, but I don't have time to teach you to ride. In the few days we have left before the wedding, he can start and I'll finish your lessons later. Right now I've more important matters that draw my attention."

He finished the last bite of food on his plate and stood. "I think I'll go to the parlor for a cigar."

Liberty saw her chance. "I think I'll retire. I've a headache."

Samuel walked her to the foot of the stairs and kissed her on the cheek. "Good night. Get some rest, dear, you look tired."

Liberty had to force herself not to run up to her room.

She knew with all the houseguests Samuel wouldn't follow her, but she needed to put as much distance as possible between them. He'd been obnoxious all evening. Since their kiss in the garden, he seemed to believe that he had a firm grip on his bride-to-be.

"Well, he has another think coming," Liberty mumbled as she climbed out of her clothes and tossed them aside. She wasn't one of his men and she didn't have to follow orders.

Joy, her maid, followed behind her, picking up. When Liberty stepped behind her beautiful china silk screen to remove the last of her clothing, Joy handed her a night shift.

"Is everything all right?" Joy whispered.

"It's fine," Liberty lied. "Go on up to your room. You've got to be as tired as I am."

Joy yawned. "It's been a long day and tomorrow we have to start packing. Stella said she would help me. She'd like my job, I fear. Would like to move upstairs, if you know what I mean. Thinks she's too good to be in the kitchen all the time."

Liberty didn't want to think about the staff. "Good night," she said as she took the warm cocoa from Joy and waved her farewell.

After the maid closed the door, Liberty strolled to the window and stepped out on her tiny balcony. The back of the house was dark. The barn only a shadow. Most of the guests had long ago gone to bed. This quiet time of night usually calmed her. She loved listening to the wild sounds of the night on the rare trips to Texas. Everything seemed so untamed, so free. Everything but her.

Liberty's thoughts grew dark. She could almost feel the cage that was being built around her. Her father already had too many worries; he didn't need to know hers. In a few days Samuel would control not only her, but all the money, she had. In a few days the cage would be completed and the door locked and she'd have no choices left . . . no life to call her own.

Samuel said once that as the senator's son-in-law he would naturally inherit all the Mayfield support if he wanted to run for Congress one day. Liberty didn't think it worked that way, but that might explain why Samuel spent most of his time with her father.

"In a few days," she whispered, trying to think of some way she could change her fate. All her life she'd dreamed of freedom, but for her there never seemed to be more than a few moments in time when she could slip away from her obligations. Every hour of every day she was surrounded, protected, pampered.

The horses in the corral circled, rustling the night with their stomps and whinnies.

She leaned over the railing, listening as if they were whispering to her. If she knew how to ride a horse, she could run away.

Even the possibility frightened the breath from her. If she could ride, she could escape.

She stared at the corral. As her eyes adjusted to the dark, she saw the lean shadow of a man. He stood with his back to her, his legs wide apart, his arms resting on the corral fence. The faint sound of a low whistle drifted through the air as if he were calming the horses. Even in the dark, she knew who it was.

Tobin McMurray.

Maybe her one real chance to escape before the cage door closed.

CHAPTER 6

Tobin tried to ignore Stella at breakfast, but it was hard to not be thankful for her buttermilk biscuits. They were, as she'd promised, the best he'd ever eaten. When he finally looked at her, he was surprised that the biscuits didn't seem to be the only things that had risen in the kitchen. Stella's bosom seemed to have doubled in size and looked like it might erupt out of her blouse at any moment.

"You're up early," she said with a giggle. "The men who help out around here aren't in until after daylight unless the senator needs them." She glanced over at Anna. "Of course, that doesn't include Dermot. He lights the morning fires for Anna and banks them at the end of the day." She smiled at Tobin. "He says he likes starting and ending the day at her side. Don't you think that's about the most romantic thing a man could say?"

Tobin had no idea how to respond, but he tried to make conversation. "I like to be working by dawn." He didn't add that around Whispering Mountain, Martha threw out leftovers to the hogs by sunup. The memory made him wish for home, but he'd promised the senator last night that he'd stay another day.

"You're not romantic?" Stella leaned closer.

"No." Tobin swallowed without chewing a bite. "I'm not."

He tried to keep his gaze respectable, but it wasn't easy when she kept leaning over to pass the butter or to ask if he wanted more coffee. He remembered once Teagen had commented about a well-rounded saloon girl in Austin during Tobin's first trip off the ranch. His older brother said that a man can appreciate beauty without making a fool of himself. Tobin, almost sixteen at the time, went back into the bar that night for another look and ended up climbing the stairs with the saloon girl.

Every part of her was pretty, and when she undressed she smiled with a look in her eyes that made him feel drunk. In a violet robe that covered little, she'd taught him how to kiss and how a woman liked to be touched. She took her time, welcoming his advances as she told him all the things he could do to please a woman.

When he unbuttoned his shirt, she saw his scar crisscrossing over his heart. She'd laughed nervously and asked about it as she toyed with touching the twisted flesh as if she'd been asked to stroke a snake. He told him of his family and how he'd been hurt defending his ranch. He even told her of lying behind his horse with both of them bleeding. The outlaws kept yelling at him, trying to figure out if he was dead so they could move on to killing the rest of the Mc-Murrays.

Tobin couldn't remember why he'd talked so much, it wasn't his nature, but that night he wanted to be understood.

Before he finished his story, he noticed that the saloon girl wasn't listening. She pulled her hand away from his chest and averted her eyes, and he knew she was trying to shove the ugliness from her mind.

He'd been embarrassed, but he asked her to look at him, all of him. The scar was a part of him. He wanted her to see him, not just another customer, not just a damaged body, but him.

He hadn't come here to talk, he thought, so what did it matter? But suddenly the girl wasn't nearly as pretty as he thought. He dressed and left money on the bed, deciding he didn't want his first or any time to be like that. He needed more.

Looking at Stella, her cheeks red from the stove and her eyes wide with possibilities, he found himself asking her if she liked horses. She answered with a giggle and he looked for his hat. As he stood, he pocketed two apples and thanked her for the breakfast.

"Come back any time. The senator takes his breakfast in his study and Miss Liberty usually doesn't get up until after nine, so the kitchen is always quiet in the mornings." Stella waved good-bye from the doorway.

Walking back to the barn, he called himself a fool. Most men his age had slept with every willing woman they ran across. Most had stories to exaggerate. And as near as he could tell, none had regrets. Just because he never planned to marry didn't mean he couldn't enjoy a woman. He suspected both his big brothers had tumbled into bed a few times, though they never bragged like some men. Maybe something was wrong with him. Maybe he couldn't be all that attracted to a woman.

As he stepped into the dawn shadows of the barn, Tobin collided with Liberty. His hand went out to steady her, accidentally brushing the side of one of her breasts with his open palm as he put his arm around her waist.

On second thought, there was nothing wrong with him at all. He was definitely attracted to one woman. Unfortunately, she couldn't have been more out of reach if she had lived on the moon. She was a senator's daughter and he was just a man who delivered horses as far as she was concerned.

"Remove your hand, sir," Liberty snapped.

"Sorry," he managed to say. "Next time I'll let you fall."

"Next time don't run into me." She looked as jumpy as a filly around fire.

Her beautiful eyes were more gray than green this morning and he thought she looked like she'd been crying.

As he stared, her gaze filled with anger.

Confused, he asked, "Did you need something, Miss

Mayfield, or did you come out before daylight just to stand in the way?"

"You said you'd teach me to ride."

"It's not even seven o'clock in the morning."

"I want to try before I change my mind."

He saw it again. The fear in her gaze, and he knew the anger was not directed at him. She was fighting fear with any tool she could find. "I thought you said you wouldn't learn?" He lowered his tone.

"I've changed my mind. A woman has the right to change her mind, at least in some matters."

He guessed the truth even if she didn't know him well enough to be honest. She feared something, or someone, more than she did horses.

He moved to the stall where Sunny waited.

Liberty backed into the corner by the door while Tobin saddled two horses. He watched her out of the corner of his eye as light danced across her china smooth face. She wore a plain white blouse and a split skirt for riding a regular saddle. The jacket she carried over one arm didn't look thick enough to offer any warmth. Her midnight hair, which had been curled and tucked back last night, now flowed straight down her back. Her boots looked new.

He grinned. Even in simple clothes, she still looked every ounce a princess. She was a woman who got everything she wanted when she wanted it, he guessed.

"What do I do?" she asked when she seemed to be able to stand the silence no longer.

"Tie back that hair. It might get in the way," Tobin ordered.

She looked around. "With what?"

He looped the reins over a railing and walked over to her. "Turn around."

She raised one eyebrow, then did as he asked.

Tobin tugged off his gloves and gently moved his fingers into her hair. It was even thicker than he would have guessed. "When I was a kid, I always had to braid my little sister's hair." His fingers twisted the strands of silk into a long braid.

"Don't you do this?" He'd assumed all women braided their hair at night. Sage always did when she changed into her nightclothes.

Liberty turned her head. "No. Joy, my maid, combs it around damp rags so it will be curly in the morning. I've never worn a braid. My father doesn't think they're lady-like."

Tobin twisted off the end with a strip of leather. Her hair was beautiful even in the braid down her back, but bore not one turn of curl. "What happened last night?"

She gave him a sharp look, then said simply, "I didn't bother with the damp rags. Not that it's any of your concern, but I was tired." She brushed her hand over his handiwork. "Thank you."

"You're welcome." He wondered when he'd ever talked to a stranger so much.

He shoved on his gloves and motioned her toward the horses.

She didn't move. She simply stared at the animals. "I can't," she whispered. "They're so big."

He thought of grabbing her and lifting her up on the horse's back just to show her there was nothing to fear, but he wouldn't know how to handle the hysterical female she might turn into. She would frighten Sunny if she yelled and, if the animal bolted, he'd never get her near a horse again.

"All right." He tried to assure her that he knew what he was doing. "We'll take this one step at a time." Maybe now would be a good time to tell her he'd never taught anyone to ride. They'd carried Sage with them from the time she could walk, and as soon as she could reach stirrups his little sister outrode them all.

He put the horses back into their stalls and closed the gates so only their heads hung over. "How about we say hello first?"

To his surprise, she took a step forward. Knowing that the horse could not get any closer seemed to calm her.

"Hold the reins firm with one hand. That way he won't shake his head and frighten you."

She took the reins.

"Now, stroke his head, nice and gentle." Tobin moved behind her, circling his arms around her, showing her. "Talk to him, Miss Mayfield. I'll be right here if you need me. And if he nudges you, that's just his way of saying hello, so don't be frightened."

"Hello, boy," she said, her voice shaking slightly. "I'm not going to be afraid of you."

Sunny snorted, making her jump. Tobin steadied her and whispered, "Easy now. It's all right. You're doing fine."

She looked at him. "Are you talking to me or the horse?"

Tobin shrugged. "Does it matter?"

She huffed. "I guess not."

Twenty minutes later she'd fed the horse an apple and relaxed a fraction. Sunny's head movements and snorts no longer made her jump.

Tobin opened the gate and taught her how to walk the horse out. He explained where to stand and how to circle close behind the animal. She touched Sunny the way he did, listening to every word he said. "Now walk him outside," he finally said as he handed her the reins.

After a few steps, she turned back to him and said, "Stay close."

"I'm your shadow," he answered.

Her step steadied and he guessed she believed him. He stayed within easy reach of her as they walked the beautiful horse into the cool morning light.

Sunny liked the attention and was on his best behavior.

Absently, as he'd done hundreds of times for his sister, Tobin lifted Liberty's hat and put it on her head. "I'll tell you a secret about horses, Miss Mayfield. Most like to please. Problem is, sometimes they don't know what you want from them. You let Sunny know you'll take care of him and he'll run his heart out for you."

She patted the horse's neck.

"Why don't you give him a drink while I get my mount?"

Liberty nodded, but she didn't look too happy about him leaving if only for a minute.

Tobin collected his horse and a lead rope to tie onto Sunny. He wanted Liberty to ride, but if she got into trouble, he'd control her horse for her.

As he stepped behind her, he asked, "You ready to get up now?"

She shook her head. Her hat hid her face, but he stood so close he could sense her fear.

His hands circled her waist. "I'm going to sit you up in the saddle nice and easy, miss. There's nothing to worry about. I'm right here."

She shook her head again. "I can't." She twisted in his hold. "You don't understand. I saw my mother fall from a horse when I was four. Her head hit a rock and she just closed her eyes as if she went to sleep."

Tobin felt her entire body shake beneath his grip.

"I was only ten feet away, but by the time I reached her blood circled around her." Liberty's intense gaze met his. "I had to kneel in her blood to touch her."

Tobin pulled her to him, holding Liberty tightly against him while she shook. He might have been two years older when he'd been ambushed, but he remembered how it felt to be surrounded by blood. The smell of it. The taste of it deep in his throat. The thick feel of it on his skin.

"It's all right, Liberty," he whispered against her ear. "It's all right."

After a moment, she calmed and pulled away. "I'm sorry. I thought I could do this, but I can't."

"You can do this," he answered.

"No."

"Liberty, the horse didn't kill your mother. The fall might have, or the rock she hit, but not the horse. I've seen a few horses that people have mistreated who turned mean, but your father would never have let your mother ride a horse like that. What happened was an accident. A terrible accident."

She faced him. Tears swam in her stormy eyes. "I have to learn to ride. I have to."

He saw it then, the strong determination. And, once more,

he knew without doubt that this lady feared something far more than riding. She had to rule one fear to survive another.

"We'll do this together." Before she could argue, he gently lifted her onto the saddle and swung up behind without letting go of her.

She gripped the saddle horn as if it were a lifeline. He leaned his body against her back and circled his arms around her. With a tug, he dropped the lead rope to his horse, and with a low clicking sound he'd known how to do all his life he nudged the horse into a walk.

They moved away from the barn and headed down a lane shaded with trees on both sides. Once out of the early morning sun, the air chilled and he enjoyed the warmth of her so close. After a few minutes, she relaxed against him and he let his arms rest next to hers.

"Put your hand on top of mine," he said. "Get a feel of the reins before you take them."

She waited so long he wasn't sure she planned to follow his direction, but finally she put one hand on his.

As they rode, slow and easy, he told her how to handle the horse. Tobin did his best to ignore the fact that several parts of their bodies were touching. He wasn't here to come calling. He was here to teach her to ride and then be on his way back home. For what her father was paying for the horse, Tobin could afford to spend an extra day.

"You ready to take the reins now?"

She shook her head, but he turned his hand over and passed the two leather straps to her. His fingers laced between hers as he covered her hold, and he found himself wishing there were no gloves between them.

"Tell him where to go," Tobin whispered in her ear. "You're the boss."

She nodded stiffly and he moved his hand away.

For a while, she let the horse have his head. Sunny seemed content to continue down the road. When he tried to stop or wander to the side for grass, Liberty tugged him back, each time her movements more fluid, more sure.

"That's the way, Libby," he coached. "You're doing fine."

"Don't call me Libby. It's not my name."

"All right, what should I call you?"

"Miss Mayfield will be fine." He could feel her back stiffening.

"At least for three more days and then I guess you'll be Mrs. Buchanan." Tobin wished he hadn't said the words the moment they were out of his mouth.

Her back went rigid. She didn't speak.

He waited her out. Finally, she said, "How do I turn around? I'm ready to go back."

He talked her through the rest of the ride. When they arrived at the barn, he stepped down and helped her as politely as if they were total strangers, and for all he knew that was exactly what they were. Two people who'd shared a riding lesson, nothing more.

"I'll be back at one for another lesson."

He tipped his hat. "We'll be ready, Miss Mayfield."

Watching her walk away, Tobin couldn't help but wonder why, for a lady who hated horses, she sure was in one hell of a hurry to learn to ride.

"McMurray!" A sharp northern accent snapped through the air.

Tobin faced Captain Samuel Buchanan. The man looked like a painting of the perfect young officer. His uniform pressed and brushed, his buttons and boots polished.

Tobin, on the other hand, looked like he had slept in his clothes, which he had. "Morning, Captain."

Buchanan didn't bother with pleasantries. "I saw you had my fiancée riding this morning. I commend you. She's a beauty, but a coward of a woman. You're the last of a long line of people who've tried to teach her to ride. Most, she simply ordered off the property. As far as I know you are the first to actually get her in the saddle."

"Maybe she was motivated." He remembered how she'd stiffened when he'd mentioned that she would be Mrs. Buchanan soon.

"Or maybe she's learning to follow orders," the captain said more to himself than Tobin. "We have little time left. Some of the guests are already moving to the hotels in town so they'll be ready for our Saturday morning wedding."

Tobin didn't comment. If the captain took the time to look in Liberty's eyes, he'd know that she was neither a coward nor learning to follow orders. He'd also realize that she had none of the signs of a bride counting down the hours.

"The point is, she's learning to ride." The captain straightened. "I've other matters to think about. See that the lessons continue."

Realizing he'd been dismissed, Tobin grabbed the reins and walked Sunny back to the barn.

At the barn door, he turned to watch the captain and several of his men mount up and ride away as if they had important matters to attend to. The soldiers were camped in small tents a few hundred yards from the house. Judging from the tents, Tobin would guess about a dozen men traveled with the captain. They must be the chosen few, the best, for a captain on a frontier assignment would have many more under his command.

Dermot strolled out of the barn and leaned on the pitchfork he carried. For a few minutes he stood beside Tobin and watched. Finally, the older man said, "I don't much like that fellow. Never bothers to cool down his own horse."

"He's busy," Tobin murmured, but remembered how he'd heard his father say once that a man too busy to care for his horse should try walking.

"More so every day." Dermot shook his head. "The senator's always had to deal with hotheads yelling and calling him out, but lately, with the trouble with Mexico, it's a mountain of trouble I fear coming. Our Captain Buchanan there takes his job of guard seriously. If something happened to the senator he'd be losing not only a father-in-law, but a career."

After today, their troubles weren't his. One or two more riding lessons and Liberty would know enough to stay in the saddle. The senator had only asked him to stay a day. Dermot might feel trouble storming in, but the senator expected it. Otherwise, he wouldn't have made Tobin promise to get Liberty to safety if it came.

Tobin unsaddled Sunny, then picked up the reins to his bay. "I think I'll ride into town," he said. "I'll be back in a few hours."

The old man waved him away.

Tobin didn't take a deep breath until the house and barn were out of sight. He needed to ride, just ride. It seemed the only time he could think.

He pushed his powerful mount until he saw the dust of what had to be the captain and his men. Tobin pulled back. The last thing he wanted was another conversation with Buchanan. Especially if what he suspected about the man was true.

Turning off the road, Tobin stayed close to the trees, needing to feel nature around him.

Halfway between the ranch and town, he noticed a campfire's smoke drifting up from well into the woods. Tobin walked his horse toward it. By the time he was close enough to see a campsite, he'd blended even his shadow into the brush and wrapped the bridle so that his horse didn't make a sound. He guessed he was still on Mayfield land, and it looked as if the senator had uninvited guests.

Tobin would have assumed any camp this close to town was simply travelers, but the senator's fear of trouble coming today made Tobin check. From the road Buchanan and his men wouldn't have spotted the smoke. Whoever camped either was harmless or they thought they were far enough off any path to be noticed.

The men around a dying fire were rough with the markings of a band of Gypsies. But something didn't sit right with Tobin. He'd seen Gypsies before, even allowed some of them to camp next to the bridge on McMurray land. But these men were different.

He noticed the horses first. Not old broken-down wagon horses, but fast mounts with good lines. Except for a pot of coffee near the fire, there were no signs that the band had cooked or killed their meat. Gypsies lived off the land as they moved around. The campsite was far too organized to have been new. What kind of men build a camp and then don't use it?

There were no women about, or any signs of them. Gypsies always traveled in families.

The last thing Tobin noticed were the rifles stacked military-style. These men would not welcome a stranger. Tobin knew better than to walk into their camp alone. Whatever they were doing, they had chosen a site far from the road. They wanted no visitors.

He marked the way to their camp with an old Indian sign his grandfather taught him as he backtracked to the road. No traveler would notice the marking, but Tobin could find it easily when he returned.

He kicked his horse, and rode toward town. A few minutes later he took the window seat at the boardinghouse café and watched people moving about a town just coming to life with business for the day.

He'd almost finished his second breakfast of the morning when he noticed the captain riding in. Tobin wondered how he could have arrived ahead of Buchanan when they traveled the same road. Obviously Buchanan had stopped. Somewhere along the way. Somewhere off the road.

Tobin relaxed and finished his meal. Buchanan must have been checking out the strangers as well. Maybe they were some of his troops, out of uniform so they could guard the perimeter of the ranch.

Watching the captain, Tobin crossed the street to the mercantile. Buchanan seemed nervous, strung tighter than drying rawhide. He not only had to guard one of the most powerful men in Texas, but the captain had to do it during a public wedding—his own.

After buying a fresh shirt and a foot of ribbon, Tobin headed back to the ranch. One day, he thought. One day and he'd be out of this place and on his way home. He'd heard Stella say that everyone in the wedding party would be moving to the hotels in town tonight. After that he could forget the second promise he'd made the senator. Both the senator and Liberty would be surrounded by every Texas Ranger, marshal, and sheriff in the area.

Tobin could go back to Whispering Mountain and forget about them all.

CHAPTER 7

LIBERTY SMILED ALL THE WAY BACK TO THE HOUSE. She'd done it—or at least she'd begun. Somehow she'd managed to climb on a horse and stay there long enough to learn something. Tobin McMurray had been bossy most of the time, but his touch had reassured her again and again. It was almost as if they were communicating on two levels at the same time. There was such caring in his touch and such formality in his speech. She sensed that talking was harder for him than the contact. Growing up in politics, it was unusual to meet a man who preferred silence to talk.

She couldn't make up her mind if she liked the man or not. Half their conversations seemed to be arguments. But when he communicated silently with a brush of his arm, or a touch on her shoulder, she sensed no anger. No hostility.

"Miss?" Joy greeted Liberty at the door and fell into step. "Will you be wanting a bath?"

"Yes," Liberty said, "and lunch in my room." For the first time in days she was truly hungry. "Then I'll need an hour's rest before my next lesson."

Joy, as always, hurried to take care of Liberty's needs.

"Captain Buchanan said you would, so I've already got the tub ready."

Liberty slowed on the stairs. She resented his comment to her maid but did not bother to point it out. Joy, she knew, idolized the captain and thought he was the most handsome man she'd ever seen.

"Is my father here?" Liberty asked.

"He's in a meeting," Joy said as she opened the door to Liberty's room. "And we all know what that means."

"He's not to be disturbed."

"Right," Joy agreed. "Captain told me this morning that the senator had a mountain of troubles to deal with today."

Liberty's shoulders drooped slightly. She understood. No one had better bother the senator unless the house was on fire.

"I'll catch him later," Liberty said as she pulled off her clothes and slipped into a soft robe.

"What did you do to your hair?" Joy asked.

"I braided it." Liberty didn't want to tell Joy that a man had done the task.

The maid shook her head. "I'll comb it out for you."

"All right, but then braid it back."

Joy raised an eyebrow but followed orders without comment.

Liberty closed her eyes as the maid twisted her hair back into a thick braid. She could almost imagine it was Tobin McMurray's hands working through her hair and surprised herself by thinking how much she might enjoy that.

Despite her worries, Liberty slept soundly after she ate. The day grew cloudy and the promise of rain whipped in the air. By the time she crawled out of bed and dressed, she was late for her next riding lesson.

Tobin McMurray stood holding the reins of two horses as she ran into the barn. He raised his eyebrow in rebuff, then walked the mounts past her without saying a word.

He certainly hadn't mellowed since this morning, she thought, as she followed him out. In fact, now his mood seemed as dark as the clouds gathering on the western horizon. Liberty stood a few feet away, her arms crossed.

Tobin messed with the horses, adjusting, checking until he finally had to look at her.

She waited.

He grumbled, "The next time you're late you'll saddle your own horse."

"I'm sorry," she raised her chin slightly. "I was unavoidably detained." If he had any comment, she planned to remind him that he worked for her.

"We'll be lucky to make it back before the rain," he answered, then closed the distance between them. "I got you something." He dug into his vest pocket.

Taking the tiny paper sack, she pulled out a thin strip of blue ribbon. "What is it?" she asked, more aware of his nearness than the ribbon.

"It's for your hair," he said.

"Oh." She didn't know what to say. She had a hundred ribbons upstairs. She certainly didn't need this stranger buying her a piece. An engaged lady should never accept a gift from a man, but a penny bit of ribbon surely didn't count. "Thank you," she said awkwardly.

He looked embarrassed. "I just thought it would look better than the leather."

She tied it to the end of her braid. "You're right. It does. Shall we start the lesson?"

When she moved beside Sunny, she felt Tobin's hands go round her waist. He lifted her up onto the horse, then brushed the calf of her leg as he shoved her boot into the stirrup.

"Aren't you getting up behind me?" Liberty fought to keep panic from her voice.

"No," he answered. "This time you ride alone, but I'll be close if you need me, miss."

She started to tell him to call her Liberty. She couldn't even remember why she'd insisted on Miss Mayfield.

She laced the reins like he'd taught her as he tied a rope onto Sunny's bridle and led him over to where the other horse waited.

"Mr. McMurray, I don't think I'm ready for this. I need more time."

He patted her leg. "Of course, you are. I'll be riding right beside you. You'll be fine." There was more warmth in his touch than his words.

Anger sparked along with fear. "Stop talking to me as if I were a horse you could calm and stop patting me."

He said something under his breath and mounted his horse. "We ride north." He glared at her. "And put your damn hat on."

He made a sound and both animals moved.

She straightened, trying to remember everything he'd told her, but wasn't fast enough. He reminded her to relax, guide with her legs, loosen up on the reins.

"I guess being nice is over," she said when he went over the rules for the third time in a tone that was less than friendly.

"I guess it is." Tobin pulled his hat low to shade his eyes. "Now kick it up a little. I could walk faster than you're riding."

They rode north into a field without trees. After almost two hours her legs and arms ached from trying to do everything he told her. She didn't know if she was more angry at him for bossing her or at herself for never seeming to remember all he told her. She'd been so busy following orders she'd forgotten her fear.

"Can we stop for a minute?" she asked removing her hat to wipe her forehead with her sleeve. The air seemed as thick as soup.

He stared at her awhile. She guessed he thought she must be the weakest female in the world. She'd read about men who stayed in the saddle from sunup to sundown. She hadn't even made it two hours.

Tobin pointed. "There's a stream another half mile ahead. We can rest the horses there, but not for long. A storm looks like it might be moving in."

"Good," she said replacing her hat. "Maybe it will cool off." She hadn't missed his point that it was the horses he was considering, not her. "How do you know there is a stream on our north border?"

He didn't look her direction. "I rode in this way."

"But there is a road to our place. You didn't need to ride across the land."

He shrugged. "I like riding across open land. You don't run into many people."

"You don't like most people, do you, Mr. McMurray?"

"Nope."

"And I fall into that 'most' category?"

Surprised he didn't answer, she guessed what he thought of her and told herself she didn't care. Putting up with him was just a means to an end.

After a few minutes of riding silently, he pointed toward a bare spot between cottonwoods. "There's a place where we should be able to get to the water easy enough. When we head down toward the stream lean back, not forward, and let the horse find his own footing."

She did as told, adding "close eyes" to the list of directions while her mount picked his way down the bank. When she opened her eyes, the horse had stopped and stood a few feet from the water.

"Get down," Tobin said as he swung off his horse. He held the reins for her.

"I can't," she said. "I don't know how."

He moved to her side, touching her leg again. "Keep this leg in the stirrup and swing the other one high over the horse's back."

When she did what he said, his hands caught her waist and guided her down.

"That's good," he added as both of her feet touched the ground. "Even if you'll probably always have people to help you mount and dismount, it's a good idea to know how to do it yourself."

Liberty had had enough of him. "Don't bother to pat me on the head or try to be polite. I'm fully aware of what you think of me and I don't care. Just teach me to ride."

He handed her Sunny's reins. "Water your horse, then tie him over where the grass is high so he can graze. Once he's taken care of, you've got half an hour to rest before we head back."

Liberty wanted to scream that he should water the horse, but she didn't say a word. Somewhere in his mind he probably thought he was doing her a favor by insisting she learn how to take care of her own mount. Her backside might be killing her, but she wouldn't complain. He'd probably just pat it and say it would be fine.

She did as told. When she looked back, he was stretched out on the grass a few feet from where his horse grazed. His hands were behind his head, his hat covered his face. She had a feeling he wasn't asleep, but at least he wasn't watching her and correcting every move she made. Tobin McMurray could have been one fine-looking man if he made half an effort to be nice, but the frown he wore seemed permanently tatooed across his face.

Sitting on a rock beside the stream, she tugged off her boots, wishing she owned a pair of the knee-high moccasins like he wore. One of her stockings had slipped down and the leather of the boot rubbed her skin raw near her knee. Checking to make sure he hadn't turned in her direction, she tugged up her skirt and slipped her leg into the cold water all the way to her knee.

Smiling, she realized she felt freer at this moment than she had in months. Washington, D.C., was exciting, but there were always people watching, judging her every move, evaluating everything she said. No one watched her now. Except for the sleeping man behind her, no one even knew where she was. She could wiggle her toes in the stream without worry that it would appear in Mrs. Prescott's social news column the next day.

Thunder rumbled in the distance. Tobin lifted his hat showing no sign that he'd been dozing. "We'd better be getting back."

A spark of lightning cracked the sky a few hundred yards away. Liberty let out a scream as she scrambled to her feet, her boots forgotten in the grass.

Tobin rose in one fluid movement and reached for his horse as the storm rolled across the land like a downhill train.

"Grab your mount!" he shouted, but it was too late. Sunny had pulled free from the bush he'd been tied to and was in full gallop toward the barn.

Liberty ran a few feet, then stopped and stomped her foot in frustration. Tobin rode up beside her and offered her a hand. "Climb up. We'd better race him to the barn or we'll be soaked."

She'd expected him to give her a lecture about keeping her horse tied, but he didn't. In fact he smiled down at her as the first raindrops splattered her face.

Taking his hand, she swung up behind him and wrapped her arms around his waist. She felt the powerful muscles in his legs kick the bay into action, and suddenly they were racing the storm.

Liberty laughed. She would have thought she'd been frightened at the speed he took, but she felt safe against his solid back. He knew what he was doing. The man had probably been born in the saddle.

As the wind and rain increased, Liberty and Tobin sliced through the air toward the barn. His back protected her from the rage of the storm. Someday, she thought, I'll ride like this. I'll be one with the horse and have no fear.

Twice, Tobin's arm covered hers where she held tight. Both times he rubbed her hand, warming it with his own.

The downpour had soaked through their clothes by the time they reached the barn. Dermot waited, ready to take the horse. "Thank the Lord ye made it, Miss Liberty. I was worried about ye when that horse came in alone."

Tobin lowered her to the ground, then climbed off laughing. "What about me, Dermot? Were you worried about me?"

The old man shook his head. "Ye were riding like the devil was chasing ye, lad. My guess is 'tis not the first time ye've outrun the lightning."

"You're right." Tobin turned and winked at Liberty. "That's the way to really ride—fast on a good horse."

Liberty grinned back thinking of how he looked younger when he smiled and wondering why he did it so rarely.

"Riding that fast didn't frighten you, did it?" he asked, concern in his voice.

"No. I loved it."

Dermot moved away with the horses.

Tobin glanced down the length of her. "You're soaked." He frowned. "Where are your boots?"

Liberty hugged her sides. "By the stream."

Tobin took a step toward her. He opened his mouth to say something, then changed his mind. With a swift movement, he lifted her into his arms. "I'll get you through the mud and to the back porch."

"Thank you, Mr. McMurray," she whispered, leaning her cheek against his shoulder already feeling the warmth of his body through wet clothes.

A moment later they were back in the rain. His arms held her tightly as he ran for the house. Circling her arms around his neck, she did what she'd done when they'd been riding, she hung on tightly. Tobin McMurray was tall, a bit on the slim side, but he seemed to be made up of solid muscle. She felt no fear of falling as they splashed toward home.

When they reached the porch he set her legs down gently, letting them brush against his as he lowered her. Then, far too quickly, he stepped away.

She shivered with the sudden absence of warmth.

A moment later, he was back in front of her and the blanket kept on the porch swing circled her shoulders.

Liberty snuggled into its comfort, laughing. "Thanks," she said looking up at him. "But you're dripping wet also."

Lifting one blanket-covered hand, she wiped the rain from his face. Then, without thought of anything but warmth, she circled her arms once more around him, enclosing him within the blanket.

For a moment he stood still letting the heat from their bodies blend. Then he lowered his mouth to hers, his hands closed over the sides of her ribs and pulled her hard against him.

His kiss was soft, but held no hesitance as he shifted her body to fit perfectly against him. When she didn't pull away, his kiss grew bolder, drinking her in as if he were dying of thirst.

The rain curtained them off from the rest of the world, but she didn't feel the cold. All she felt was his firm, hungry mouth pressed against hers, tasting her lips. And his hands, sliding over her back, pulling her closer. With each breath, her breasts pressed against his chest as both their heartbeats pounded.

They were once more in a storm, only this time they raced full speed ahead. Every caress he made along her body sent lightning dancing through her veins and his warm kiss thundered a passion she'd never before felt cross her mind.

When she opened her mouth to him, he moaned low in his throat and the kiss deepened. His hand slid over her hip and cupped her bottom, holding her boldly.

The storm beyond the porch drifted away and all Liberty's world began and ended in the circle of Tobin's arms. His hands. His mouth. His body against her. He smelled wild and free and tasted of a pleasure she craved.

Her grip around his neck tightened. She feared he might slip away before she could have her fill. She felt the rumble of a laugh more than heard it as he straightened without loosening his grip around her. Lifting her off the ground, his caress took her breath away. She melted in his embrace knowing he wouldn't let her fall.

When he finally lowered her back to earth and broke the kiss, he whispered low in her ear, "You all right?"

Closing her eyes, letting the paradise float through her, she whispered, "Yes, Mr. McMurray, I'm fine."

He nuzzled her throat as he responded. "Don't you think you should call me Tobin?"

His kisses along her neck were sending waves of heat all the way to her toes. "All right."

He pulled away so only his breath brushed her damp throat. "All right, what?"

"All right, Tobin," she answered and felt his mouth return hungrily to the spot where her blood pulsed.

She heard the creak of the kitchen door a moment before he did. She didn't move, as if by staying still no one could interrupt them, but he raised his head.

"Miss Liber . . ." Stella's voice trailed off.

Beneath the blanket Liberty felt Tobin's arm tighten protectively around her middle; then he moved in front of her like an ancient warrior shielding his mate.

She was flattered, but she didn't need protecting from the kitchen help. "Yes, Stella, what is it?" Liberty snapped in her most proper voice.

Stella looked down at Liberty's bare feet. "The captain sent me to see if you were back from your ride. He wishes to have a drink with you in the study before dinner. Said he has pressing matters to discuss."

Liberty moved around Tobin, feeling his resistance to step aside. "Tell him I'll be there in twenty minutes."

The maid nodded and rushed back inside.

Liberty closed her eyes. She had to say something to Tobin before she stepped back into the real world. What had just happened between them had been wild and wonderful, but it didn't belong in her world. Tonight, or tomorrow morning at the latest, she'd talk to her father and convince him to allow her to break the engagement and return to Washington. Soon neither the captain nor this rancher would be a part of her life.

She faced him, but when their eyes met she saw anger, not understanding as she'd expected.

"I owe you an apology," he snapped as if he'd already read her mind. "That shouldn't have happened."

His dismissal hit her hard. Even though she knew there could be no future, she would liked to have cherished what they shared for a little longer, and to believe that he would also.

But he hadn't. He'd already buried it.

"Forgotten," she snapped back, then pulled propriety over her like a cape. "Thank you for the lesson."

He was off the porch and back into the rain before she finished. His long legs took him into the gray rain, washing him from her sight in seconds.

"Tobin," she whispered, before turning and running all the way up the back stairs to her room.

CHAPTER 8

TOBIN STOMPED THROUGH THE RAIN NOT CARING that mud splattered all the way to his knees. Most of his anger was turned inward. He'd made a fool of himself. He'd acted on impulse, not reason. All his life he'd prided himself on holding back. His brothers might fire up and act, but he thought things through first. Only this time—this time he'd kissed Miss Liberty Mayfield, a senator's daughter. And he'd kissed her full out, no light hesitant first kiss, but one that promised more, far more.

Liberty wasn't to blame. She'd simply hugged him for warmth and he'd taken it from there. She was stubborn, and proud, and more beautiful than any woman had a right to be. "And," he mumbled to himself, "about to be married to another man."

But when he'd looked down at her deep green eyes, something misfired in his brain. The next thing he knew he was pulling her so close he could feel her heart pounding. If Stella hadn't stepped out on the porch, Liberty would probably still be in his arms.

Liberty had every right to tell her father, and the senator

would more than likely have him shot on sight. He went way over the line of teaching her to ride a horse. If he had any sense, he should roll up his bed now and head out while it was still raining. He'd be harder to track in this weather. If Liberty told anyone what had just happened, there would definitely be men gunning for him.

He stopped suddenly and raised his face to the rain, no longer caring that he was soaked. One thought kept him rooted . . . she might want to forget the kiss . . . she might even have run inside . . . but she'd kissed him back.

The warm rain did nothing to wash away the feel of her lips, or the taste of her tongue timidly exploring his mouth. She might be engaged. She might be a senator's daughter. She might have even been surprised when his mouth covered hers. But she'd welcomed his touch. She hadn't protested when his hands moved over her.

She'd kissed him back!

Tobin straightened and walked the rest of the way to the barn. If he'd gone mad on the porch, he wasn't the only one.

As he stepped out of the downpour, he slung his hat and shook his head to remove a little of the water. The musty, familiar smell of hay greeted him, anchoring him in the real world.

Dermot tossed him a towel. "Enjoy the riding lesson, lad?"

Tobin smiled. "I did." He'd ride all day in the rain if he could spend a few minutes alone on the porch with Liberty again. "What's happening here?" From the sound of it, the number of horses in the barn had doubled since he'd left a few hours ago. Two carriages now blocked most of the entry.

"All the guests are moving into the hotel in town. Buchanan asked the Texas Rangers to return with these two carriages. The captain and the rangers have been inside meeting with hisself for an hour." Dermot shook his head. "Trouble's coming in like a loaded freight train. I can feel it."

Tobin knew even if he wanted to leave, he could never desert Liberty if there was even a small chance that Dermot was right. He remembered how tired the senator had looked when he'd asked for two favors. Teach her to ride, he said, and promise to kidnap her if I'm attacked tomorrow.

The senator must want her out of harm's way if trouble thundered in, and the old soldier in him sensed the danger and prepared.

Late last night Tobin had lain awake trying to think of why the senator had used the word *kidnap*. Not *take*, or *rescue*, or even *escort*, but *kidnap*. It was almost as if Mayfield had asked Tobin to commit what everyone would consider a crime. Tobin frowned. Everyone including Liberty probably. Maybe the old man just didn't want to take time to explain to her, or anyone else, why Tobin was taking her.

Tobin didn't want to think of how much she would hate him if he grabbed her and took her away from not only her wedding but also her father when the senator might be in danger. She'd fight him with all her strength and he'd have to tie and gag her. Tobin had never forced a woman to do anything in his life, but if the senator needed the favor, he would. Not because he'd promised, but because Mayfield wouldn't have asked unless Liberty's life was on the line.

"I got coffee warming by the tack room. Ye want some?" Dermot watched the storm from the doorway. "It'll be dinnertime soon. Maybe the rain will let up enough for us to walk to the kitchen without getting soaked." He glanced at Tobin. "Not that ye'd care."

Tobin disappeared in what had become his stall and changed into his new shirt and his only pair of dry trousers. Funny, he thought, how comfortable he was bunking in a horse stall. He liked the smell of hay and the sounds the animals made. Maybe he really did have a bit of horse blood in him. He wouldn't have traded this stall for a room in the mansion.

He poured himself a cup of coffee and pulled up a barrel to join Dermot at the door. The rain had slowed to a drizzle. Water plopped from the roof into mud holes near the barn making a strange kind of music. The pale sun hung low on the horizon, with thin fingers pushing between dark clouds. Any other day it would have been a peaceful time, but Dermot was right—Tobin could feel trouble humming in the distance.

Tobin whistled softly knowing the horses must feel the air changing as a storm rumbled somewhere along the distance.

"Want to make a run for the house? Me Anna said she'd make us a shepherd's pie. She'd already made the dessert for tonight. We'll have our choice of pie or cake."

Tobin shook his head. He wasn't hungry and he didn't want to run into Stella in the kitchen. The girl seemed shy around Liberty, but she'd probably put him in his place if she got the chance. "I think I'll just finish the pot of coffee."

"Suit yeself," Dermot mumbled as he pulled his hat low and limped for the house, dodging puddles like a man crossing a battlefield.

Tobin sat on the bench just outside the barn, drank his coffee, and wondered what Liberty was doing only yards away. Was she thinking about the kiss, or had she done what she said? Had she forgotten it? Had it meant anything to her? Did one kiss mean anything to him? He wasn't in love with her. Most of the time he wasn't even sure he liked her.

One kiss meant nothing. She was right. They should both forget it. After all, it wasn't like he'd taken her to his bed.

Once the thought of them together in bed crossed his mind, it didn't want to leave. He'd thought of mating with a woman, but never of sleeping with one. What would it be like to hold Liberty all night in his arms? To hold her with no clothes between them?

Tobin swore at himself. He was thinking like a young pup still wet behind the ears. He was a man with far more important things to worry about than one kiss.

He stood and went for another cup of coffee. At this rate he'd finish the pot before sunset.

Twenty minutes after Liberty left Tobin on the back porch, she walked into the small library that Samuel had commandeered for his office. She'd changed clothes and tucked her wet hair into a tight bun at the base of her neck. Everything about her looked flawless from the shine of her midnight hair to her pale cheeks.

"You look quite presentable, tonight, Liberty." Captain Buchanan seemed to take in every inch of her. "Beautiful, in fact. I can hardly wait to see you all in white. You'll be the loveliest bride these Texans have ever seen."

"Thank you," she managed, without caring about the compliment. His clipped formalness hung in the room like an invisible noose waiting to snare her. She might like the man less every time they were together, but she was learning his moods. His smile that wasn't quite a smile. His compliment that manipulated. The tight way he held himself as if fearing he might slip and be less than perfect.

Stella served Samuel tea but looked away when Liberty neared. Liberty decided the girl must be embarrassed at having seen her kissing the rancher. When she got Stella alone, she'd explain that she felt no shame or regret for what had happened. It might have been an impulse but Liberty would never be able to lie to anyone, not even herself, to wish it hadn't happened. She and Captain Samuel Buchanan were finished. Any feeling for him was dead. If they hadn't been over, she never would have allowed Tobin to kiss her like that.

But she and Stella weren't alone. The captain seemed, as he always did, to fill the room. He thanked Stella for the scones, swearing that if she'd join the army men would flock to enlist just for her cooking.

Stella smiled shyly. Like Joy, Liberty's maid, Stella was completely charmed by the captain.

Samuel pushed a bit further, giving her one of his winning smiles. "Thank you, dear," he said lowering his voice with the endearment. "You've been a jewel. Now if you'll close the door on your way out, I have some business to discuss with my fiancée."

Liberty saw her chance. "Before you go, Stella, could you ask my father to join us? I believe he's in the formal dining room." In truth, she had no idea where the senator might be, but the dining room was as good a guess as any.

Stella didn't look at Liberty, but she shook her head. "He's at the other end of the house, miss, talking to a couple of rangers. He told me not to disturb him."

Stella turned her attention back to Samuel. "I'll see that you're not disturbed either, sir."

"Thank you," he said with such kindness that even Liberty almost believed him.

For a moment he stood at attention until he heard the click of the door. Then he faced her and the angry man she'd seen at the ball returned. Perfect features twisted slightly, distorting like reflection in cheap glass.

"I understand you're on very friendly terms with Mr. McMurray." His words sliced the silence as he pulled a heavy wooden chair out for her.

Liberty ignored the chair, refusing to sit.

She wasn't sure if his comment was a question or a statement. Either way, she didn't want to be interrogated about McMurray. She also had no doubt where Samuel got the information. What loyalty Stella possessed had shifted. The little cook had become an informant.

Samuel set his cup down carefully, not allowing even a slight click of china. "I'll not have you embarrassing me days before our wedding. I've made no secret of my plans one day to run for office. To do so I, and now you, must live a life that is above reproach."

Liberty raised her head as she faced him. "I plan to talk to my father as soon as he's available. I hope I haven't caused you any inconvenience, Captain Buchanan, but I'm afraid there will be no wedding." A clean cut seemed the only way to end it. He was not the man she thought him to be.

To her shock, Samuel smiled. "Yes, my dear, there *will* be a wedding," he answered calmly. "I feared this might be stewing in your thoughts since last night's little spat. But I've taken steps to ensure that it's too late to change your mind. Everything has already been set into action." His laughter held no humor. "In fact, I think the wedding should happen sooner."

Liberty stood her ground. "As soon as Father is free from

his meeting, I plan to tell him I will not marry. No matter what he said, he won't make me marry a man I have no wish to spend an evening with, much less a lifetime. And, sir, I'm afraid there is nothing you can do about the matter. I'm not a nervous bride. I'm not your bride at all."

Samuel moved, positioning himself between her and the door. "And what, pet, has brought on this sudden change of heart? One bothersome rancher? Maybe one too many riding lessons?"

"Tobin has nothing to do with this." She realized her mistake before the words died in the air.

"Tobin?" Samuel smiled a smile she was beginning to hate. "I'll have to deal with Mr. McMurray later. He needs to learn a lesson."

"There will be no later," she answered, furious that he thought she'd be so easy to dismiss. "It's time you and your men leave, Captain Buchanan. My father made his career as a soldier for years. I'm sure he can defend himself. We no longer need your guard, and I no longer wish to be in your company." She'd man a gun herself and stand guard if it would cut this man out of her life faster.

"You're wrong, my dear." Samuel stepped forward so suddenly, Liberty jumped backward. "You'll change your mind. You only need someone to guide you."

His arm went up. She thought he was reaching for her, but instead he shoved her.

A moment later, her side slammed into the wooden arm of the chair, knocking the breath from her lungs. She stumbled backward more in shock than in pain and tripped over a footstool. The hard landing on her backside brought reality back in full focus.

Samuel towered over her. Hate flickered in his eyes an instant before he bowed and offered his hand. "I'm sorry. I tend to lose my temper, my love." He laughed. "I never realized how clumsy you were."

Timidly, she took his hand and he pulled her off the rug. Rage at the way he'd made his point infuriated her, but she held her tongue. Arguing with a man who would do anything to win could prove dangerous. Until this moment she hadn't realized just how dangerous Captain Buchanan could be.

Holding her side with one hand, Liberty almost had her footing when she saw him raise his free hand. There was no time to block. Nowhere to run. He slapped her hard across the face.

She would have fallen backward again, only this time he had a firm grip on her.

"You spoiled child. This time you'll not have your way." The next slap, with the back of his hand, knocked her head back and she saw stars. "A wife needs discipline, and we might as well get a few things straight tonight. I've invested too much time in this quest to give up now. We're a fine match, even the president says so. You'll thank me for this one day when I'm in the White House and you're first lady."

"I'm not your . . ." She thought she must be losing consciousness for she barely felt the next slap, or the next. She tasted blood and watched as crimson drops fell on her pale green gown.

She thought of screaming for help, but Samuel had chosen the one place in the house were no one would hear her.

He didn't turn her loose when she wilted, but pulled her roughly up and laced·her captured hand over his arm. "Now, love, we'll have no more of this discussion."

His grip was crushing as they crossed to the door, but when she looked up she saw no anger left in his face. He'd calmed as quickly as he'd fired.

"We'll talk more later." He bruised her arm with his hold as he opened the door with his free hand. "And we will have no more talk of delaying the wedding."

He didn't bother to wait for her answer. Quickly pulling her up the stairs, he said in a caring voice, "I'll tell your cook that you are too tired from riding to have dinner downstairs. Your father leaves for town in a few minutes, so I'll have her fix us a tray and I'll bring it up myself to join you. By the time he realizes your carriage didn't follow, it will be too late for him to return to the house."

Liberty tried to pull away. Her ears were ringing with the

pain. Her hair had tumbled from the bun. She didn't know or care if it was her nose or her lip that continued to bleed.

When she jerked hard, he released his grip. She fell across the railing, almost tumbling back down the stairs.

As she gasped, he lifted her into his arms, then carried her to her room, looking very much like a caring fiancé. No one could see the bone-crushing grip he had on her arm or the red marks already bruising across her face. In the shadows, if he were seen, he would appear to be helping.

"Clean yourself up," he whispered as he reached her bedroom door. "You look disgusting."

She thought of screaming, but the maids would be half the house away helping with dinner. What could she tell them? That she'd fallen in the study? And on the stairs, he'd hurt her by merely letting go.

He had slapped her. But slapping one's wife, though frowned upon, wasn't a crime. If her behavior on the porch were known, some would say she deserved it.

Liberty needed time to think.

"If you leave your room tonight, I'll tell everyone you fell," he said as he dropped her on the rug. "I'll tell them now that you've suffered an accident. I'm sure everyone will understand if we have a small wedding. We'll be married by dawn. With all his troubles, the senator will be happy to leave early for Washington. The guests will be disappointed, but accidents can't be helped."

Samuel fought down a laugh.

She didn't say a word, but she wished Samuel dead. No one in her entire life had ever struck her in anger. She'd been unprepared. Unarmed. She wouldn't make that mistake again.

He bowed slightly and turned toward the door. "I'll be back as soon as I've seen to your father."

Liberty heard him laugh as he closed the door. She didn't breathe until his footsteps tapped their way down the stairs. All she could think of was that she had to run. But where? His soldiers were probably at every door. The bedroom window would be a death drop. Samuel would see her go down the front stairs, and everyone would see her if she went down the back ones.

Forcing herself to take deep breaths, she fought back tears. She wanted to go to her father.

One dark thought overcame all others. Once her father left for town, she would be alone with a madman. Scrambling to her knees, Liberty pushed aside pain and stood. She had to find him before he left, assuming she'd be right behind him.

Holding her ribs, she walked to the washstand and grabbed a towel, blotting away blood as she rushed to the door.

Locked. Samuel must have taken the key from the inside.

Liberty fought tears, trying to think. Her head still rang from his blows and pain seemed to be sending messages from every part of her body. But there was no time to take inventory of where she was hurt. She had to get to her father. He'd take one look at her, and not only would he call off the wedding, he'd probably kill Samuel Buchanan as well.

The sound of horses drew her to the window. She fought to open it as her father's lean form stepped into a carriage. The rain splashed against her face as she heard her father's quick shout. "Tell Liberty to take her time. I don't want her following too closely. If we run into trouble, I want to know she's well behind with you and your men."

Before she could push her way onto the tiny balcony, he was gone and her cry sounded like that of a wounded animal carried on the wind.

She changed quickly into her riding clothes, a simple white blouse, tan trousers, and a cotton jacket, braiding her hair as she moved.

Gasping for air, she crossed to the far wall. A panel slid allowing her into a storage room for her clothes. Without light, she crossed to the opposite door and slipped into a hallway used by servants.

She had to hide. It was her only choice. If the hour grew late, her father might think to send someone to look for her, but she couldn't bet her life on it. She had nowhere to run and no one to run to. Her plan was simple. Samuel could turn the house upside down, but he wouldn't find her.

Eventually, Samuel would start searching for her between the house and town. When he did, she'd make her move. She'd run to the barn and beg Tobin McMurray to saddle her a horse. Then she'd ride as fast and as far from this house and town, and the captain, as she could.

Liberty hurt too much to think the plan through much further. She'd get somewhere safe and notify her father. He'd probably come for her and they'd be on their way back to Washington. Perhaps after he'd horsewhipped Samuel.

Liberty straightened slowly like a tired, battered soldier ignoring all pain. She was an expert at hiding. This was her home. She knew a place where the captain would never think to look.

Her life depended on it.

CHAPTER 9

Half an hour earlier, Tobin watched the last rays of sun disappear as the lights came on in the house. He wished he were home. A thousand times he'd ridden in after dark and knew as soon as he saw the lights which of his siblings were home. Sage lit her lamp as soon as the shadows grew long. She hated the dark. Teagen always washed up in the mud room and left the light burning if he made it home first. On the rare occasions Travis was home, the study light would be on. If Travis's little wife, Rainey, was with him, every light in the house would be burning because their adopted son everyone called Duck would be running from room to room.

Smiling, Tobin thought of those first few months Travis had Duck. The boy had been taken by outlaws, probably during a raid. Travis had saved him, but odds were good the boy had seen his parents die. At about five, Duck might not talk, but the child bonded, first with Travis and then with all the McMurrays. Within a month Martha swore he was so ornery, he had to have McMurray blood in him. Duck was wild as a raccoon trapped indoors, but they all loved him.

Rainey suggested once that he circled the house checking on everyone just to make sure no one had been taken.

Tobin closed his eyes. He could almost see Whispering Mountain. Home rested thick in his thoughts.

A few minutes later, two men walked from the house. Both were big and wore their guns visible. One was dressed in black, almost like a gambler and the other wore buckskins like a second skin. Tobin took one look and knew they were rangers.

They both nodded as they entered the barn. "You Tobin McMurray?" the one in buckskin asked as he passed.

Tobin touched his hat in greeting. "I am."

"Other than size, I wouldn't have taken you for a McMurray." Eyes that looked like they'd seen a hundred more years than the man had lived stared at Tobin with half caution, half curiosity. "Name's Wes. I rode with your brother last year fighting the raiders along the border. Your brother and you look different."

Tobin knew what the ranger meant. His brother Travis was the only one in the family who favored their mother's Apache blood. Tobin straightened, preparing to defend his family if need be.

"Yeah." The other ranger laughed as he bumped his way between them and reached for a mug on the bench beside the coffeepot. "He's good looking and Travis is uglier than a coyote."

The man in buckskin agreed. "And meaner than a rattler even all dressed up in his fancy lawyer clothes." He pointed with his head toward the man in black. "This fancy dude is Dakota. Don't let his store-bought clothes fool you; he can fight with the best of them."

Tobin relaxed, knowing the men liked and respected his brother or they wouldn't be teasing. While he shook hands, Tobin thought for the hundredth time about how much fun it would be to serve with the rangers. They might look ragtag, but they were a brotherhood to rival knights of old. But he didn't know if he could stand being away from his land for a year or more, and he'd had his fill of gunplay when he'd been a kid.

"Give us a hand, McMurray?" Wes asked. "We need to saddle our two horses and hitch one of the carriages."

Tobin joined them, guessing they trusted him because they knew his brother.

Dakota explained as they worked. "We're taking the senator to town ahead of his daughter and her maid. He's had more death threats. One came flying through his office window in town. Wes and I will ride with him and stand guard at the hotel. There's a young ranger already checking out the road to town to make sure it's clear. The captain and his men will close up the house and follow with Miss Liberty in the second carriage."

Wes added, "Word is, the senator will be leaving for Washington the minute the wedding is over." He downed the hot coffee all at once, then added, "Makes more sense to me to take both of them in the same carriage, but the senator insisted. The captain claims he'll be responsible for the girl and she'll need a while to pack. Says he wants the perimeter secure before he brings her in, whatever the hell that means."

Tobin worked beside them. "I'd rather have three rangers guarding me than a dozen of Buchanan's army."

The man in black laughed. "My sentiments exactly. Captain Buchanan just wants to be in charge. He's real protective of both the old man and his bride-to-be. Whenever he wants his way with the old man, he tosses in a few sentences about Miss Liberty's safety and the senator gives in."

Wes bit off a chew of tobacco as he watched the other two men finish the work. "You ask me, Senator Mayfield is as tough as they come. He don't look like a man who listens to anyone else's counsel or who frightens easily."

Tobin had to agree.

He drove the carriage to the front and hopped down when two of the senator's house staff took the driver's seat. Tobin watched from the shadows as Captain Buchanan and Mayfield walked out.

Mayfield climbed into the carriage, and the two rangers flanking the carriage mounted up.

Then Mayfield opened the carriage door and yelled back
to the captain, leaving one last order. "Tell Liberty to take her
time. I don't want her following too closely. If we run into
trouble, I want to know she's well behind with you and your
men."

"I'll see you in town," Buchanan said with a cursory
wave, but his words were almost drowned out by the clatter
of the horses as the carriage set off.

The horses pulled away from the house and were at a full
run by the time they reached the line of trees marking the
way to town. Two of the captain's guards followed. The rest
of the troops remained, probably planning to ride in with the
second carriage.

Tobin watched the senator's carriage disappear and knew
his time here was almost over. In a few minutes the second
carriage would be pulled up and Liberty would be gone.

Without thinking of why, he saddled his horse and rolled
up his bedroll. He didn't want to be here after she left. He
might as well ride in with the guards surrounding her. Once
he knew she was safe in town, he'd turn toward home and
make a few miles before midnight. Tobin couldn't help but
hope that he'd get to see Liberty again, maybe even talk to
her, but with the captain near it wouldn't be easy.

Once saddled, he walked to the front and waited. The carriage was ready in the barn, but no one had ordered it pulled
to the front. She must be taking a long time to pack.

Time passed and Tobin thought the faraway thunder
sounded like gunfire. The house remained quiet as a tomb.

Though she'd never said a word, he had the feeling Liberty wasn't sure about marrying Captain Buchanan. Maybe
she was stalling upstairs, trying to make up her mind.

Minutes ticked by and a soft rain began to fall. Tobin
leaned against the side of the house and waited. He wasn't
sure how he felt about Miss Liberty, but if he had the chance,
he'd kiss her again.

He heard a horse coming toward the house at full gallop.
Tobin pushed away from the house and walked a few feet
into the rain. Dermot joined him, listening.

"You hear that?" the Irishman whispered.

Tobin reached for his gun.

A lone horse cleared the blackness and the rain, fifty feet from the porch. The rider was uniformed and leaning low trying to stay on the animal.

Dermot grabbed the horse and pulled him to a stop. Tobin caught the soldier as other troops came running.

He passed the bleeding man off to his friends and heard the soldier say, "The senator was ambushed."

As one soldier ran to get the captain, the others asked questions in rapid fire as they worked to help their comrade. "Was the senator hurt? Did they return fire?"

The wounded man mumbled a few words Tobin couldn't make out, then slumped. Tobin didn't have to lean closer to see the wounded man; he could read all he needed to know on the soldiers' faces. Their comrade was dead.

Buchanan ran from the house shouting orders. He wanted half the men ready to ride immediately and the other half on full guard of the house.

Tobin stood as all around him took action. He wanted to rush to the senator's aid, but all he could hear in his head was Mayfield's voice asking for a favor if trouble came.

Rushing toward his horse, Tobin was joined by Dermot.

"You know what he asked me?" Tobin said when they were out of earshot of the others.

"I know." Dermot's voice seemed to have aged. "If I thought I could make the journey, I'd take her meself and I told hisself that."

"It's really necessary then?"

"I would say so."

"Who can I trust?"

"No one except Anna and me. No one," he repeated.

Tobin nodded. "I'll saddle her a horse."

The old man shook his head. "I'll saddle the horse. Anna will get what ye'll need from the kitchen. Pack yer things and then find Miss Liberty."

"Find her? Isn't she in the house?"

Dermot nodded. "She is, but she's hiding. Ye have to find her fast. Before we knew the senator was in danger, I was running to tell you that Miss Liberty needed you. Now you got to follow hisself's orders and get her out of here."

Tobin glanced back at the house.

"Why didn't the senator take her with him?"

Dermot shook his head. "Where hisself is going will be no safer than here, lad."

Tobin began to run. "I have to get her out. Have the horses ready."

"Ye have to find her first," Dermot called after him. "And fast."

CHAPTER 10

Tobin reached the porch of the main house at a full run. When he barged through the kitchen door, he was surprised to find only Anna, the cook. She glanced up with fear in her round eyes, then relaxed when she recognized Tobin.

"Where is everyone?" he asked, allowing no time for small talk.

"Max and Andy were with the senator's carriage. Buchanan is with his men, but he told Joy and Stella to search for Liberty and have her ready to leave." Anna continued stuffing supplies in a flour bag. "But they won't find the little princess. Not now."

Tobin walked closer and lowered his voice. "You know where she is, don't you?"

"I've always known where she runs when she's been frightened."

"I'm not going to hurt her, Anna, but I need to get her out of here fast. Will you trust me?"

The old cook stared at him a moment with crystal-clear gray eyes, then nodded as if she'd found what she'd been looking for. "I've been traveling here with the family since before she lost her momma. When she used to hide as a child I'd bring her food and water, but I'd never tell anyone, not even the senator, where she was."

Tobin knew he was asking a great deal. "Will you tell me?"

"You'll get her far away from here? Away from this trouble? Away from that captain? I don't know what he did, but if she's hiding, it's bad."

"I swear. I'll keep her safe."

She looked at the back stairs. "Climb all three flights, then open a door just to the left when you step out onto the third floor. It's almost invisible, no more than a panel, but it'll get you to the attic."

He took a few steps to the slim stairway.

"Make sure no one sees you. I told the maids she always hides in the study or front parlor. They're both in there, but not for long." She patted his shoulder. "When you open the panel you'll see more steps, but there is no light in the passage. You'll have to close the opening and make your way up in the dark. If you leave it open even a sliver, someone may see it."

Tobin nodded, silently promising.

Anna continued, "She's behind a dresser along the north wall. You'll swear there is no room, but she's there. I'd bet every dime I have on it."

Tobin took the stairs two at a time. On the third floor he quickly found the panel door and climbed up to the attic.

The cluttered room was dark except for thin beams of watery moonlight coming in through slotted shutters. For a moment he thought he was looking at slices of a room with every other piece missing.

Slowly he moved among the trunks and forgotten toys, a graveyard of outgrown treasures from a little girl who had everything. A three-foot dollhouse, a rocking horse, a crib with yellowed lace.

"Libby," he whispered as he moved toward the far wall. "Libby, it's me."

The dresser was no more than a shadow, but Anna had been right—it was huge. Drawers columned both sides with a six-foot mirror in the middle. Little pedestal shelves framed the mirror ending at a marble desktop almost four feet long.

Tobin slid his hand across the wood just below the marble. No drawers, just wood from desk to floor. If it was hollow, it would make the perfect hiding place.

"Libby," he whispered. "I know you're back there. It's Tobin." He didn't know what to say. *Come out so I can kidnap you* didn't seem right. She knew nothing of the favor he'd promised her father. She hadn't said a word about wanting to call off the engagement even though he'd guessed her feelings in her actions.

If he took her to Whispering Mountain, she'd miss her own wedding. The captain and she were having a fight last night, but for all he knew their fights might be routine.

He could see a space between the wall and the dresser where she could have slipped in. Once through that small opening, provided the back of the desk was hollow, she'd have a nice hiding place. He tried to look in but could see nothing in the blackness.

"Libby, I have to take you away. I know you may not understand or want to go, but I have to get you out of here now." If he had to, he'd carry her out by force, but he'd not trick her. "Libby, one way or the other, I'm taking you with me tonight."

He heard a slight cry, then movement, and suddenly she was in his arms.

Trembling, she whispered, "Now. Take me away now."

Tobin frowned. This kidnapping wasn't proving as hard as he thought it might be. "All right," he said and lifted her up. He had no idea what she'd been through since they'd kissed on the porch, but whatever it was had frightened her. She held on to him as if she feared for her life.

He carried her down, pausing just before each floor landing to make sure he couldn't hear anyone about. When he reached the kitchen, Anna had turned down the lamps and was waiting for him. She tossed a long coat over Liberty, still cuddled in his embrace, her face dampening his shoulder with tears. "I packed any supplies you'll need," Anna said. "You take care of her, McMurray, or you'll be answering to me."

Tobin thanked the cook with a nod and crossed the kitchen thinking this had to be the world's strangest kidnapping. It came catered.

"You'll tell the captain I took her." He wanted Buchanan mad at him, not at Liberty. "She didn't run away." He didn't look back to see if Anna agreed; he knew she would. "Tell him I forced her." Tobin suddenly understood his duty. He knew why the senator had used the word *kidnapping*. Once Tobin stepped off this property, to all the world he'd be an outlaw.

Dermot waited by the back door with Tobin's two horses. "I told the only guard when saddling up I heard a sound out behind the barn. He's checking it out. Ye've only got a few minutes."

Tobin started to lift Liberty on her own mount, but she wouldn't turn loose of his neck, so without a word he carried her with him.

When Dermot handed him Sunny's reins, Tobin whispered, "Sometime tonight, when it's safe to slip away, can you get word to a ranger by the name of Wes—if he's still alive. He rode into town with the senator. Tell him what's happened here. Tell him not to pass the news along to anyone but the senator."

Dermot nodded. "I know a back way to town that I can travel even in the dark. If he's with the senator, I'll find him."

"Tell Wes if he needs to talk, I'm near the north creek property line in a patch of cottonwoods. I'll wait there until first light, then we'll be riding out hard and fast. I won't be leaving any trail for someone to follow after that."

Voices came from the house. Dermot stepped away and Tobin nudged his mount west in the direction of town. Their tracks blended with countless others in the road. Within a few feet they'd melted into the night. Tobin listened. He thought he heard the captain's voice yelling orders. Liberty hadn't moved in his arms, but he could feel her breathing against his chest and knew she'd relaxed a little. For the first time he wondered at what had frightened her so.

They'd have plenty of time to talk later. He kissed the top of her head, wishing he could tell her they were safe, but the truth was they were a long way from being out of danger.

Watching the trail, it took twenty minutes before he made out what he was looking for in the darkness. A rocky spot wide enough to turn the horses without leaving any trail. Slowly, not wanting to disturb even the dirt, he moved off the trail and circled around until he was crossing open land thick with grass. Finally, they headed north. Even moving carefully, he knew the signs would be there for an expert tracker to find. Tobin was betting no one with such skill would be with the captain. Tobin knew once Buchanan had the senator safe, he'd come after them.

He frowned. This life of crime was new to him, but not tracking. He and his brothers had played a game often when their grandfather visited them. He'd been an Apache who knew nothing of games the settlers play. He taught them games he'd played as a child and one was the Indian version of hide-and-seek. Travis had been the best at tracking, but Tobin was the most skilled at leaving no trail to follow. He used those skills now, riding over rocks, twisting different directions, riding down creek beds where tracks vanished in the water.

By the time he reached the cottonwoods on the north border of the property, Tobin doubted even Travis would have been able to follow.

Liberty was asleep in his arms, her hands still locked around his neck. Carefully, he climbed down and settled her in the knees of one of the hundred-year-old cottonwoods. With the shadows of the branches lacing across her, no one would find her if they didn't know exactly where she slept. He would have liked to light a fire but knew it would be too dangerous tonight. So he settled for covering her almost completely with her coat.

Unsaddling the horses, he left them several yards down the stream. Tobin wanted them close enough that he could hear them warn him if someone was around. He placed the saddles and gear beneath a tree across the clearing from where Libby slept so that it looked like someone might be sleeping there, then carried his rifle and one blanket back to Liberty.

He crawled in between the roots beside her and she shifted, curling into his warmth as he covered them both with the blanket. If they were lucky they had four, maybe five, hours until dawn; then they'd face a hard day's ride.

Tobin didn't sleep. Somehow all the pieces didn't fit together. He'd expected to have to pull her away from the house. It was her home. She was only a few days away from her wedding. She'd been mad at him after he'd kissed her, so why had she trusted him so completely in the attic? Why was she hiding away like a frightened child in the first place? Surely not simply because her father left. An only child of a senator must be used to having her father leave, and Liberty was no longer a child.

Something had happened between the time they'd kissed and when he found her. Something bad.

It also bothered Tobin that if the senator had wanted his daughter away so desperately, why hadn't he asked the captain or taken her himself? Unless the captain were incapable of protecting her. But if that were so, why had Mayfield left his only daughter alone with the man?

Tobin leaned his head against the tree and mentally listed what he knew. One, she must have been in real danger, a danger that the senator had feared earlier or he wouldn't have made Tobin promise the favor. Two, it didn't matter whether he had proof or not, Tobin didn't trust the captain. And three, he didn't plan on stopping until they were back on Whispering Mountain property. They'd travel no roads and he'd make sure no one saw them along the way. It would take a few days longer, but he'd get her to his ranch safely.

The call of a mourning dove drifted in the predawn light. Tobin sat up slowly and answered in kind. He knew, thanks to his brother, that if a ranger had made the call, once it was answered there would be a short whistle to follow.

The short shrill blast came from the trees near where Tobin had placed the saddles. A ranger. Tobin relaxed.

A buckskin-clad man stepped out from between two cottonwoods. He stood tall, thin, and well armed. "Almost fooled me with those saddles, McMurray. If I hadn't had some light, I might have thought you were sleeping there." He spoke matter-of-factly as if he just happened to be walking in the woods.

Tobin stood, leaving Liberty beneath the blanket.

"I didn't know if you'd come." He crossed to the trees and motioned for Wes to follow so that they wouldn't wake Liberty.

Wes rested his rifle across his shoulders. "Why'd you take the senator's daughter?"

Tobin saw no need to lie. "I promised."

"Dakota and I kind of figured something like that even though we haven't had time to talk to the senator about it. One thing about you McMurrays, come hell or high water, you always keep your word."

"What's happened?" Tobin guessed there was something Wes wasn't telling him.

"Last night, halfway to town, we were ambushed. Michael, that pup of a ranger we had with us riding ahead as lookout, was hurt bad. Both men from the senator's house were hit, but they'll recover. The two soldiers riding drag weren't so lucky. One died fighting. The other, I heard, made it back to the house to warn Captain Buchanan. The fight was over by the time Buchanan and his men arrived."

He shook his head in frustration. "It was far too organized to have been anything but a planned attack, and that road is rarely used by anyone but the senator and his people, so the trash who rushed us had to know who rode in the carriage."

"Is Mayfield all right?"

Wes laughed. "You should have seen the old man. He came out firing like the fast draw in a stage show. Took the gang trying to surround the carriage by surprise. Dakota covered his back and no outlaw could get close."

"And the senator? Was he hurt?"

Wes shook his head. "He was swearing and laughing when the gang turned tail. He said he was grazed a bit but not enough to slow him down. He would have given chase if I hadn't stopped him. He's one tough old bull, I'm telling you. Washington hasn't softened him one bit."

Tobin relaxed. "Does he want me to bring Liberty to him?"

Wes shook his head. "I don't think so. Between getting the wounded in and guarding him, it's been a wild night. Someone is out to get him and Captain Buchanan doesn't have the skill to stop them. The senator needs to know why and who. He has to move freely and fast, and he can't do that unless he knows his daughter is safe with you. He wants an end to this. I could see the determination in his eyes. He plans to get all those involved. Killing half the snakes in a hole don't make it no safer."

"But why did he leave her last night?"

Wes shrugged. "I'm just guessing, but I figure the senator knew he was the target of a real threat or he wouldn't have asked for a ranger guard. He didn't want his daughter getting caught in the cross fire last night."

Wes pulled out a chew of tobacco. "What I don't understand is why she went with you so easy. She's one wildcat from what I've seen. How'd you get her out of that house without her screaming to high heaven?"

"Because"—Liberty's voice reached them loud and clear—"I wanted to leave."

Both men turned toward her and stared as she sat up and shoved her midnight hair from her face.

Wes swore.

When he saw her face, Tobin felt as if he'd been punched in the gut. "What happened?" he asked, not sure he wanted the answer.

Wes grabbed his arm. "If you did this, McMurray—"

Tobin jerked away. "Save it, Wes." He knelt down beside Liberty waiting for her answer.

Liberty tried to smile, then winced in pain. Her tongue brushed across dried blood on her lip. "The groom wasn't too happy when I broke our engagement. All at once I became very accident prone."

Tobin tucked his first knuckle beneath her chin and lifted her face to the light. "I'll kill him," he said calmly, promising, not threatening.

Wes knelt on the other side of her and frowned down at her. He didn't seem to notice that swear words flowed like air out his mouth.

Liberty looked back at Tobin. "How bad is it? Do either of you have a mirror?"

Both men said no at once. Then Tobin forced a smile. "It's not so bad. Your cheek is bruised, your left eye is almost swollen closed, and your bottom lip is split."

"On the bright side," Wes added, "you still got all your teeth and your nose don't look broke."

Liberty frowned at the man's idea of the bright side.

Tobin brushed a strand of her hair back. "Why didn't you say something last night?"

She shook her head. "It doesn't really hurt that bad . . . compared to my side."

Tobin met Wes's questioning look.

"Are you shot?" Wes asked as he almost touched her shoulder, then seemed to reconsider.

"No. Samuel made sure I hit a chair arm when I turned to run from him. It hurts right here." She placed her hand just below her left breast. "I think he planned to knock the breath from me. I thought once I could breathe it would be all right, but it still hurts."

Tobin stood. "You need a doctor."

Wes shook his head. "The only doc within a hundred miles is at the fort and we can't take her there without the captain knowing about it."

"What if she broke a rib? The kind of riding we are going to do could be very painful on her."

Wes scratched his chin. "She made it this far. Maybe she just bruised one or cracked it. If so we could wrap it. I've seen plenty of men wrap their chests after a bar fight when they get one too many knuckles plowed into them."

Tobin looked hopeful. "Can you check it? Then wrap her if you think it needs to be."

Wes shook his head. "No. I don't know nothing about women. My number one rule is to spend my life avoiding the fairer sex, and I practice it religiously except on the rare occasions when I get too drunk to remember how to count. You got a sister. You do it."

Liberty stood, holding her side. "Stop talking about me like I'm a dumb animal. The next suggestion from you two will probably be that you have to shoot me and put me out of my misery."

Tobin opened his mouth to argue but then thought better of it, knowing it would be a waste of time. "How can we help? If you want a doctor, we can ride until we find one. Maybe Austin."

"I could leave her here and go over and get one. Two, maybe three, days I'd be back, depending on how much the doc protests," Wes offered.

"There's been enough kidnapping," she said. "But I don't know if I can stand the pain of the ride without doing something. Wes is right, I think, wrapping it might help. I can't stay here. Samuel would find me before you could get back with a doctor. He seems to want to marry me so badly he's willing to kill the bride."

Tobin walked to his saddlebag and pulled out his new shirt. Without hesitation, he ripped it into strips and handed them to Liberty. "Can you do this yourself?"

"No," she answered. "I don't think I can." She looked at first one man and then the other. "Hold out your hands."

"What?" they said at the same time.

Liberty frowned and repeated. "Hold out your hands."

Both men did. Tobin's were rough and calloused, but clean. Wes's looked like they hadn't been washed in weeks.

Liberty frowned up at Tobin. "You're elected. You'll help me."

He nodded. He wasn't sure he would know what to do,

but he didn't especially want Wes's hands touching her. If Libby had an idea he'd try to help. "What should I do?"

Liberty studied the trees. "Follow me. If we do this, we do it in private."

Glancing over her shoulder, she ordered, "Get my boots down by the creek, will you, Ranger? I left them there yesterday and I'll need them when I get back."

Wes looked relieved at only having to fetch boots. "I'll stand guard."

Tobin walked beside her as they moved into the trees. He let her set the pace amazed that she hadn't complained last night. The princess was far stronger then he'd thought.

CHAPTER 11

THE MORNING SUN OFFERED SOME WARMTH, BUT AS soon as they moved into the shadows of the cottonwoods along the creek Tobin felt the chill. Liberty said she needed to make sure they were alone while he wrapped her ribs, but they could have asked Wes to turn around. At least then they'd be in the warmth and light.

Tobin followed her across the dead leaves, guessing Liberty also worried about someone riding into the clearing before he finished. She reminded him of a wounded animal wanting to stay in the shadows until she was strong enough to fight.

Glancing at her stockinged feet he realized he should have noticed she had no shoes last night. As a kidnapper, he must be somewhere close to the bottom of the bucket. It seemed a stroke of luck that she'd left her boots here yesterday when the storm started. Or, for all he knew, she had boots and shoes abandoned everywhere in her world.

He tried not to think about how he planned to beat the captain to a bloody pulp for what he'd done to Liberty. He'd spent his life avoiding fights. He would make the time for this one. When he got through with Samuel Buchanan, his face would look far worse than Liberty's did now.

She would probably be frightened if she knew how dark his thoughts were, but Tobin had never seen anyone hurt a woman. He'd heard of it, of course. Travis, during his days as a ranger, had arrested several men who'd hurt or killed women. His brother told him once that a few of the rangers down near the Big Bend country got together and tied an outlaw up the same way he'd tied a rancher's wife he'd robbed. The outlaw had left her to almost starve. Only when the rangers left the outlaw, he was nude and tied across a six-foot red-ant bed.

At the time, Tobin thought the rangers cruel. Now he understood. A man who hurts a woman deserves the pain returned in spades.

"Have a seat, doctor," Liberty interrupted his plotting. "We've work to do, though I'm not sure what." Her light mood was forced.

"Neither am I." He sat on a stump the height of a chair. "The only things I've ever doctored are horses. Maybe you should have brought Wes after all?"

"Just pretend I'm a horse." She didn't laugh. "You can be no worse than that leather-clad mud man out there. Wes must work to stay that dirty." She pushed between his knees and handed him the strips of cotton he'd made. "This has to be done and you are the only one to do it."

Tobin smiled. She might be pampered and beautiful, but she had a bit of her father in her. "General" was a better nickname than "princess" right now.

"First," she said as she began unbuttoning her shirt, "you have to tell me if you think I've got a broken rib. I don't think so, but if you do, we're on our way to Austin."

He nodded. He could take her to Travis and Rainey's place a few blocks from the capitol. It wouldn't be as safe as the ranch, but it would do if they had to stay somewhere and find a doctor.

As Liberty pulled open her shirt, he saw the white lace of

her camisole. She tugged it from her riding trousers and lifted the material up to reveal her middle.

Tobin tried to swallow. The fullness of her breasts was clearly visible, and the top of the undergarment lacked an inch being decent, he thought, but he didn't plan on complaining about it. She looked better than any painting of a woman hanging over any bar he'd ever seen.

Except for a dark bruise the size of a man's fist that lay just below where she'd bunched up the material, her flesh was white, almost porcelain, making the mark appear even darker.

Liberty moved closer resting one hand on his shoulder for balance. "Well, feel it. Is a rib broken? It hurts like the devil."

Tobin swallowed and placed his hand gently over the mark.

She flinched.

"I'm sorry," he whispered and brushed her undamaged skin gently with his other hand. "I'll try to be careful. Tell me if you feel a sharp pain."

Liberty nodded for him to continue. He saw the forced control in her eyes and the paleness of her cheeks.

"You're not going to faint on me, Libby?"

She shook her head, but he wasn't sure willing it so could stop her from passing out. He gently spread his other hand out across her back to brace her just in case.

One rib at a time Tobin felt along her skin examining each bone. His other hand, holding her still, prepared to catch her if she fainted. When he reached the last rib exposed, he felt the bottom of her breast brush along his fingertips as he moved across the rib.

Her skin was so soft. So perfect. He couldn't resist moving his fingers down the middle to where the waistband of her riding pants stopped his progress.

"Are you finished?" Her breath came quickly.

He pulled his hand away. "Yes."

"And?"

"I couldn't feel a broken bone and your breathing doesn't seem to be hampered. I think we're just dealing with a bruise."

"Good. I'm glad that's all *we* are dealing with. Would you mind wrapping me?"

He picked up the strips. She lifted her arms, still holding the camisole tightly in place. She was so close he could have leaned forward slightly and tasted her warm flesh. And he might have done it if it weren't for the fact that she'd made it plain she wanted no more of his advances. What had she said after the kiss? Something about forgetting it ever happened. Or maybe she'd just thought it and he'd been the one who said it. So much had happened in the few hours since their kiss, Tobin couldn't remember exactly who said what.

He couldn't resist taking extra care as he smoothed the cotton strip around her.

"Tighter," she ordered. "It will feel better if it's tighter."

He followed orders aware that her fingers gripped his shoulder as he worked. He was hurting her, he could feel it, but she didn't make a sound. When he circled the dressing around her back, she leaned forward and the side of one of her breasts brushed against his cheek.

"Sorry," she whispered as she moved away.

His hands stopped. He looked up into her beautiful eyes. Even with one surrounded with dark and swollen flesh, he could still see the fire in her stormy gaze. He wished he could think of something light to say, but he couldn't. The soft pressure of her breast had branded him and he knew that somewhere, sometime he'd have his fill of it. He didn't bother to try to hide his need as he stared.

She must have understood, for her breathing quickened, making her rib cage move lightly beneath his touch.

Now was not the time, he knew. Not when she was hurting and frightened. But there had been something between them from the beginning, and one day they'd both have to deal with it.

"Done," he said as he straightened. "That should help."

She let the camisole fall over the binding, then crumbled

into his lap. For a moment she seemed to want to let her guard down and not be the brave little general. He understood and offered what he knew she needed, comfort.

Tobin held her gently, rocking her back and forth as he had his little sister when she'd been hurt as a kid. "It's all right, Liberty. It will be better tomorrow."

She buried her head in his throat and gulped down silent sobs.

He kissed the top of her head. "Go ahead and cry. You're safe now. No one is ever going to hurt you again."

Brushing strands of her hair away from her face, he wished he could hold her tighter and make her believe that she really was safe. She'd been broken when he'd found her last night, too terrified to talk. But she was rebuilding, strengthening, and he wanted her to know that he'd be there when she needed him.

After a few minutes, she raised her head. "I'm ready. Don't tell anyone I cried. It never happened."

Tobin nodded slowly.

They stood. He watched her button her shirt; then she turned and walked ahead of him to the edge of the trees.

Wes stood just beyond the shade of the cottonwoods with his back to them. "Someone's coming," he mumbled. "Don't come out till we know who it is."

Tobin pulled her back a few feet and they waited. After a moment, he heard the sound of two horses coming up fast.

Wes walked a few more feet into the open and lifted his rifle. He knew his duty. He was the first line. Anyone coming to harm Liberty would have to leave him dead first.

Two horses broke through to the clearing from the south side.

"Dermot," Tobin whispered, the moment he saw the old man leaning low over his horse as if he could barely hang on to the animal.

"You recognize them?" Wes whispered.

"I know the first one. The old man is the one I sent to ask you to meet me."

Wes squinted, then nodded. "It was dark, but I remember

the make of him. He'd be the only one who knew you were here for I told no one."

Dermot motioned to the other rider to slow and they turned their horses toward Wes.

"That's far enough," the ranger shouted. "State your business, Mr. Dermot."

The old man slowly climbed from his mount, but the second rider, covered in a black cape, stayed back.

"Ranger, I need to speak with Tobin McMurray and I wouldna be riding out here if it weren't urgent." He limped toward Wes. "I been praying all the way that he'd still be about."

Wes wasn't giving any information away. "What's your business with him?"

Dermot looked around. He might be old, but he was no fool. He knew the ranger wouldn't even be bothering to talk to him if Tobin and Liberty were already away. "Got a lass here who claims 'tis a matter of life and death that she talks to him."

"Tell her to step down. I'll talk to her."

Dermot shook his head. "She says she'll talk to none but Tobin or Miss Liberty."

Tobin looked past Dermot to the woman with him. The hood of her cape had slipped back enough that he could see red hair. Stella.

When he started to move forward, Liberty stopped him. "She told Samuel about our kiss. That's what made him so mad last night." She leaned close. "I don't trust her, Tobin."

"Neither do I," he answered. "But let's hear what she has to say. If she talked Dermot into bringing her, she already suspects more than I'm comfortable with her knowing."

Nodding, Liberty whispered what they were both thinking. "She's not to know where we're headed."

He tightened his grip slightly over Liberty's hand. A pact formed. They walked out of the shadows. Wes frowned when he saw them. Dermot looked relieved.

"What is it, Stella?" Liberty asked without greeting.

The maid scrambled down from her mount and rushed toward them, falling on her knees in front of Liberty. "I'm so sorry, Miss Liberty." She locked her hands and raised them as if begging for her life. "I didn't know he was going to hurt you. I swear I didn't. I just told him what I saw because I thought he wasn't paying you any attention. I didn't think he'd hit you." She looked up at Liberty. "Oh, my Lord. Look at your face. This is all my fault. All my . . ."

She let out a cry as though she'd been stabbed and continued, "He was so nice, sweet really, when he thanked me for pointing out that he'd been neglecting you. I never thought he'd hurt you. Not you, Miss Liberty. I'm so sorry."

"Stop," Wes ordered. "Enough chatter. My ears are starting to hurt."

Stella looked at the ranger as if he were simply being rude and not addressing her. She added in a whisper, "When Anna told me she saw a bit of your face and thought you were hurt, I almost died. I could never live with myself if my actions brought you sorrow. I'd have gladly taken the pain and not you. I wish I were dead."

Liberty patted the girl's shoulder. "You didn't know what he was capable of. Neither did I."

Tobin noticed, though her gesture seemed caring, Liberty's eyes were as cold as the morning breeze. Part of her didn't believe the maid any more than he did.

Stella wasn't finished wailing. "I should kill myself for having been any part of hurting you. I want to die for it. I just want to lie down and die in a puddle of mud. I wish I were dead. Oh, God please let me—"

Wes lifted his rifle. "I can make it happen, miss. One bullet to the brain. You'll hardly feel a thing."

Stella's eyes widened in panic and she shut up.

Dermot finally got a word in. "She told me she'd kill herself if I didna bring her out here." He lifted his palms to Liberty. "What was I to do?"

Liberty stepped forward, her back as straight and proud as a queen. None of the shattered, frightened girl Tobin had held only minutes before remained. She took charge as she'd been born and raised to do.

"You did what you had to, Dermot," she said to the old man, then turned to the maid. "It's all right, Stella. I understand. It wasn't your fault."

Stella produced a handkerchief from her cleavage and blew her nose. Her fit was over as quickly as it started.

Wes looked disappointed he wasn't going to get to do the lady a favor and shoot her. "McMurray, you'd better be heading out. Looks like folks are wearing a road to your hiding spot."

Tobin agreed. "Help me saddle up."

As they moved into action, Stella's voice drifted to them. "Thank you, miss. You've always been very kind to me." She followed Liberty to the old cottonwood where Wes had left Liberty's boots.

Stella knelt, helping her mistress slip the boots on. "I've been thinking, miss, and the only way I can pay you back is to go with you. With you hurt and all, I could be a great help to you."

"No!" All three men said it at once, but Stella barely paused.

"You'll need someone to take care of you and your things and I'm a good cook and I know how you like your clothes ironed and your breakfast cooked, and—"

"No," Tobin repeated. "We're traveling fast and she has no things to look after."

Stella was insulted. "I was raised on a farm. I can ride as fast as any woman."

"No," Tobin repeated.

Stella started to cry, big tears bubbled from her summer-blue eyes and rolled across her freckled face. "I have to help you, miss. I just have to. I got a sense about the future and I know mine is black for what I did if you'd don't let me make it up to you. I'll die if you don't let me help you through this time of trial."

Wes leaned closer to Tobin. "Should I offer my services to shoot her again?"

Tobin grinned. Just as he mumbled, "She's not going, so it doesn't matter," they both heard Liberty say, "All right, you can come along, Stella, if it's that important to you."

Tobin took a moment to think about his options. He could protest, but he wasn't sure what Liberty would do. She was fragile right now. Maybe she thought she needed the magpie. Maybe she was too tenderhearted to leave her behind. Stella probably had good reason to fear the captain now. If he'd hit a senator's daughter, there was no telling what Buchanan might do if he found out Stella saw Liberty and didn't tell him.

Tobin looked directly at Wes. "Change of plans. Shoot *me* now and put me out of my misery."

To his surprise, the hard ranger laughed. "My pa used to say one woman in your life is heaven, but two is hell." He slapped Tobin on the back. "Welcome to hell, McMurray. I've half a mind to change my plans and ride along with you."

Tobin frowned wondering how, for a man who loved solitude, he managed to get in this parade.

Wes grinned. "Look at the bright side. Now you've got more to worry about than half the soldiers in Texas hunting you down."

He looked at Liberty. "We can't—"

She raised her hand and said simply, "End of discussion."

Tobin raised his eyebrow. He hadn't planned on discussing anything; he'd planned on ordering, but she beat him to the draw. The beautiful little general was definitely back.

He watched Dermot help Liberty into the saddle. Her movements were stiff as she tried to avoid any more twisting than necessary. She was fragile and for now she needed protecting, but he knew before this trip was over they'd have a long discussion . . . with or without words.

"Mount up, Stella," he ordered. "And keep quiet."

Wes, to his credit, helped the maid up as she chattered. "I won't say a word. You won't even know I'm along. I'll be like a mouse following along in total silence, I won't even—"

Wes pulled out a rag of a handkerchief that was so dirty it was stiff in spots. "You want me to gag her, McMurray?"

Stella's eyes rounded into saucers again.

"No. She'll be quiet," Tobin said.

Wes looked like he doubted it but added, "Dermot and I will stay around for a few hours and make sure no one follows you. Then I'm riding to join the senator. If he's going hunting, I'm not missing the fun."

Tobin glanced to make sure Liberty was in the saddle and had a good hold on her reins. "Ready?"

She nodded.

He pulled his horse close to her and whispered, "I'll take it slow the first hour. You let me know if you're in pain and remember all the rules I taught you about riding."

He swore he could feel Liberty push fear aside with determination. Her knuckles were white as she gripped the reins. Today she'd learn to ride. Not because she wanted to, but because she had to.

CHAPTER 12

LIBERTY FOUGHT THE PAIN IN HER SIDE AS THEY RODE
the rough ground between the creek and the tree line. She
knew Tobin wanted to stay out of sight, but as the morning
passed she prayed for even ground. She didn't have to look at
him; she knew he was watching her, expecting her to crumble.

Most of her body ached—her face and ribs, thanks to
Samuel—her back and legs thanks to the horse. Tobin had
taken the time to tell her how to hold her body so that the
movements didn't hurt so badly. He'd even used his bedroll
to brace her back. But nothing she did helped for more than
a few minutes.

Stella made little effort to keep her promise to be quiet.
She seemed to see the escape as an outing and complained
about the pace, the wind, the tree branches that snagged her
clothes. The third time Tobin threatened to leave her behind
if she didn't keep up, she believed him. Liberty had no doubt
that he would do just that if she tried to delay them again.

They stopped at noon at an old well that had been abandoned on an early homestead. The water had long ago turned
bad, but the remains of a barn and house offered shade and

shelter from the wind. Except to give orders, Tobin hadn't said more than a few words to her all morning. He'd said even less to Stella.

As he helped Liberty down, he held her next to him and whispered, "I want you to lie down and try to rest your back. It should be safe on the porch."

"I'm fine," she lied.

"No discussion," he retorted with a frown. "No argument."

He moved away and offered Stella a hand down, but his orders were sharp. "Spread out a few blankets for Liberty to rest, then see if you can find something for lunch in that bag." He pointed at the flour sack the cook had packed. "I'll take care of the horses."

Liberty wanted to argue that she could help, but in truth, she could barely walk. Riding seemed no harder than breathing to them, but she'd been fighting to stay in the saddle all morning. As soon as Stella spread the blanket, Liberty melted on top of it.

Tobin poured enough water from his canteen to dampen a scrap left from the shirt he'd ripped apart. He knelt beside her and lay the cool cloth atop the bruises on her face. "This'll help," he said.

"Thanks," she whispered, and closed her eyes.

She heard Tobin mumble something to Stella about leaving her behind if she bothered Miss Liberty. Then Liberty heard nothing. She slept.

When she woke and moved her arm, she felt Tobin's leg next to her shoulder. Liberty rolled her head and saw him sitting a few inches away, his arms folded, his hat low as if he were asleep, his boots crossed. Only the rifle within easy reach reminded her that he was on guard.

"You awake?" she asked.

"Yep," he said, "but don't tell your maid or she'll start talking again."

Liberty laughed, surprised at how much the nap had lifted her spirits. "Where is my chatty helper?"

He shoved his hat up. "She left about ten minutes ago, saying she needed some time to herself. I figure if something attacked her over by the privy we would have heard about it by now."

"You don't trust her." Liberty whispered the obvious.

"Nope, but I figure you had your reasons for letting her come along."

Liberty nodded.

"And as long as she doesn't know where we're headed, she's not likely to run back to tell anyone like the captain."

Liberty winked. "We'll know her true colors long before she knows where we're headed."

Tobin smiled and she saw the silent compliment in his gaze. "Something about keeping your friends close and your enemies closer?"

She grinned, then touched her painful lip. "Something like that."

He traced his thumb along the side of her cheek and gently caressed the corner of her mouth where a scab had formed.

"How long have I been asleep?" She rested her hand on the rough wool of his trousers, wishing she had the words to thank him, not only for last night but also for sticking with her this morning. If Captain Buchanan claimed he'd kidnapped her, Tobin could be in real trouble. But Tobin guessed Buchanan would prefer to believe the lie of kidnapping than any truth he might hear. Which suited Tobin fine. He'd rather have the captain mad at him and not Liberty.

"Almost an hour." He made no move to pull away.

She felt the warmth of the muscle just above his knee even through the heavy fabric.

"Do we have that much time to spare?" They both stared at her hand lightly brushing his leg, ironing the material flat.

"We'll make time." He met her gaze but still didn't move.

Liberty felt his warm skin beneath the trousers, but it was nothing compared to the fire she saw in his eyes. She looked away, not because the raw need she saw frightened her, but because his openness surprised her. She wouldn't speak of it, this attraction she knew they both felt. They seemed to have some unwritten rule that as long as she didn't, he wouldn't. A silent pact to ignore an attraction they both felt.

"How long until we get to Whispering Mountain?"

"Five days if we push hard."

She twisted, stretching her back against the solidness of his leg and felt his hand lightly brush across her hair. His rough hand was feather light as it caressed her cheek just beneath her swollen eye.

"Does it hurt?"

"No." She didn't want to think about the pain. If she did, she'd have to think about Samuel and what he'd done so easily, almost casually. "Tell me about this ranch called Whispering Mountain."

He was silent so long she wasn't sure he planned to grant her request.

Then he began like a man who'd never told a story in his life. "My father was from Ireland, a teacher. He met my mother at a mission when he was seventeen. My mother said she fell in love with him when their hands touched beneath a book. They were married within days. He took all the money he'd inherited from his father and applied to Mexico for a land grant. By the time it came through, they were living on the ranch and my brother Teagen was on the way."

"They homesteaded at seventeen?"

"Yep. My father loved the place he found because it was so isolated, bordered on two sides by hills and two by rivers. And he loved the mountain the Apache called Whispering Mountain. They told him of a legend that says if a man sleeps on the summit of Whispering Mountain, he'll dream his future. So one summer night my father climbed the mountain."

"And . . ." Liberty waited, but Tobin had stopped. She poked his leg. "And?"

Tobin caught her fingers in his before continuing. To anyone watching, the gesture could have looked light, almost playful, but there was nothing casual in the way he gripped her hand, firm and solid. He didn't let go as he continued. "My father dreamed his death that night, right down to how old his sons would be when he died, Teagen almost twelve, Travis ten, and me six. He spent the rest of his life preparing both the ranch and us for that day. He knew my mother wouldn't be allowed to claim the land because of her Apache blood."

Liberty turned so that she could see him. "And the three of you held the land."

"Yes, we did. We burned the only bridge over the river and fought off those who swam across. We fought for months before finally outsiders decided it wasn't worth the risk to step on McMurray land. But we never let our guard down. Not then. Not now." His eyes were suddenly hard. "Whispering Mountain remains a fortress even though it's in our names now and no one can ever take it away."

Liberty squeezed his hand and he turned loose of her fingers as if he wanted no comfort. "And your mother?" she asked as her hand brushed past his knee to the leather of a high moccasin boot he wore. "Did she help?"

No emotion reflected in his face as he said, "She died in childbirth a few months after my father was killed at a mission called Goliad. My baby sister, Sage, lived." He smiled suddenly. "She's small like my mother was, but she's no less of a McMurray. By the time she could talk she was giving orders."

He lifted Liberty's braid and added, "Reminds me of you."

She started to react, then caught the hint of teasing in his dark eyes. "I have a feeling I'll like your sister."

Liberty rested her hand back on his leg, wanting their conversation to continue. "You kept the ranch, just like your father planned. Now your children will inherit, and their children, and . . ."

"Maybe Travis's children, or Sage's, but Teagen is a confirmed bachelor and I have no plans to ever marry."

"You've slept on the mountain and you know your future?"

He shook his head. "I don't need to sleep on the mountain. I saw my future when I was six covered in blood. I tricked death that day, but it's bound to catch up to me sooner or later. The only thing I can control, I made a promise to do.

I'll not leave any children to have to grow up like I did with one eye watching for trouble and a gun always close. I'll never marry."

Liberty felt his determination, heard it in his voice, saw it in his eyes. Nothing she could say would change his mind. She admired him for that. Unlike her, he knew the kind of life he wanted. Lacing her fingers in his, Liberty wished a little of the solidness that was Tobin McMurray would rub off on her. She'd spent her life floating between goals like a butterfly in a garden.

"After knowing Samuel," she said more to herself than him, "I think I've reached the same conclusion. I don't want to pass control of my life from my father to some husband. I want the freedom. Out here, the life of a woman living alone would be hard, but in Washington it would be easy."

He looked away and for a moment they were silent. Then, he said in his low, quiet way, "There's Stella. We'd better get saddled up." He slipped his hand from hers without meeting her gaze.

Tobin stood in a smooth motion that men his height rarely show. "We'll ride until full dark." He offered his hand and she let him help her up. "You think you can make it without falling out of the saddle?"

"I can make it," she promised.

Late that afternoon, she realized she had lied.

The third time she almost tumbled, Tobin stopped the horses and climbed down from his mount. She'd expected him to help her down so they could rest, but he pulled her foot from the stirrup and climbed up behind her.

Without a word he took the reins with one hand and pulled her against him with the other. His arm rested low on her waist, holding her in the saddle but avoiding her bruise.

Liberty was too tired to protest. She leaned against him and fell asleep knowing that he'd keep her safe. This quiet man she barely knew seemed part of her life now. His body, his touch, were becoming familiar to her.

There was a wildness about him, as if not all of him had

been civilized or tamed, but there was goodness too, and a protective nature.

She woke when he finally lifted her from the saddle. It was full dark as he'd promised and they'd stopped in the shadows of the trees as before. Liberty couldn't see her, but she heard Stella complaining about wanting a fire.

Tobin told her to take care of the horses first.

Liberty rested her head on his shoulder, too exhausted to comment.

Tobin carried her to a grassy spot about six feet from a stream so narrow she could have stepped over it. Gently, he lowered her to the ground. "You want anything to eat?" he whispered, his cheek brushing hers as he spoke.

Liberty shook her head and watched him move away to help with the horses. It was late and the sounds of the night were all around her, but she was too tired to be frightened.

Stella offered her a canteen and a blanket, then made her bed a few feet away. Because no one would answer her chatter, the maid finally stopped talking. Using her saddle for a pillow, she wiggled beneath her blanket and fell asleep.

Liberty closed her eyes and dreamed of dancing at one of the fine Washington balls. All the gentlemen were dressed in black evening clothes and her feet glided across the polished floor as if she were floating. She belonged there, she almost whispered aloud, before promising herself that when this was over she'd go back to Washington and never return to Texas. She had her mother's trust fund. She was a woman of means even without her father's fortune. No matter what her father said, he'd welcome her back to Washington.

Just before she drifted back to sleep, she felt Tobin spread his blanket over her; then he sat down on a rock a foot away. It was so dark she could only make out his shadow and the outline of the rifle at his side.

As if he knew she watched him, he ordered, "Get some sleep."

Liberty swallowed hard. "I have to ask. Do you think we're safe now?"

"No," he stated without hesitation.

She fought down a panic like she'd never known. There had been times when she'd sensed danger, but not like this. She had no doubt Buchanan's men were riding hard and fast to come *save* her. If they picked up the trail, eventually, no matter how hard Tobin pushed, the soldiers would overtake them. Liberty had no idea what Samuel would do with Stella, but she had a pretty good idea Tobin would be killed and Samuel would do his best to make her wish she were dead. By going with Tobin, she'd ruined the captain's plans.

Liberty hated the thought of ever seeing Samuel again, but another fear overshadowed that of her ex-fiancé.

"Tobin."

"Yes," he answered as if not surprised she wasn't sleeping.

"The men who tried to kill my father . . . will they try again?"

"They might, but he'll be ready for them."

After a few minutes of silence, she asked, "Tobin?"

"Yes," he said, a hint of laughter in his voice as if he'd made a bet with himself that she'd have more questions.

"Do you think they'll come after me also?" Part of her reasoned they wouldn't. After all, she had nothing to do with politics.

"They might," Tobin answered. "If for no other reason than to hurt your father."

She studied Tobin's tall frame. He was a strong man, but he was one against an army of men. One man between her and Samuel. One man between her and assassins.

"Tobin?"

"Libby?" he whispered back as if he liked saying her name.

"If you promise to tell me when we are safe, I'll not ask again."

"I promise," he answered. "Now get some sleep."

She dreamed again of dancing in Washington at a fine ball.

Just before dawn, she rolled stiffly to her side and came full awake with the pain. Carefully, she sat up and opened her eyes. The air was cold. The first violet of dawn washed over the horizon. Stella's blanket was folded over her saddle, but Liberty didn't see her or hear her. Tobin was also nowhere in sight.

Liberty took a deep breath, feeling the air push into her lungs as she touched her side. She smiled. She felt better. The bruise across her ribs was still tender, but it no longer hurt to breathe. Her eye also seemed less puffy, and the cut on her lip had scabbed to a thin rough line.

Slipping from her blanket, she followed the stream until she found a place surrounded by trees. Kneeling, she cupped her hands and took a drink. The cold water tasted better than any wine she'd ever had. She drank her fill, then lay her cold hand over the side of her face, thankful that she couldn't see the bruise there.

Slowly, finding comfort in the simple ritual, she washed her face with her satin handkerchief. She found a small comb in her coat pocket she must have used to pull her hair back the last time she'd worn the wool jacket. Sitting back on the grass beside the stream, she untied her braid and began combing out her hair.

The first light of morning sliced through the trees making the stream sparkle. She smiled remembering something an old nanny had told her when she was small. The woman had said that in the time between first light and when the sun appears, there is magic. The nanny had sworn it was the wishing time.

Liberty closed her eyes and could almost feel herself dancing on a polished floor with crystal chandeliers above her. If she could have one wish, it would be to be back were she belonged.

"You all right?" Tobin's sudden question shattered her dream as if the chandelier had tumbled. "You looked stiff when you crawled out of your bedroll."

Liberty noticed him standing on the other side of the stream watching her. "I'm fine," she answered, a little more sharply than she'd intended.

"Good, we leave in ten minutes." He turned to leave.

"Tobin?" She stopped him with one word.

"Yes?"

"Are you mad at me?"

"No," he answered, without looking at her.

"Then what is it?" She knew he was worried, but it was more than that. Maybe he was mad about having to take her to safety. Maybe he resented all the trouble she'd caused him. Maybe he was still angry about the kiss on the porch, which seemed like it had happened a lifetime ago.

She had no idea, but she planned to find out. He'd treated her with kindness when he touched her, but his words were crisp and to the point.

"Nothing," he finally answered, but he didn't look at her. "I've got a job to do. A promise to keep. I need to remember that above all else."

Liberty stood and tucked her comb back into her pocket. "And I'm the job."

He slapped his gloves against his hand. "And you're the job. I'll get you to the ranch and keep you safe until your father can come take you back to the world where you belong. I feel like I've got fine china out here in the wilderness."

He couldn't have made it any plainer.

"Great," she said as she unbuttoned her blouse. "If it's nothing personal, would you mind rewrapping my ribs? The strips seem to have loosened."

He stepped over the thin stream and looked down at her. "Wouldn't Stella be better at this?"

"I don't know where she is." Liberty tugged her camisole up. "Plus, you already know how." She raised her chin. "We wouldn't want fine china getting broken."

"All right." He knelt as she straightened on her knees.

Every part of her body took the nearness of him like a caressing blow. Part comfort, part pain.

His fingers fumbled with the knot on the bandage; then he seemed to be trying not to touch her as he unwrapped the strips.

For a moment he leaned back staring at her bruise. When she shivered, he remembered his duty and began rewrapping her ribs. Finally, his hands were gentle and caring, caressing her flesh as he worked.

There it was again, she thought. A touch that was almost an embrace, from a man who frowned as if he didn't like anything about her.

"Too tight?" he whispered, holding her steady with one hand as he wrapped.

She shook her head afraid that if she opened her mouth she might cry out.

His hands moved around her, brushing the strip of cloth smooth across her ribs. The last few circles he made were high on her ribs. The side of his finger slid slowly just beneath her breasts.

When she sucked in air, he paused. "Am I hurting you, Libby?"

"No, it feels good."

Tying off the end, he whispered so close she could feel his words on her cheek. "That should feel better."

"Thank you," she answered when he looked up. Nothing in his stare told her that she was only a job to him. She guessed she was more to him then she should be and probably far more than he wanted her to be.

He stood, then offered his hand.

When she got to her feet, he didn't turn her hand loose for a moment. Then suddenly, with an embarrassed look, he let go of her fingers. "I'll get the horses."

He looked back, his gaze on her open blouse.

She glanced down. Her breasts were clearly outlined beneath the camisole. The nipples peaked in the cool air. Liberty raised her chin, daring him to say anything.

For a moment he just stared, then turned away. She heard him taking a few deep breaths before he managed to ask, "Have any idea where your maid is?"

Libby smiled as if she'd won some kind of victory. "You didn't see her get up?"

"I walked over to check the horses. When I came back she was gone. That was half an hour ago."

Liberty could fill in the blanks. Stella might be missing, but Tobin wouldn't leave her to go look for the maid. She had no doubt he'd been watching her since she first awoke. "I'll be right there," Liberty finally said. "If she's not back, we'll look for her together."

She took another drink and walked slowly back to the horses. Tobin was saddling up. By the time he had all three horses ready, they heard Stella tromping through the underbrush, mumbling to herself.

Tobin nor Liberty asked, but both heard all about Stella's adventure while trying to find a secluded place to wash up. Halfway through the rant, Tobin moved behind Liberty and gently helped her onto her horse. When he was close to her ear, he whispered, "Too bad she found her way back."

Liberty tried her best to frown, but she couldn't stop one side of her mouth from lifting. Their gazes met and held but neither spoke. Sometimes she swore she had an entire conversation going on silently with this man.

Stella chatted on about how she had a gift for knowing when trouble stood near. She swore she was part Gypsy and could sense things better than a hound dog could smell a fresh trail. "Trouble is riding full out for us all," she voiced. "I don't know where it's coming from but it's bad."

All day Liberty and Tobin played a game of cold politeness. He'd ask her how she felt, and she'd lie, as always, and say fine. The land stretched in rolling hills with no sight of settlers, so the riding was easier. Stella asked Tobin one question after another as to exactly where in Texas they were. Most of the time he ignored her, but when he did give out any information it was directed toward Liberty, not the maid.

As the day warmed, the buttons on Stella's blouse began to open. By noon the top of her bosom looked like it might come out of the material at any moment. Liberty watched Tobin, but as near as she could tell, he wouldn't have noticed if Stella had been riding nude. When he'd made no comment by late afternoon, Liberty watched the buttons close one by one as the temperature dropped.

That night they ate in silence, too tired to even try to talk or bother to say good night to one another. About the time Liberty heard Stella's snoring, she began to cry. She'd felt better all day but worried more about her father. She told herself he was all right. He was always all right. Her father had been a fighter all his life and a threat on his life, even an ambush, wouldn't slow him down. He had rangers with him. It would take an army to get to him. But none of this stopped her worry.

She thought she'd muffled the sound of her crying but knew she hadn't when Tobin's hand touched her shoulder. Without a word, he pulled her up into his arms. Liberty cuddled against his warm chest and wept. She didn't need to tell him about her fears. He'd asked for no explanation.

As the warmth of him moved over her, her tears stopped. She looked up but could only make out the shadow of his face.

His thumb brushed gently over her face, then lightly over her bottom lip. "The cut is almost healed," he whispered.

She rested her head against his chest. "I'm sorry I cried," she said.

"It's all right, Libby. Get some sleep." His words were a gentle order as he lay her back down and pulled her blanket close. "We've got a long day tomorrow."

Then, as silently as he'd come to her, he was gone, and Liberty wondered if he'd been there at all.

The next day and the next were the same. They rode, taking only minutes to eat. No one bothered to talk more than was necessary. Tobin kept turning, never going in a straight path, never venturing into the open if there were shadows they could ride through.

On the fifth day, an hour before dark, it began to rain, a slow drizzle that seemed to cool in the wind. Tobin told them it was a blessing, making tracking almost impossible, but as the rain soaked through her clothes, she didn't feel blessed.

Stopping before dark, Tobin built a fire. With the rain and fog, no one would see the smoke in the tall pine. For the first time, they had coffee. As they huddled near the fire the rain finally stopped, but the clouds were so thick they looked like they were resting on the treetops.

Tobin rigged a line to hang their damp coats and Stella made a stew from the leftover bits of food in the flour sack. Since no one had anticipated the maid's coming along—there were only two cups, plates, and forks—Tobin insisted the women eat first; then Liberty washed her plate with a bit of water from the canteen and handed it to him. While he ate, Tobin and she silently agreed to share the cup of coffee.

The hot food seemed to have wound Stella up again. She talked about how her family traveled by wagon to Texas when she was a girl. "Once," she said with a laugh, "my baby brother, Fred, rolled out from under the tent and Ma thought the Indians got him. We were running around screaming and crying for an hour before Dad found him in the trench he'd dug to keep the water out of the tent." She looked at Tobin. "You ever get frightened by any of those savages?"

"No," Tobin answered, and stood.

For the first time in days Liberty smiled, just thinking how Stella would react if she knew Tobin were half savage. The maid might stop flirting with him if she thought he'd scalp her in her sleep.

When Tobin walked into the shadows, Stella said, "I swear that man must think every word he says cost a dime and he's only got two bits to last a lifetime."

Moments later, Tobin returned with wood.

As he stepped into the firelight, Liberty asked, "Where will you sleep?"

He tossed the logs on the flames. "In the shadows." His words were so low they couldn't have reached Stella. "If someone should come upon us, it will be by accident in this fog. I want to know he's here before he figures out where I am."

Liberty watched him disappear again, then curled close to the fire and tried to sleep. Stella complained until she fell asleep in midsentence. With the fire almost smothered in fog, the night took on an eerie glow. After spending an hour trying to get comfortable, Liberty finally stood, wrapped her blanket across her shoulders, and poured the last cup of coffee. Then, feeling more than seeing her way, she circled the fire.

On her third round, she spotted him. If Tobin hadn't moved she never would have seen him. He sat against the trunk of a fallen tree, almost invisible. His hat, as always, was low hiding his face but she guessed he'd been watching her every movement.

She walked toward him. "Want half of the last cup of coffee?"

He made room for her. "Sure."

She sat almost touching him as they shared the coffee. She couldn't see him, but she could feel the warmth of his nearness and it comforted her. They passed the cup between them.

"I feel out of harm's way tonight, wrapped by the fog."

He nodded. "If we're being tracked in this mess, it's by someone who knows more than I do."

Liberty passed him the cup. "And that wouldn't be Captain Buchanan?"

"Nope." Their hands touched casually as he took the cup. "More likely one of the savages . . . or a half-breed."

They both laughed. She rocked and bumped his shoulder with hers before relaxing beside him once more. This time, their arms and legs brushed, warming Liberty more than any blanket could.

"Why are you still up, Libby?" he finally asked.

"I noticed tonight that you gave your blanket to Stella when she complained."

He stiffened, telling her he didn't like to be questioned.

"This far from the campfire can't be warm." She pushed.

"What is your point?" He crossed his arms.

She spread the blanket over them both and leaned against his shoulder. "Point is," she said just as coldly as he had, "we're sharing a blanket and you'd better not snore."

He lifted his arm and she lay her head on his chest.

Finally, she let out a breath and added, "And, remember, tomorrow not a word to Stella. Nothing about sleeping next to you is proper."

His chin brushed her hair as he nodded. "Seems to me we're developing quite a list of improper activities."

"Swear you'll never tell."

He laughed. "I swear."

She closed her eyes and slowly relaxed into his warmth. If he wanted to chatter on, he'd have to do it alone like Stella did. All she planned to do was sleep.

CHAPTER 13

NO MOON GAUGED THE HOUR OF NIGHT. LIBERTY shifted with the usual discomfort in her side, only this time she wasn't cold, or alone. Another body warmed her. Another heart beat next to her own.

Spreading her hand across Tobin's chest, she realized exactly where she was. She lay cuddled into and halfway on top of him. His arm warmed her back and his hand spread over her hip as casually as if he were familiar with her body. Her leg rested over his muscular thigh. His steady breath brushed against her forehead.

Slowly spreading her fingers beneath his vest, she felt the beat of his heart against her hand. He slept soundly, probably for the first time in days. The night had grown black, but she would have known if he watched her. For days now she'd felt the gaze of his dark blue eyes protectively observing her every move.

The firelight was no more than a red glow in the distance. Liberty smiled. She couldn't see. She had no choice but to feel her way across the sleeping man beside her. He might be content to watch, but she wanted to touch him. Since that first night in the barn, the hunger to be closer to him had built inside her, disturbing her thoughts, haunting her dreams. In her privileged life, she usually did not have to wait for the things she wanted. But she had waited to touch Tobin.

Liberty knew her longings were short-lived. Her father had once called her a flitterbug, rushing from one interest to another. She'd want something, beg and demand to have it, then abandon it just as quickly. Yet she'd never longed to be close to a man. She wasn't sure she even liked Tobin; he acted angry at her most of the time. Since the night he'd carried her out of her home, however, she'd craved his nearness.

She told herself that his presence gave her a sense of safety . . . but she knew it was far more. She wanted him close, very close.

And tonight, she had just that.

His arm felt solid as she moved her hand up his sleeve. A week's worth of whiskers tickled across her fingers as she crossed his jaw and touched his full bottom lip. She'd spent days trying not to think of the way his mouth had captured hers that night on the porch. He might be a quiet, shy man, but there was nothing quiet, or shy, in the way he kissed.

She leaned closer. His skin smelled of spring water and she wondered when he'd had time to bathe. She trailed her finger down his open collar and unfastened the first button of his shirt, wanting to know what his chest hair felt like. In the darkness she became an explorer, a blind voyeur discovering her obsession. Tobin McMurray had been just that since he'd walked into her life . . . an obsession.

He was the first man she felt she knew well enough to have no fear of letting near. She'd trusted other men, but Liberty had always been aware of who they were and, more important, who she was expected to be. Her father would allow no scandal. She had to be the proper senator's daughter every moment.

But a part of her deep inside ran wild and free. With Tobin she knew that what happened between them would stay between them and no one else.

When he didn't wake with her touch, she moved her face

closer lightly brushing her lips against his. She could never remember craving anything the way she craved another kiss, and here in the silent darkness there seemed no border to stop her from tasting once more.

For a moment, he didn't move; then she felt his mouth slide into a smile.

"You're awake?" She would have pulled back, but his arm held her atop him.

"Did you plan to have your way with me while I slept?" His low laugh rumbled through his chest and she felt it echo through her body as well.

"Maybe," she whispered, moving her fingers into his hair, loving the thickness of it. "After all, I've got you surrounded." She balled her fist into the dark brown mass as if trapping her prey.

"Then do your worst, Libby, because I'm tired of wanting what I had a taste of on the porch."

He wouldn't advance this time. He would wait for her to make the first move. Before she changed her mind, she closed the inch between them and kissed him. His mouth welcomed her, teasing, playing, tasting.

After a long moment, she raised her head. "How about I do my best? I really want to kiss you again. A taste for you seems to be something I've acquired of late."

She knew he was smiling when he answered, "You're hungry for me and that's how you kiss? That's the best you have to offer a man you woke from a deep sleep? Seems like if you really set your mind to something you could do better."

The second time she kissed him, there was no teasing and playing. She kissed him long and hard, tasting the passion that their first kiss had only promised. She felt his entire body warm and harden against her. He made no effort to hide his need for her and she played no game of being shocked.

When she finally pulled away from her captive and rested her head on his shoulder, it took several seconds for their breathing to slow. She'd thought to quench her thirst for him, but as his chest rose and fell beneath her all Liberty could think about was kissing him again. The man was addictive.

"We can't be doing this," he finally said, his hand brushing lightly over her hip in a gentle caress that made his words a lie. "Much as I enjoy it, we can't. Not here, not now."

She understood what he meant. This was certainly not the way a young lady and gentleman courted. But then nothing about Tobin McMurray was ordinary and they were not likely ever to court. He would never fit into her world of parties and dances. When they reached his ranch she would be the one out of place. But the ache for him went all the way through her. It had nothing to do with the gratitude of him saving her. It was something far more basic.

"I've never felt this . . ." If he asked her to explain, she wasn't sure she could. She felt like a part of her had been missing for years and when she met him she found that piece.

"I know," he answered as uncertain of his words as she was of hers.

Feather-kissing her forehead, he groaned. His fingers tightened over her hip even while Tobin silently argued with himself. He didn't belong in her world nor she in his, but right here, right now in the darkness between worlds, they could touch. They could feel. They could be together.

As if she read his mind, she moved closer, molding her body against his. She showed no embarrassment as she touched him.

"If I deny what is between us, I have a feeling I'll regret it all my life." She moved her cheek against his chin. "I want to be closer to you, Tobin. Closer than I've ever been to a man."

"We can't . . ." He was having trouble forming thoughts.

"You're right," Liberty whispered, her words brushing against his ear. "We can't do just this. I want to do more."

"No" had formed on his lips when she kissed him again.

For a moment he didn't respond. Then, like a dam shattering, all the longing he'd felt, all the loneliness he'd known, broke through. He could have pushed her away with one hand, but the flood of need deep within him wouldn't allow it. He knew what was right, what was proper, but he couldn't fight her and himself. If wanting her was wrong, there could be nothing right in the world.

Twisting onto his side, he pulled her against him and turned her kiss to fire. They were no longer experimenting, but giving and taking newborn desire. They began a dance that only lovers know, a dance set to the beat of two hearts.

Her tongue matched his, sending lightning skimming in their blood. In their hunger, all the earth slipped away and there was no time, no world outside to hear, or see, or touch. There was only Liberty in his arms.

He tugged at the buttons of her blouse, needing to touch what he'd seen when he wrapped her ribs, knowing how her breast would feel in his hands even before he uncovered them.

To his surprise, she helped with the unbuttoning, pushing her shirt aside and lifting the camisole. When he hesitated, fearing he might hurt her ribs, she lay her hand atop his, guiding his movements.

He felt her sudden intake of breath when the cold air reached her chest and then the sigh when his hand covered her and began to move. "Easy now," he whispered against her cheek. "I don't want to hurt you."

She relaxed, leaning back, moving slightly as he stroked her.

Tobin would have given anything to have seen what he held. He could feel the perfection of her. With his hand gently circling her breast, he kissed his way across her face until he found her mouth, already open and willing.

He tugged her bottom lip into his mouth as his thumb brushed over the tip of her breast, then swallowed her soft cry of pleasure. She was molten in his arms, responding to his every move. He kissed her lightly, playfully, letting her need for more build before his tongue moved into her mouth and drank his fill of the taste of her.

His hands on her breasts were gentle, ever aware of the bandage just below. He wanted to give her only joy tonight. Libby in his arms was a gift.

Lost in her kiss, he barely noticed her opening his shirt until she moved closer, pressing herself against his bare chest. The shock of pleasure as her warm soft skin touched his made him feel half drunk.

She moved her hand over the scar covering his heart without hesitation, accepting it as a part of him, nothing more and nothing less. When he felt her perfect breast press against the twisted flesh, Tobin fought back a groan of pure satisfaction.

His hand moved gently over her bandaged ribs. He wanted to feel more of her, but he'd not risk unwrapping the strips of cotton. At her waist, he shoved her trousers down. When the flesh of her hip filled his hand, Tobin felt himself tremble. For a man who rationed feelings as if joy came rare and far between, the nearness of her was overwhelming.

Liberty pulled an inch away, her hands still framing his face. "It's all right, Tobin. I want this." He shoved his hand lower on her hip as she murmured, "I want you to feel all of me."

"But . . ."

"Just this once," she whispered as she moved against him. "And then we can go on pretending nothing ever happened. You don't have to care for me, just hold me tonight. Be mine tonight as if there is no world outside this place."

He closed his eyes and pulled her hips toward him, letting her settle against him.

He felt her surprise at the intimacy of what he'd done, but she wasn't shy with him. Instead, she wrapped her arms around his neck and held tight. "Please love me. No matter what happens tomorrow, or every day of my life, I want to have this one night to remember. Please, Tobin."

Tobin hoped his tender touch told her she wouldn't have to ask again.

This might be the first time for them both, but Tobin and Libby had no desire to tread lightly. Her fingers fumbled with the buttons of his trousers. "I'm tired of worrying about dying; for tonight I want to think only of living."

"All right, Libby," he whispered as he moved his hand between them and unbuckled his belt.

He'd meant to go slow, to be careful of her bruised body and inexperience, but they were both new to this game and neither knew how to slow down. He kissed her with almost violent need as his hands stroked her, claiming every part of her, body.

"Love me," she whispered softly when he opened her legs. "Please love me."

She was hesitant when he brushed against her, more afraid that he'd pull away before he loved her than that he'd hurt her.

"You feel so good," she heard him whisper as he touched her in her most private place.

Rolling to her back, she waited, trying to control her breathing as he explored her.

His fingers, then his mouth, moved over her. He took deep breaths, breathing her in like an animal finding his mate. He tasted her flesh, then kissed each spot as if wanting to erase his hunger for her. Again and again, he returned to her mouth, each time with more fire, more need. His low groan of pleasure whispered in her ear, driving her mad with excitement.

She felt cherished, truly cherished, for the first time in her life.

She'd expected him to move on top, but he stayed on his side, gently pulling her to him until he entered her. When she cried out in surprise, he pushed hard, his hands on her hips keeping her from moving, his mouth against her ear whispering an apology.

Liberty buried her cry in his chest as he began to move inside her. She felt as if he were splitting her in half, body and soul . . . shattering her thoughts until there was nothing but him and what they were doing. His words were gentle, his hands firm, his entry into her consuming.

She whimpered as she clung to him, drifting with the hurt as she learned to move with him . . . as they became one.

He rocked back and forth until he washed the pain away with slow, even strokes of pleasure, each easing deeper inside her.

"Take all of me," he whispered. "Open up to me, Libby." He nuzzled her cheek. "There you go. Let me in."

His words calmed her and his hands once more became a

gentle caress over her body. She sighed and tasted his throat, biting softly where blood pulsed. When he kissed her forehead and turned her mouth to his, she opened wide to his familiar kiss, knowing what he wanted as he knew her.

He felt it when she began to enjoy their mating. She leaned her head back and pushed against him no longer passive, but now demanding attention. He let go of her hips and moved up to stroke her straining breasts as he rained kisses down her throat.

He tried to hold back as she began to moan softly, but this was all too new to him, too wonderful. With one last push, he shoved deep inside her and felt like his entire body exploded.

Holding on to her, he drifted free from gravity.

When his heart finally settled and his mind could form thought, she had moved a few inches away from him. Her fingers were still tangled in his hair. His hand spread wide across the soft flesh of her stomach.

"Libby," he whispered having no idea what to say. She'd just given him heaven.

"I know." She laughed nervously. "It was nice."

Tobin's head fell back against the tree trunk with a hollow sound and he wondered if it were his head or the tree that was void. His universe had just shattered, the earth had stop rotating, the sky had fallen into his heart, and all she could say was that it was nice. *Nice* wasn't the word he would have chosen to describe his feelings.

He didn't know if he had felt too much or she too little. What they'd done was something grand and wonderful, an act that bound two people together. She acted as if they'd just played a game of checkers.

He pulled his trousers up and buckled his belt. "Yes," he finally managed. "It was nice." The feel of her was still on his skin, the taste of her in his mouth, the dampness of her . . . He had to stop thinking of what they'd just done—as she apparently had.

He could hear the sounds of her dressing. He leaned back and waited for her to regain her senses. She had every right to yell at him. He should have stopped them. He should have been reasonable even if she were not. Or maybe she'd start crying any moment. After all she'd just given him her virginity. Tobin groaned. Knowing her, she'd probably demand it back.

"You all right?" she whispered.

"Yes," he said. "You?"

"I'm fine." She leaned back against him and he circled his arm around her once more as if they were old friends. "You're not going to say something insane like you love me, are you?"

"No." He figured the less he said the better at this point.

"Good. If there's one thing I can't stand it's a man who mutters of undying love when everyone with a brain knows love is a fleeting thing at best that's as likely to go as stay."

Tobin rested his arm behind his head and stared up at the starless sky. All he wanted to do was lie awake thinking of the paradise he'd just lived through and she wanted to talk. "You have a lot of experience with love, I suppose?" he finally said.

"Of course I do. I've had gentlemen callers dropping by the house since I was fifteen. A few wrote poetry, most brought flowers, some flattered me and everything I said." She laughed. "One even said he'd kill himself if I wouldn't marry him."

Tobin thought of asking how many had touched her as he had, but he knew the answer. He also knew, thanks to his sister, that when a woman is thinking something through she likely as not does it out loud. So he let her talk. Cuddled up against him this way she could talk all night if she wanted to.

"I only let a few of them kiss me," she said simply. "Mostly on the cheek."

"So, why did you let me"—he paused, then decided to take the safest route—"kiss you?"

She lay her hand over his chest. "You have it wrong." She yawned. "I kissed you."

Libby straightened and Tobin felt the point of her elbow sink into his chest. "I had a longing for you, something awful, but now it's past and we can go back to being friends."

Before Tobin could think of an answer, she curled back against him. Within minutes her slow breathing told him she was asleep.

Tobin tried to sleep. Maybe in the morning he'd find out this had all been a dream. One hell of a dream. At some point tonight reality and wishing collided. He wasn't even sure how it had happened.

But he did know one thing. Dream or real, come morning the longing for Libby would still fill his every thought. It might be over for her, but for him it was just starting.

CHAPTER 14

WHEN TOBIN WOKE, LIBBY WAS GONE. FOR A moment he felt her loss like a blow. Then reality registered and he wondered if she'd ever been by his side. He'd thought about her endlessly in the midnight hours of each night when he couldn't sleep. A few times he'd even walked over to where she rested, and pulled her blanket up to her shoulder, wishing he could join her there. But then he'd walked away and waited for dawn in the shadows thinking of what it would be like if she came to him.

And last night she had.

He didn't think he had the imagination to dream up what had happened between them. He could still feel her skin on his fingers and the scent of her hair lingered in his lungs. She'd been wild and free, not the proper princess he'd seen before.

Tobin stood suddenly. He had a job to do. He had to get her to Whispering Mountain. He'd not spend time thinking of what happened last night. There would be time enough for that when he got her to safety. Even without the captain following, there were dangers this far north, dangers she probably didn't even want to know about.

As he walked toward the cold campfire, he noticed both Libby and Stella were still asleep. Sometime in the night she'd left him. He felt a strange mixture of sadness and anger. She'd left without a word. Liberty Mayfield had changed his world forever, then simply walked away.

Fog still hung over the camp in spiderweb wisps. He built up the campfire and had coffee on by the time Libby rolled over.

She smiled up at him. "I had the nicest dream last night."

That word again, he thought. He'd never considered the possibility anyone could hate a word, but that one was starting to get on his nerves.

"Me too." Stella stretched, unaware she'd barged into a private conversation. "I dreamed I was eating at a banquet with food spread all over the table. About the time I was ready to dig in, I glanced over and saw a six-foot rat sitting next to me, all dressed up like King George. He smiled at me with his pointed teeth like I was the next course."

Libby laughed. "I've been to a few state dinners just like that."

Now they were both giggling. Tobin didn't see anything funny so he kept quiet. He wanted to hold what happened in the night close to him for a while, just the way he'd held Libby.

"What's for breakfast?" Stella asked as she shook her curly hair sending it into a tumbleweed style.

"Coffee," Tobin answered, "and a few pieces of jerky. But, if we ride hard today, we could be at the ranch tonight for supper."

Libby accepted a cup of hot coffee without touching Tobin's fingers as she had the evening before.

He watched her in silence. In truth, he wasn't sure what to say.

"We leave at full light," he said as he moved to the horses giving the girls time to do whatever women do when they need time alone. He almost wished Libby would follow him.

If she did, he'd pull her out of the maid's sight and revisit a few places along her body that he'd gotten to know quite well. He'd never known a woman could be so soft or taste so good.

Tobin muttered an oath. He had to get his mind on the danger ahead and away from the shadows of last night. He had to think of her safety, not of her ripe body that welcomed his touch, or the way she'd kissed his throat when she'd first felt joy in their mating.

He swore again. At this rate he'd be lucky to remember the way to his own home. He had to think of what needed to be done, not what he wanted to repeat.

When he returned with the horses watered and saddled, the women were ready. Tobin avoided looking at Libby as she walked past him and took the reins of her mount.

"Morning, Sunny," she whispered as she showered the horse with more attention then she'd shown him.

Then, to his surprise, she swung up on her saddle before he had time to offer help. Stella did the same.

Tobin led them toward Whispering Mountain. He knew this last leg well. The land was, for the most part, open and sparsely settled. It was also the most dangerous portion of the journey. If Buchanan hadn't been able to pick up their trail from the senator's ranch, he might send men ahead. It wouldn't take much investigating to learn that as far as everyone knew, there was only one way into Whispering Mountain. Men on good horses could have taken the wagon road and already be at the bridge. A dozen men could be waiting for them to arrive.

Tobin knew they had to get to the bridge that joined his land to Texas before dark. Otherwise, they could easily be ambushed.

He considered taking them through the hidden route over the hills, but no one had ever traveled that way except family.

Besides, to go that way would take him too close to town and increase their chances of being seen.

Tobin grinned remembering one exception to the family-only rule: Martha, the housekeeper. Teagen had been forced to bring her that way because the boys had burned the bridge that spring when they learned of their father's death. She'd been all spit and vinegar when she'd seen them, claiming the boys were more animals than human, but she'd loved baby Sage so the brothers tried to follow her orders.

"What's so funny?" Libby asked as she pulled her horse up beside him.

Tobin smiled at her. "I was thinking it will be good to be home."

Libby nodded. "I feel the same way when I get close to Washington." She wrinkled her forehead. "Do you think we're still being followed?"

Tobin shook his head. "If Buchanan thinks you were kidnapped, he's not likely to think I'll bring my kidnapped victim home. But if the captain is smart enough to realize you weren't kidnapped, but rescued, then Whispering Mountain will be the first place he'll look."

Libby followed Tobin's thinking. "The men who ambushed my father, if they're looking for me, will think the same thing."

Tobin hated to admit that he agreed. But whoever came would have to kill him first to get to Libby, and he didn't plan on making that easy.

As the day wore on, Tobin knew he was pushing the women. Stella complained, but Libby didn't say a word. In fact, most of the time she didn't even look at him. But he watched her. He was aware of every time she gripped her side or dabbed water on her handkerchief, then put it to the back of her neck. She might have been pampered all her life, but there was steel in her.

He admired her silence at the same time he felt her pain. The need to comfort her was an ache within him, but he guessed she wouldn't welcome his attention. She'd been even more distant than usual all morning and twice she'd pointed out how much she wished she were back at the capital. If she got any colder, he'd need a coat even to ride next to her.

By late afternoon they were riding parallel to Elmo Anderson's trading post. They would have had to cross through the edge of town to reach the back entrance to Whispering Mountain.

Tobin knew if he rode into town Elmo would tell everyone for miles around that Tobin McMurray had two women with him. Half the town would have him married off to one or the other by sundown and the other half would be trying to guess who the women were and why they'd agreed to go with the likes of him.

Stella saw a signpost to Elmo's Trading Post and begged to be allowed to go into town for a few personal supplies, insisting she had to have them.

When Tobin met Libby's gaze, she shook her head slightly. Silently, they both agreed to keep Stella close and uninformed. After spending almost a week with the maid, neither thought she might be a danger, but she did rattle on. Once when she'd lagged behind, Liberty had suggested that she might be a spy for whoever had tried to kill her father. Tobin had laughed. If the assassins were depending on Stella's help, they must be pretty hard up for recruits.

Because he and Liberty never talked about the senator around her, Stella seemed to believe they were on the run because of what the captain had done. As the days passed and Liberty's bruises faded, Stella began to make excuses for Samuel. Making Tobin wonder if she were on a mission to somehow get the couple back together.

When they passed the sign to Elmo's place, Tobin thought he might have to tie Stella up to keep her from bolting toward what she called civilization, but Libby ended the discussion by saying that as soon as they reached the ranch she'd make a list of all they needed and have someone go after the supplies while they rested.

Stella whined but didn't argue. Tobin wondered who Libby thought ran errands around a ranch. They had no butler waiting around to be sent on a mission.

As they neared the bridge, Tobin rode ahead, making sure there were no fresh tracks. It looked as if only one wagon had passed onto Whispering Mountain land since the rain. That would probably be Sage picking up supplies or

Teagen riding into town to check on a letter he'd been expecting from Chicago.

Tobin lifted his hand to his mouth and made a bird call. An answering call came from the trees. Tobin knew it was safe.

He rode back to the women and told them they were almost home. He pulled close to Libby. "Can you travel full out for just a few more miles?"

She patted her horse but didn't meet his gaze. "Sunny seems to smell home. He's been fighting to run for an hour."

Tobin reached for the horse's neck, almost touching Libby's hand. "After we walk the bridge, give him his head and we'll be home."

Tobin wanted to say something about what they'd shared. He wanted her to know that it meant something to him. But now was not the time and Stella might overhear. When the maid wasn't talking, she seemed to be studying the two of them carefully, almost as if she planned to file a report.

He started over the bridge. The familiar sounds of the wood creaking beneath the horses welcomed him.

A moment later he was riding hard with Libby keeping pace beside him on the beautiful palomino. Over their days on the trail she'd learned to ride and they made quite a pair racing the wind.

Stella tried to keep up as they rushed toward the bridge.

Minutes later all three hit the wooden bridge at full gallop. Tobin took the lead now and pointed them toward the ranch house. Home. He almost said it aloud. Finally he'd made it back.

Liberty watched the McMurray home come into full view. She didn't know what she had expected. A log cabin. A hut in the woods maybe. Not a huge two-story ranch house with a wide porch running around it like a ribbon. The roof reflected the last of the sun as they neared and the mountain behind seemed to stand guard over the entire ranch. She noticed barns, corrals, a bunkhouse, a wide garden lot. Whispering Mountain wasn't just a ranch house; it was a world within itself.

A small woman in trousers, her hair in a braid to her waist, jumped off the porch and ran down the walk.

Tobin jumped from his horse in one fluid movement and lifted her into the air.

"Tobin! We were so worried!" She laughed, halfheartedly trying to wiggle out of his hold as she noticed Liberty riding up.

"We're safe," he said simply when he finally set her down.

Liberty slowed her horse and to her surprise, the girl rushed, not to her, but to the animal. "Hello, Sunny. Came back, did you, old boy?" Then the girl hugged the sweaty animal as if he were family.

Tobin reached for Libby and she let him help her down. "Sage, I'd like you to meet Miss Liberty Mayfield. Libby this is my little sister, Sage. Don't let her size fool you. She runs this outfit, or at least thinks she does."

Liberty offered her hand to the girl. "Pleased to meet you," she said, with her best smile. "I apologize for my appearance."

Sage laughed nervously. "You're here in one piece. That's what's important. We got word yesterday from Travis that you were coming. He thought the stage, making a direct path, might beat you here."

Tobin and Libby stared at Sage for a moment, before Libby whispered what they were both thinking, "You've heard from Ranger Travis? Is there news of my father?"

Sage shook her head and tried to smile. "The letter was short. Only the fact that Travis guessed Tobin would bring you here so we'd best get ready for company. But," she hurried to add, "I'm sure the senator is fine or Travis would have written more."

Liberty relaxed a bit, almost leaning against Tobin. She'd spent the long days on the trail worrying about her father. Maybe that was why she felt she had to be with Tobin last night. Maybe she just needed someone. If her father, her only living relative, died she wasn't sure she could take the blow. Since her mother died, her father, the housekeeping staff, her governess—everyone—had always protected her, sheltered her. Who would protect her when the senator was gone?

She'd needed Tobin last night, wanted him all the way to her bones, but she wasn't sure she needed Tobin now or just someone to hide behind. Until she had time to think about it, she'd keep her distance and nothing like last night would happen again. She wouldn't allow her armor to fall until she knew her own mind.

Liberty straightened. She'd not be needy again. No matter how good it had felt in his arms.

While introducing Stella to Sage, Tobin put his hand on Libby's back. She let it rest there a moment, then reluctantly shifted away.

His little sister stepped into the role of hostess. "Please come in. You are both welcome. I'm happy to have the company."

In spite of her welcoming words, Liberty felt something was wrong. Sage's gaze darted to her brother as if she needed to tell him something that wasn't meant to be shared with company.

As they moved up the walk, Liberty didn't miss how Sage hung back with Tobin and she watched the McMurrays out of the corner of her eye. Meanwhile, Stella was exclaiming how thankful she was to finally be safe and how much she was looking forward to a good meal after days of eating food covered in dirt.

Behind them, Tobin put his arm around his little sister's shoulders. Liberty heard him whisper. "What is it?"

Stella greeted an older woman at the door, but Liberty watched and waited as Tobin held Sage comfortingly.

Liberty hadn't missed the puffiness of the girl's eyes. Over her years playing the games of politics in her father's world, she'd learned to watch for signs . . . for what people didn't say. She almost guessed what was coming before Sage spoke. Sorrow clung to the girl like a second skin.

"My Michael was with the senator the night he was attacked. The same night you took Liberty. Travis wrote that the other two rangers had sent Michael on ahead to make

sure there would be no trouble when the senator passed."
Sage raised her chin, refusing to allow a single tear to fall
while others watched. She didn't seem to notice Liberty was
close enough to overhear. "Travis joined up with the rangers
at Victoria the morning after you kidnapped Miss Liberty.
He wanted to catch up to you and add his gun as guard for
the senator's daughter, but when he saw Michael hurt he decided he'd better stay with him."

No one had to tell Liberty what the young ranger must
have meant to Sage. She could read it as plainly as if the Mc-
Murrays were actors on a stage.

Tobin pulled his sister into a hug. "I was worried. The
morning after we left an old ranger named Wes caught up to
us. He said one of his men named Michael had been hurt.
The thought crossed my mind that it might be your friend."

Sage gulped back sobs as she pressed her face into her
brother's chest. "The note Travis sent says he's bad, Tob.
What am I going to do?"

To Tobin's credit, he didn't try to come up with easy
words. He just held her.

Liberty turned her attention back to the porch as Stella
began the introduction of Martha. Liberty shook the old
housekeeper's hand. Martha hesitated taking her hand, making Liberty wonder just how bad she must look after almost
a week on the trail and bruises still along her jawline.

By the time Sage joined them, she'd shoved her tears
aside. She invited them inside with a wide wave of her hand.
"While you wash up, I'll help Martha put supper on the
table. We didn't know when you'd be in, but we got plenty of
food that will be ready by the time you shake the dust off
you. Tobin will take care of the animals and wash up in the
bunkhouse. Teagen, my oldest brother, never makes it in until well after dark so the mud room is all yours, ladies."

Liberty had meant to simply glance back in Tobin's direction, but when she did their eyes met and held for a few
seconds, and she swore she could feel his touch in the
warmth of his blue eyes.

She hurried to join the others, not wanting to deal with

what she'd done last night. She had done more than she'd ever dreamed she would with a man without being married to him. She couldn't blame Tobin for anything. After all, it had been she who went to him. It had been she who touched him first and begged to be loved. He'd only done what she asked and nothing more.

Stella was already undressing when Liberty reached the mud room. The area, tucked between the porch and the kitchen, reminded her of a bathing chamber except that there were no frills. The walls might not be cloth or the fixtures porcelain, but all the necessities were there. A big hip tub, soaps, clean white towels, and a small stove in the corner to keep the room warm and the water steaming.

An hour later, with her hair still wet, Liberty felt like she'd washed away pain and aches along with the dirt. Thanks to Sage and Martha's pampering, she and Stella had baths and clean clothes. Stella chose a dress of navy blue that looked almost exactly like the dress Martha wore. Liberty had been offered the same but decided on a big shirt and a faded pair of trousers. Both were far too big, but she knew she'd be too tall for Martha's dresses and she'd never fit into Sage's petite clothes. Plus, etiquette demanded she dress similarly to her hostess, and Sage wore pants. So Liberty belted the trousers as tightly as she could and thanked her hostess for the clothes.

Liberty loved Sage's honesty. In a world where most people guarded every word said, Sage was refreshing. Open, friendly, and full of curiosity. It didn't take Liberty long to learn that Sage worshiped all three of her big brothers. She bragged about them like a proud momma.

When they returned to the kitchen, Sage asked, "Mind if we eat supper in the kitchen? It's routine. Unless we are all together, no one eats at the dining table."

Liberty set her at ease by saying, "You've made me feel like family. Thank you."

"As of right now, you are family," Sage replied, visibly relaxing. "Which means you may have to help me clean up. Martha goes to bed at sundown no matter what shape the kitchen is in."

Liberty pulled her chair out from the table.

Sage laughed. "I read in the paper that you were an only child. You must have had a quiet life without brothers."

Before Liberty could answer, Tobin commented from the doorway, "I remember not having a sister."

Sage pointed her finger at him. "I bet it was so horribly sad and dull."

Tobin shrugged. "It was quieter."

Before anyone could react, she picked up a hush puppy and threw it at him.

He ducked behind Liberty and the corn-bread ball brushed past them.

Sage looked mortified. "Oh, I'm so sorry. I shouldn't have done that with company. Please forgive me, Miss Liberty. I almost hit you."

Liberty smiled. "It's just Liberty, Sage. To tell the truth I've thought of throwing a few things at your brother this week, even if he did save me."

Sage didn't look surprised. "Travis said Tobin was keeping you safe, but the news coming by stage says he kidnapped you."

Sage frowned at Liberty and added, "You're the only one in the state who hasn't heard how you were kidnapped. Martha and I knew Tobin wouldn't kidnap anyone unless there was a real need. Travis's letter said once you got here to do whatever we have to do to keep you safe, so we figured you were in some kind of trouble." Sage glanced at her brother. "I've got two of Grandfather's braves guarding the bridge. If anyone tries to cross we'll hear the shots."

"I know." Tobin shrugged. "I signaled them when I rode in."

Liberty raised a questioning eyebrow and Tobin explained, "Apache braves. Now and then, if my mother's father thinks we could use a little help, he sends a few of his men. They cross through the hills and no one in town even knows they're here."

Stella looked appalled. "Apaches? What if they kill us in our sleep? Or maybe the men trying to kill the senator will come for Miss Liberty and storm the place?" She looked from Sage to Tobin. "The two of you can't stop them. Either way we are doomed. I can sense it as plain as if it were written on the wall. Death's coming. It may not be calling my name, but I'm bound to get run over in the stampede."

Sage ignored Stella completely as she motioned everyone to take their seats at the table. As they began passing huge bowls of food, Sage said calmly, "Teagen says Tobin can take Liberty into the hills where no one will find her and the rest of us will meet trouble with rifles on the porch. We've done it before."

Tobin laughed. "You were a week old, kid, the last time someone stormed this ranch. I don't remember you fighting from the porch."

Sage frowned. "I would have if one of you would have handed me a gun. I'm a McMurray too."

He tugged on her braid. "That you are, little sister. You're the best of us all. Now, can we eat? I'm starving."

As everyone began to eat, Stella shook her head still seeing only blood in her future. "Well, don't give me a gun. I've never touched one and the day I do will be my last on this earth, I fear. My father used to try and make me learn to shoot. I'd cry so hard he finally gave up even mentioning it. When I was old enough to earn my way, he took me to the nearest town and told me to stay there 'cause I wasn't meant for the country."

Liberty looked at Tobin. "I've fired both a pistol and a rifle. If there is a fight, you can count on me. I doubt if I could hit anything, but anyone riding in wouldn't know that."

Tobin nodded. "I'll see that you have both tomorrow."

CHAPTER 15

TOBIN ENDURED ABOUT AS MUCH OF THE WOMEN'S chatter as he could stand. He left for the barn, wondering why Sage wanted to know all about society in Washington, D.C., when she'd never go there, or why Liberty cared that the big frame tied to the ceiling of the dining area was a quilt frame. The princess would never quilt. And Stella, he'd discovered days ago . . . Stella just talked to hear the sound of her own voice. Her bust might be fully developed, but her brain was the size of a peanut.

In the silence of the barn, the muscles in Tobin's jaw relaxed. Liberty was safe. There were guards on the bridge. Teagen would be home soon. It would take an army to reach the ranch house and long before then he'd have Liberty hidden in the hills. He'd kept his promise to the senator and he'd made it back home. Now all he had to do was wait for word from Liberty's father.

In the meantime, he should be glad Sage had someone to talk to. Unlike Martha, Sage needed people. If she married the young ranger, she'd probably be happy living in Austin. And if the look in Michael Saddler's eyes when he saw Sage was any indication, the young ranger would agree to live anywhere Sage suggested.

Grinning, Tobin decided he needed to talk with his sister about Michael. It didn't take an expert to tell that Sage was falling in love, but Travis had mentioned more than once that Michael loved being a ranger. Somehow the two facts didn't quite go together. Judging by how upset she was over the ranger's getting hurt, though, it was probably too late for the "don't fall in love" speech.

As he always did when he worked with the horses, Tobin thought everything through. If Michael's injuries were bad, maybe Travis could bring him to the ranch to recover. That would give Sage and him time to get to know each other through more than letters. In a year or two, if he measured up, Sage and Michael could think of getting engaged.

When Tobin closed the last stall, he turned to find Liberty standing in the doorway. The lamplight behind her formed a halo around her. She looked just as beautiful in his old jeans and shirt as she had in her fine ball gown that first night he'd seen her.

"Hello," she whispered, glancing around to see if they were alone.

He didn't answer. Tobin had known this talk was coming all day from the way she'd refused to look at him at dawn to how she'd avoided even his slight touch. He'd tried not to think of what would happen when they finally found a moment to themselves, just as he'd forced the memory of what they'd done last night to the back of his mind.

But now he let the memories flood him. If he was about to take the pain of her turning away, he wanted to remember it all first.

"I thought we needed to talk." She took a step toward him. "There may be little time now." Lacing her hands together, she raised her gaze to his.

Uncertainty blended with a bit of fear in her bottomless eyes. Part of him wanted to make it easy for her, but his pride wouldn't allow him to move. She'd been the one who came to him last night and now she'd be the one to walk away.

"You told me you never plan to marry and I respect that. In fact, after realizing my mistake in almost marrying the wrong man, I'm considering the life of an old maid myself. Neither of us is naive enough to believe that what happened last night was anything more than two people clinging to each other out of need."

She was being what she'd been trained to be, diplomatic. She wasn't apologizing or asking him to. She was simply setting the record straight.

"It was nice," he repeated her words.

Smiling, she nodded. "Nice."

He didn't miss the blush of red in her cheeks. They both knew that what they shared was a hell of a lot more than nice. He gripped the stall gate, fighting not to reach for her.

Straightening, she finally added, "I never thanked you for saving me. I hid in the attic thinking my father would come, but deep down I knew that if he didn't I would run to you. I knew you'd help me."

"You can always run to me," he said, wishing the Libby he'd held last night would run to him now. But only the proper princess stood before him.

"Thank you for the offer." She lifted her hand. "I will always be in your debt."

When he closed his fingers gently around her hand, their eyes met and Tobin knew they were thinking of other times they'd touched. To anyone who might have walked in, they looked quite formal, but memories flooded over him like a tidal wave. Last night in the darkness he'd memorized how every curve of her body felt. He knew how she breathed, how she slept, how she smelled. How she felt against his heart.

Without another word, she turned and walked away. Tobin tried to ignore the tightness in his chest. He told himself he was too old to fall in love. They were just two people who met and needed each other one night. Any fool could see

they didn't belong together, but he had a feeling that for the
rest of his life when he thought of a woman, he would see
Libby. They may have only touched once, but he'd sleep beside her a thousand times more in his dreams.

As his last chore, Tobin filled water buckets from the
well between the house and the barn. It crossed his mind
that he seemed to plan everyone's life out but his own.
What happened with Liberty hadn't been part of any plan
and there could be no future to think about. A senator's
daughter wasn't likely to fall for a rancher in the middle of
nowhere.

After placing the buckets just inside the mud room, Tobin
grabbed his rifle and began to walk the perimeter of the ranch
house grounds. It was a duty either he or one of his brothers
did each night. When his father left to fight for Texas, he'd
tucked away a letter in his desk drawer with instructions on
how to hold the ranch. When the boys found the letter after
his death, they called the instructions "the rules."

The list had saved not only the ranch but their lives as
well. Simple precautions their father had put in place, basic
knowledge he'd taught them to use until the rules became
routine, never neglected, never broken.

In the moonlight Tobin studied the signs, listening to the
sounds in the night, watching for anything out of place that
would tell him a stranger hid on McMurray land. The circle
he walked lay just beyond the lights of the house where the
stars lit the way. When he finished his rounds, he climbed
fifty feet up the hill behind the house and perched on a
ledge. From there, he could see all the way to the bridge in
one direction and far to the north pastureland in the other. As
still as stone he watched the shadows for movement.

With trained eyes, Tobin finally spotted what he'd been
hoping for. Teagen moved across the pasture, heading toward home. Teagen, the oldest, who'd become a man at
twelve and never thought of anything since but the ranch and
the family.

Tobin watched his brother move closer. At first Tobin
thought Teagen looked tired, for he slumped in the saddle.

But as he neared, Tobin stood knowing something was wrong even before he could make out trouble.

Something long and dark lay over the front of his saddle and Teagen's right arm hung limp from his shoulder. Tobin broke into a run toward the shadowed rider.

By the time Teagen reached the light of the yard, Tobin was there to meet him. Tobin grabbed the horse's reins when Teagen made no effort to stop the animal.

Teagen's head lifted and he nodded once to Tobin, then crumbled from his horse as if he'd used the last ounce of energy.

"Sage!" Tobin yelled as he caught his brother.

The weight of him took Tobin to his knees, but he managed to break Teagen's fall. "What's wrong?" Tobin asked. "Where are you hurt?"

"I'm fine, it's only a few wounds. Get"—Teagen bit back pain—"the Roak tied in the barn."

Tobin had no idea what his brother was talking about. "Where are you hurt?" He tugged Teagen's hat off and felt warm sticky blood covering the scalp.

The back door slammed. Once, twice, three times.

"Stay with me," Tobin demanded as he heard footsteps stampeding toward them. "Don't drift off, Teagen. You've made it this far. Stay with me."

Sage reached them first, her body dropping to the ground beside Teagen, her hands feeling what the darkness wouldn't allow her to see. "What's wrong?" she asked.

"He's bleeding from somewhere along his hairline, I think," Tobin said almost calmly as Sage patted Teagen down for other injuries. "Something may be wrong with his right arm. I don't know what happened. He's talking out of his head."

"I am not." Teagen spit out the words as if each one were an effort. "Get the Roak tied up."

Tobin and Sage looked at one another.

"What is a Roak?" she whispered.

Tobin started to shake his head, then stopped suddenly. "It's who, not what," he said as the word registered in his brain. "I think that's the name of the lowlifes who live north of here in that old outlaw camp." As he commented, he remembered that something had lain across Teagen's saddle.

One glance told him what Teagen carried rolled up in a blanket. A Roak. One of the band of outlaws some thought were more animal than human. They were so mean not even the Indians would trade with them.

"We've got to get him in the house." Sage stood, trying to hold half her brother's weight across her shoulders. "If it's a head wound, we've no time to waste."

Tobin noticed Libby and Stella standing a few feet away. When he turned to them, Stella took a step backward.

He met Libby's frightened stare. "Can you help?"

She nodded once and moved closer.

Tobin lifted Teagen's arm over her shoulder. "Will you faint at the sight of blood, princess?"

"No, I don't think so."

As her body took part of Teagen's weight, Tobin whispered, "Can you help carry him?"

"I can walk, damn it." Teagen sounded angry, which made Tobin smile. If he was mad, he couldn't be too far gone.

"Good, then get in the house so Sage can stitch that head wound. I'll take care of the Roak. You try not to bleed on our guest."

Teagen mumbled something. Tobin couldn't tell if it was directed toward him or the pain.

As the women half carried his oldest brother, Tobin went to the horse and pulled the bundle to the ground. He untied the rope. A boy, not quite grown, rolled from the blanket, fighting like a bobcat even though his hands and feet were tied. He got in three good blows and almost knocked Tobin off his feet before Tobin caught him in a bear hug.

The boy was all arms and legs with little meat on his bones and slipperier than a water moccasin.

"Stop!" Tobin demanded holding the boy so tightly he feared he might break bone.

"Or what?" the youth swore. "You'll skin me alive like

your brother promised he would? Well, I'm not afraid of you. I'm not afraid of any of you. If I'd have got in another hit on your brother, he'd be dead at the river about now."

Tobin started for the barn, ignoring the kicks the boy managed to land every few steps. The kid smelled worse than a skunk and swore more than any five drunks. If Teagen had him captured, that could mean only one thing: the boy had been on Whispering Mountain land, and no one, not even a kid, was allowed on their land.

Tobin reached the barn and tossed the captive in the first stall. He didn't take the time to see if it was clean. Grabbing a rope, he looped one end around the Roak's bound hands and pulled tight, drawing the kid up to a sitting position with his hands high above him. Then, before the Roak could start kicking, he looped the rope around his feet and pulled his legs straight out.

Roak fought against his bindings and Tobin wouldn't have been surprised if the wild kid tried to chew his arm off to get away. All the time he jerked and twisted, he swore using every foul word Tobin had ever heard and a few he could only guess at the meaning.

Frustrated, Tobin pulled out his bandanna and gagged the boy. "There," he said in the sudden silence. "You were offending the horses."

Dark gray eyes stared up at him with enough hate to set the barn on fire. Tobin had no doubt that if the kid got free he'd kill them all. After checking the ropes, he pulled his gun hoping to frighten the boy. "I have to check on my brother, but when I come back, if one rope is undone, I'll tie you upside down next time."

The kid didn't look the least bit scared. Tobin frowned. His brothers would have threatened to shoot him, but despite the several spots of his body that would be sore or bruised tomorrow, Tobin couldn't bring himself to promise anything he wouldn't carry out.

He ran back to the house, wanting to get away from the son of Satan as fast as possible. There was only one reason the boy would risk trespassing on their land. He was stealing horses, or trying to.

Tobin almost collided with Stella on the back steps. She sat curled in a ball crying softly. When she looked up at him, she increased the volume.

He pulled her up by the shoulders fearing that somehow in the chaos, she'd been hurt. "What is it?" he asked, brushing her arm in awkward comfort. "Are you hurt?"

She shook her head. "I can't stay here. I can't. I hate this place. Death is coming here. I can feel it. I can almost smell the blood in the air."

She reminded him of an actress he'd seen once on stage, but Stella had no reason to be acting. Something must have frightened her.

"Will you take me to town, Tobin?" she begged. "I can't stand fighting. I just know something bad is going to happen here. I felt it the minute we crossed the bridge." She knotted the front of his shirt with her fists. "Your brother is just the beginning. Miss Liberty will be the death of everyone on this ranch. I saw evil in the shadows around your brother and it's only a matter of time before it closes in to claim us all."

Tobin thought of shaking her hard. He couldn't tell if she just wanted her share of attention or if she had truly snapped. One thing for sure, he already had his share of trouble tonight and he didn't need a hysterical woman too. He'd wanted Stella gone from the first. "All right," he said, hoping he wasn't lying. "I'll get you to town first thing in the morning."

"No," she cried. "Please take me tonight or I swear I'll find the way on my own. I'm not staying in this place." Stella now had a death grip on his shirt.

He needed to get to Teagen. His big brother was hurt and bleeding. Tobin didn't have time for Stella's private blend of crazy and Gypsy witchcraft now.

He grabbed her by the shoulders. "All right. I'll be glad to take you out of here."

She nodded as if she'd finally won.

Before she could say anything, he added, "Only first, I'll

know that my brother is out of danger." He pulled her into the kitchen. "So sit down and wait."

Stella opened her mouth to argue, but for once Tobin was faster. "Not a word. When Teagen's been doctored, I'll saddle up and not before."

He turned and headed down the long hallway to the library expecting to hear her complain, but for once Stella remained silent.

He found the others where he knew he would, in the library. Teagen sat on a low stool near the fire. Every lamp in the house circled around him. Libby was on his left, Martha on his right. Sage leaned against the desk behind Teagen. All three women looked determined in what they were about to do.

"Get it done," Teagen said between clenched teeth.

Tobin stepped closer as Sage turned to the supplies littering the desk. She lifted a needle in one hand and a towel in the other. "This is going to hurt," she said calmly as she moved toward Teagen.

Teagen lowered his chin to his chest. "Just do it, Sage. I've been putting up with the bleeding long enough."

Tobin circled in front of his brother and braced his hands on Teagen's shoulders. If he jerked, Tobin would hold him down. If he passed out from the pain, it would take all three of them to keep him from falling. Teagen didn't have an ounce of fat on him, but he was over two hundred pounds of solid muscle.

Sage moved up behind her brother.

Tobin looked at Libby. Her hands braced the back of his brother's bloody scalp. Hair and blood covered her fingers, but her grip was steady. Wet rags were piled at her feet. Tobin guessed it had been Libby who cleaned the wound.

Martha watched Teagen's face. She didn't touch him or comfort him in any way. As always, the housekeeper saw herself as an observer even though she'd been part of the family for eighteen years.

Sage brushed the towel across the wound. It spotted red. She took a deep breath and began to stitch.

Tobin felt his brother's muscles tighten in pain, but he didn't move, didn't cry out. No one said a word. There was no comfort or lies for what had to be done.

Finally, Sage whispered, "Can you pour the whisky, Libby?"

Libby reached behind her for the bottle. Whisky splattered over the stitched wound and onto them all. No one seemed to notice.

Sage patted the wound once more with a clean spot on the towel. There was less blood this time. She straightened. "It's done. The wound is closed and with luck will stay so. Try not to get clubbed again before it heals."

Teagen raised his head slowly and took the bottle from Libby with his left hand. He downed a long drink then said, "Now my arm."

Tobin had forgotten about Teagen's arm. He helped his brother to the big leather chair. Martha folded a towel to pillow the back of his head while Teagen stretched out, took another drink, then closed his eyes.

He didn't move while Sage examined his arm.

Martha handed her supplies as she cleaned and wrapped scrapes and cuts.

Tobin looked up to see Libby standing straight as a sentinel in front of the fire. He moved behind her and circled his arms around her, pulling her into his chest.

She leaned against him and slowly relaxed while they watched Sage work her magic. His little sister had been fascinated with nursing ever since their grandfather told her that their mother had been a healer. By the time Sage was sixteen, she'd helped deliver babies and acted as nurse when the traveling doctor made his yearly visit. Tobin was proud of her skills.

He leaned close to Libby. "You all right?"

She nodded. "I've never done anything like that. I'm glad I was here to help."

"So are we," Sage said as she wrapped Teagen's forearm. "No broken bones here, but looks like a horse dragged him by the arm."

"That's about what happened," Teagen mumbled, without opening his eyes.

"I'll make you a sling. Three weeks and it will be healed." Sage looped a medicine pouch over Teagen's head. "Wear this until I tell you to take it off."

Martha, loaded down with bloody rags, bumped her way toward the door. "I'll toss these in water, then get him something to eat." Tobin knew she wouldn't be leaving the room unless she believed he was on the mend. "Tobin, you need to get your brother to his room before he's too drunk to climb the stairs."

"I'll be all right," Teagen said after the housekeeper left. "Did you tie up Roak?"

"I did." Tobin motioned for Libby to take the other chair by the fire while he sat on the wide ledge of the fireplace. "What happened?"

Sage abandoned her cleanup on the desk and propped on the arm of Teagen's chair not wanting to miss a word.

"I caught the kid taking down the fence in the far north corner." Teagen took another drink. "I think his plan was to rope a horse and make the swim with him back across the river. Near as I could tell, the kid must have swam over and walked on foot until he saw the herd."

Tobin shook his head. "That river is hard enough on horseback—to just swim it this time of year would be almost impossible."

"That's what I thought too. But we've lost two horses in that pasture since you've been gone and I've checked every day. No one else's horse went near the river but ours, so the kid had to have come on foot."

When Libby raised an eyebrow, Tobin explained, "We make a special horseshoe used only on our horses. Travis swears he could track a McMurray horse in a buffalo herd."

Tobin continued questioning his brother. "You're trying to tell me that kid caught them on foot and then rode them, no saddle or bridle across the river?"

Teagen nodded, then winced at the pain. "He gave me quite a fight. I don't know why he wanted a horse—he can run faster than any stallion raised and set traps better than most. But the fact is, he's a horse thief. We'll turn him over to the marshal."

"How old is the Roak?" Sage asked.

"Fifteen or sixteen. Another year or two and he'll be full grown. I'm not sure I'd want to wrestle with him then."

She stood. "The marshal will treat him like a man, not a boy."

Teagen nodded. "He did a man's thieving. It's not our problem how the marshal treats him."

Sage frowned but didn't say more.

Libby leaned forward, almost touching Tobin's knee. "What will happen to this Roak when the marshal comes?"

Tobin didn't lie. "He'll hang. He's a horse thief. A man who steals another man's horse in this country is risking his life. He'll have a fair trial, then he'll hang."

She nodded slowly. He guessed she didn't like the answer any more than any of them did, but of all people in the room, Libby understood the law.

For the first time Teagen focused on their guest. "You're Liberty Mayfield. I remember now about your coming, but I almost didn't recognize you all dressed up." He raised an eyebrow at her trousers belted tight at her waist and her shirt that was far too big. "How'd you get here, Miss Mayfield?"

She blushed. "I rode, Mr. McMurray."

Tobin grinned remembering Teagen's account of the spoiled senator's daughter. She must look nothing like the girl he'd tried to sell a horse to a month ago.

"I'm glad," Teagen said as he took a glass Sage had mixed water and a powder into. He took a mouthful then washed the medicine down with whisky. "Thank you for your help, Miss Mayfield. You're welcome here."

They all stepped back as Martha brought in a tray of soup and bread. Sage packed up her medicine box, while Teagen complained that he wasn't hungry.

Tobin went to the gun case and pulled out a gun and holster for Libby. While he punched an extra hole in the belt so that it fit around her small waist, he told the women about Stella's determination to go to town.

Teagen, between bites, suggested they put her in the stall next to the Roak. Then the boy could swear and she could cry all night without anyone in the house losing sleep.

Libby looked from Sage to Tobin as if waiting for someone to tell her the oldest McMurray was kidding.

No one did.

Sage and Tobin agreed that Tobin should take Stella into town and put her up at the Widow Dickerson's place. She'd be safe enough there for a few days. After listening to her through supper, neither Sage nor Martha suggested comforting her to try to get the maid to stay.

Tobin didn't want to leave Libby, even for the short time it would take him to drop Stella off in town. Walking to the barn, he tried to figure out what to do. With Teagen hurt there was no one else to make the ride.

He wasn't surprised when Libby fell into step beside him.

"I don't think I should leave you," he spoke his thoughts.

"I feel safe here and I'm ready to have a break from Stella."

Tobin smiled. "You don't think she might be in league with the assassins?"

Libby laughed. "I think we both gave up on that idea days ago. I've come to the conclusion that Stella lives in a drama of her own making."

"She's still not convinced that you won't forgive Buchanan and marry him anyway."

They moved into the darkness of the barn. She stood close as he lit the lantern. When the light washed over her, Libby's beauty took his breath away as it always did. In the light he could no longer see the reminders of her injuries.

"How are you feeling?" he asked, watching closely for a lie.

"I'm fine," she answered. "But not so fine I'll ever forget what Samuel did. The bruises will heal, but my memory won't disappear. I've heard Stella's hints about forgiving him, but I'll never be that big a fool again."

He brushed his hand along her arm. "What do you want me to do?"

"Take her to town. She's miserable here and she'll make us all miserable too."

"But I don't want to leave you."

"Sage is right. If you take the back path, you'll be back in a few hours. It's twice as fast as the road and no one will ever know you've left the ranch. This time of night no one in town will see you deposit her. You could blindfold her to keep the way a secret. Not that she'd probably be able to find it anyway."

"And if she gets to town and somehow contacts the men who ambushed your father, or Buchanan?"

"Then we'll face that together. I wasn't lying when I said I know how to use a gun. If trouble comes, I stand with you."

She looked up, the light playing across her face. The general and the princess were both there.

"To hell with being friends," he said as he pulled her to him. "I need to kiss you once before we go back to being strangers."

His mouth covered hers before she had time to argue. For a moment she was stiff in his arms, frozen. Then she melted into him and kissed him back. He'd meant the kiss to be hard and fast, but it turned tender with farewell.

A thud against one of the stall gates reminded them they were not alone.

When she pulled away, he didn't try to hold her. He knew he had to let her go. They'd finish out these last few days together, but not as lovers.

"I'll take her as fast as I can. Promise you'll keep a gun near until I get back."

She nodded. "Sage and I will be on the porch waiting for you to return."

She turned and walked away. He saddled the horses and checked on Roak. Then he rode out with Stella complaining incessantly about the blindfold.

All the night closed around him, but Tobin didn't look

back at the house. His mind filled with the memory of Libby in his arms and nothing else seemed real.

He didn't want to marry her, he reminded himself, and she didn't want him.

Why, then, did the thought of never holding her again make his whole body ache with loss?

CHAPTER 16

"Teagen will sleep the night, and Martha never opens her door once she retires unless someone yells fire. You ready?" Sage whispered at Liberty's bedroom door.

Liberty grabbed a slip of ribbon and tied back her hair. A quick pat at the handle of her holstered gun and she was dressed. Excitement danced in her's eyes. "Ready."

Smiling, Sage decided Miss Liberty looked very much like she belonged at Whispering Mountain. The senator's daughter had gone along with her plan the moment she heard about it. It had been hard on them both to wait until they knew Tobin was well away. Sage had a feeling Liberty rarely hesitated.

Like two thieves in the night, the women slipped out the back door of the house and moved toward the barn, their arms loaded down with supplies, buckets of water, and the medicine box.

Sage almost giggled. She couldn't believe she'd talked Liberty Mayfield, their houseguest, into collaborating with her. But Sage had to act fast before Tobin got back from delivering Stella to town, and she needed someone to serve as her guard.

They moved into the barn and turned up the first lantern.

"Know which stall the Roak is in?" Sage whispered.

"The first," Liberty answered.

They crossed like two children approaching a caged bear.

"I just want to check him out. If he did that much damage to Teagen, he's bound to be hurt. I could never sleep thinking of him out here bleeding." Sage opened the stall door, reflecting that her need to take care of people would probably get her killed one day. "I wouldn't let an animal suffer and I can't see letting a Roak."

Liberty set down her load and pulled out her gun. "I know my part." She didn't bother to lower her voice. In fact, she seemed to be talking more loudly than usual. "I'll shoot if he makes a move toward you. So if he knows what's good for him, he'll lie still and let you doctor him because I'm already nervous and everyone knows nerves make a trigger finger jumpy."

Sage nodded, fighting down laughter. Liberty was going to be a fine guard. She could hardly wait to tell her brothers.

They moved both barn lanterns into the stall. A boy, not much taller than Sage, sat tied up in the center of the back wall. His hands were bound and then tied to the rail above his head. His feet were pulled straight out in front of him so that he couldn't kick at them.

"He looks uncomfortable," Liberty whispered.

"We're not untying a single rope. We're just here to check him." She knelt down beside the boy while Liberty took her post at his feet.

The boy's eyes were wide open and he watched them with a mixture of fear and rage. The only clean spot on him was the white of the gag cutting into either side of his mouth. The rest of him looked like he'd been dragged through the mud everyday since birth. His rag clothes hung on his thin frame and his shoes were more moccasin than boot.

"I'm not going to hurt you, boy," Sage said. "I just want to doctor you."

He shook his head and tried to mumble something around the gag. His lean body jerked against the ropes like an animal fighting for life.

Sage wasn't surprised by his fear. In the back country where people lived like wolves, doctoring, if there was any, was crude and often deadly. She could make a pretty good guess at what this boy's life had been. His mother was probably one of the prostitutes who ran with the outlaw gang. She'd look forty at twenty and only cared for any child she bore when sober. Sage had seen the likes of them at the trading post a few times. They were always dirty and unkempt with kids following after them like pups.

Somehow this boy had survived long enough around camp to make himself useful or, Sage guessed, he would have been starved out. His dark hair was blocked off at his collar as if someone had cut it with one whack. His clothes were crude linsey-woolsey and made by someone with little skill. Judging from the scars she could see on his face, neck, and hands, he was no stranger to fighting, or maybe beatings.

She lay her hand on his arm. "I'm not going to hurt you. I only want to see if you're injured."

He watched her like a wild animal.

Sage moved her hand down his arm. His frame seemed made of bone and rawhide. She crossed to the other arm. No broken bones. Teagen had said he'd fought full out. She was thankful her brother hadn't done the same.

Then she moved to a small cut across his nose. The blood had dried, but she washed it and coated it with ointment to keep the cut from getting infected. When she washed his face, she found skin so brown it seemed the same color as the dirt she removed. His cheeks were hollow, telling her he didn't have regular meals.

The boy jerked when she touched his chest, but there was nowhere for him to go. Her hands moved down his thin frame until she felt dried blood. Carefully, she unbuttoned his shirt and found another wound, this one more a puncture.

His chest was also tanned and bore not a hair. The wound lay a few inches above his waist and appeared too old to have been inflicted by her brother.

Sage set to work forcing herself not to look at the boy's face. She guessed, at the very least, he must find this terribly embarrassing. While she worked she hummed, filling the silence. With gentle strokes she washed around the wound, praying that whatever had poked him hadn't gone too deep. The wound wasn't new. Maybe two or three days old. It didn't seem to be infected probably because it continued to seep blood a few drops at a time.

Sage doctored it with a mixture of root and ashes the Apache had told her about, then made a patch soaked in aloe oil to go over the wound. Wrapping the area carefully so that the patch wouldn't slip even if he wiggled, she said a silent prayer for him. Finally, she buttoned back the rag he wore as a shirt.

"I'll check it again tomorrow," she said, meeting his eyes for the first time. If she knew her medicine at all, the oil would have already eased the pain around the wound and by tomorrow he'd be on the mend.

The fear and anger were gone from his eyes, but he still watched her warily.

"I'll offer you water if you promise not to speak when I take off the gag."

He nodded once.

Libby leaned closer. "Are you sure, Sage? He might try to bite you."

Sage studied the kid. "Will you promise not to try to bite me?"

He nodded once more.

Turning to Liberty, Sage winked and said, "Shoot him if he tries anything. I'm in no mood to be gnawed on."

Liberty nodded and did her best to frown at the kid, but tough wasn't a role she could pull off.

Sage untied the gag and leaned back, waiting.

He didn't say a word.

Carefully, she lifted the dipper and set it to his lips. He drank long gulps, spilling a little on his chin in his haste. It was obvious he hadn't had water or food all day, maybe longer.

Sage finally pulled the dipper away.

"Thanks," he mumbled, then bit his bottom lip as if remembering he wasn't supposed to say a word.

Sage grinned. "What's your name?"

"Drummond."

"Well, Drummond, open your mouth. I have to put the gag back on."

He shook his head.

Sage raised an eyebrow. "Open your mouth. I won't tie it so tightly tonight, and tomorrow morning I'll bring you breakfast if you cooperate now."

He followed orders, but she could see the mistrust in his eyes. She couldn't help but wonder how many times he'd been promised something that never happened.

Touching his bony shoulder, she whispered, "I'll be back at dawn. I promise."

He looked away as if not wanting to hear a lie.

As they walked back to the house, Sage asked Libby, "Did you see that boy's eyes?"

Libby leaned closer. "They looked cold. Like they would just as soon kill you as look at you."

"Outlaw eyes," Sage said as she stepped on the porch. "In a few years he'll be a gunfighter or a bank robber."

"Either way, he'll be a killer." Libby joined her on the top step.

"Maybe," Sage answered. "Maybe not."

CHAPTER 17

LIBERTY RELAXED INTO THE OLD ROCKER ON THE front porch of the McMurray ranch. It had been one of the longest days of her life, but she knew she couldn't sleep until Tobin made it back. She told herself it was because she needed to know that Stella would cause them no more trouble, but in truth, she wanted Tobin back beside her.

Sage bumped her way out from the kitchen with two cups of coffee. "You can go on to bed, Liberty. I'll be fine on guard."

Liberty shook her head. "I'm wide awake," she lied. "But you turn in. If I so much as hear a mouse sneeze, I'll wake you."

Sage laughed as she handed her a cup. "I'll wait up for Tobin too, I guess, but if you don't mind, I'd like to write a note to Michael. It's been almost a week since he was injured and I haven't heard a word. Even if he's really hurt bad, I know Travis will read him my letters."

Liberty patted her arm. She felt she'd known Sage for years instead of hours. "You go ahead. Your ranger is a brave man, but a letter might help with recovery."

Sage shrugged. "He's not my ranger yet, but I'm hoping he will be one day. Did I tell you how we met? I turned a corner in Austin and we just ran into one another. He grabbed me to keep me from falling and I laughed." As if to demonstrate, Sage giggled, looking even younger than her eighteen years. "You should have seen his face when my brother, Travis, came storming around the corner ready to fight the man who had his arms around his little sister. I should have panicked and jumped away, but I was in no hurry to have Michael turn loose of me. His arms just felt right, you know, like I should have been close to him."

Liberty smiled, understanding exactly and wishing her life could be so simple. Sage had turned a corner and bumped into her love. Liberty wasn't so lucky. She didn't fit with the man she cared about and he didn't want to marry anyone, much less her; meanwhile, the man who wanted to marry her, Liberty could never care for. Samuel's arms had been a trap, Tobin's hold a shelter. But it was only a temporary shelter.

She and Tobin were far too different ever to think of a life together. There was something untamed about him. He was perfectly at home sleeping out beneath the stars or in the barn at her father's home. In fact, the only time she'd seen him ill at ease was inside the house. She, on the other hand, was made for fine linen and bubble baths. So how was it possible that they could be attracted to one another? The gods had a sense of humor.

Liberty touched the bruise on her cheek knowing it would fade, but her doubts about her judgment, when it came to men, never would. How could she have thought Samuel would be the perfect husband? Why had she acted like such a child and insisted on a quick wedding? If she'd waited a few months, she would have seen the man beneath the uniform long before a wedding had been planned.

Maybe that was her problem. Liberty never waited for anything in her life. Her father probably figured that by sending her here to do nothing but hide, he was sending her to hell. Liberty smiled. The senator might be surprised to know how interesting she found this place. She could almost feel herself changing and growing. Once she returned to Washington, there would be little left of the girl who had left three months ago.

Sage went inside the house to check on Teagen one last time. Liberty curled her legs beneath her in the chair and watched the night sky. This place was different from any she'd ever known. There was a quietness about it, a stillness. She might like the wild beauty of it, but she knew that if she stayed long the loneliness of the place would ultimately bore her.

A gentle wind moved her chair, rocking her to sleep. She drifted in her dream free of all worry. She danced a waltz across a polished marble floor.

"Some guard."

For a moment the words seemed a part of her dream; then Liberty came fully awake to the sound of Tobin's low whistle.

She jumped almost tumbling from the chair. "I only nodded off," she tried to explain as he loomed over her. "You didn't have to frighten me to death."

He ignored her complaint. "How's Teagen?"

"He's fine. Sleeping." She tried to stand but one leg remained asleep.

He laughed as he offered her a hand. "Where's Sage?"

Liberty pointed, then followed him to the study. Sage lay sound asleep at the desk, the pen still in her hand. Without a word Tobin picked her up and carried her to the room across the hall. "When we were kids," he whispered to Liberty as he took Sage's boots off, "she wouldn't go to bed until we did. Almost every night she'd fall asleep while my brothers and I were talking. At first we tried to wake her, but finally we just took turns carrying her. When we built the bedrooms on upstairs, Teagen insisted Sage take the downstairs bedroom just in case she grew up fat."

He covered his sister with a quilt and kissed her on the cheek. "She could sleep through any storm. She's probably spent as many nights in her clothes as her nightgown." Turning the lamp down by her bed, he added, "She hates the dark so we leave a light burning because she usually wakes before dawn."

Liberty couldn't say a word. She just stared at the caring reflected in Tobin's actions. She'd bet all three big brothers had a soft spot for their little sister. She had a feeling that if any man ever hurt Sage he'd be triple dead.

As they stepped into the hallway, Tobin looked back at his sister, and to Liberty's surprise, she saw sadness in his gaze.

"What is it?" she whispered, fearing that something might be wrong with Sage that Tobin hadn't mentioned. She was small but seemed healthy. A dozen illnesses came to mind and Liberty didn't want to imagine dear Sage having any of them.

He shook his head and walked toward the kitchen. "It can wait until morning. Let her sleep."

Liberty followed him. "It can't wait. I know something is wrong. Now I can't sleep."

She circled round him as he reached for the plate Martha had left in the warmer box over the stove.

"Go to bed, Libby. The morning will be soon enough for bad news." He poured the last of the coffee and downed it all at once.

"No," she said thinking that he looked truly tired. "I'll know tonight." She folded her arms over her chest and prepared to wait him out.

He frowned at her.

She waited.

"All right," Tobin said as he turned toward the table. After setting his plate down, he reached for a whisky bottle tucked behind the flour tin. "Want a drink?" He pulled two glasses from a shelf.

"I didn't know you drank."

He poured a round in each glass. "You don't know me very well at all, do you, Miss Liberty?"

She knew he was right. But in some ways she knew a great deal. The way he smelled of leather and spring water and male. The way he moved in the saddle. The way he touched her. The way he talked to her when she was nervous, telling her to be calm.

But in other ways, real-life ways, she knew little. She knew how he felt inside her, but she couldn't name his favorite food, or song, or color.

She almost swore aloud. Something was definitely wrong with her perspective when it came to men.

She took the drink. "What's wrong, Tobin? I have a right to know."

When he pulled a letter from his pocket, Liberty thought her heart stopped beating. Bad news! Her father?

"Has something happened to the senator?" she whispered. Maybe if she avoided calling him Father the news would not hurt as much.

"No." Tobin shook his head, his food and the drink forgotten. "As far as I know your father is alive and well."

Liberty took a deep breath, swearing that once she got her father back to Washington she'd never let him come west again.

"It's Michael," Tobin said, unfolding the letter and looking down at it as if hoping the words on it had changed. "Elmo keeps the back door of his post open in case someone needs supplies after he closes for the night. I stopped in to pick up the mail after dropping Stella off at Mrs. Dickerson's place. The old schoolteacher had an extra room upstairs for her, but Stella didn't seem too happy with it."

Without taking her attention from the letter, Liberty whispered, "Forget Stella. Tell me what's happened."

Tobin nodded. "Travis knew the stage would make it in before he could, so he wrote to let us know about Michael."

For a moment the name meant nothing to her; then Liberty whispered, "Sage's ranger."

Tobin nodded. "Travis says he's bringing Michael home—to bury."

A cry escaped her mouth before she could stop it. Michael, the young ranger who'd been shot protecting her father. Michael, Sage's secret love. Dead.

She wasn't sure how it happened, but she was in Tobin's arms, crying. All the strength she'd mustered for a week vanished. She didn't know if her tears were for the ranger or for

Sage and the love she'd never be able to hold. On the porch earlier Liberty had imagined Sage and Michael's love as enduring. She'd been almost jealous. It hurt Liberty's heart to realize that the ranger had already been dead several days when Sage had giggled and told of their meeting.

The ripple of Sage's loss circled round them all. Suddenly there were not just threats and plots. A man had been killed. A war had begun.

Tobin lowered into a chair and pulled her in his lap. He held her gently as she cried, never once telling her to stop. His hand moved up and down her back, comforting her when no words would have. The familiar smell and feel of him soothed her.

Finally, she leaned her head on his shoulder and took a deep breath. "When will you tell her?" Liberty asked wishing Sage had more time to dream of her ranger.

"Tomorrow. After breakfast. They'll be here by nightfall. Travis sent the letter on ahead with the stage, but they're traveling in a wagon and moving slower. Travis said once that Michael didn't have any family left. We'll bury him on McMurray land. I think he would have been one of us soon."

"I think you are right. Sage already loves him."

"I was afraid of that."

For a while they were silent. Liberty thought of how hard this part of the country was. She wished she were far away. "I'll help out any way I can tomorrow." She wasn't sure she'd ever said those words before, but somehow they seemed called for.

"Thanks." Tobin lifted her to her feet. "You better go on to bed now. I need to make rounds."

She suddenly felt as if they were once more strangers. Without another word, she climbed the stairs.

The door to Teagen's room was open, a light burning by his bed. Liberty checked on him, touching his forehead lightly to make sure there was no fever. He slept soundly, probably owing to the powder Sage had given him. No blood spotted his pillow. The stitches in his scalp were holding.

Liberty studied him for a moment. In the low glow of light

he and Tobin looked so much alike. There was no mistaking that they were brothers, but Teagen's features seemed harder, maybe because he was six years older, maybe because he'd borne the weight of the family on his shoulders since he was twelve. Despite his roughness, she had to admire a man who could take on the world at twelve with only his younger brothers at his side.

Liberty decided she like the oldest McMurray. He might be hardened, but he reminded her of her father. She let a tiny smile lift the corner of her mouth as she remembered the senator. If her father had told Tobin he'd come for her, he'd be here.

"Good night, Mr. McMurray," she whispered, backing out of Teagen's room. "We'll talk in the morning."

She passed the next door. Tobin's room. Empty. Dark.

Opening the door to the third room, Liberty noticed someone had put clean towels on the washstand. She'd planned to share the room with Stella. With the maid gone, it seemed strange to be upstairs with two men.

She laughed suddenly. One man was hurt, the other had slept within a few feet of her for days. The only one of the three of them who had wandered from a bedroll had been Liberty. Maybe the men should fear for their safety.

Stepping into her room and closing the door, she almost said a prayer of thanks for the privacy. She needed to be alone tonight. Her body felt so tired she was sure she could sleep standing up. Quickly washing and pulling on a nightgown several inches too short, Liberty slipped into the first bed she'd seen in almost a week.

But sleep didn't come. Life seemed too raw here, too real. In Washington she'd worry over having the right clothes or saying the right thing. Here she worried about staying alive.

When she turned on her pillow, she thought she caught the hint of Tobin's scent and found it comforting.

An hour passed before she heard Tobin climb the stairs. He didn't strike a light, but moved about his room in the darkness.

Liberty closed her eyes almost seeing what he was doing.

Tossing off his clothes. Letting his moccasins fall with soft thuds. Walking across and opening his window. Falling into bed.

In the darkness, separated by one wall, she thought of how they had made love and wondered if he were lying in his bed, staring at the ceiling thinking the same thing.

Lovemaking hadn't been what she'd expected. She'd collected stories and thoughts of it for years. Once she'd heard a maid describe it as heavenly. She'd read a report of a rape in the *Washington Post* that made her flesh crawl and, for a long while she thought that sex must be a kind of hell. Her married friends placed it somewhere between duty and delight.

None of the descriptions fit what Tobin had done.

Liberty blushed even in the darkness. No, she thought, not what he'd done, what she'd asked him to do. Begged him to do. And even though he'd been drafted into his part, he'd done it with tenderness. His hands had hesitated several times as if testing her reaction before moving on. His mouth, however, had been hungry for her—hot and demanding—making her forget all rational thought.

He could probably be everything she wanted in a man, in a lover, but he was the right man in the wrong place. He belonged here as clearly as she belonged in society and no amount of lovemaking would ever change that fact.

CHAPTER 18

SAGE WOKE UP EARLY, AS USUAL, TIPTOED TO THE MUD room, and changed out of her wrinkled clothes from the night before. Though she put a pot on to boil, she washed in cold water hoping to be ready for the day before Martha started breakfast. But halfway through her morning ritual, she heard the housekeeper banging around in the kitchen.

The family had long ago settled into the rule that the mud room, off the kitchen, was woman's domain before breakfast and man's at night. It made sense, with all the tubs for bathing and washing there, that not only dirty clothes but clean ones too were left in the mud room. Each brother had a dresser in his room for personals, but they saw no point in carrying clean clothes upstairs and then dirty ones back down. So four sets of shelves that no one bothered to identify with tags, lined one wall with neatly folded clothes in each.

The rule was simple: when the boys got in at night, they washed and changed before entering the kitchen, then left their clothes on a chair in their room before sleeping and wore them the next morning. No brother owned a nightshirt or robe.

As she pulled on her leather vest, Sage paused, realizing that Liberty had slept all alone upstairs in the extra bedroom. Sage had meant to warn the brothers to keep their doors closed. Martha might not care if she saw them in their underwear, but Liberty was a fine lady, anyone could see that. She'd be shocked.

"It ain't normal," Martha mumbled as Sage stepped into the kitchen.

Sage first thought the housekeeper might be worried about Liberty as well, but Martha continued, "A full-grown woman don't sleep in her clothes. That's why I made the boys buy you gowns, girl."

Sage shrugged. "I fell asleep."

Martha clicked her tongue. "That's another thing. You got the sleeping habits of a town drunk. It ain't normal, your brothers having to carry you to bed because they can't wake you."

"I'd wake if they yelled." Sage tried to blame it on her brothers. None had the heart to startle her awake. The few times they'd done so when she was small, Sage had ended up frightened and crying half the night.

Martha shook her head. "What if someday a killer or thief breaks into this house and steals you away. You'd be halfway to the gulf before you woke."

Sage laughed. "Speaking of thieves, have you got any breakfast for the kid tied up in the barn? Teagen may have ordered us to keep him bound, but we don't have to starve him as well while he's waiting for Teagen to recover enough to take him to the marshal."

Martha handed her a plate of biscuits and eggs. "That's another thing. I don't like the idea of keeping him here. Those Roaks ain't much more than animals. You might as well keep a bear tied up in the barn. Tobin should have taken him into town last night when he took Stella."

Sage grabbed a cup of milk and started out the back door. "He already had his hands full with Stella whining and clinging to him. Besides, where would he leave the kid in town? No one would watch him until the marshal rides up from Austin. They'd just let him go and we'd be losing horses again in a week."

Martha didn't answer. She was better at stating wrongs than righting them.

Sage crossed to the barn just as the sun colored the horizon. This was her favorite part of the day. The air blew cold and fresh down from the hills and she could almost hear the world yawning.

The boy was still in the stall, tied as solidly as he had been the night before, but his arms were tied low against the bottom rail now. Sage had an uneasy feeling as she neared. Maybe she should have waited for Liberty or Tobin to stand guard. It might not be a good idea to be alone with a horse thief, even one too young to shave.

But he hadn't hurt her last night, and he was tied up. Surely she could manage to feed him a few bites. If he started swearing like Tobin said he did, Sage decided she'd simply walk away and let him starve.

As she stepped into the stall the first thing she saw were his dark outlaw eyes watching her. He looked more worried than glad to see her.

Sage decided she'd kill him with kindness. "Morning, Drummond. I brought you breakfast."

He only stared as she pulled up a milk stool for the plate. "I see you have one of the horse blankets." She knew Tobin must have thrown it over the kid last night. Her brother Tobin wouldn't even let an outlaw freeze. She wasn't so sure Travis or Teagen would have been so kind.

She leaned forward and untied the gag. "The same rules apply. Be nice, understand?"

He nodded. "Your brother tossed me the blanket," he said in a rush, as if he feared she might have thought he stole it.

Sage smiled. The kid was trying.

She started to wrap a kitchen towel around his neck and then realized his clothes couldn't possibly be any more stained or dirty.

"I hope you like eggs, Drummond." She lifted a fork full.

He took the bite and said as he chewed, "Drum. Just call me Drum."

"All right," she said, and lifted another bite.

He took it greedily and she wondered how long it had been since he'd eaten. "You're Sage McMurray," he said as soon as he swallowed the next bite. "I heard tell of you."

Sage wasn't surprised. Folks around here liked to tell stories, good and bad, about the McMurrays. She kept feeding him, stopping now and then to make him take a drink of milk.

He frowned but swallowed. "I'm too old for milk," he said.

She looked surprised. "What do you drink?"

"Whisky," he said, bragging. A smile raised the corner of one side of his mouth.

"Well, no wonder you're so thin. My brothers are all grown and they drink milk every morning."

He looked surprised. "They do? Hell, you say."

To his credit, the boy was quick. He realized his mistake. He froze as if waiting for a blow.

She saw it then, a pride in his dark eyes. Sage had a feeling that she could beat him half to death and he wouldn't apologize. She hadn't grown up around men without learning a few things. "I'm sorry," she said. "I didn't hear what you said."

Drum watched her as if he feared a trick. "I said I was surprised grown men drink milk."

"Oh." She offered him a bite of biscuit. "Well, our cook is Martha and she believes her job is putting food on the table and our job is eating it. She never asks what we want and she never cooks more until everything is eaten. If she sets a pitcher of milk on the breakfast table, she expects it to be gone before anyone stands up to leave."

He raised a dark eyebrow and Sage decided that if he lived another five years he'd be a fine-looking outlaw. "One snowy winter"—Sage offered him another bite—"we ran out of supplies. Martha made cabbage stew. The boys refused to eat it, so we had stew the next morning for breakfast. We all got her point."

He ate a few bites without talking as if he were thinking over what she had said.

She heard the back door slam and guessed Tobin was up. He always headed to the barn before sitting down to breakfast. He'd stop and fill two buckets of water before he reached them so she'd probably have time to finish feeding the kid.

"You full grown?" Drum asked as he chewed the last piece of biscuit.

Sage wasn't sure it was a proper question, but she said, "Yes."

"You been with a man?" he asked as if he thought the question quite proper.

Sage fought down a blush. She guessed in the outlaw camp a woman was considered grown when she'd slept with a man. "That's none of your business. Do you want the rest of the milk?"

He studied her as if he'd never encountered anyone like her.

She lifted the cup.

He nodded once and downed the last of the milk. "Thanks," he said as she wiped his mouth.

"You're welcome." She stood, wishing her face didn't feel so warm. "Tobin will check on you later."

She was halfway back to the house before she realized she hadn't retied the gag. Marching on, her head down, she decided she would not go back. Let Tobin deal with the boy.

Just a boy! One half-grown kid had embarrassed her with a simple question. Of course she was a woman fully grown even if she hadn't slept with a man.

Her cheeks burned even warmer as she thought of the way Michael had kissed her. It had been far more than a friendly kiss. And when he'd helped her on her horse that last day, he'd let his hand brush along the side of her breast. It was probably an accident, but she'd looked in his eyes and known what he was thinking. He might have been too scared of her brothers or too much a gentleman to say anything, but she knew that the next time they met they'd be doing more than kissing.

Sage almost giggled. She was ready. Michael might be shocked at how ready. The first time they could manage to be alone again she planned to surprise him with her boldness. She'd had almost six months to think about the way he "almost" accidentally touched her, and she planned to make sure the accident happened again.

The thought of her ranger's big hand on her bare skin made her body warm all the way to her toes. She'd be nineteen next month, almost an old maid. She not only wanted his touch, she planned to do some exploring of her own. The idea that Michael might allow her, even want her, to explore made Sage laugh at how absolutely, positively wicked her thoughts were.

"Morning." Tobin startled her as she stepped on the porch.

She'd expected him to be by the well, or already in the barn, not just standing on the porch. "What is it?" she asked. Of all her brothers, Tobin was the most predictable. She could name the day of the week by what color shirt he had on. Blue, she noted, smiling. It was Wednesday.

"Want to ride the border with me before breakfast?" Tobin said.

Sage nodded and they turned toward the corral. Five minutes later they were riding a wide circle around the ranch and Tobin hadn't said another word. Sage gave him time. Travis might storm with anger and Teagen often mumbled for hours about a problem before he shared it with anyone, but Tobin was usually silent when something bothered him. As always, he'd have to find his own time to tell it.

One thing they both loved dearly was riding. All the McMurrays lived on horseback. When Tobin stopped near their parents' graves and stepped down from his horse, Sage did the same.

She knew Tobin visited this place more than any of them. Maybe because he'd been at the house with their mother when she'd died. He'd only been six, but somehow he must have felt he should have done more. Once he told Sage that when their mother called for him to come get the baby, he hadn't even asked if there was anything he could do for their mother. He'd just carried Sage to the porch, fired a round, and waited for his brothers to come home. By the time they rode in, their mother was dead.

Sage walked to the beautiful spot where the boys had buried Autumn McMurray. They'd put up a cross for their father too even though his body had been burned on a pile after the mission at Goliad fell. It didn't matter that his body was missing, they all knew Andrew's heart was here on the ranch he loved, lying next to the woman he loved.

"I like this spot." Tobin took her hand.

"Me too," she whispered. "It's the most beautiful place on the ranch. Even though I never knew them, I can feel our parents here."

"Me too," he answered. "It's where I want to rest some-day."

Sage had never thought about her own death. It seemed too far away.

For a while, they sat in silence on a natural rock ledge that shielded the graves from the north wind. Sage waited, knowing her brother would find his time.

The air was still cold, but the sun warmed her face. She could hear mourning doves in the pasture below them making soft calls to one another. Tobin took her gloved hand in his.

"I've got something to tell you and I didn't know where would be the right place. I thought here, next to Mom and Dad, might be right."

Sage nodded wondering what could be so important to say that he brought her all the way out here. She mentally counted down the people she loved. Travis and Rainey were in Austin, safe as far as she knew. She'd checked on Teagen before dawn and he was snoring like a bear bedded down for the winter. Martha looked the same as always and Tobin sat right beside her. All had to be well.

"I stopped by the trading post last night and checked to see if we had any mail. I knew Liberty would want to know any news about her father as soon as possible."

Sage nodded again, feeling a knot in her stomach tighten. Something was wrong.

"Is the senator all right?"

"As far as I know. There was a letter from Travis. He said he was on his way home." Tobin closed his eyes, then finished, "With Michael's body."

For a moment Sage felt nothing. She tried to put his words together so that they made sense. "He's bringing Michael here to recover."

"No," Tobin answered. "To be buried here."

Pain, raw and hot, lanced through her. "No," she whispered, tugging away her hand.

Tobin reached for her but she was on her feet.

"No!"

Before he could catch her, she was running. In seconds she was on her horse riding across the open country trying to outrun what he'd told her.

She didn't look back. She couldn't look back. Not at the place where they would be burying her only love. Rubbing her mouth, Sage wished she could rub away the memory of Michael's kiss. She wanted to forget all about him—all the hours and days of dear memories of how they'd met and when they'd talked and how he'd held her against him like he'd never let go. She wished she could drain the sound of his gentle words from her mind. Promises. Endearments. Whispers of a forever.

Only he'd lied. He'd let go.

The wind dried her tears as she rode toward Whispering Mountain. At the base, she jumped from her horse and ran up the rocky slope until she fell, scraping her hands and knees on the rough rocks.

Sage slammed her fist into the mountain and yelled, "It's not fair! I don't even get to dream my future. I have no future. Michael is dead." He'd been the only man she'd met all her life that she thought she could love forever, could grow old with, could sleep beside, and he hadn't loved her enough to stay around long enough to make her a real woman.

She curled between the rocks and sobbed so hard she

thought her insides would fall out. Tears fell on the ground, pooling against her face, but she didn't care. Michael was dead.

A few hours later, Tobin found her. She didn't open her eyes when he picked her up and carried her to his horse. He rode slowly home with her holding tight to his shirt.

He didn't try to say anything. He knew no words would comfort her.

When they reached the barn, Tobin carefully stepped down from his horse and turned toward the house. Her face was buried against his shoulder.

As he moved past the first stall, the Roak shouted, "What'd you do to her?"

Tobin glanced over at the boy. He'd forgotten all about him. "Nothing."

The kid struggled against his ropes. "If you hurt her, McMurray . . ."

For a moment Tobin just stared. The kid looked as if he'd gladly kill him. Then Tobin realized Roak thought he'd hurt his own sister. The idea made him angry and then sad that the boy would even think such a thing was possible.

Tobin softened slightly. He stared straight at the dark eyes so full of anger. "She's not hurt physically. She just learned that the man she cared about died."

The kid looked from Tobin to Sage. "Oh," he said, almost in a whisper.

Tobin moved toward the house as he felt Sage cry softly against his shirt.

CHAPTER 19

LIBERTY WATCHED TOBIN WALK TOWARD THE HOUSE with his little sister in his arms. She'd known when Martha said they'd gone riding that Tobin was telling Sage about Michael.

She rushed toward them, then fell into step beside Tobin. He carried Sage to her room and Liberty wiped dirt from the girl's face. Sage always put on such a big front as if she were as tall as her brothers, but now, curled beneath a blanket, she looked small and very young.

Tobin watched helplessly from the foot of his sister's bed. Sadness lined his handsome face. Liberty knew he'd take Sage's pain if he could.

Sage was so still she frightened Liberty. A part of her seemed to have died with Michael. They waited as the youngest McMurray took the loss into both her mind and heart.

Finally, Sage looked at her brother and whispered, "You're right. We'll bury him on McMurray land. Then at least I can visit his grave." Turning into her pillow, she let grief overtake her.

Tobin knelt beside his sister's bed and spread his big hand

across her back in comfort. "He was a good man, Sage. You were right to care about him."

She turned toward him, brushing aside tears. "I know. I loved him, Tob."

Liberty thought of the rangers who often rode guard with her father. They all looked pretty much the same to her. She could have seen Michael and not even known it. In fact she couldn't remember that she'd ever addressed one of them directly. They put their lives in danger often and this was the first time Liberty thought about the fact that they had families and loved ones. She felt shame for being so shallow.

Sage lay silent for a while as though forcing the pieces of her mind and life to meld back together. Slowly, she sat up and shoved a final tear aside with her fist. "We have to be ready for them. There's much to do."

Tobin looked relieved that his sister was back with him.

"I will help anyway I can," Liberty offered.

Sage reached for her hand, silently sealing their friendship. "Will you check on Teagen this morning? You may have to bully him, but I don't want him trying to do too much until he recovers."

"There is no need," an angry voice sounded from the doorway. "I'm fine. I found Travis's letter." He didn't need to say more.

Liberty met his hard eyes and guessed Teagen McMurray wasn't too happy to have a stranger among them. He might have a bandage on his head and one arm in a sling, but nothing about the man looked soft. She'd have more luck bullying a rattler than the oldest McMurray.

She nodded her greeting and he returned with a slight bow of his head toward her before continuing, "I'll stand guard and see no one comes after our guest today." His attention turned back to Sage. "You and Tobin do what needs to be done."

Liberty saw it then, the way the McMurrays almost read one another's thoughts. She'd never been that close to anyone. No wonder Tobin rarely talked: he'd grown up knowing what all around him were thinking without asking.

They moved to the dining room table and sat down. Martha brought coffee then stood at the door to listen.

"First, Michael will need a coffin." Sage looked at Tobin. "Do we have time to cut a few of the tall pine for the job? I think he'd like that."

Tobin nodded. "There are only two carpenters left over at the site where Travis's house is being built. They're working on doors and windows, but I'll have them start on the coffin as soon as I get back with the wood."

"And I'll get Travis and Rainey's room ready here. It's too cold for them to sleep out at the building site." She fought tears a moment, then added, "I'll ride into town and get navy wool to line his box. Michael told me once that he liked blue."

Liberty remembered that Tobin said the McMurrays didn't have ranch hands often, so she guessed there would be no mourners except family. "When will the funeral be?" she asked.

They all seemed to figure it out at the same time, but it was Teagen who said, "Dawn tomorrow, assuming they make it in tonight." The coffin needed to be ready when Travis arrived with Michael.

As if she'd been part of the team forever, Liberty worked readying rooms and helping Sage make a blue blanket and liner for the coffin. Just before noon two men rattled across the pasture with a wagon load of carpentry tools. They set up in the bunkhouse waiting for Tobin to return with the pine.

Martha took the news of Michael's death without comment. She did what she did every day of her life. She cooked and cleaned. Teagen did as promised, he stood guard. When Tobin returned with the wood, he talked with Teagen for a few moments, then headed toward the corral.

Liberty stepped out on the back porch in time to watch Tobin go. They hadn't been alone all morning and she wished he had enough time to hold her. It seemed a tornado of emotions flew around her and Liberty needed his comfort if only for one touch. But he had other problems, it seemed, far more important than she was right now.

She lifted the cup in her hand toward Teagen. "Martha thought you might want a cup."

"Thanks," Teagen said, without looking at her.

"You're welcome," she answered, wondering if the man ever smiled. Tobin and he were so much alike physically and so different in all other ways. She had a feeling the oldest McMurray never backed down from a fight or hesitated when he thought something needed saying.

He didn't disappoint her now. "Miss Liberty," he started with a half cough.

"Yes, Mr. McMurray." She smiled, not willing to offer him the use of her first name as she had everyone in the house.

He looked at her then. Blue eyes like his brother. But Teagen's were more the color of steel. Liberty met his gaze. She'd been around powerful men all her life and would show no fear of this one.

"I don't remember much but the pain last night, but I know you were there helping to patch me up."

"I was," she answered.

"I thank you for that. I have few friends in this world, but I'd like to count you as one."

Liberty knew he didn't say the words lightly. "I would be honored."

He frowned but nodded, looking half embarrassed.

She guessed that would be the end of his speech, so she asked, "Teagen, is Tobin coming in for his lunch?"

He shook his head. "There's work to do. Ranch work doesn't stop to grieve or to entertain."

"I haven't asked to be entertained." She resented his words. She'd worked as hard as Sage and Martha all morning.

"I know you haven't . . ." A hint of a smile almost lifted the corner of his mouth. "Liberty."

She moved to the edge of the porch. "Can I help Tobin?"

"You can offer, but you'll have to ride."

She winked at him as she stepped off the porch. "It seems I lied to you when I said I'd never learn to ride. I've developed a fondness of it."

Liberty thought she heard him laugh as she ran toward the barn.

She found Tobin saddling a fresh mount. "What's going on?"

"Teagen said there's a mare about to foal in the east pasture. I need to ride out and check on her."

"Want some company?"

Tobin stared at her as if he didn't understand the question, then nodded slightly and saddled another horse.

He might be happy with the silence, but she wasn't. "I helped Martha with the bread making. I used to do that with Anna when I was a child." She followed him out of the corral. "Sage is in her room. I think she needs some time alone. She said she wanted to finish her letter to Michael."

Liberty couldn't tell if Tobin was listening to her. "Teagen let me change his dressing, but he grumbled through the whole thing. I helped Sage move her things upstairs to your room. She said Travis and his wife can have her room and she'll take yours. I guess that leaves you downstairs in the study. I saw Martha toss a few blankets in there by the fire. They were for you, though that doesn't look like a comfortable spot to sleep. At least it's better then the outdoors on this gray day. I've almost lost track, but I think it's the first of October."

Tobin patted the horses and turned to her. For a moment, he just looked at her, then he moved closer until he was almost touching her.

Liberty forced herself to remain still and not step away.

"Are you planning on talking all the while you tag along," he asked, his mouth almost touching her ear.

"No." She swallowed.

"Good." He lifted her onto the saddle.

Before Liberty had time to think about his rudeness, they were riding at full gallop toward the east pasture. The cold air felt good on her face and her movements on horseback seemed natural now. She smiled, deciding she loved riding.

She watched Tobin when he reached the small herd of beautiful animals. First, he counted them, then scanned the area, as if making sure there was plenty of water and grass.

He swung from his horse and whistled as he moved among them like an old friend, brushing his hand along their backs in greeting, letting them smell and nuzzle against him. He checked their hooves and ran his hand beneath one's swollen belly making sure she was all right. He talked in a low voice, having more to say to the horses than he'd said to her all morning.

Liberty couldn't help but smile. Sage had told her the story of why Tobin loved the horses, and she'd seen his care before, but not so completely as now. Even from twenty feet away she could hear him.

Finally, he came back to her and his mount. "The mare's all right." He sounded relieved. "Dropping a little in the flank, but not as close to delivering a colt as Teagen thought, but this time of year it pays to be safe."

"You're waiting for your ranger horse," she whispered.

He frowned. "What are you talking about?"

"Sage told me. You've worked with breeding speed along with the stamina of the horses running free in these hills. Sage said you've tried to produce the perfect horse for your brother Travis."

He smiled. "Maybe. I never really thought about it being a ranger horse, but I guess Sage is right. My father brought a stallion born to run with him. The wild horses around here are offspring of a herd the Spanish explorers left over a hundred years ago. They're survivors and strong like my sister's horse, Glory. Blend the two and I'd have a mount fit for a Texas Ranger. It's not what I think a lot about, but with each colt it's a possibility." He swung into the saddle. "I'll check on this one tomorrow. If she seems closer, I'll bring her in."

They rode on to the next small herd and the next. Sometimes he checked fences, sometimes they rode along the creek bed as if he were looking for strange tracks in the mud, but always Tobin saw to the horses.

Three hours passed before he turned back toward the ranch house without another word spoken to her. Part of the afternoon she wasn't even sure he knew she followed. She felt as if the hours she'd shared with him in the darkness on the trail had only been a dream. How could a man make love to her and then look at her as if he barely remembered her name?

When he helped her down near the back steps, he asked, "How's your side?"

She wouldn't have been surprised if he ran his hand along her just as he had the horses. "Fine," she answered. "I left the bandage off this morning."

He simply nodded and led the horses away. Liberty guessed she'd have to attack him to get him to pay even the slightest attention to her. She knew he was trying to do her a favor by making it easy to stay away from him, but something about him drew her. Maybe, once she was back in Washington society, there would be other distractions and she wouldn't find Tobin McMurray the least bit attractive, but for now even the smell of him attracted her.

An hour before sunset, Liberty stood on the porch and watched a wagon moving toward them. A man, as big as Teagen and Tobin, drove with a small woman and a child sitting beside him.

As if the world cried with Sage, it began to rain softly as the wagon drew near. No one but Liberty seemed to notice.

Tobin opened the barn doors wide and everyone walked through the mud following the wagon.

Once inside the shadowy barn, Liberty watched as the McMurray family greeted one another. The middle brother, Travis, passed a sleeping boy from his shoulder to Tobin's. She remembered Sage's saying Travis had an adopted son they all called Duck. She felt very much the outsider that she was as she witnessed their grief.

Travis helped a small woman down from the wagon with a tenderness that surprised Liberty. Travis McMurray was leaner than his brothers with a hint of Apache features, but his care of his wife spoke more beautifully than any love sonnet could have. He didn't just love and respect her, he cherished her.

Once his wife had thanked him with a pat on his sleeve, she turned to Liberty.

While the men moved to the buckboard, she extended her hand. "I'm Rainey, Travis's wife and of course you are the beautiful Liberty Mayfield. I've a message from your father," she whispered with a smile. "He says he's well and hardy and much comforted to know you are safe."

Liberty liked the woman at once. She had kind eyes and a soft voice. "Thank you, Rainey."

The little woman squeezed Liberty's hand before turning to Sage, and Liberty realized she no longer felt like an outsider.

Travis pulled the tarp back from the wagon bed. A body lay wrapped in a thin blanket and tied with rope. Even though the days had been cool, the body already smelled of death.

"What do we do?" Sage asked choking back a sob.

None of them answered.

Finally, Teagen spoke. "We wrapped Mother in one of her Indian blankets."

Tobin looked down at the body. "We have the coffin ready. I guess we put him in it, then tomorrow at dawn we'll bury him. Mother once said that the good should always be buried at sunrise for they have no fear of meeting the next day."

Sage spread her hand over the blanket. "We can't bury him like this." Tears streaked her face. "The blanket has dried blood and mud all over it."

Liberty understood and stepped forward, putting her arm around Sage's shoulders. "I know what to do," she whispered. "I've helped prepare others to make the last journey. We'll see that he's ready."

All three brothers stared at her, but Sage smiled in understanding.

Liberty realized this family hadn't buried anyone since they were all children. "I'll help you wash all the blood and dirt from his body and then we'll put his best clothes on."

"And his badge and gun," Sage whispered. "He'll want to have them with him."

Travis's wife joined them, her kind eyes full of understanding. "I'll help also. We brought his belongings. I'll pick out his best and make sure they're washed and mended."

While Travis and Tobin carried the body to the bunkhouse, Liberty helped Sage collect all the things they would need. She reminded herself that she hadn't lied about knowing what to do; she'd watched twice. But both deaths that Liberty had assisted with had been from old age. Not violent deaths.

As the women began to work, Sage hummed, reminding Liberty of the way Tobin had whistled low when he walked in among the horses, calming them with his familiar sound.

Sage seemed to be doing the same thing, only Liberty knew it was to calm herself this time. When Sage would pause, having trouble continuing the hard duty, Rainey, Travis's wife always stood near. She would offer a word or a touch that would help Sage walk over the bridge of pain and grief.

Liberty couldn't help but wonder how the sweet little lady who smelled of cinnamon and flowers could have ever matched up with Travis McMurray, a legend in the Texas Rangers. Her father liked to tell the story of how Travis and two other rangers had saved his life once. In the telling, Liberty always saw Travis as a giant warrior of a man not afraid of anything, but now, seeing the way his eyes always followed Rainey, she saw a different side.

In watching them, she felt a sadness, wondering if she'd ever be loved so dearly. Would a man ever look at her as if he'd cross hell's fire to get to her?

While they worked, Teagen and Tobin sat on the bunkhouse porch with rifles ready and talked.

Liberty heard Travis join them.

"I got the boy to sleep," he said. "Duck doesn't like sleeping out on the trail."

"You think his family might have been attacked while they were traveling?" Teagen asked.

"I think it's a possibility. The raiders I saw the boy with looked mean enough to ride in and kill a family just for the food supplies. Strange they didn't kill the boy."

"Maybe they figured he was too young to remember what happened to his folks."

Travis shook his head. "They had him tied up like he was a pet. It makes me sick to think about the way he looked that day in the camp. He looked at me and I think he knew I was there to help him."

Teagen laughed. "He sure took to you."

"He took to us all. I've tried every channel and found no one who knew of him or his family."

"He's ours now," Tobin observed, joining the conversation.

His brothers agreed that it didn't matter that Duck had no past or name; he was McMurray now.

While Liberty worked she listened, comforted by the good in the men a few feet away. They were tough, strong, and rough. Sage said folks walked a wide circle around her brothers. But they were more, far more than they let the world see.

She glanced up at Rainey and in her eyes, Liberty saw understanding and knew they were thinking the same thing.

Suddenly, Liberty understood how Rainey could love the wild Texas Ranger she'd married.

Liberty turned back to the body of Michael Saddler and knew she was strong enough to do what had to be done. They all were.

She bit her bottom lip as she cut away the blanket from the young ranger's body. He spilled his blood saving her father and the least she could do was help. If the young ranger had no wife or mother to wash him, she would. If nothing else, she seemed to have given Sage a purpose.

When Sage washed away blood from her Michael's arm, she whispered, "My brothers don't understand why we're doing this, but you do, Libby."

Liberty shook her head. "It's the last way we can say we care."

She noticed Sage turn her washrag over, brushing the back of her hand along his cold skin. She seemed to be silently saying good-bye to what might have been.

An hour later, with Michael's body dressed and in a coffin lined in blue, the family returned to the house and all sat down at the dining table for a simple meal of soup and corn bread. No one talked much, but Liberty noticed a pride in the lift of Sage's chin even though she ate nothing. She'd said her farewell to her ranger.

The family said good night, everyone too tired and drained for conversation. Within half an hour, the house was quiet. Liberty and Sage were upstairs, but Sage left to sit with Michael for a while and Liberty guessed she'd spend the night in the bunkhouse beside the coffin.

After washing up, Liberty tiptoed downstairs to the kitchen. She wasn't sleepy yet. Too many emotions flooded through her. This ranch was a strange place, a world where life was lived with all the senses. It frightened as well as fascinated her. She was closer to Rainey and Sage than she was to all her Washington friends.

She made coffee and sat drinking it quietly, reflecting that she'd felt more today than she'd felt in years. These people didn't play any of the games of society. She wished she could take some of the honesty of their lives back home with her.

When she passed the study, she noticed Tobin sitting by the fire staring into the flames.

"Couldn't sleep," she whispered from the doorway.

He lifted an eyebrow in understanding. "I've always had a problem with sleep, maybe because I spend so much time trying not to dream."

She was about to turn and leave, when he stood and walked to her. Without a word, he bent and kissed her gently on the mouth.

Liberty couldn't hold back a sigh. He felt so good. "Again," she whispered. "If you don't mind." After all the sorrow of the day his light kiss felt like heaven.

He touched his mouth once more to hers. When she didn't move, his arms encircled her waist and lifted her off the floor. She couldn't help but laugh. His hold reminded her she was alive.

Without a word, he carried her back to the huge leather chair by the fireplace and sat, settling her atop him. For a moment he studied her, then kissed her again.

This time his mouth was hungry as his tongue pushed between her lips, tasting her, warming her. When she didn't pull away, he tugged at the robe she'd borrowed and opened it. Only the cotton gown blocked his bold touch.

Liberty almost cried out in pleasure as he slipped his fingers over the gown and filled his hand with her breast. She leaned back and let him kiss her neck, loving the way his hands molded her boldly to his liking. Loving the craving in his touch.

"I want you, Libby," he whispered against her ear. "God, how I've wanted you since I awoke that morning without you by my side. I've tried to keep my distance, but it's been torture."

"I want you too," she answered as the sadness of the day washed away. "I need you." The words seemed so simple, so poor a voicing of the desire to be near him, but they were the first true words she could remember saying to a man. No games, no flirting, no innuendos.

Suddenly, his hand was gone from her breast. He lifted her up as he stood and carried her to a pile of blankets in a shadowed corner.

She felt cold and alone when he walked away. He crossed to the door and closed it. She heard the clank of a lock falling into place. Then he was back beside her, kneeling over her.

She'd expected him to lie beside her, but he remained above her, studying her. Slowly, he began to remove her clothes. The robe first, then he unbuttoned all the buttons of her gown and spread the cotton aside. After staring for a moment, he shoved up the bottom of the borrowed gown and tugged it over her head.

Liberty lay back, completely nude. She knew she should have been shy, embarrassed maybe, but all she felt was alive. Stretching her hands above her head, she closed her eyes and smiled as he began to explore.

His hands molded down the sides of her body, outlining every curve.

"I want to look at you," he whispered, his words full of need. "I want to remember every inch of you."

Liberty remembered her friends telling stories of lovers who were only interested in lifting their skirts. It appeared her lover was interested in far more.

"Lover." She whispered the word against his shoulder as he bent to kiss the soft curve between her breasts. That's what he was, her first lover. Maybe she'd be one of those rich old maids who took lovers and never married.

He stilled. "What did you say, Libby?" he asked, still hovering so close to her flesh she could feel his breath.

"Don't stop," she answered. "Please don't stop."

He laughed and ran the tip of his tongue down the center of her from her breast to her naval.

She jerked with sensation and he cupped his hand around her thigh to steady her. With a tug he parted her legs and continued his journey lower.

When he returned to her mouth, she was panting for breath. "I thought about this," he whispered as he kissed her lightly. "I swore if you ever came to my bed again, this time we would do it right, Libby. I promised myself that we would do it where I could see you, all of you, and I'd take my time. I promise we'll do it slow even if it takes us all night."

She'd thought they did it right in the darkness in the fog, but he quickly corrected her opinion. She thought she knew herself, knew her body. He proved her wrong.

Fire flowed in her veins as he moved over her. She loved the way he kissed, then tasted, her flesh, making all the nerves come to the surface; then when he'd had his fill he kissed the spot, leaving a promise to return.

Finally, he leaned close and wrapped her arms around him. "Hold on," he whispered as he lifted her and carried her to the chair by the fire. "I don't want you getting cold."

He sat down with her atop him once more. This time his need for her was obvious, pressing against her hip.

Kissing her so deeply she could think of no world but his arms, he moved his hand slowly down her body. Without breaking the kiss, he spread her leg over the arm of the chair and pressed his hand against her wetness. Gently, at first, he explored her. Then his touch grew bold and a warmth spread from the very center of her.

When he moved his hand away, she cried softly in protest, but he only laughed against her ear and promised more. His kiss grew bolder as his hand moved once more to her breast.

"I'm going to get to know you tonight," he whispered. "All of you." Then his mouth found hers.

When he finally ended the kiss, she tore at the buttons of his shirt wanting to be closer. He leaned his head back and closed his eyes as she rained kisses down his neck. Her hands moved over his chest loving the strong, solid feel of him.

His arm closed around her waist pulling her against him. As the soft flesh of her breasts pushed against his chest, he moaned in pure pleasure.

Smiling, she moved against him, skin on skin. The hair of his chest tickled across her. When she lowered her mouth, his kiss was so tender it almost made her cry. She broke the kiss finally and settled into his arms, her cheek against his shoulder.

He pulled her braid free of the ribbon he'd given her and twisted her hair around his hand, then gently tugged until she raised her mouth to his. This time when he found her, his kiss grew deeper, demanding and giving at the same time. His hand stroked her once more with a need building in each embrace.

She moved in his lap loving the way she fired his passion with a slight shift of her hip.

Suddenly, he lifted her up and carried her back to the blankets, only this time when he lay her down, his body covered her, heavy and hard with need.

She unbuckled his belt and he unbuttoned his trousers, feeling his longing for her pressing against the soft flesh of her stomach as he kicked the last of his clothes aside. He entered her hard and fast, but she felt no pain. She loved the weight of him pressing down on her, warming her, touching all the parts of her body at once. His big hands moved around to her hips and he lifted her to him. She went, a willing sacrifice to passion.

Drifting with first one pleasure, then another, she tried not to wake the entire house by yelling for more. His hard kiss bruised her lips and drank in her sighs. His chest pressed her breasts making them ache for his hands to caress them as his lower body built a fire that spread through her.

When she thought she'd lose all grip on the world, his hands finally moved up, gripping her breasts as he shoved into her. She cried out as pleasure shot threw her body.

He covered her mouth with his and continued filling her again and again. The waves of passion kept washing over her. She fought, suddenly thinking she could endure no more without losing her sanity.

And then she did. Without warning one wave of pleasure crashed into her, shattering her body and soul. Libby shuddered and felt she would have left the ground if Tobin hadn't anchored her to earth.

He pushed one more time deep inside her and she knew no matter what happened for this moment she was one with him. Joined body and soul.

For a while, she barely breathed. Then slowly, as the world around returned to her, she tried to figure out what had happened.

He moved to her side and pulled a blanket over them both. She couldn't form words to tell him that she wasn't cold.

Cradling her in his arms, he kissed her cheeks lightly, washing away tears she hadn't known were falling. The warmth of him, the feel of him, the nearness of him, were a part of her now, just as she was a part of him.

"Are you all right?" he whispered as he combed back her damp hair from her forehead.

"I think so," she mumbled. She felt his hand rubbing against the skin of her stomach.

"And was that nice, my Libby?"

She buried her face against his throat, trying to think. Finally, she managed to whisper, "No, that was far more than nice."

He laughed and held her against his heart.

CHAPTER 20

Sage spent most of the night next to Michael's coffin, reliving every minute they'd spent together. Then, almost welcoming night for once, she crossed to the house and climbed the stairs without light. Curling beneath the covers, Sage slept a few hours without dreams.

She woke long before dawn and slipped from her bed, hardly feeling the cold air that greeted her. Achy and heavy with grief, Sage moved like a ghost through the house. Not only must she bury her ranger at dawn, but she'd also have to bury her dreams of a life that would never be.

In total blackness, Sage tiptoed downstairs and lit a lamp when she reached the main room. She hated the darkness. Maybe that was why she feared death so much. She saw it as a dark place.

After crossing the kitchen, she dressed in the mud room thinking only of all that must be done. Her life seemed to stretch before her now in endless days of routine with all hope of love gone. She knew she was still young, but she also knew all the men in the area. Not one came close to measuring up to Michael. He'd been handsome and funny and loving. He'd winked at her once and said she was the prettiest little thing walking God's earth.

Sage smiled. That was the moment she fell in love, she decided. Now that she'd known him, no one else would ever measure up by half.

Where would she find another man like Michael when part of her didn't even want to look? She'd grow hard and cold like Teagen or start avoiding people like Tobin. The three of them would grow old together, meaner than rattlesnakes, just like the town folks already claimed. They'd work from dawn to dusk then sit around too tired to talk to one another at night. She'd mark the years in wrinkles and think of what might have been.

She slipped into the kitchen. By the low glow from the coals, she collected supplies for the kid tied up in the barn. When Teagen brought the Roak home, he'd planned on taking him to the marshal the next day, but Teagen had been hurt and Tobin had to stand guard. Then Travis arrived with Michael's body and the problem with Roak was forgotten. Sage understood all the reasons, but she didn't like thinking of the boy still tied up. It wasn't right. The least she could do was feed him. Maybe Teagen would take him to the law after the funeral.

Closing her eyes tightly, she tried not to think of what would happen to him once he was delivered to the marshal. But an old memory drifted into her thoughts. She must have been about ten. Teagen was taking her to school, and because of snow, they'd stayed on the road for a change. Just as they got to town, Sage saw two men hanging from the big tree behind Elmo's place. One hung straight, his head lowered to his chest, but the other's head lay sideways as if all the bones had been snapped by the noose.

Teagen had sworn when he'd spotted them and tried to turn away, but Sage saw. She'd cried all day at school even when Mrs. Dickerson told her the men had been tried and found guilty of stealing a horse. That afternoon, when Teagen picked her up, he rode back by the tree. The bodies were gone, but Sage never forgot the sight.

She cut off slices of bread now in the shadowy kitchen, trying not to think of Drummond Roak's thin body swaying in the breeze beneath that old tree limb.

A door creaked somewhere in the house and Sage leaned to glance through the dining room to the main room.

In the shadows of the lamp she'd lit, she saw Liberty slip from the study. Just before she stepped free, a man's arm circled her waist and pulled her back into the room for a moment as if he couldn't part with her so easily.

Sage heard Liberty's laugh as she tugged away and ran up the stairs on bare feet.

Jerking back so that if anyone looked he wouldn't see her spying, Sage hurried across the kitchen with her tray of food. As soon as she was out the back door, she mumbled to herself. "So much for Tobin fearing people. There seems to be one he doesn't avoid." Sage slipped off the porch. "Great. That leaves just me and Teagen to grow old and cranky together. He's pretty well got the job sewn up."

She crossed the yard, still thinking about Liberty and her brother and wondering what they had been doing until almost dawn. If she knew Tobin at all, it wouldn't be talking. Of course, she must not know him, because she would never have guessed that Liberty Mayfield would be a woman he'd be interested in knowing.

Sage set down the food she'd collected and lit the barn lantern. She wanted to get the boy fed before everyone woke up and it was time for the funeral.

"Morning," she murmured as she entered the stall.

He shifted and opened his eyes, having obviously been sound asleep beneath the blanket. "What time is it?"

Sage was glad to see that no one had gagged him again.

"Almost dawn. I thought you might be hungry."

He studied her, then tossed his head to the side so his straight dark hair would stop obstructing his vision.

The hair fell back in place, half covering his eyes.

Sage reached to brush it aside for him.

He jerked back as if reacting to a blow.

"I'm not going to hurt you." She frowned wondering how many times he must have been hit to react that way when anyone came close. "Be still."

He didn't look like he believed her motives, but he didn't move as her hand rose again. This time she brushed her fingers in his hair and combed it back. "Let's start again. Good morning, Drum. Are you hungry?"

He nodded.

"Good. I brought bread and cheese and cold bacon cooked up yesterday. I'm sorry I have no eggs this morning, but I didn't want to wake the house by cooking." She offered him a bite of bread. "I also brought cookies. Martha always makes them when she thinks Duck is coming." She lifted a napkin full of cookies from the tray.

He frowned as if he had no idea what would be in the napkin.

"For dessert." She smiled. "Though I don't think breakfast has a dessert." She winked. "We can play like it does."

Drum didn't smile back. In fact, he acted like he didn't know what she was talking about.

They were quiet as she fed him one bite at a time.

She thought of how long this day was going to be and how hard it would be to get through. But she'd make it. She was strong and she'd started with a kindness.

"Can I ask a question?" he said between bites.

"Sure," she said, glad to have a distraction from her darker thoughts.

"What'll happen to me when I'm turned over to the marshal?"

"I don't know," she lied.

He frowned. "Yes you do. Tell me."

Sage fought back tears, but one escaped and drifted unchecked down her cheek. "I guess you'll be found guilty of stealing horses."

"Then what?"

She didn't want to think about it even though both Tobin and Teagen had explained how important it was to have laws.

"If they consider you still a child, you might go to prison for a few years. If the jury thinks you're old enough to be a man, you'll hang."

Drum shrugged. "That's what I figured." He smiled. "How about I promise not to steal any more of your horses, will you let me go?"

She shook her head. "Even if you promise, I couldn't."

She fed him another bite and decided that talking about him hanging was as sad as thinking about the funeral to come.

Sage patted the thick blanket covering Drum to almost his shoulder. "Were you warm enough last night?"

He looked confused by her question.

"I worried about you because it always seems colder when it rains."

"Your brother tossed this over me after he walked me to the privy last night."

Sage nodded. Tobin would have thought of that need. And, since Drum's hands were down, Tobin hadn't bothered to tie his arms above his head again. No wonder the boy slept soundly.

Drum chewed a bite of cheese. "I could have gotten away in the dark out there. Your brother seemed to have something else on his mind."

She lifted the mug of milk, smiling at the boy's arrogance. "Sure you could have."

He lifted his hand from beneath the blanket and took the mug from her.

Sage froze.

Still drinking, he stared at her over the rim of the cup, his dark eyes studying her every move.

She stared at his hand, wondering if she should make a run for it. She hadn't even thought to strap on the holster and gun this morning. Suddenly, this boy she'd felt sorry for presented a real danger. She knew he was a thief, but would he go as far as murder too? It seemed a short walk from one crime to another. He could grab her and knock her out with one blow, or maybe choke her to death. His hands were thin, but she'd guess plenty strong enough.

He handed her back the empty cup. "Thank you," he said calmly, but his gaze never left her.

Sage lifted her chin, waiting for a chance to run or fight. Either way, she figured there was a good chance she'd die today. "You're untied," she said, making conversation to give herself time to think.

He looked like he had no idea if she were asking a question or stating a fact.

"Yes," he finally said, pulling the blanket aside.

"Why didn't you run?" The thought crossed her mind that maybe he wanted to hang around and kill them all first. "You could have been off McMurray land by dawn."

His outlaw eyes seemed to drink her in. "I wanted to say good-bye to you."

He stood slowly and offered his hand.

As she stood beside him, she realized he was a few inches taller than she'd thought. Tall enough to be tried as a man.

"If I yell," she said, thinking aloud, "my brothers will shoot you before you get out of the yard."

"Maybe." He shrugged as if his life were of little matter. "That ranger you're burying today, was he your man?"

Sage shook her head. "He might have been one day."

Drum backed a step away from her and Sage drew her first breath. "I have to go. If you'll give me till dawn before you start screaming, I promise never to steal a McMurray horse again."

Sage nodded. He wasn't planning to kill her. He only wanted away. "I planned to try and talk my brothers into letting you go."

"You did?" He looked surprised.

"I didn't want you to hang."

He reached for the cookies wrapped in a napkin. "Why?"

"Because you're still a boy."

He frowned down at her. "How old are you?"

"Almost nineteen."

"I'm almost sixteen." He hesitated. Anger salted his words. "If you'll wait for me, Sage McMurray, I'll make you a full woman one day."

Sage didn't know whether to laugh or scream. Before she could answer his insult, he added, "I'll make you my woman."

She shook her head. "I'm no one's woman and I don't plan to be. Now run, Drummond Roak. If you make it to the bridge before dawn, you might be able to slip across on the south side without the guards in the woods seeing you."

He leaned suddenly toward her and Sage closed her eyes, waiting for a blow.

A moment later she felt the slight touch of his lips on her cheek. When she opened her eyes, he was gone. She wasn't surprised she didn't even hear his steps. He'd probably spent his life sneaking in and out of places.

Sage walked slowly back to the house, wondering what she could tell her brothers. By the time she stepped onto the porch she'd decided on the truth, or at least most of it. Sometime during the night the boy had gotten loose from the ropes.

She smiled at his childish kiss. In a few years he'd grow up and forget all about what he'd said, but at least he'd grow up.

CHAPTER 21

TOBIN WATCHED AS LIBBY WALKED OUT OF THE HOUSE, her arm around Sage. The ache to hold her again was already in his blood, but now was not the time and there might never be a place again.

He turned his collar up against the October wind and followed. The men had loaded the coffin into a wagon and saddled the horses for everyone except Travis and Rainey, then waited.

Though it had been months since Travis took a bullet in his leg, he still preferred a wagon to a horse. Rainey and the boy called Duck already waited for him on the bench. They'd all agreed that Duck was old enough to go to the funeral, but Rainey held his hand tightly. Travis's wife had a gentleness about her that took the edges off of Travis who'd spent ten years along the border fighting outlaws before deciding to study law. A year ago they would have all agreed that Travis was the wildest brother, but now, in his starched shirt and dark coat, he seemed more and more like a lawyer and less like the tough ranger he had been before he met Rainey.

Watching Liberty comfort Sage, Tobin couldn't help but wonder if she'd changed him in some small way owing to the days they'd spent together. Because of her, he'd learned the touch of a woman—the nearness of Libby—and he had a feeling he'd ache for that comfort the rest of his life. She'd crossed not only into his thoughts and actions but into his heart too. He knew she would only be with him for a few more days. He knew he'd never stop missing her.

Tobin should have been thinking only of the funeral and Sage's pain, but here he was, staring at Libby. Her midnight hair reminded him of how the glow from the fireplace had danced across it. His fingers twisted, fighting the desire to pull it free of her braid as he had last night. He wished he'd never taught her how to braid her hair.

How could she look so strong, so prim and proper, when only hours before she'd been in his arms soft as velvet with nothing between them? He could still smell her scent on him, still feel her skin on his, still hear the echoes of her sighs in his ears.

Even in her borrowed shirt and trousers, all he could think about was the way she'd looked, pale as ivory atop the blankets. He had to admit that he'd never seen a woman fully bare. He'd seen parts now and then in saloons—women who showed off their breasts or opened their legs to invite customers—but seeing Libby had been different. The saloon girls had somehow made their wares seem dirty. Libby's body was a work of art. He didn't just want to look and touch, he wanted to worship.

Fighting down a smile, he thought of the way she'd silently begged him for more with her movements. And he'd taken the time to do it right last night. He'd left her satisfied. If they had no more memories together, he'd take pride it that. What they'd shared hadn't been sex—they'd made love. Then she'd slept in his arms. He'd stayed awake watching her. Her fingers had spread across the scar over his heart as if her slender hand could hold all the hurt of life at bay.

Frowning, Tobin realized that while he was daydreaming

about Libby, Travis had moved forward to help her onto her horse.

He'd wanted to do that. But short of shoving his brother out of the way, he had no choice but to wait until later to touch her again. With all the family around, it wouldn't be easy, but maybe they'd find a few minutes to be alone. He knew it would only be a matter of days, maybe hours, before her father came to claim her. Liberty had said more than once that she planned to get back to her home in Washington as soon as possible. She always talked of going, never saw any alternative. Leaving him.

Tobin felt guilty thinking of Libby when he should be worrying about Sage. His little sister had aged in the past twenty-four hours. The girl she'd been would never return.

He helped Sage up, wishing he could take all the sorrow from his sister's eyes. She looked like she hadn't slept at all. He wondered if she'd spent the entire night in the bunkhouse sitting with Michael's body. Her eyes were red and her cheeks far too white.

She'd loved Michael, Tobin thought. As far as he knew, she'd never done more than kiss the ranger, yet she loved him. As Tobin followed the wagon to their small cemetery he realized that what he felt for Libby wasn't love. It was need. A basic need like animals finding their mates.

Only they weren't mates. Neither one of them wanted to love or marry. Libby might change her mind in time, after the hurt of Samuel healed. But he never would. He'd grown up without a father and sworn since he was six that he'd never do that to a child. The only way he could keep his promise was to never marry and have children.

Luckily, Libby was also in need, but not in love. She needed someone to comfort and protect her. What had she said when she'd stepped into the study? I want you. I need you. But nothing about love. He wondered how many times she'd told the captain that she loved him. Maybe she figured she'd used the word enough for a while.

Which was fine with him. The last thing he wanted was a woman falling in love with him. He'd been honest with her from the first, making it plain that he wanted no attachments. She'd said love was for fools and she'd been right. Why couldn't two people who were attracted to each other share a few hours of pleasure without getting all wrapped up in illusions of love?

Libby needed him to protect her and if she needed him physically as well, then that was all right with him. When it came time for her to return to her father, they'd both shake hands and say good-bye like two adults.

He ignored the nagging feeling that he was full of bull and resolved to stop thinking about Libby. He had more important things to worry over.

Dawn cleared the horizon as they reached the tiny cemetery backed by ancient willows. Here Tobin often thought of his parents watching over them all.

The two carpenters had dug a grave the day before and covered the spot with a tarp so the rain wouldn't fill the hole. Tobin helped Travis carry the ranger's coffin noticing the men had taken the time to carve a circle star on the box.

Sage cried softly as they lowered it into the grave. Teagen read from his father's Bible about there being a time to live and a time to die. Then the McMurray men raised their guns and fired three shots as they'd done when they buried their mother. Although they couldn't have said why, it had seemed a fitting ending to a funeral; they'd done it as children and somehow it gave a proper salute to the ranger.

As they filled in the grave, Libby and Duck gathered wildflowers. They would be gone in another month, but today they still bloomed in the shelter of the trees. Rainey sat on the grass with Sage. They talked of Michael for a while; then slowly, carefully, Rainey turned the conversation to the view of the ranch. She asked questions Tobin guessed she already knew the answers to, but it gave Sage a chance to calm down.

The sun had grown warm by the time Sage climbed on her horse and rode away from them all.

"Where's she going?" Libby asked, returning with a handful of flowers.

Travis stopped shoveling to answer her. "When troubles get the better of her, she rides. Don't worry, she'll cross from the bridge to the mountain, but she'll not go off Mc-Murray land."

Libby did not look comfortable with the answer, but she didn't say more.

Once they loaded the shovels, everyone left except Tobin and Libby. She lingered, arranging fall leaves and flowers over the mound of dirt. Tobin stayed watching her.

She looked up and seemed surprised everyone had gone. Tobin offered his hand and they walked back to their horses.

His hands went around her waist to help her onto her horse, but instead of lifting her, he let his hands rest there. "Libby," he whispered, loving the feel of her. "You were beautiful last night. The memory of you drowns out all other thought."

She didn't look up at him. He buried his face against her hair and breathed deeply of the scent that could only belong to Libby.

Kissing her forehead, he wished he could read her mind. He couldn't tell if she was embarrassed, or if she regretted what had happened in the study, or if daylight made her shy.

Slowly he tugged her chin up and kissed her as gently as he knew how. He wanted her to know what a gift last night had been to his life.

She didn't move, didn't respond at all.

"Libby? Are you all right?" His fingers moved along her back. Maybe this wasn't the time or place to mention what happened between them in firelight.

She nodded, then whispered, "I don't want to bury you, Tobin. I don't like the thought of your body turning cold in the ground."

His arms closed around her then, warm and secure. He wanted to promise that she never would, that he'd live on forever, but Tobin didn't know how to lie to her. A memory flooded his thoughts and he voiced it. "When I was hurt at six, my mother doctored me, but I didn't seem to be getting better. She sent word to her father. A medicine man showed up about a week later. Most of my fever had passed by then, so I remember what he said. He took one look at me and whispered, 'You cheated death but it waits for you. Be prepared for its return.'"

Libby frowned at him. She grabbed his coat. "Swear to me you won't die." Tears bubbled and fell from her beautiful green eyes. "I don't like the story you told me about dreaming of being covered in blood or this one about cheating death. Tell me another."

"Libby, I can't change fate."

Anger sparked in her eyes, so he added, "But I swear that my last thought will be of you and the way you looked last night."

As he leaned to kiss her, she shoved him away. Before he could understand her anger she was out of his arms.

"After I leave, when I think of you, I want to think of you on the ranch, not in this place buried under the ground." She turned and ran.

Tobin watched her go, trying to understand. Finally, he swung onto his mount and followed her, deciding his older brother was right about the fairer sex. Teagen always said women were a world unto themselves and trying to understand them was like trying to breathe underwater. Why couldn't she just be happy that they were both alive now?

When he made it back to the barn, his brothers both stood waiting for him. For a second he thought Liberty had shared their fight with them all.

"What's wrong?" he said as he climbed down.

Teagen stepped forward. "The Roak kid is gone."

"What?" Tobin yelled, then was thankful his brother didn't bother to repeat the news. Once was bad enough.

"We should have left a guard on him," Travis said. "He's probably grown up wiggling in and out of places he didn't belong, but how hard could one kid be to keep an eye on?"

Teagen shook his head. "The Roak almost killed me before I caught him. He'll be stealing horses again by nightfall. Now we not only have to keep a guard on Liberty, we have to ride the north pasture waiting for the little thief to swim the river and try again. Hell, knowing him, he probably picked one of our best mares and rode bareback out of here."

Tobin felt a sickening feeling in the pit of his stomach. He'd retied the boy last night after taking him to the privy. The ropes had burned his wrists raw, so Tobin had not bound them as tightly as before. He would have sworn the knots would hold, but maybe the Roak managed to get them loose.

"It's my fault," he said.

"No," Teagen corrected. "It's no one's fault. We have a few other major problems on our hands right now." Teagen never allowed anyone to take all the credit or the blame for anything that happened on the ranch. "I'll grab a few provisions and go after him." He tugged at the bandage on his head. "I've had enough time to heal."

"I'm the better tracker." Travis shrugged. "It's time I got accustomed to a saddle again. I'm getting soft. I'll say good-bye to Rainey and hit the trail. When we came in last night, I left an old ranger who rode out with us at the bridge with the two Apache guards. I don't think Liam wanted to see another ranger buried. I'll send him in to take my shift on guard here and I'll find the kid."

"No." Tobin held up his hand. "Teagen, you're still recovering and, Travis, you can guard Libby as well or better then I can. Sage can look over the sorrel mare about to deliver. I'm the one to go."

He didn't miss the glance Teagen and Travis exchanged. Their little brother's volunteering to leave the ranch was a first.

Travis nodded. "I'll tell Ranger Liam to go to town this morning and pull in a few favors. It will take a day or two, but we'll have more rangers here as soon as they can ride in. We can put them up at the bunkhouse and with Martha's cooking they'll think they hit high cotton."

Teagen shook his head. The brothers knew he wanted only family on the ranch, but for once he didn't argue with Travis. Maybe because Teagen knew Travis would be asking help from rangers, no one else. Up until now rangers had been their only houseguests. Travis might be a McMurray, but he was also part of a brotherhood of lawmen. They'd come if he asked.

Ten minutes later Tobin rode off, following the boy's tracks as they headed straight for the bridge. With the rain the night before, the kid was smart not to try and swim the swollen river, but the muddy ground made tracking easy.

Neither Tobin nor his brothers had bothered to check on the Roak that morning. Each thought the others had opened the stall gate and made sure he was still tied. If the Roak left before dawn, he had at least a three-hour start on Tobin. Three hours wasn't much, but if he reached the trees before Tobin caught up with him, it would be hell tracking him. On horseback Tobin would have to move slower than a kid running on foot through the brush.

Tobin pushed hard, but the tracks soon disappeared into the tree line on the other side of the bridge. Somehow the boy had even managed to cross the bridge without either the Apache or the old ranger seeing him. Liam offered to help with the hunt, but Tobin knew it was his responsibility.

The ranger took the rejection with a smile, saying he guessed he'd have to ride onto the ranch and have one of Martha's meals.

Tobin waved farewell and went back to work. Tracking wasn't going to be easy from now on. Not only did he have to follow the signs through the undergrowth around the trees, he had to watch out for an ambush. If the boy had been smart enough to cross the bridge on the side, never stepping foot on the bridge where the Apache guards would have seen him, he might be smart enough to figure out clobbering Tobin would be less trouble than running. He'd already split one McMurray's head open. One more wouldn't worry the kid.

Tobin headed into the brush, hard pressed to figure out which he'd rather be doing, tracking a Roak or home continuing the fight with Libby. Her worry over his dying would be the death of him, he figured. He couldn't make her a promise he knew he wouldn't be able to keep, and Libby had spent her life demanding and getting what she wanted. She seemed to think she could demand he keep living and he'd follow orders.

He laughed suddenly. God help him, breathing under-water seemed the easier of the two choices when it came to reasoning with Libby.

The air hung heavy in the trees as though the dying leaves held last night's rain. By the time he'd gone a few hundred yards, Tobin's hat and shirt were wet. Without the sun's warmth, he felt the cold and guessed the boy ahead of him would also. Tobin had a coat he could put on, but Roak didn't.

The kid was good, Tobin would give him credit for that. He left little sign. Most men walking in this thick a grove would break branches and crush leaves, leaving a trail easy to read. But the kid must have been picking his steps, staying to rocks and fallen branches. Wherever he'd learned his skills, he'd learned them well.

Tobin knew how to read even the smallest clue. Wet mud pressed flat on a fallen tree trunk. Brush combed back into place too carefully. Spots on branches where the dew was gone in the same width as a palm's grip.

He kept moving, following the boy, knowing he was gaining.

A little after noon, Tobin lost the trail near a shallow creek. He blamed it on his lack of sleep and the fog that had settled in among the trees, making it easy to miss something. After calling himself an idiot, then backtracking half a mile, Tobin started again covering inch by inch.

Three hours later, he picked the kid's sign back up. Only now the trail was colder, along with the weather. By nightfall, a light rain dribbled on him, making it impossible to see more than a few feet. Tobin chose a big oak tree with enough foliage left to offer some shelter. Disappointed, he curled into his bedroll. There was nothing to do until first light and then, he knew, any trail would be almost impossible to follow.

Tobin thought he would fall asleep immediately, but Libby filled his thoughts. The memory of her warmed his blood and unfortunately made other parts of his body ache. He dreamed he was home, in the study, waiting for the house to sleep so she could join him. While he waited, he thought of how he'd touch her. In his dreams he decided that every time he touched her, their lovemaking would be different so that every mating would be like the first time.

Once he drifted off, he slept so soundly, it was daybreak before he woke.

For a moment Tobin didn't know where he was. Though he slept out often on the land, he preferred the open spaces where he could see the stars. Here in the shadows, his senses were still cloudy.

Slowly, he realized something had awakened him. Not the morning, but something else—a sound.

Though every nerve in his body urged him to jump up and defend himself, Tobin waited. He lay on his side, facing the tree, and listened.

The sound came again. One word whispered. "Hey."

Tobin reached for his gun as he rolled slowly over.

Roak stood three feet away from him, close enough to whisper, but not so close that he couldn't jump away if Tobin grabbed for him.

To Tobin's surprise, the kid smiled. "'Bout time you woke up. You were snoring like a bear. I had no trouble finding you."

Tobin slipped his gun from its holster without a sound.

Roak huffed. "Great. You're going to shoot me. I knew it was a dumb idea to come back to get you. Well, fire one shot and you'll be sorry." He shrugged. "And so will I, I'm guessing."

Tobin didn't point the barrel at him. His brain must still be dreaming. Nothing made sense. He waited, his hand still on the gun.

The boy knelt down a foot closer. "I could hear you following me yesterday. A few times, if we hadn't been in fog, you would have seen me."

"So why aren't you running. You know I came to take you back."

The kid had the brass to grin. "You came to try. I ain't going back to no hanging. I plan to miss that party."

Tobin couldn't help but smile. Roak had gotten close enough to him while he slept that if the kid had wanted to kill him, he could have. "So." Tobin sat up. "Why are you here?"

Roak accepted Tobin's truce. "I came to warn you. Though why the hell I'm doing it beats me."

Tobin waited wondering if he could trust anything this wild boy said. Tobin had tied his horse in a small clearing fifty feet away. He knew, if the kid hadn't already spotted the bay, he soon would. Maybe the boy thought he'd renew his career as horse thief by taking the bay. But if so, why wake Tobin to tell him? "What do you want, boy?" Tobin figured he'd ask directly and test the kid's lie.

"I don't want nothin'. I just came to warn you that you've got trouble heading toward your ranch, McMurray. Big trouble."

"What do you care?"

"I don't give a damn if you and your brothers die and burn in hell." Roak snorted. "I'd buy a ticket to watch. But your womenfolks . . ." He took a minute as if searching for the words. "They're all right. I wouldn't like knowing they was hurt or killed and I could have done something to prevent it."

"What do you know of the women on the ranch?" Tobin growled. He'd told them to stay away from the prisoner, but no woman he knew ever followed a direct order. Giving all them a command was about as useful as trying to get fleas to march.

Roak swore, then complained, "Damned if every one of them didn't try to feed me. If you'd left me tied up for a week I'd have been too fat to sit a horse. Even the old one, mean as they come and the queen of nagging, came out and loosened my ropes 'cause she was afraid they were hurting me." He lifted his wrist tied with one of the McMurray linen napkins. "Your sister put cream on my wrists and then gave me cookies wrapped in this. I ain't never had cookies before, but she said I should take them with me."

Tobin wasn't surprised. Now he knew how the ropes got so loose. Martha freed the boy and Sage had packed him a snack for his getaway. "Tell me of the trouble you've come to warn me about."

Roak nodded and moved closer. "I seen a man scouting just before dark last night. He was traveling light, no gear, and keeping to the tree line like an Indian would do if he was the advance from the war party. It took me most of the night, but I tracked him back to a camp about five miles from here. It was too dark to get a good look, but there were ten, maybe more, sleeping around a small fire. They were heavily armed, like they come to fight." Roak's dark eyes stared straight at Tobin. "I think they was waiting for orders to head straight for your place."

Tobin stood.

The boy jumped back, preparing to run.

"Take me to them," Tobin said. "If you're right, they're here for Miss Liberty and my guess is they have orders to kill anyone who steps in their way."

Roak relaxed a little. "That's what I figured from the bits of conversation I picked up while I was a guest in your barn."

Tobin raised an eyebrow, then laughed. "When this is over kid, you'll be our guest again until the marshal takes you off our hands."

Roak frowned. "How about we strike a deal? If I help you now, you let me go. I'm no more than a bother to you. But if I'm right about these men, they're a real threat. I heard one say that it should be no problem taking the princess."

Not a muscle in Tobin moved, but suddenly he knew the boy wasn't making up a story. The threat was real. "If you help me, and you're right, I'll not only set you free, you'll ride away on a McMurray horse."

"Really?"

Tobin nodded as he rolled up his blanket. "Now let's get moving."

CHAPTER 22

LIBERTY SAT ON THE PORCH UNTIL AFTER MIDNIGHT, waiting for Tobin to come home. He'd barely made it out of sight when she realized how childish she'd been. He wasn't some toy her father gave her. She couldn't decide when to put him in the attic.

She also couldn't treat him like only her feelings mattered. He'd played no games with her, even from the beginning. The problem seemed that she was the one playing a game. She wanted to set the rules. She wanted to be the one who said when and how far. And now, even in the middle of the game, she wanted to be the one to say when it would end.

Rocking back in her chair, Liberty recognized the problem finally. She wanted to be in control, always in control, and Tobin wouldn't be controlled. Getting closer to him had been exciting because of that unpredictability, but Liberty had a feeling that in time she'd learn to hate the very trait that attracted her.

Teagen opened the back door and stepped out on the porch. "You should go on to bed, Liberty. The rest of the house is already asleep."

Another man she wouldn't try to control and this one didn't even make an effort to be friendly.

"All right," she said. "Do you think Tobin and the boy are all right?"

Teagen nodded. "Tobin can take care of himself. As for the kid, I'll bet we never see him again. He's like a coyote. He knows this part of the country and where all the hiding places are. Tobin will be lucky to follow his trail more than a day."

"Oh," she said, then smiled suddenly. "You're not sorry the kid got away, are you?"

Teagen shrugged. "I would have turned him in. It was the right thing to do. But I can't say I would have enjoyed the duty."

She looked at the oldest McMurray. Though in his early thirties, he looked older. Maybe because he frowned at the whole world. He was solid as a rock in thought and action. "You're a good man, Mr. McMurray," she whispered, surprised she'd said her thoughts aloud.

He grumbled like an old volcano about to erupt. "Don't go spreading that rumor, Liberty. It'll do me no good."

"I won't," she said as she turned toward the door. "It'll be our secret. Good night."

Once in her room Liberty's thoughts turned back to Tobin. Part of her wanted him here and was angry that he'd left her. Part was worried about his safety. The kid had almost killed Teagen. Tobin could be walking into the same trap.

Also, she didn't like the idea that Tobin was out there somewhere probably thinking she was an idiot. All her life, when she'd thrown a tantrum over something, there had always been someone who calmed her and told her everything would be all right. Tobin hadn't done that. He'd made her face the truth.

Liberty laughed at herself. Why shouldn't he think she was completely mad? It seemed like she'd done one foolish thing after another since she'd met the man.

She rolled over in her bed facing the windowless wall.

She lay awake for a while in the dark, thinking of Tobin and wishing he were downstairs. He'd ridden out after Roak without saying good-bye to her. How could a man spend hours in the firelight touching her as if he was starved for the feel of her and then ride away without even a nod?

The next morning she was still trying to figure it out at breakfast. An old ranger named Liam had shown up yesterday. He smelled of pipe tobacco and campfires. Once he'd said the required few words after they were introduced, he directed all his attention to Travis and Teagen. Duck jumped around him, but Liam paid no more attention to the boy than if he'd been a squirrel.

Because everyone expected Tobin back any minute, they ate breakfast in the dining room as a family, saving him a chair. The table was set with good china and linen napkins embroidered with an *M* in the corner.

Just to have something to say, Liberty asked about the fine stitching on the napkin.

Sage beamed. "I did them one winter as my home project. All girls at my school had to do at least one a year."

Travis laughed. "Her teacher, Mrs. Dickerson, insisted Sage learn to stitch." He held up his napkin. "I must have one of the early set."

Teagen agreed. "Sage made us keep buying cloth until she'd made a dozen perfect ones to turn in, but Martha saw no reason for tossing away good napkins so she kept the first practice set and the second. Over the years they mixed into the drawer with the perfect set."

"Well, you learned the art quite well," Liberty said to Sage. "I love needlework myself. If you have a project going, I'd be happy to help. It will give me something to do."

The McMurrays looked at one another. The idea of a project other than the napkins hadn't occurred to any of them.

Travis's wife, Rainey, spoke up. "Travis, dear, if you'll drive us into town I'm sure Sage can find suitable material. I've always thought stitched cushions for these chairs would be nice."

"That's out of the question," Teagen snapped.

Everyone looked at him, but it was Travis who spoke. "Tell me, brother, is it cushions, Sage's judgment on material, or the trip to town you're objecting to?"

Rainey laughed. She'd obviously lost all fear of Teagen.

Teagen looked bothered. "The trip to town, of course. The fewer people who know Liberty is here, the better."

"I could go by myself," Sage offered. "Saturday is the day we pick up supplies anyway. I'll get the material then."

"If I made a list, could you pick up a few things for me?" Liberty asked thinking she'd like to have something that fit her. "And if you've time, you could check on Stella."

"Sure." Sage looked at her brothers. "Unless Tobin gets back by Saturday morning, I'll go alone. If that horse delivers, both of you will be needed here. But don't worry, I'll go armed."

Teagen nodded agreement and added, "Tobin said he left your maid enough money to buy a ticket south on the stage. I'm sure she's long gone by now."

Travis and Rainey agreed politely with Teagen, but Liberty remained silent. After a week on the trail with Stella, she wasn't so sure. The maid loved having someone to listen to her. She might find that in a small town. Also, Stella took great interest in what Liberty planned to do. The idea that Stella would have anything to do with the men trying to kill her father seemed ridiculous, but she'd been an informant for Samuel Buchanan once. Liberty wouldn't put it past the maid to be one again.

She grinned, feeling as though she'd changed since she'd left home. She'd been headstrong then; now she felt strong. She'd never go back to Buchanan, but she now knew he was a dangerous man. A man not in control of his own temper will strike like a snake at whoever is in his path.

Excusing herself, Liberty went to the study to start her list.

In the silence of the book-lined room, the memories of the night she'd spent with Tobin filled her mind. She caught herself staring at the chair where he'd held her. With a pad in hand, she crossed and sat in front of the fire, wishing he were home to hold her now.

Everyone in the house seemed to have a plan for the day, except her. Liberty leaned against the chair's worn leather back and closed her eyes, drifting back with the memories. She'd never imagined making love could make her feel so good. There were times during her night with Tobin that she felt like she was floating.

She spent the afternoon helping out wherever she could and enjoying the constant chatter of women around her. With the fall came canning and today Martha had peaches to put up so the more hands to help the better. Martha not only set up canned peaches, but she also liked to make peach preserves, which took more sugar as well as more cooking.

Liberty took her turn at stirring the huge pot with a wooden spoon wide enough to serve as a paddle. She liked the chore, the warmth of the stove, and the sweet smell of cooked peaches surrounded her. In a strange way, she felt like she was in the center of the world. Sage mixed flour, sugar, and soda with milk for a cobbler while Martha washed jars. The stores they'd make today would feed the family all winter, just as the cobbler would feed them tonight.

Strange, Liberty thought, how the floor of Congress and a kitchen could both feel the same. Both seemed to take a great deal of brewing and stirring before they concocted anything. Except Congress, with all the pipe smoke and old men, didn't smell nearly as good as peaches and sugar.

Duck, who wasn't even as tall as his father's waist, shadowed first Travis, then his uncle Teagen around the house and barn. Teagen acted like he didn't care for the boy, but Liberty noticed several times when Teagen held the door open or slowed when he walked making sure the boy could keep up.

Rainey let her adopted son roam. Duck followed the men like the little duck that his nickname implied, but Liberty didn't miss that whenever he passed the kitchen he touched Rainey or she touched him. Sometimes a pat, sometimes a hug. Travis might give him adventure of the world around, but gentle Rainey gave him unconditional love and a home.

Liberty could not remember having such a free and open world to explore when she'd been a child. Her safety net had always been a nanny or housekeeper, never her father. She knew in his way he loved her dearly, but now, after being away from his world for a while, she could see how he'd wanted to hurry the wedding to Samuel as much as she did. He wanted to pass her off, believing she could not stand on her own.

Yet the senator had asked Tobin to take her to safety. Maybe her father had started to notice the cracks in Captain Samuel Buchanan, behind his perfect image. Maybe the senator had asked the rangers to ride with him that night because he didn't trust the captain's ability to keep him safe.

Liberty sat in the darkness of the front porch and began a plan. If she was right about her father, he'd understand why she'd called off the wedding and insist on her going back to Washington with him. Maybe, for a while, they would have no talk of her marrying and she could go back to her life in peace.

She waited on the porch until after midnight, hoping Tobin would make it in, but again there was no sign of him. When she finally turned in, she could just make out Ranger Liam across the yard. He stood smoking on the porch of the bunkhouse, standing guard.

Just after dawn the next morning, Liberty waved goodbye to Sage and told the others she wanted to spend another morning reading. Once again, she planned to dream the morning away in the chair where Tobin had held her so tenderly.

It was almost eleven when Rainey shouted for everyone to come to the porch.

"Something's wrong," Rainey said as soon as Liberty stepped out of the door.

Liberty shielded her eyes and watched Sage's wagon come in fast from the bridge. She could see no driver at the reins.

Rainey stood close. "She's driving too fast. No one should drive a loaded-down wagon like that."

"If she's driving." The wagon looked more like a runaway.

Travis joined them. A moment after he caught sight of the wagon, he yelled for Teagen.

The two men swung onto horses that had been left saddled from their dawn rounds. They rode hard toward the wagon. Within minutes they flanked the wagon's team and brought the horses to a stop.

By now, they were close enough for Liberty to see that she'd been right—no one sat on the bench. To her relief, Sage crawled from beneath the seat and jumped onto the back of Travis's horse.

Teagen looped a rope around one horse's neck and led the team into the yard.

Liberty and Rainey stood silently waiting until Sage reached the porch. Her hair was wild and she'd lost her hat, but otherwise she looked whole.

"Everyone inside," Travis ordered, before anyone could start asking questions.

They followed orders, moving into the kitchen.

Martha dropped the pot she was cleaning and ran to Sage. The old woman took little interest in the happenings of the ranch, but this was Sage. She knelt by Sage's chair and pulled the girl's chin up. "Where are you hurt, child?" she demanded.

"I'm fine." Sage sounded shaky. "I fell out of the wagon when the firing started."

"From the beginning, Sage," Travis said as he took the seat across from her.

Sage nodded, folded her hands on the table and answered her big brother. "In town there's a lot of talk about who we have out here. Some even think we're holding Liberty against her will. Elmo told me there has been talk of organizing a group of men to come out and rescue the senator's daughter. Rumors fly that Tobin kidnapped her in the middle of the night only two days before her wedding."

Liberty began to pace. "That's ridiculous," she said, though many of the facts were correct. "Who could know I'm here?"

Sage stared at Liberty. "Stella didn't leave."

Teagen swore.

Liberty shook her head. "But she knows the truth. She was with us that first morning. She saw the bruises where Samuel hurt me." Even as Liberty said the words, she remembered how loyal Stella had been to the captain. How even when she'd seen Liberty's face she said that she was sure it had been an accident. But she'd said she felt bad about Liberty being hurt. She'd demanded to come along.

Liberty frowned. So much for giving Stella the benefit of a doubt. Tobin had been right about her all along. She glanced at Sage and knew their minds were traveling the same road.

"Did she try to slow you down?" Sage asked. "Did she try to contact anyone along the way?"

Liberty stopped pacing. "Yes. She complained that we were moving too fast and she was so slow that several times Tobin threatened to leave her. Twice, when we were near trading posts, she begged to go in and get supplies. I believed her, but Tobin wouldn't let her go."

Sage finished the logic. "Once she got here and knew you were staying, she couldn't get away quickly enough. Maybe she had someone to inform."

Liberty hated to think that she'd let the enemy ride along with her. Tobin had tried to stop Stella—even that buckskin ranger had said it would be best to leave her behind—but Liberty had insisted. She'd fallen for Stella's tears and pleas about wanting to help.

Travis poured himself a cup of coffee and sat back down. "Forget about Stella for now. What happened in town?"

"I collected the supplies and got out as fast as I could." Sage took a deep breath. "Before I made the second bend in the road home, I realized I was being followed. I thought about turning around. I thought if I fired off a few shots someone from the post could still hear me, but I had no guarantee anyone would come. That early most of the men were working."

"How many followed you?" Travis wanted details.

"Four, maybe five. I decided my best chance was to outrun them. But it didn't take me long to realize they were gaining on me. A mile from the bridge, I heard shots. At first I thought they were trying to get my attention, but the third shot hit the back of the bench a few inches from my elbow. I panicked and reached for the rifle. The wagon wheel hit a hole at the last curve and I bounced right out."

No one said a word. They all waited.

Sage rubbed her bottom. "I hit hard, but I think I'm just bruised. I rolled away from the wagon, landing in brush. The riders went right past me. As soon as they made the bend, they must have seen the wagon was empty and had no trouble stopping it. They hadn't seen me fall out because I could hear them swearing as they rifled through the bed looking for me. By the time they started backtracking to look for me, I'd cut across the bend in the road and was hiding in a stand of oak not far from the wagon."

Liberty tried to calm her heart. Sage was all right, she reminded herself. She'd come out of it unscathed.

Sage continued, "One man rode back to where I fell out and found my hat. He yelled for the others. I couldn't see much but I think they must have climbed off their horses to search for me in the brush. I didn't take the time to backtrack and check. I ran for the wagon. I didn't even take time to pick up the reins. I just wiped the horses once and they took off toward home. I crawled beneath the bench just in case the men got close enough to fire off a shot.

"Two of Grandfather's scouts were at the bridge ready and waiting. They must have heard the shots. The minute I crossed, they stepped onto the bridge, their feet wide apart, rifles on their shoulders like they were a gate closing.

"Since I didn't hear gunfire from behind, I guessed the gang following me thought twice about taking them on."

Travis agreed. "They thought a woman alone was fair game when they started, but maybe they figured we'd hear shots fired at the bridge. Two Apache might not stop them, but it was sure to warn us. Either way, I'm glad you made it in. Until Tobin gets back we need to all stay together."

Teagen cut in. "Tonight I'll bring the mare about to foal in from the range. Then I agree, we all stay here. It could have been drifters finishing off a night of drinking by trying to scare you, or down-on-their-luck cowhands thinking you had money for the taking—"

Sage finished his sentence. "Or men wanting to cause me harm because I'm a McMurray."

Teagen shook his head. "We haven't had trouble for years."

Martha stood. "Well, we're going to have a house full coming. Somebody better bring in those supplies."

The brothers left to follow her orders. They might run the ranch, but Martha ran the kitchen.

Liberty got Sage a cup of coffee and added a shot of whisky from the bottle she'd seen Tobin put behind the flour tin. "Did you recognize any of them?"

Sage shook her head. "I came and went from the back door of Elmo's place, but the horses tied out front, where men sit and drink, were mostly broken-down nags. I'm surprised they could gain on my wagon."

Rainey laughed. "Spoken like a true McMurray. Ignore the people, but take a good look at any horses."

"That's our business." Sage smiled. "Any word from Tobin?"

Rainey shook her head as she helped unpack the first box of supplies. When Sage tried to help, they all pushed her back toward her chair.

The clothes she'd brought Liberty were plain but well made. Liberty thanked her as if they were the finest styles from Paris. Martha seemed more interested in the fifty pounds of sugar and Rainey loved the material for the chairs. By the time the supplies were unpacked, the women had moved on to other topics.

Liberty noticed Sage motion Teagen to the corner of the kitchen and pass him what looked like a letter.

She first thought it might be news from her father. If something had happened to him, Sage might want Teagen to break the news to her. But neither of the McMurrays looked in her direction as they talked.

When Liberty finally got the chance to ask about the letter, Sage smiled. "Years ago, when the boys closed the ranch off, Mrs. Dickerson insisted on sending out messages of what books to buy with the grocery order. Teagen acted like he resented her interference, but he ordered the books. After a few years, he began dealing with a bookstore in Chicago, and he became friends with Eli Coleman, the owner. They write back and forth every few months." Sage giggled. "Eli is Teagen's only friend, probably because he lives too far from the dragon to smell the smoke and see the fire."

Liberty agreed with a laugh and they went back to work.

The rest of the day passed quietly, but every hour Tobin was gone worried her. By dawn the next morning, Liberty felt sick with panic. Surely he could have caught the kid in two days. Something had to be wrong.

She guessed everyone else felt the same, but no one voiced their fears. The men took turns guarding the house and the women sewed new covers for the chairs.

About the time Rainey convinced Liberty that all the excitement was over, they heard hurried footsteps storming up the steps.

"Sage!" Teagen yelled. "Come out here. Come armed. Rainey, run to the barn and get Travis."

Rainey swung Duck into her arms and bolted for the back door without hesitation.

Sage grabbed one of the rifles racked by the back door.

Liberty did the same. If there was going to be a fight, she planned to be part of it.

She'd stepped one foot outside when she almost collided with Teagen. "Stay inside," he ordered.

"No," she answered, staring straight at him.

To her surprise, the big man backed down. "Then stay in the shadow of the porch well out of sight."

"Yes sir," she whispered, surprised that he'd conceded.

From the porch they saw a buggy bumping its way toward them.

Teagen lifted his rifle to shoulder level and asked, "Any idea who is coming to call?"

Sage studied the old buggy. "It looks like Mrs. Dickerson's rig. But she's never come to the ranch."

"The schoolteacher?" Liberty asked.

Both the McMurrays nodded as the buggy pulled closer. Liberty had no problem making out the bonnet and shawl of a woman well past her prime.

Teagen waved at Liam, who moved back into the bunkhouse, taking his rifle with him.

Then Teagen and Sage moved to the yard as Mrs. Dickerson rattled to a stop. Teagen helped her down. "Welcome, ma'am, I don't believe we've ever had the pleasure of a visit." He'd said the right words, but his tone was cold.

For a short lady, she did a good job of looking down her nose at him. "I've never had the need to call, Teagen. Until now." She fanned herself with a starched handkerchief made mostly of lace.

When Travis and Rainey met them halfway between the buggy and the house, she looked the couple over carefully as if about to reprimand them for being tardy.

Finally, she turned her pale blue eyes to Travis. "How is that leg of yours? I heard you were laid up with it for months, but obviously my information was wrong. You look fit." She smiled. "I also heard you finally made use of those law books I suggested you boys buy years ago."

"Yes, ma'am." Travis smiled at the widow and introduced his wife before adding, "What brings you all the way out here, Mrs. Dickerson?"

Sage stepped between her brothers and offered her hand to her teacher. "First, Travis, we'll invite Mrs. Dickerson in and insist she have a drink and refreshments."

Mrs. Dickerson patted her hand. "You learned well, my

child. And I'll accept your offer. Would you believe I was almost run over on the road by a gang of no-goods? Frightened me and my horse near to death."

Liberty glanced over at the horse. In truth, he did look near death, but she had a feeling he left town that way.

Once they were in the main living room of the house, Sage introduced her only teacher to everyone. Mrs. Etta Dickerson made a fuss over Travis's new bride, Rainey, saying how proud she was that Travis found such a lovely girl to marry. Though she'd only had Travis attend school four years before his parents died and the boys cut the ranch off from everyone, she knew him to be bright and she took a great deal of pride that he'd become a lawyer.

Liberty smiled, guessing Mrs. Dickerson was not only the town teacher but also the town historian. Someone who kept up with everyone.

When Mrs. Dickerson turned her attention to Liberty, she said, "You must be Miss Liberty Mayfield. I've read about you in the Austin paper."

Liberty curtsied as politely as if she were at a ball. "I'm pleased to meet you, Mrs. Dickerson. Sage told me about all you taught her, from her fine needlepoint to her understanding of politics. You're a treasure in the wilderness, Mrs. Dickerson."

Liberty noticed Teagen raised his eyebrow. He'd never seen her play the role she'd been born to. Liberty wanted to laugh.

Mrs. Dickerson straightened with pride. "I do what I can. I'm just a poor widow in this rough country trying to earn a living."

Martha brought in tea. "Sorry it took me so long. I had to wash the dust off the pot." She clanked the tray on the table and disappeared.

Liberty grinned remembering how Tobin told her Martha didn't like the McMurrays much, and strangers not at all.

All the women took their seats as if it were a formal tea and Sage poured. The two men stood near the windows and declined any tea. They looked uncomfortable, and Liberty had no doubt this was the most women they'd ever had in the ranch house, or on the property for that matter. They looked as if they stood in the middle of one of Moses's plagues.

It took five minutes, but Teagen finally got in a question. "And why are we honored with your visit, Mrs. Dickerson?"

Mrs. Dickerson sat down her cup. "Much as I need the income from a boarder, I've come to ask you to take Miss Stella back or put her on the next stage heading to Austin. When I decided to drive out here, I wanted to make sure Miss Liberty wasn't being held, as Stella suggested, against her will." She looked at Liberty. "I assume you are not."

Liberty smiled. "I am not. I'm a guest here."

Mrs. Dickerson nodded. "I thought that from the first." She glanced at the two big men. "I've had both these boys in class and I'd reason their younger brother is cut from the same cloth. They'd never do any of the crimes Stella hints at to all in town who will listen. Now I've seen it with my own eyes, I can no longer allow Stella to stay under my roof. It wouldn't be right."

Teagen laughed. "You're one fine woman, Widow Dickerson. You wouldn't consider marrying me, would you? If I looked a lifetime, I'd find no woman with such high standards."

The old woman blushed. "If you were twenty years older, I'd consider taking you on as number four."

Everyone joined in the laughter as Teagen added, "Well, Mrs. Dickerson, you may be the only woman I ever ask. I welcome you to stay a while, and when you leave I insist on seeing you safely home." This time his words were warm and honest.

Mrs. Dickerson continued to blush. "I'll stay a while, thank you. I'd love to visit with Miss Liberty. It isn't often one gets to discuss politics with an insider."

Liberty guessed the McMurrays wanted to make plans, and like Mrs. Dickerson, she was an outsider. So Liberty stayed in the great room with the old teacher entertaining her with stories from Washington while Travis and his wife, Teagen, and Sage moved to the study.

The widow told her of the social life in what was becoming a town. The church was almost built, a hotel would be operating fully by the end of the year, and there was talk of building a real schoolhouse so Mrs. Dickerson wouldn't have to teach students in her parlor.

Liberty couldn't help but admire the widow for coming out to warn them. Behind her proper stature was a woman of deep values. She didn't just teach right from wrong, she lived it.

"How'd you get past the guards?" Liberty asked since five armed ambushers hadn't even tried.

"I told them to get out of the way, I had important business." Mrs. Dickerson chuckled. "When I use my teacher voice, few argue. Once a drunk turned left instead of right and ended up on my porch instead of Elmo Anderson's place. I ordered him to do his alphabet on a slate. He got all the way to *R* before he worked up the nerve to run."

Martha brought in cookies and tiny sandwiches made with apple jelly.

When Liberty thanked her politely, Martha nodded once and disappeared back into the kitchen.

They ate and Mrs. Dickerson complimented each dish as if it were fancy. Liberty tried to keep the conversation though she wished she could hear what the McMurrays were talking about in the study. Whatever plans they were making, Liberty had no doubt a few of them would affect her.

Finally, the door opened, but when the family returned Liberty could guess nothing from their faces.

Travis picked up one of the little sandwiches and stared at it as if trying to figure out what it was. Teagen popped a couple of cookies in his mouth and asked Mrs. Dickerson how many students she had this fall.

Liberty guessed the family must have figured something out, for they all seemed far calmer than before.

When finally the teacher stood to leave, she insisted on hugging them all good-bye. With Teagen as an escort, Mrs. Dickerson drove off.

Liberty stood on the porch and watched the buggy bump

down the road to the bridge. She could hear Travis and Sage talking about what they planned to do about the ambush as soon as Tobin returned.

She also knew them well enough to know that they didn't care what people in town were saying. But Liberty did. She'd brought this trouble on their heads and she had to think of some way to end it. It was time she stopped letting everyone else clean up her messes.

CHAPTER 23

THOUGH NOON, THE GRAY SUN OFFERED LITTLE warmth as Tobin and Roak moved among the shadows. Tobin had seen the camp the day before, but he wanted to take no chances rushing in too fast. His only opportunity to get close was to move in at twilight. Roak stayed right beside him, even spending two nights in the grass without a complaint.

The boy had been right. There were a dozen men waiting. They were all military lean and fully armed. They were obviously waiting for something, but none seemed relaxed. Their clothes were the brown of fall, making them seem almost a part of the countryside.

"If we circle, we can hear them talking," Roak whispered, taking the lead for once.

Tobin nodded. He outweighed the kid by fifty pounds. Moving between the trees wasn't as easy for him, but he managed to keep up.

It was sunset before they were within hearing distance. The kid flattened on the ground, disappearing in the dried leaves without a sound.

Tobin did the same, with less skill. As they had for two days, they waited.

Most of the men in the camp were silent. This wasn't a group of troublemakers looking for fun. A few cleaned their weapons, one slept, but the others seemed to be watching for something.

A tall man with a thin face circled restlessly about. Once he stopped to talk to someone near the fire. Tobin couldn't make out what he said, but he thought the man listening called the tall man Lieutenant Hawk. The next time he stopped his pacing, he was only ten feet from them. He rolled a smoke and talked to a shorter man who'd come from behind a tree. Tobin didn't even breathe as he listened.

"About time you got out here," Hawk said. "You won't want to have your pants down when we ride."

The shorter man huffed. "And when is that going to be, Lieutenant? We've been here for four days waiting for the word to ride, and all I can see is there are more McMurrays at the ranch than when we first arrived."

Hawk nodded. "That last one in the wagon was a ranger. I've seen him in Austin a few times."

"I don't want to be no part of killing a ranger."

Hawk's voice rose slightly. "Not even if he's part of the kidnapping?"

The shorter man shook his head. "Maybe he's gone there to talk his brother out of a life of crime. It's a sure bet he wouldn't be traveling with his wife and kid if he thought he was heading to a fight."

Hawk swore. "From what I've learned in town, they're a family that sticks together. Some say they'd kill for one another. If so, you can bet the brother is there to stand with his kin even if he did take a senator's daughter."

"I don't know," the shorter man mumbled. "If the princess was kidnapped, she's probably dead already. It don't add up. If he took her for money, looks like he would have named his price. If he took her to hurt the senator, why not kill her right off instead of dragging her out here? She couldn't have been nothing but trouble on the trail."

"I'm thinking the same thing—all the pieces don't go together—but are you going to be the one to tell the captain? I think he went insane when he found out she was gone. I've seen him lose his temper before, but never like that."

"You'll probably see it again when he gets here and finds out all we've been doing is waiting. Maybe Warren got word today. But unless he gets here quick, it will be too dark to ride in tonight. None of the men like the idea of crossing that bridge in the dark."

Tobin had heard enough. These were Samuel Buchanan's men out of uniform and the boy had been right, they were headed toward Whispering Mountain. Somehow, he had to get home and figure out how to stop them. He didn't like the idea of killing soldiers who thought they were doing their duty, but he also had no intention of allowing them to ride onto his ranch and take Liberty.

He motioned for Roak to back out.

The boy nodded once and slipped backward as silently as a garden snake.

Tobin waited a while longer, making sure none of the men noticed the boy leaving. Then, as silently as possible, he stood and turned to follow.

From nowhere, something slammed against his head, knocking him to his knees before he could react.

"Help me out here!" a man shouted. "I caught me a spy."

Tobin reached for his gun, but before he could clear the holster, someone grabbed him from behind.

He struggled and a powerful fist slammed into his gut, almost knocking the breath from him. He counted three, no four men surrounding him.

The man pinning Tobin's arms gripped tighter as another punch found his jaw.

Tobin saw stars and stopped struggling.

They dragged him into camp. Tobin was only vaguely aware of the other men joining the crowd.

"What do we do with him?" one yelled.

"Kill him," someone answered. "If he was sneaking up on our camp, he was up to no good."

"Maybe we could beat information out of him. He might be one of the McMurrays."

"I doubt it," said the one called Hawk. "Why would a McMurray leave the ranch? They don't even know we're here."

The man who suggested the beating must have agreed for Hawk added, "For all we know, he's just an outlaw thinking this would be an easy camp to rob."

The short man, who'd been talking to Hawk earlier, barked a laugh. "If he's not a McMurray, he's one dumb outlaw." He grabbed Tobin's hair and pulled his face up. "I've only seen them from a distance. He's big enough to be one, but I can't tell. Why else would he be out here?"

Tobin shook his head, trying to clear his mind as the men continued to argue while the two holding him shoved his back against a tree and tied his hands around the trunk.

When he kicked at one, the man punched him again in the gut. It didn't seem an angry hit, just a necessity to control the prisoner.

Hawk walked up to Tobin and looked straight into his eyes. "Who are you and what are you doing here?"

Tobin didn't answer. If he told them the truth, Liberty might be in more danger. If Samuel found out that Liberty had gone willingly with him . . . that her father had asked Tobin to take her . . . there was no telling what the captain would do. From what Libby had mentioned, Buchanan was counting not only on her money when they married but also on her father's help to advance as an officer and later to enter politics.

Buchanan's dreams were shattered and he would blame Libby.

Another fist landed in Tobin's gut, but he still didn't speak. The blow to his face knocked his cheek against the trunk and split his lip. Tobin tasted his own blood, but he still didn't speak.

"Forget him," Hawk said. "Warren is due back any minute. He said he saw McMurray hanging around the barn. If he's a McMurray, we'll leave him tied up here and have one less to deal with when we get to the ranch." He laughed. "If he's not, we'll still leave him here tied up. What happens to him then is not our problem."

The man who'd tied him hit Tobin one more time for good measure, then walked away.

Tobin's anger filled his thoughts so completely he didn't even feel the pain and hardly noticed blood dripping from both his nose and lip. He didn't care. All he cared about was getting back to the ranch and warning the others. These men weren't just soldiers—they were a special group the captain must have handpicked. These were men who were doing more than just following orders.

Night settled over the camp with no sign of the man called Warren arriving. Tobin tugged at the rope, but couldn't free his hands. To his surprise, the men seemed to have forgotten about him. They moved around the camp, drinking coffee and talking quietly.

When Tobin calmed down enough to listen, he realized several were talking about the money they planned to spend. One said he'd buy a ranch down south, one said he planned to stay drunk in a whorehouse in San Antonio, and another planned to go back east and never come west again.

They were being paid, and paid well. Tobin knew a captain in the army didn't make that kind of money, so where would Samuel get it? Slowly, it came to him. The senator had to be rich, and Liberty would inherit everything. She would have not only her money, but her father's. A woman's wealth all went to her husband on the day they married. Samuel's reason for wanting to marry Liberty became crystal clear.

A sick feeling hit the bottom of his stomach, hurting worse than any blow could have. If Samuel married Liberty for her money, he wouldn't care how long she lived. The "accidents" she experienced the night he kidnapped her would continue to happen until one killed her. Then Samuel Buchanan would be a rich widower.

Tobin struggled, fighting to get free as the men bedded down for the night.

He watched them, looking for one who might see reason. The one called Hawk was cold and wouldn't listen, but the shorter man he'd seen talking to the lieutenant had said he didn't like the idea of killing a ranger. So, he must have some standards. But there was no way of talking to him without others hearing.

Tobin would have to wait.

An hour passed and then another. Tobin watched and waited.

Something moved slowly across his arm and Tobin jerked. He hated snakes.

Then it dawned on him that it was far too cold for snakes. He forced a long breath out to relax.

The touch came again, right at his wrist. Something pulled against the rope. *Roak*. Tobin almost said it aloud. The kid had come back for him.

While he felt a knife hacking through the rope, Tobin smiled. He'd see Roak had the best horse on the ranch for this.

When the rope broke, Tobin had to force his hands to remain still. Not all the men were asleep. He had to wait.

He thought he heard leaves crunch and guessed Roak had disappeared back into the blackness.

The wind began to howl. One of the men tossed a huge log onto the fire and several others rolled up tighter in their bedrolls.

Tobin studied each one. They were too far from a road or town to worry about anyone passing by, so the fire was safe and they hadn't bothered to leave a guard.

One man sat near the horses, but as a midnight fog settled in he disappeared from Tobin's view.

Tobin, his arms still stretched backward, moved a few inches around the tree. When he was no longer in view of half of the men, he stepped away from the tree and vanished in the blackness of a moonless night. His moccasins left no trail as he moved silently.

An hour later when Tobin made it back to where he'd left his horse, Roak was waiting for him.

Tobin swung up and offered his arm to the kid.

Roak shook his head. "I'm not going back with you. This is not my fight and I don't want to be in the middle of it. With my luck, both sides would shoot at me. But when this is all over, I plan to walk across that bridge and right up to the house to claim my horse."

"It'll be waiting for you." Tobin offered his hand. "Thanks."

The kid hesitated, then took his hand. "Drummond Roak," he said. "That's my name, if you're interested."

Tobin wasn't surprised the boy had a strong grip. "I'll not forget you."

Drum stepped away. "I promised Sage I wouldn't steal no more horses. Tell her I've decided to be a man of my word, will you?"

Tobin laughed. "I will."

He turned his horse toward home and rode hard. By first light they had to be ready for trouble. Big trouble.

CHAPTER 24

Liberty stood in the shadows at the corner of the long porch and waited for Ranger Liam to step into the bunkhouse for another cup of coffee. She'd studied the old man all evening and found him quite predictable. He allowed himself one smoke an hour and drank one cup of coffee when the cigarette was gone.

He'd been nice enough, polite even, but she couldn't help but wonder what he would be like if he knew all this mess was her fault. If she hadn't been fooled by Captain Samuel Buchanan, Ranger Liam wouldn't be here losing sleep while he watched over her. She also reasoned he hadn't come to help her, but simply because the McMurrays had asked him. To the old man, who probably spent most of his life fighting outlaws along the edges of civilization, a Washington senator's daughter would mean little. But the McMurrays were friends, and in this country that meant offering your gun when needed even if it was to protect a woman who'd been a fool.

Her father was right. She always acted before she thought. She'd been rushing through life since she was born:

running before she had walking down, jumping into things before she thought them out. But this time not only her well-being was at stake, but others might be harmed. She could not stand by and let that happen.

Liberty waited for her chance to run. Ranger Liam would go in for coffee soon. The barn would be an easy distance to make if she could dart straight, but she couldn't risk being caught in the light. She had to skirt the corral, doubling the distance to the barn.

Liam stood and lifted his cup. He tossed the leftover grounds in a neglected flower bed and studied the darkness in the direction of the bridge one last moment.

Liberty stepped off the porch and watched his back as he opened the bunkhouse door. She took a deep breath when he disappeared inside.

"Run!" she whispered as she bolted.

The night air was crisp with a dampness that stung her cheeks. She crossed just outside the light. If Travis and Teagen were still up, they wouldn't be able to see her from the house. She thought they were both asleep, but she hadn't checked. She'd heard Travis say he'd relieve Liam an hour after midnight.

With luck, no one would miss her until morning.

Liberty made it to the barn. She glanced back toward the bunkhouse, relieved to see no sign of Liam's returning to his post.

Once inside the barn, she pulled Sunny from the stall and began to saddle him. She'd watched the chore a dozen times and helped with it a few, but she hadn't realized the saddle would be so heavy. It took three efforts to plant the saddle atop Sunny, and then she had to remove it because she'd for-gotten the blanket. By the time she finished, Liberty was sweating from the effort.

She hesitated when she reached under Sunny's belly to cinch up the saddle. "Begging your pardon," she whispered.

Sunny turned his head to watch her, but he stood still. His big brown eyes almost looked like he felt sorry for her.

Liberty laughed and patted him, surprised at how fond

she'd grown of the horse. He was ornery, nipping at her braid sometimes or taking one step just as she tried to shove her foot in the stirrup. Once, when he'd done his one-step trick, she swore he looked back at her and smiled.

Finally in the saddle, Liberty headed toward the corral entrance at the back of the barn. That way she could stay out of Liam's sight.

Sunny protested. The horse didn't seem to think this was a good idea even if she did, but his jerks no longer frightened her. She held a strong grip on the leather straps.

"Come on," Liberty mumbled. "You can't stay in the barn all nice and warm. We have to go."

Sunny snorted and moved along.

Once outside, Liberty crossed the corral to the back gate. Slowly, so she didn't make any more noise than necessary, she headed across the pasture and finally to the road.

In truth, it wasn't much of road, more like two ruts in the grass worn by a wagon. The parallel lines darkened the land in the pale moonlight. She rode between them, knowing she was heading directly toward the bridge and her only way off the ranch.

She worried that the Apache at the bridge would try to stop her. If so, she'd make a run for it. Maybe their orders were to keep anyone from entering and not to bother those leaving. She felt like her heart hammered as loud as Sunny's hooves when they reached the wooden bridge.

She guessed right about the guards. When she clomped across, she saw both men standing by the trees. Neither made a move to bother her.

Once over the bridge, the road was far more traveled and easy to follow in the moonlight. She turned to what she hoped was the direction toward town. Liberty had no idea how far Elmo's Trading Post was, but judging by how long Teagen had been gone when he'd seen Mrs. Dickerson home, it must be at least an hour away from the ranch, maybe two. Calculating her progress in the dark compared to Teagen's in daylight, Liberty figured she'd be lucky to make it to town an hour before dawn.

Liberty planned as she rode. She'd heard everyone talk about the trading post . . . the first building in the area . . . the center of the settlement.

All she had to do was find Elmo's place and cross the road. Mrs. Dickerson had told the story of a drunk turning left instead of right when he was heading toward Elmo's. Liberty would do the same and have no trouble finding Mrs. Dickerson's home. From there, she'd allow the old schoolteacher to advise her how best to inform everyone in town that she wasn't a victim being held against her will. Once she finished her public speech, everyone would see Tobin for the hero he was. It seemed the only answer. This charade had gone on far too long.

Teagen had told Travis at supper that he almost had to toss Stella and her belongings out the second-story window because she didn't want to catch the afternoon stage. She seemed to be enjoying spreading lies while she shopped and stayed free, thanks to the McMurray credit in town.

Liberty would look left of Elmo's for a two-story home as her double check. Simple, she thought.

Once there, she'd wait on the porch until morning. When she saw a light on, she'd knock at Mrs. Dickerson's door and hope she'd be invited in. Maybe the old teacher would offer her breakfast while they waited for the town to wake up. As soon as it did, Liberty planned to end all the talk once and for all. By noon she'd be back on Whispering Mountain land with one less thing for the McMurrays to worry about.

Liberty smiled. She'd almost like to be there when word got back to Samuel and he could no longer claim his fiancée had been kidnapped. His plans were shattered and as soon as she got back to civilization, his career would also be ruined.

Without any self-pity she knew Samuel would mourn the loss of his career far more than he would her. She'd been a means to an end, nothing more. It bothered her more that she'd allowed herself to believe his lies than that he'd lied. People had been lying to her all her life it seemed. The crime was hers for believing. She found no comfort in knowing her father had also been fooled by his charm.

Tobin was the only person she'd ever known who didn't lie. He'd said he'd never love her. He'd made no promise of marriage.

Liberty closed her eyes, wishing she couldn't hear the echoes of his words telling her he'd cheated death once and knew it waited for him. She wouldn't, couldn't face the thought of his dying young.

Sunny stumbled over a hole in the road and Liberty almost tumbled out of the saddle.

Holding on to the reins, she slipped down, afraid if she tried to stay on they'd both fall. Sunny stomped back a few feet and balanced.

Liberty knew the first thing she had to do was make sure Sunny was all right. She'd seen Tobin run his hand along the horse's leg. It couldn't be hard and she had to check him.

The first whisper of fear entered her mind. She hadn't worried about the journey. No one would be out this late. All she had to do was follow one road. But what if her plan had hurt the horse? Tobin would never forgive her. She'd never forgive herself.

Liberty felt the left front leg.

All seemed solid.

She reached for the back leg. Dark shadows from the trees crossed over the path cutting any moonlight. She continued her search for injury. When she circled behind Sunny, she walked close to the horse so he couldn't accidentally kick her.

Restless, Sunny shifted, catching her little toe beneath his hoof.

Liberty yelped and jumped back, dancing in a circle with the sudden pain.

Without warning, the palomino jerked on the reins, pulling free of her grip. Before she thought to reach for them, he turned and galloped back toward home.

Liberty ran after him for a few steps, forgetting her toe. "Stop!" she yelled, but Sunny had disappeared into the night. "Whoa! Halt!"

More angry at herself than the horse, Liberty stomped her foot in frustration, then yelled in pain. This was *not* going as planned. She circled round as if looking for a way out of her adventure, but there was nothing but the sounds of the night closing in around her. Liberty had no way of knowing if she were closer to town or the ranch.

Suddenly the midnight road didn't seem so safe to travel. She considered finding a place to sit and wait out the night, but that would be hours. Even with no people traveling the road, there must be animals out. Animals looking for food.

Liberty stood in the center of the road and fought down tears. "I'm not helpless," she whispered. "I'm strong. I'm a survivor, the daughter of a senator."

One tear dribbled down her face as she walked to a break in the shadows where the road glowed pale in the moonlight. She'd thought the spot might feel safer. It didn't.

Liberty shoved the tear away with her glove. Think. Don't do something stupid. But she knew it was too late. She already had.

Moving along the road a few yards, she found a large rock and sat down to try and figure out what to do. As soon as she was still, she heard the whinny of a horse not far away.

"Thank the Lord," she said out loud. "You came back, Sunny."

Standing, she moved in the direction of hooves coming toward her.

A horse and rider crossed out of the blackness and almost toppled her before she had time to think of turning around.

The outline of a man, tall and too lean to be a McMurray, seemed to take up the entire road. His mount was black and snorted a puff of white smoke in the chilly air.

Liberty stood frozen, staring.

"Evening, Miss Liberty," the rider said with a hint of a northern accent. "Remember me? I'm Sergeant Warren."

Liberty couldn't place where, but she'd heard Samuel or her father mention the name. She relaxed enough to breathe.

"Have you come to escort me back to the ranch?" She hadn't been missing long enough for the McMurrays to organize a search, and besides, she had a feeling that if they missed her they'd come after her themselves.

"No, miss, I've come to take you back to the captain."

Liberty widened her stance. "And if I don't want to go?"

Warren leaned back in his saddle and pushed up his hat. She had the feeling he was smiling though his face lay in shadow. "I have my orders, miss. The captain's worried sick about you, so we'd better be going."

Liberty frowned. He was talking to her as if he seriously considered her touched in the head. And in all honesty, she couldn't blame him. What kind of woman in her right mind would be standing in the middle of a road after midnight?

She had to stay calm. She could talk her way out of this, but first she had to get the facts. "Sergeant Warren, how did you know where to find me?"

"Your maid, Stella Brady, told everyone in town you were on Whispering Mountain Ranch being held captive. I wasn't sure it was true until yesterday morning when the McMurray woman bought clothes that looked like they'd be about your size." He glanced at her gray split skirt and leather jacket. "Though they're not near fancy enough for your taste, I heard the girl say she wanted the best in the trading post. She even helped me out by describing you to the old man running the place. 'Tall,' she said, 'and every inch a lady.'"

When Liberty didn't comment, he added, "I figured I'd hang close to the bridge and wait. It took some skill staying out of the sight of those two Apache guards, but I managed. I never thought you'd escape and come across that bridge alone. I figured we'd have to fight our way in to rescue you."

Liberty straightened. "I wasn't kidnapped, Sergeant, and I'm not being held captive at Whispering Mountain."

She couldn't see his eyes, but his head moved slowly from side to side. Finally he said with a touch of pity in his voice, "All of us who've worked the fort line have seen captives who suffered like you, who resisted being saved. We've seen rescued children captured by Indians who tried to escape and go back."

"But I'm not—"

Warren shook his head. "Save your breath, miss. Buchanan told us the facts. Don't you worry, we'll get you back safe and sound so you can marry your true love. You'll thank me later."

Liberty was appalled to see that this soldier would follow orders no matter what she said. One thing Samuel insisted on was loyalty. She wanted to throw a fit, to start crying and begging, but she guessed the sergeant would probably gag her, toss her in a sack, and take her away.

Her only chance was to stay calm.

"We?" Liberty kept her voice low as she glanced past Warren.

"Yes, miss. Captain Buchanan sent a dozen of us. The others are a few miles away waiting for me." The sergeant straightened slightly with pride. "Captain Buchanan even promised us a bonus if we brought you back safe and sound. He said he didn't care what we had to do to rescue you. He even hinted that if Tobin McMurray were killed, it would save the time for a trial." Warren hesitated before adding, "He also said no matter how you might be ruined by the half-breed who took you, he plans to marry you the minute we get you back. So you can take comfort in that, miss."

Liberty wanted to scream that Warren was all wrong and she had no intention of going with him anywhere much less back to Samuel. Of course Buchanan wanted to marry her at once. Then he could keep her from talking to anyone.

And it didn't take much to figure out how he planned to pay the bonuses to these men. The minute they were married, what money she had became his. Her trust fund from her mother's family would split into twelve nice sums.

"I wasn't *ruined*." She resented even the hint that Tobin might have taken advantage of her. If anything, it had been the other way around.

"I'm glad to hear that, miss, but he's a dead man for what he did."

How could she have been so dumb to leave the ranch? She'd been safe. Her father's voice drifted in her mind. "Just once," he often said, "I wish you'd look before you leap off a cliff, because one day I won't be there to catch you."

Swallowing her panic, Liberty tried to think. She could run, but on foot her chances were not good. And if Warren thought she was deranged, he'd never hear reason. The sergeant didn't seem a bad sort. More like a man doing his duty. He was a soldier and Liberty had been raised by a soldier. If she wanted to change his thinking, she had to use the only weapons she had. Reason.

"Will you help me?" Liberty tried to sound frightened. Tobin was also off the ranch and in danger. She had no doubt that if they caught him, he'd be killed.

"Of course, miss." He swung from his saddle. "If you don't mind riding double, I'll get you to the camp. By first light we'll be well on our way."

"To where?" she asked as she took a step toward him.

"The captain is at the fort north of here. We can be there in five days if you're up for a hard ride."

Liberty nodded. "I have to stop by a home in town first. Stella promised she'd leave a few personal things for me there."

"I don't—"

"I insist, Sergeant."

Warren opened his mouth, but nothing came out. She knew she'd played him right. She'd agreed to his plan, but she'd asked for one small change. Her father used to call it "wormholing" in politics. She could almost hear the senator saying, "Talk the opponent into one small hole in his plan and pretty soon you'll have enough room to shoot a cannon through."

Warren nodded. "All right, but we have to be quick about it. I don't want the McMurrays noticing that you've escaped."

"Oh, they won't know anything is wrong until morning. We have hours and I'm only asking for a few minutes."

He offered her his laced hands as a step and she swung

into the saddle. A moment later he was behind her holding the reins in front of her while trying not to touch her.

"I'll tell you where to go as soon as we get near Elmo's Trading Post." She held her back stiff and kept her voice formal. "While I collect my things, I think you should get me a horse."

"We've already thought of that detail, miss. We have an extra one waiting for you at camp. I'll just stand guard while you retrieve your belongings."

Neither said another word. She needed time to think and Warren seemed occupied watching the shadows for any sign of trouble.

Thirty minutes later, they arrived at Mrs. Dickerson's house.

The poor woman looked frightened when she answered the door but managed a smile as she recognized Liberty. A moment later she turned a raised eyebrow at the stranger who followed Liberty into her parlor that doubled as a classroom.

Warren's tall thin frame with a rifle crossed over his arms looked out of place in the tiny school.

Liberty gave her no time to talk or ask questions. She insisted on picking up her things left in Stella's room. All the while she talked, she moved between the desks toward the back of the room where a stairway rose, pulling Mrs. Dickerson in her wake.

Warren, thankfully, took up his station at the room's only window.

When Mrs. Dickerson looked confused, Liberty said simply, "Please show me the bundles left for me. I'm sure they're there even though you may not have noticed." When the teacher hesitated, Liberty added with a tug, "I may need your help in finding my things."

Mrs. Dickerson finally seemed to catch on to the game. She took the lead and moved up the stairs, frowning when Warren followed. When he stood at attention on the top landing, she said, "You know, my third husband was in the cavalry."

Warren eyed her with a raised eyebrow.

Mrs. Dickerson smiled. "I can always tell the stance of a military man, with or without a uniform."

Liberty passed the teacher and walked into the first room. She lifted a slate and chalk from the small table by the bed as Mrs. Dickerson told Warren details of her life as a soldier's wife.

Warren looked uncomfortable at the old woman's complaining. When she followed Liberty into the bedroom, he waited in the hall. He seemed to have no desire to continue his conversation with Mrs. Dickerson.

Liberty turned her back to him and scribbled, "Tell McMurrays I'm being *taken* north to fort. Tell Tobin *not* to follow."

Mrs. Dickerson made a fuss of looking under the bed and in several drawers. When she asked Warren to hand her the lamp in the hallway, Liberty slipped her the slate.

In one glance the teacher read the message and looked up at Liberty. Her thin eyebrow lifted, sending ripples of wrinkles across half her forehead.

Liberty whispered, "Do you understand what is happening?"

Mrs. Dickerson glanced back to the door as Warren returned. She leaned to check beneath the pillows and when she straightened the slate had disappeared. "I can think of one other place to look," she said loud enough for Warren to hear. "She might have left something in the laundry."

The old woman took the lamp from Warren and crossed the hall. A moment later she returned with a small bundle of clothes. "Reach and hand me that carpetbag on the shelf, young man."

Warren did as told. He even held it open while she stuffed it with her find.

"I'm sorry, Miss Liberty," Mrs. Dickerson said. "I would have washed these right away if I knew you'd be leaving so soon."

"Oh, that is all right." Liberty took the bag. "I thank you for keeping them for me." She fought down a laugh. Mrs. Dickerson had taken to the farce like a pro.

They moved to the door, forcing Warren to head down the stairs ahead of them.

"Thank you," Liberty whispered.

"You're welcome. I'll expect you back soon for tea."

Liberty wished she could tell Mrs. Dickerson just how much trouble she was in, but at least she knew Tobin would not come for her. She'd be safe, at least until she reached the fort and Samuel found time to be alone with her, but if Tobin followed he'd be outnumbered.

CHAPTER 25

Tobin hit the bridge at full gallop. Daybreak already dusted the eastern horizon. If he managed to move away from the camp unnoticed and if no one checked on him to see that their prisoner was still tied, Tobin figured he had two, maybe three, hours' head start on the soldiers.

He waved at the braves on guard and knew they'd be no match for the storm of a dozen trained soldiers. Though he hated to lose time, he had to let them know he only wanted them to fire one shot when trouble crossed, then disappear into the trees. He no longer needed warning if someone came; he only needed to know when. The soldiers might already be riding toward Whispering Mountain, but with luck, he and Libby would be well into the mountains before the Apache fired off a shot.

Tobin spoke to the two Apache in their native tongue. They nodded and began breaking camp sensing their time on guard would be ending soon. All his life Tobin had felt his grandfather watching over them, but the old man never interfered. In his eyes his daughter had joined the white man's tribe when she'd married Andrew McMurray, and her destiny, as well as the destiny of her children, lay with them.

Tobin whirled his mount and rushed for the house. Minutes later he wasn't surprised to see Sage, fully dressed, running toward him from the barn. By the time he slowed his horse, Teagen had stepped out on the porch.

"You're home," Teagen stated the obvious. "Good, that sorrel mare is getting close to giving birth."

"We've got trouble." Tobin barely heard Teagen's words as he dismounted and ran toward them.

"More than you know." Sage gulped for air. "Liberty's gone."

Tobin slowed. "She's already safely in the mountains?" He spoke his hope even though he knew from the faces of his siblings that his words couldn't be true. Teagen looked surprised. Sage showed only worry.

Sage shook her head. "She must have left some time in the night. She apparently took Sunny, but he returned a few minutes ago. I just finished cooling him down."

Teagen was the only one who didn't look worried. "Maybe she just went for a ride. We all know Sunny heads for home if he gets the chance."

Tobin hadn't slept in two days. It took his tired mind a few seconds to run through all the possible explanations. She wouldn't have gone riding by herself and certainly not before dawn. No one could have gotten onto the ranch and taken her out, not with the ranger watching from the bunkhouse and the guards at the bridge. Even if someone could have made it onto the ranch and passed the old ranger, Teagen was asleep next to Liberty's room, and Travis slept directly downstairs. One of his brothers would have heard something. Travis woke when the first snow fell each winter.

There was only one way she could have left . . . under her own power. Liberty had chosen to leave. But why?

Maybe she'd thought she needed to help him? Maybe she wanted away from him? He tried to remember what the fight they'd had earlier had been about. How could he remember being angry at her and not remember why?

Tobin continued to try to think of some reason she would leave while he told his brothers about the camp of soldiers. Travis came in halfway through and started asking questions in rapid fire.

"They'll be on their way here as soon as they discover I'm gone," Tobin said.

"Great." Travis shrugged. "Sage said when she was in town she heard talk of men organizing to come out here and save Liberty thanks to all the lies that maid of hers told. Mrs. Dickerson mentioned they planned to have a meeting last night and organize."

"Drink, you mean," Sage said.

Teagen shook his head. "We've got townspeople coming from one direction and soldiers from the other." He tossed his brothers rifles. "With any luck they'll all run into one another at the bridge and start fighting over who gets to kill us first." Teagen didn't crack a smile, leaving his brothers to wonder if he was serious or joking.

When he handed Sage a rifle, she straightened proudly.

Teagen said what was on all their minds. "We're in agreement. No one steps foot on McMurray land uninvited."

They all nodded. For a moment, no one said a word. They just stared at one another, knowing they were all thinking the same thing. Today they'd fight, maybe even die, but they'd stand or fall together.

They'd follow the first rule their father set down on paper almost twenty years ago. No one invades McMurray land.

Tobin glanced at Sage. The brothers had spent their lives protecting her from harm, but she was an adult now . . . and more . . . She was a McMurray.

Teagen took charge. "Travis, make sure your wife and Martha know what is going on. Their safest hiding place might be the cellar."

Rainey stepped outside. "I heard everything, Teagen, and I stand with my husband. Martha can take Duck to the cellar."

Travis shook his head as he blocked her way. "No, Rainey."

He widened his stance as if preparing to fight the little woman before him. "Darlin', you can't risk being hurt, not now."

She touched his arm gently, having no fear of the bear within her husband. "I can't risk losing you now."

Tobin noticed the look they exchanged. Love and worry. The kind of love that lasts a lifetime.

Rainey didn't back down.

Finally, Travis ended the standoff. "Take one of the rifles to the upstairs window, Rainey. You'll have more cover there but still be able to fire if they storm the place."

"I'll take another window." Sage looked at her sister-in-law. "These rifles are heavy. If the firing lasts a while, we'll be glad we have the window sill to use as a brace."

Rainey nodded and they moved inside as Travis and Teagen loaded all the extra rifles and stacked them along the railing while Tobin saddled the horses and brought them around to the back of the house. No one planned to leave, but it wouldn't hurt to have horses ready to ride.

Duck ran onto the porch with Martha yelling for him. He took one look at what was happening and jumped toward Travis.

The tough ranger held his son tightly for a few seconds and then pushed him away enough to see the little boy's face. "You got to go with Martha, son."

He shook his head wildly.

Teagen lifted him from Travis's arms. "We need you, Duck," Teagen said. "You're the next generation of Mc-Murrays. You're the most valuable thing we got on this ranch, so just for today we want to know you're safe."

Teagen spoke to Duck, but he looked at his brothers as he said, "If something happens to us, there's a letter in the bottom drawer of the desk in the library."

Tobin hadn't heard those words for twenty years, but he remembered his father saying them as if it were yesterday.

The tiny boy looked from one of the McMurrays to the other. Tears bubbled over his eyes and down his cheeks, but he nodded. Teagen passed him back to Travis, and Travis held him tightly as he walked back inside and handed the boy, their future, over to Martha.

When Travis stepped back outside he didn't look up. He just reached for his rifle preparing to do what had to be done.

Tobin looked at his brothers. The three of them were nothing like the children of yesterday, but they all believed the same thing. No matter what. Hold the ranch.

The brothers spread across the porch watching a winter sun sparkle across their land as peacefully as it had for years.

"Do you think they know Liberty is gone?" Teagen asked in a low voice.

"No," Tobin answered. "From what I heard at the camp, the soldiers were just waiting for a scout named Warren to return and then they planned to attack. But now that I've escaped, my guess is they won't wait on him."

Travis grunted. "If the town is firing up after a night of drinking, they're probably on their way as well. The ones sober enough to stay on their horses should be here soon."

Tobin didn't comment. He'd heard Travis's stories of when the Texas Rangers had to deal with mobs. The men coming from town wouldn't be in any mood to listen to reason. Though they probably couldn't shoot straight, they might hit someone by accident. Tobin had no desire to shoot anyone, but if they came he'd have to fight.

Seconds ticked by. No one moved. Tobin thought of how much he loved this place his father had found. He loved the hills at his back and the rivers that bordered. He loved the way the wind sounded in the trees and how frost blanketed the rocks in winter. This one spot of earth offered him all the beauty and comfort he'd ever wanted.

Until now. Now he ached for the sight of Liberty. She drove him nuts most of the time. Bossy as a general. Pampered like a princess. But he missed her so badly even his bones ached. The knowledge that she'd left him willingly bled like an open wound across his soul. He'd always thought they'd have time to say good-bye. Maybe they'd share one last night together . . . one last night to remember.

Why had she run? If not from him. Not from here. Then why? If she wasn't running from something, she had to be running to something, but what?

He knew how she felt, how she smelled, how she tasted, but he had no idea how she thought. She was afraid of horses, afraid of riding, afraid of the dark, yet she'd ridden out alone in the night. He might never get the chance to ask her.

"Something's coming over the bridge."

Teagen's warning jerked Tobin out of his thoughts.

The brothers raised their rifles.

A few minutes later, a buggy cleared the bridge.

"It's a trick," Teagen said, without lowering his rifle. "Five men could be hiding inside."

Tobin watched, thinking his brother must be right, but as the buggy rolled closer he saw only one person. The Apache on guard hadn't fired a shot. They must have seen no danger.

"It's Mrs. Dickerson." Travis laughed as he lowered his rifle. "Great, the old woman has come to call again. She's like a stray cat. We shouldn't have fed her those jelly sandwiches."

All three brothers swore in unison.

The buggy rattled closer.

"What do we do?" Tobin mumbled. "She's going to be caught in the middle of a war. She'll have about as much chance as a rabbit in a stampede."

"We tell her to go back," Teagen suggested.

"If we do, she's bound to run into either the soldiers or the town drunks." Tobin sat his rifle against the railing, out of sight. "Maybe we ask her how she feels about a visit to the cellar."

Teagen still hadn't moved. "Well, we're sure as hell not inviting her in for tea." He relaxed slightly. "Any votes for shooting her? From the looks of her, she'd only be getting to heaven a few years early. She'd probably be glad to get to see all those husbands she buried."

"Hush, Teagen," Sage said as she stormed out onto the porch. "We can't shoot the only teacher for miles around."

Teagen groaned. "It was just a suggestion."

With all their rifles hidden behind the railing, the brothers followed Sage out to meet the buggy.

Mrs. Dickerson started talking before she came to a stop. "I got important news. Important news for sure. I couldn't wait for dawn. I had to come fast even though it's a real danger traveling at night."

Teagen offered his hand to help her down. "What is it?" He raised an eyebrow when she didn't take his offer.

The old school teacher breathed deep like she was about to dive in and looked straight at Tobin. "I've seen Miss Liberty. She's in trouble, but she says she don't want you to come."

Tobin felt like someone had slammed the butt of a rifle against the side of his head. He stepped forward as Mrs. Dickerson continued. "She came by my place before daylight. About scared me to death banging on my door so early. A man followed her in like he was standing guard. A military man."

Mrs. Dickerson pulled a handkerchief from her sleeve and patted her face. "I knew something was wrong, but I couldn't tell what. The man wasn't frightening, but he didn't seem to want to let Liberty out of his sight." She took a few breaths as she wiggled something from her knitting bag on the seat beside her. "The minute we got in the house, Miss Liberty insisted I had to follow her upstairs to get something Stella left. Well, I knew that Stella didn't leave a thing—I'd already cleaned her room. If she would have left so much as a hairpin, I would have noticed. I know how to clean a room from top to bottom."

Tobin considered shaking the old woman to get her back on track but figured he'd frighten her more.

Teagen said what they were all thinking. "What happened?"

"Well, of course, at her insistence, we went upstairs. All three of us. The man waited in the hall. I noticed Liberty turn her back to him, so I tried to distract him by telling him how horrible the army treated me when I was married to Mr. Dickerson. He wasn't an officer, you know, so he didn't have any say about where we were stationed. He ended up being mustered out in Texas without enough money to return home."

Teagen looked like he was about to do something that might truly frighten the schoolteacher, so Tobin ordered, "Please, continue about Liberty. Is she all right? Is she safe?"

"She's safe enough, I guess, for the moment, but she handed me this." Mrs. Dickerson pulled the slate from her bag.

Tobin took the message and read it aloud. "Tell McMurrays I'm being *taken* north to fort. Tell Tobin not to follow."

He looked up. "She underlined *taken*."

Travis reached for the slate.

Mrs. Dickerson pointed. "I think she wants us to know that she's going against her will."

"The fort is almost a week of hard riding from here. Why would they be taking her there?" Travis asked to no one in particular. "It would be a far easier ride to go back to Austin."

"Maybe her father is there," Sage offered.

Mrs. Dickerson corrected her as if they were doing a lesson. "No, dear. If he were there, she would have said she 'was going' to the fort. After talking with her, I believe she wanted to be reunited with him as soon as possible."

Tobin felt the sting of her true words. Libby had never once said she wanted to stay with him. He'd been no more to her than temporary shelter.

Sage turned to her brothers. "What do we do?"

Tobin gripped the buggy. He felt like his body was splitting in half. He had to go to Libby, no matter what she wrote, she needed him. But he had to defend the ranch. If the man with Libby was Warren, the scout, he'd take her first back to the camp. If they got there before the men left, then Libby would have a dozen men guarding her on her journey to the fort. If Warren was late, he might miss the rest of the army men. If he was an army man, he'd follow orders and take Libby to the fort, not go looking for the other troops. The other men might even now be riding full speed toward Whispering Mountain still thinking that Liberty needed to be rescued.

He couldn't leave his brothers to fight alone, yet he had to get to Libby before she reached the fort. What if Samuel waited for her?

Before Tobin could move, shots rang out from the bridge.

To everyone's surprise, Mrs. Dickerson grabbed the reins of her buggy. "Oh, I forgot to tell you. That will be the men from town. I heard them talking in the barn when I got my buggy ready. Not one of them offered to help me and I plan to take them to task about it. What kind of self-respecting man stands by talking while a lady harnesses a horse and pulls her own rig from the stall?"

She raised her whip. "I'll just be a minute," she shouted as she slapped the reins against the back of her horse. The buggy jolted forward.

Sage tried to stop her, but for once the horse seemed to have found a bit of energy.

Teagen shouted for her to wait.

Mrs. Dickerson just waved and answered as she kicked up dust turning. "I'll be back in a minute. Now don't you worry."

By the time the McMurrays collected their rifles and climbed on their horses, the teacher was halfway to the bridge.

When they caught up to her, she was blocking the end of the bridge with her buggy and her old horse looked even closer to dead than usual.

Men were shouting for the teacher to get out of the way, but Mrs. Dickerson didn't look the least bit scared.

"Now, Frank, you stop that yelling, and, Harry, I'll thank you not to use that language in my presence or I swear I'll wash your mouth out with lye soap again just like I did ten years ago. Philip! What kind of example are you setting for your children jumping around and yelling like a monkey in a tent show?"

The mob settled. Tobin couldn't tell if it was because of Mrs. Dickerson's orders or the fact that McMurray rifles were pointed at them.

One man, looking more sober than most of his comrades, stepped forward. "We're here to save Miss Liberty Mayfield.

We hear she's been kidnapped by Tobin McMurray and is being held here against her will."

"That's a lie," Teagen shouted.

"Then you won't mind us seeing for ourselves," the man yelled back.

"No one steps foot on our land."

The men mumbled as if Teagen's words had proven their theory.

"We'll see for ourselves," someone shouted from the back of the crowd. "Why should we believe any McMurray? If you've nothing to hide, let us in."

Teagen shouldered his rifle. "Any man crossing the bridge is trespassing. I don't care if you believe me or not."

The men all took a step forward, then hesitated as if each waited for someone else to be the first. Mumbled oaths rose from the crowd. Someone near the back shouted, "Of course he's lying. Don't believe killers or kidnappers."

"Then believe me!" Mrs. Dickerson's voice rang clear in the cold air. "Believe me." She stood straight and tall on the step of her buggy. "Have I ever lied to any of you?"

No man answered.

"Liberty Mayfield was here. I had tea with her and she swore to me that she wasn't being held against her will. She was a guest."

The men mumbled some more like a pot just beginning to boil. Finally, one voice popped out from the group. "Well, if she's here why can't we see her?"

"That's a good question, Daniel," Mrs. Dickerson said. "She left last night with a military escort. I gave her a weapon to protect her on her journey myself." The teacher smiled. "So you see, she's not here to save, or to meet. But I must say, you are all very brave to come when you thought she needed saving. To think you were willing to die to help. A very fine lot indeed, for surely, with all the rifles aimed at you, many would have died if you'd crossed this bridge."

The men looked behind the wagon at the four riders with their guns ready. And beyond they could just make out the ranch house with rifles in every window.

"We'd do what we have to," one man mumbled, "if we thought a woman was kidnapped, but if Mrs. Dickerson says she ain't, that's good enough for me."

"Me too," someone else yelled.

"Fine, gentlemen," Mrs. Dickerson said. "Now, if you'll be so kind as to escort me back to town."

They all agreed, turning their horses as her buggy passed. The McMurrays watched them go.

"That's one hell of a woman," Teagen admitted. "I almost asked her to join us for breakfast."

"We've only fought off one wave. There may be another one coming." Travis turned back toward home.

Sage sighed. "This may prove a long morning."

CHAPTER 26

THE OCTOBER SUN BROUGHT NO WARMTH AS LIBERTY and Warren rode into the soldiers' camp just after dawn. She could see several men moving about, saddling horses, preparing weapons.

Warren whistled, then yelled, announcing their arrival.

Liberty counted eleven men who stopped what they were doing and stood silently watching as Warren picked a path between the trees into camp.

He rode within ten feet of the fire and swung down, then lowered her to the ground so carefully Liberty almost laughed. His touch was formal, impersonal, holding none of the warmth Tobin had shown her even during those first few touches weeks ago.

A tall, thin man stepped forward. He looked first at Warren, then back to her. "Miss Liberty Mayfield?"

Liberty nodded.

"I'm Lieutenant Jeremy Hawk." He looked at Warren and smiled.

The sergeant didn't say a word.

"You've arrived just in time." Hawk gave her his full attention. "Another ten minutes and we would have been riding toward the McMurray place." When she didn't comment, he added, "We planned to ask for a surrender and your return. There would have been no blood shed if they had cooperated and no one harmed except for the man who kidnapped you."

Liberty knew she was looking at the second soldier who would not listen to reason. She wanted to scream that the McMurrays would never have surrendered and many of the soldiers would have died crossing the bridge, but she could barely bring herself to think of the battle. McMurrays would also die and all because of her.

"And if I swear that I wasn't kidnapped?"

Hawk looked at Warren.

Warren moved forward finally. "You are safe now, Miss Mayfield. No one will harm you or carry out any threat toward you if you tell the truth."

"But—"

Lieutenant Hawk broke in, "We've been informed of the truth by Captain Buchanan and we have orders to see you safely to the fort north of here." With a nod to Warren, Hawk turned his back and began issuing orders to break camp with all haste.

"But I wasn't . . ."

Warren moved closer. His sad gray eyes looking like he felt sorry for her. The kind of sorry a person might feel for a senile grandmother. "Don't worry, miss. This is all going to be over soon. Don't talk no more about it. You've been through a great deal and we're here to help."

"What's your first name, sergeant?"

"William, miss. William Daniel Warren."

Liberty thanked him with a nod for being honest. She tried again. "And are you married?"

"Yes." He smiled. "My wife calls me Billy D., but no one else would ever dare."

"I know what you mean. Someone calls me Libby no matter how many times I correct him, but I don't mind." The sergeant didn't know it but he'd calmed her. She'd need all her strength to think of how to escape from men loyal to Samuel without getting anyone killed in the process.

The times she could have stopped the madness before it reached this point tumbled through her mind. She could have run to her father that night at the ball and demanded he listen. Or when they'd first arrived in Texas, she could have stopped this chain of events by simply saying no to Samuel's proposal. Other times came to mind, but all she could think was that she had to stop this now, before someone was killed.

The men in town would have believed her, but these soldiers were under orders. And—she closed her eyes—they were under orders to kill Tobin on sight. The farther she got from Whispering Mountain, the better.

"Lieutenant, do you know of my father?"

Hawk nodded. "I had word three days ago. He's in San Antonio." The officer straightened. "Despite all urging by Captain Buchanan, he refuses to leave Texas until he can leave with you."

Liberty tried to read between his words. Maybe her father had come to his own conclusions that Buchanan wasn't the man for her. She suspected part of the reason he stayed looking for the men who attacked him was that her father never turned away from a battle, but maybe, just maybe, he stayed to take her back with him.

"I wish to go to my father," she said as calmly as she could.

Hawk didn't hesitate. "We've orders to take you to the captain."

"That's what I told her." Warren stepped forward and offered her a canteen. "But, having a daughter, I can understand why she'd want her father."

A stocky man joined them, whispering to the lieutenant, "Ain't we riding for the ranch? I've been itching for a fight."

"No need, Frazier," Hawk snapped. "We've accomplished our mission. Miss Mayfield is safe."

"What about Tobin McMurray?" The soldier called Frazier looked disappointed. "The captain wants him dead for what he did."

Liberty forced down a swallow of water and tried to act like she wasn't listening.

Hawk mumbled something to Warren. Liberty guessed the young officer might need advice from the more seasoned sergeant.

Warren shrugged, then seemed to agree.

The lieutenant looked back to Frazier. "Pick two men and ride to the bridge. Get as close as you can to the ranch and wait for him to come out. He'll have to leave the place sometime. When he does, do what you have to do."

"But how will I know which one of those McMurrays is Tobin?" The stout soldier didn't look happy at having to stay behind.

Warren moved closer to him. "The one who was a ranger walks with a limp and looks like he might be part Indian. I saw him once with the senator. When I saw Tobin McMurray last, he was wearing knee-high moccasins. A fella in town said he has a scar that runs right over his heart, so he should be easy to identify."

The soldier still didn't look happy. "I can't exactly ask every man riding by to open his shirt. What if I shoot the wrong one?"

Hawk looked bored with the conversation. "Set up camp where you can see that damn bridge that keeps all away and do your best."

Liberty noticed Warren didn't look comfortable with Hawk's order, but he didn't say anything. She'd listened to soldiers talk all her life and had long ago given up reacting to anything she heard, but not this time. This time she knew the men they talked so casually about killing. This time she knew they'd done nothing wrong.

Fighting exhaustion, Liberty forced her back to remain straight. She wanted to ask if they could rest a few hours before leaving, but she knew it would be safest for both the soldiers and the McMurrays, if they were as far away from the ranch as possible. If the McMurrays knew where she was, they might try to save her even if she had told them not to. They didn't seem a clan who followed orders well. If they came, men would be killed. Her best choice was to put miles between the ranch and the soldiers until she found someone in authority who would believe her.

"I'm ready to leave," she said to Warren. "Can we go now?"

Warren nodded. "I'll saddle your horse, miss."

While she waited she saw the stout soldier pick out two men to remain behind with him. She guessed that he'd chosen the two best marksmen. She also knew that the first man who rode out of Whispering Mountain would have three bullets in him by the time he cleared the bridge.

He'd be covered in blood. Tobin's nightmare would come true.

Liberty turned, walked to the nearest tree, and vomited. With the image of Tobin lying on the ground in her mind, she threw up until there was nothing left.

His dream was about to come true and she'd be the cause.

Warren stood behind her ready to help. She tried once more, desperate to have him believe her. "I wasn't kidnapped, Sergeant. I don't need saving."

He showed no hint of believing her.

"I was riding into town to convince . . ." Liberty stopped, realizing how crazy she sounded even to herself. No sane woman would have been standing in the middle of nowhere in the middle of the night with no horse.

Warren handed her his handkerchief with his initials embroidered on it.

"Thank you, Sergeant."

"You are welcome, miss," he answered formally.

Ten minutes later when they rode away, Liberty forced her mind to think of nothing but the ride. She studied everything around her, filling her brain with facts that didn't matter, counting trees, rocks, birds, listening to every word the men said, anything to keep from thinking about the three men waiting just off McMurray land. Three men planning to kill Tobin.

When they stopped for lunch, she forced down a few bites, not because she was hungry but because she knew she had to be strong for the battle to come. Warren told her the fort was five days away. If Tobin got her note and didn't follow, maybe she'd have a few days to convince one of these men that she hadn't been kidnapped.

"Warren," she whispered as she handed him back the tin plate. "Do you think me mad?"

"I'm not paid to think," he answered.

"Please answer me."

"Yes," he whispered. "But I'll watch over you every minute. Nothing or no one is going to bother you again. You'll be safe until we get to the fort and then you'll be with Buchanan."

Liberty closed her eyes and heard what he hadn't said. He'd be making sure she didn't escape.

"Sergeant Warren?"

"Yes, miss."

"You plan to protect me even from myself, don't you?"

"Yes, miss."

Liberty wanted to ask who would protect her from Samuel, but she didn't. The sergeant wouldn't understand. She'd never wanted Tobin so much as right now.

Thinking of Tobin, her senses wished him near so strongly she could almost feel him close. His riding instructions drifted through her mind as she rode. As the hours passed, she relived every moment they'd spent together and the longing for him became an ache within her.

She studied each one of the soldiers. A few were young. They might be convinced, but they didn't look like they'd disobey orders. Even if she talked one of them into taking her back to Whispering Mountain, there was a good chance she'd never be able to convince the shooters at the bridge to turn away.

By the second day, she reasoned that she had one chance and that chance would be Sergeant Warren. He seemed the most reasonable and the other men respected him far more than they did Hawk.

Warren worried about her, making sure she had a blanket and a bit of privacy when she needed it. He even talked to her from time to time about his wife in Tennessee and his daughter named Natalie.

Slowly, so no one would notice, she began to make friends with Warren. She thanked him for helping her up and for taking care of her horse. She asked him innocent questions about the land and how much farther it was to the fort. Liberty even asked about his child and laughed when he told a story about her having a skunk for a pet.

By the third day, they were talking easily and no one, including Lieutenant Hawk, seemed to be paying much attention. Liberty wanted to scream each morning for she knew they were moving farther and farther away from the ranch, but if she didn't cooperate fully Hawk would suspect something.

The lieutenant tried to accommodate her needs by starting later in the morning and slowing the pace when she looked tired. If he thought she was plotting something, the ride could become far more grueling.

Hawk seemed a nervous man, always pacing and fidgeting. Warren whispered once that the lieutenant had to keep moving or he'd worry a hole in the ground.

The good news was Hawk had little interest in speaking to her except when necessary. He seemed far more concerned with the route and the safety of his men. He even took his turn scouting ahead. Liberty decided that would be the time she could approach Warren and tell him the truth. The worse he'd probably do was not believe her. The best might be that he'd agree to take her back.

Liberty tried to bide her time and calm her nerves by telling herself that the McMurrays only left their ranch when they had to. Sage said she made the trip to town once a month. If she was the one who usually made the trip, surely none of the shooters would mistake her for a man. Liberty also knew that if the men rode in for mail, they crossed the back way through the hills. With any luck the soldiers would get tired of waiting long before a McMurray man crossed the bridge.

Another fear haunted her thoughts. If she convinced Warren to take her back, the others might consider him a traitor, or worse, think that he was in league with Tobin. She didn't like to think that she could be putting a little girl's father in danger.

When Sergeant Warren talked of his Natalie, his gray eyes didn't look so sad. He may have been in the army more than half his life, but his heart now stayed back in Tennessee with his wife and child. Liberty needed his help, but she understood why he could not risk his future even if he had believed her.

At night, she tried to think of a plan, but most of the time she found herself wishing Tobin were near. He was so thick in her thoughts she could almost feel him holding her. But she wouldn't really want him here: he'd be in danger.

On the evening of the fourth day, Lieutenant Hawk decided to take two men and ride ahead to inform Captain Buchanan that his bride-to-be was safe and arriving before noon on the next day. Liberty knew this would be her last night on the trail and maybe her only chance.

The men seemed content to sit around the fire and talk of how they planned to spend their bonuses now that the mission was almost complete. By lunch tomorrow, they would be eating in the mess hall.

Liberty moved away from the others and waited, knowing that Warren would bring her a plate for dinner. She hadn't waited long when he showed up.

"Miss," he said politely. "Sorry the meal's so poorly tonight."

She took the food, thanking him, then asked, "Sergeant, what if this were all a mistake and I'm not crazy? What if I wasn't kidnapped from my father's house? What if I ran from Captain Buchanan for my own reasons and Tobin McMurray's only crime was helping me? What would you do?"

Warren stared at the toe of his boot for a while. When he looked up his smile didn't reach his eyes. "I've less than a year of finishing my tour. My Sally and I plan to farm when I get out." He looked at her directly, his eyes full of sadness as he said, "I wouldn't do anything, miss."

"But innocent men may be killed," she tried again.

"Innocent men get killed all the time. I'd feel sorry for that, but if I disobeyed orders and got kicked out now, I'd have nothing."

"So you wouldn't risk doing the right thing?"

He shook his head. "What's right is following orders for a soldier, nothing more."

She understood. He'd answered her question. Without saying another word, she ate the half-cooked beans with hunks of tough jerky chopped in. The food was bad. The water tasted alkaline.

Liberty threw up her meal with Warren standing a few feet behind her. When she turned to him, she tried one more time to reason with him. "Would you let me go? I can't face Buchanan tomorrow. I have to get back to Whispering Mountain."

It had grown too dark to see his face, but his word reached her. "No," he said. "You'd be in a great deal of danger out here alone. It wouldn't be safe. No matter what you face at the fort, it can't be as dangerous as you being out here alone."

Liberty wiped her mouth on a bandanna he'd given her two days ago. "It isn't safe where I'm going either."

She expected him to argue, but he remained silent.

CHAPTER 27

JUST AFTER DAWN ON THEIR FIFTH MORNING OUT, Liberty refused breakfast and asked if she could have some privacy to wash before they rode into the fort.

Warren looked reluctant but agreed.

She found a spot by a stream where trees sheltered her on both sides to the waters' edge. The morning was damp with rain. Fog seemed to close in around her little bank by the stream like a thin curtain. She picked up her small carpetbag as she heard Warren post men to the right and left of her location.

Warren walked her to the clearing and asked for her boots. He said he'd have a man polish them for her, but Liberty guessed he thought she'd be less likely to bolt with no horse or boots.

She smiled and handed them to him. "Thank you, Sergeant, you are very kind."

He seemed embarrassed and walked away. He was still polite, but the friendliness between them was gone. She found little comfort that he questioned his duty but still planned to do it.

Liberty stripped down to her undergarments and slowly began to wash one part of her body at a time. She had to prepare her mind for the next battle. If there was a commander at the fort, she'd demand to see him. Or maybe she'd act glad to see Samuel, then faint and claim she had to rest before the wedding. But somehow, even if she had to shout no during her vows, she would stop the wedding.

The morning air felt crisp against her damp skin, the water almost ice, but she still took her time, needing a few minutes to plan. Pulling one of the two towels Mrs. Dickerson had shoved into the carpetbag, Liberty carefully made sure the knitting needle didn't poke out of the bag. The old woman had probably packed it as a weapon, but Liberty saw little use of a knitting needle against armed guards.

She heard a branch splashing at the water just as she pulled on her blouse. "One minute, Sergeant. I'm not quite dressed."

Something moved behind her and a low voice whispered, "That's the way I like you best."

Liberty swung around and collided with Tobin. Before she could scream, his arm circled her waist and his hand covered her mouth. For a moment he just held her tightly against him. Then his mouth replaced his hand and he was kissing her wildly.

Liberty dug her hands into his hair as he lifted her off the ground. She wrapped her legs around his waist and kissed him back, starved for the taste of him.

He pulled away suddenly. "I'm furious at you."

She saw the fire in his eyes, but it was not the fire of anger. Kissing his throat, she felt his hands move over her hips greedily. "I can tell," she whispered as she worked her way to his mouth. "You're really angry at me."

He kissed her again, hard and fast, then circled her waist and pulled her off his body. "We can't do this, Libby," he said. "We need to talk."

Liberty knew he was right, but the attraction she felt for him every time they were close was back ten times stronger than it had been before. She wanted to beg him to make love to her right here, right now.

Tobin's blue gaze looked at her as if he would do just that, but he forced his mouth into a frown. "Why'd you leave?" He may have stood her on her feet a few inches away, but he couldn't seem to stop his hands from caressing her.

"How did you find me?" She took deep breaths to calm down and saw him watching her breasts rise and fall. "There are men planning to kill you."

"Did you leave *me* that night?" Tobin forced himself to look up. "Were you running from *me*?"

He was starving for her, drinking her in, but denying himself. Liberty didn't want to talk. She didn't even want to run. She only wanted to feel.

"You're in great danger. These men have orders to kill you on sight."

He pulled her so close she could feel his breath on her cheek. "Were you leaving me, Libby?" he demanded in a whisper that seemed to come from deep within.

"No," she answered, and felt his control break.

He crushed her against his chest and buried his face in her hair. "Then nothing else matters."

His big body was warm and comforting surrounding her. She felt his heart pounding as his hand tugged her hair until her mouth lifted once more to his. This time his kiss bruised her lips, but she didn't care. All the longing and fire and need pounded inside her until she felt she would vanish into dust if he didn't hold her against him.

Tobin mumbled her name, then lifted her high in the air. As he slowly lowered her, he kissed the swell of each breast.

Liberty laughed wishing no clothes blocked his kisses. Her whole body strained, aching for his touch.

"When I get you somewhere safe," he whispered against her ear, "I plan to have my way with you."

"I was thinking the same thing." She combed her fingers through his hair. "A week is far too long to sleep alone."

Tobin kissed the corner of her mouth. "I have no plans of sleeping."

"I'll wake you if you even try." She giggled. "Now, how do we get out of here?"

Reluctantly, he stepped away. "Get dressed. I've been watching you for days, waiting for a chance to get you alone. Now that I have, I know we only have minutes left before that guard dog comes to find you."

Liberty tugged on her stockings and buttoned her blouse. "I'm ready."

Tobin raised an eyebrow. "Where are your shoes?"

Before she could answer he added, "Never mind. We have to get out of here fast."

As Tobin took her hand and turned, the click of a gun's hammer being pulled back stopped him.

Warren appeared from between the branches. "Not so fast, McMurray."

Tobin didn't move, but Liberty did. She rushed between the two men. "Don't, Sergeant! Don't shoot."

Warren didn't lower his rifle that now pointed straight at Liberty. "I'll not let him take you again, miss."

Anger flared as Liberty took a step forward, daring Warren to shoot. "He's . . ."

"Step away, Libby," Tobin's voice came from behind her.

"No," she said, without looking at Tobin. "I left the ranch that night to go to town and tell everyone you hadn't kidnapped me. I'm tired of the lies. One could get you killed."

"Step away, Libby." Tobin's voice bore an edge she'd never heard him use.

"No." She glared at Sergeant Warren. "If he shoots, he'll shoot me. This is all my fault. I'm the one who believed Samuel loved me."

Warren didn't lower the gun, but she saw sweat trickle down the side of his face. He was a good man, a fair man, a good soldier. Her only question hinged on which he was most, a man or a soldier.

She felt Tobin's hands circle her and pull her gently to the side, but she stared at Warren. "If you fire, kill us both because I'm leaving with Tobin, one way or the other."

"No," Tobin said as he moved in front of her. "I'm the one he has orders to kill."

Liberty twisted beneath his arm, wanting to be as close to

him as she could, wanting the warmth of him to blanket her. Tears bubbled in her eyes as she knew Warren's bullet would strike him at any moment. At this range, the sergeant could not miss.

She thought of begging for Tobin's life, but knew it would make no difference. If he reached for his gun, Warren would fire. If he ran the bullet would land in the center of his back.

Libby rose to her tiptoes and kissed him softly on the cheek thinking of all the times they'd touched.

Tobin faced his death in silence. He'd not beg or bargain.

To Liberty he whispered, "For the last time, stand clear, Libby."

The morning breeze seemed to hold its breath a moment as Tobin stared into cold gray eyes. Then, slowly, the sergeant lowered his rifle.

No one moved.

"He called you Libby," Warren said. "You told me only one person called you that."

A slow smile brushed over Warren's mouth before he straightened back into military attention. "I'll give you a few more minutes, Miss Liberty, and then I'll send a man with your boots."

The sergeant took a step backward. "He may have a little trouble finding you in these trees since I don't remember the exact spot where you were."

Liberty understood completely. "Thank you, Billy D."

"No need. Just doing my job of checking on you. I see you are all right." He turned to Tobin. "Take care of your Libby."

"I will," Tobin answered.

Then, as quietly as he appeared, Warren was gone.

Before Liberty could take a breath, Tobin tossed her over his shoulder. "We're not waiting around for the boots." He ran into the branches and splashed across the stream toward his horse.

Before Liberty could grasp what had just happened, they were riding through the stream and away from where the soldiers had camped last night. She leaned against his chest and tried to slow her heart.

"I don't know how long Warren can allow us, without looking like he had something to do with your escape," Tobin whispered, "so hold on. I'm going to make as much ground as I can."

She nodded knowing even though running through the stream wasn't as fast as on land, they had to get away without leaving any hint of a trail. The soldiers at the camp would have to spread out to look. Still, with only a few minutes' head start, escape would be hard.

"Where are we going?" she asked as the horse plowed through water.

"To the fort," Tobin said against her ear. "It's the only direction they won't search."

Liberty thought of arguing, but decided Tobin might be right. If the troops found no trail, they'd probably assume she went back. Warren wouldn't say a word about Tobin, so they'd think she was on foot.

They rode for two hours before Tobin climbed out of the stream and into a field of dried corn stacks. He asked for the ribbon from her braid and tied a brush to the tail of the horse. The weed swished away their tracks as he walked the horse into the field.

"I can walk too," she offered.

"Not without shoes. But lean forward over the horse's neck."

Tobin moved slowly, guiding the animal between the rows.

"Tobin," she whispered. "You didn't die."

He looked at her for the first time since they'd left. With his standing and her leaning down, they were at eye level. "The day's not over." He winked.

His mood surprised her. She'd never seen him like this. They were in more danger than she'd ever been in her life and yet she felt fully alive.

"Tobin," she whispered again. "How'd you get past the three men at the bridge waiting to shoot you?"

He smiled. "The Apache spotted them about noon. We'd

been ready to defend the ranch, but by then realized no army was coming. I had my pack ready to cross the hills and catch up with you, but the mare decided to deliver her colt so I lost an hour. I was still there when one of the Apache rode in to tell us what was going on at the bridge."

Liberty frowned. "You delayed your rescue of me to deliver a horse?"

Tobin shrugged. "Priorities."

She swung out toward him and almost toppled off the horse.

He gently shoved her back on and said, "Aren't you the one who told me not to follow you?"

Liberty frowned having a feeling she wouldn't win this argument. "Was the colt what you hoped for?"

Tobin smiled. "You should see him, Libby. Long legs and deep girth. Lean in the flank. He's born to run with the heart to never stop. He'll be the best horse ever bred for the rangers."

She knew he'd been working for years breeding and training horses, hoping for the perfect one. One day a ranger's life would depend on the speed and endurance of his horse, and Tobin planned to make sure the lawman rode a Mc-Murray mount.

"I couldn't believe the markings," Tobin continued. "Chestnut brown with black mane and stockings, just like I knew he'd be. Before we could wipe him down, he was bucking to run."

Libby studied the man walking beside her. "At what point did you remember me and all the trouble I was in?"

Tobin frowned. "I'm always thinking of you. Lord, you fill my every thought, Libby. I was even thinking of naming the horse Liberty."

This time Libby tumbled off the horse when she swung at him. Tobin caught her easily as he laughed. "Could you wait to kill me until after I've saved you?"

He kissed her soundly and lifted her back on the horse. His finger brushed her lips as he whispered, "We'll fight this out later."

She looked up and saw the guard tower of the fort. The dried corn stacks snapped beneath the hooves, but they moved slowly forward.

"We can't go in," she whispered. "Samuel is there."

Tobin shook his head. "No. I'm guessing the captain is out looking for you by now. Besides, we're not going into the fort. We're heading toward that barn."

Liberty studied the direction he pointed until she saw a shack about a hundred yards from the outside wall of the fort. It looked no different than a dozen others she'd seen. Freighters traveling from fort to fort often built such primitive structures for their rigs to stay in. The army might welcome their trade, but not necessarily their company for days. Men who drove the mule teams preferred to keep to themselves and not have to follow the army's rules. So they stayed close enough to feel protected by the fort guard but far enough away that the captain couldn't smell their liquor while they rested up before moving on.

Libby dreaded to think what a place inhabited by mules and drunks would smell like, but as they neared, the heavy gray clouds opened up, drenching them both.

"Great," she whispered.

"Isn't it," Tobin answered. "If this keeps up a few more minutes, no one will be able to find any sign of our trail." He untied the weed from his horse's tail. "You want your ribbon back?"

She glared at him.

Tobin shrugged, tucked it in his pocket and added, "I'll buy you another."

The rain blew so strong that Libby felt like they were wading through water by the time they reached the barn.

Tobin lifted her from the saddle and carried her to a dry spot. Then, without a word, he went back into the rain and walked the horse inside. In almost total darkness between the lightning strikes, he pulled the saddle and brushed down the animal with the saddle blanket.

Libby tried to see where she was in the flashes. The barn was long and leaked in several spots, making tiny indoor waterfalls. The barn floor was dirty, covered with trash and horse dung, but the loft in the back looked relatively clean. Hay had been stacked in one corner and it looked dry.

"Libby, you all right?"

She jumped when Tobin said her name. "Yes. Just cold."

"Don't move," he said. "Stretch your hands out so I can find you. Don't move."

She followed his order. A moment later his hand touched hers. He lifted her up and carried her to a crude ladder. "Can you make it to the loft?"

She gripped the rough-cut boards. "I think so."

"Good. Climb up and strip off those wet clothes."

A flash offered her a glimpse of where she was going. Libby climbed. Her stocking feet planted firmly on cold boards, she pulled off her blouse and skirt, then waited for another flash to show her where a rafter was so she could hang the wet garments.

By the time she heard Tobin climb the ladder, she'd stripped down to her undergarments and was shivering.

The thump of his saddle hitting the loft floor echoed across the barn. A few seconds later, Tobin wrapped his bedroll blanket around her. "It's wet on the corners, but I think my oil slicker kept it pretty dry."

Through shivering teeth she thanked him. "I guess a fire is out of the question."

"You guessed right." He laughed as if all this were great fun.

She heard him moving in the hay; then, in a flash of lightning, he reached for her hand and pulled her down on the wool inside lining of the slicker. She tumbled into the hay and into his arms.

As she shivered, he tucked her beneath his arm and pulled the blanket over them both. It took her a moment to realize that though she was wearing only a thin layer of silk, he was wearing nothing.

"Let's try to get warm," he whispered as he pushed her wet hair back and kissed her neck.

"I'm too cold," she said as she chattered.

He held her close as his hands moved over her back, gently caressing as he warmed. "Do you have any idea how hard it was to lay out in the grass only a few yards from you every night and not move in to share your bed?" His words whispered against her ear. "I thought I'd go mad, I wanted to touch you so badly. Once in a while I'd hear you say something and I'd grip the earth to keep from coming to you. Last night I swear I heard you whisper my name in your sleep."

Libby stopped shivering. "How long were you there?"

"Every night, from the first night. I told myself that as long as I knew you were safe, I'd wait for just the right time to take you so that no one would get killed." He moved his big hand over her hip. "But you have no idea how the thought of you so close tortured me."

She breathed deep of his scent and spread her hand over the warmth of his bare chest. The scar over his heart reminded her of the men who'd planned to kill him. "Tobin, what happened to the men hiding at the bridge?"

She felt his laugh more than heard it. "We let the Apache handle them. They asked if they could pester them and Teagen told them to have fun. If I were guessing, I'd say the first night the men would be bothered by spiders and ants. The Apache consider it a prank to dig up an ant bed at night and plant it beside someone sleeping. The soldiers probably woke up with ants crawling in their noses and ears."

Libby kissed his neck, loving the taste of him. "And the second night?"

Tobin leaned his head back and groaned. "Do we have to talk about this now?"

"No," she said as she licked the rain away from his throat. "What would you like to talk about?"

"I don't want to talk at all." His hand slid beneath the lace of her camisole and caressed her tender breast.

When his thumb crossed over her nipple, she sighed. "All right," she managed to whisper before his mouth found hers.

He rolled on top of her and pressed her into the soft bed of hay. She no longer felt the cold. Stretching, she let his body move over her cuddling her into him. He felt heavy and hard and oh so wonderful. The storm outside seem to drift away and there was only him and her in the world tonight.

When he finally ended the kiss, he rolled to his side and tugged at the ties of her undergarments until they fell away. Then he spread his hands over her, pushing his palms from her knees to her throat, feeling every inch of her.

She sighed again and began to move with his touch. He leaned, barely brushing her lips with his as his hand continued to burn across her flesh. As her body warmed and responded, his kiss deepened until all thought but the pleasure he offered vanished and she reached for him.

He gently shoved her hand away and continued exploring her body, touching every part while his kiss teased her mouth offering pleasure, then pulling away before she had her fill of the taste of him.

She reached for him again and again he shoved her hand away. Finally, he held her hands with one of his so that she couldn't touch him. He began to kiss his way down her body, taking his time first at her throat where he tasted her neck and then kissed each spot. Slowly as if he were working his way through a banquet, he moved to her breasts.

Here, he paused, enjoying every soft inch of her, moaning when she shifted shoving her breast further into his mouth. The tenderness she'd felt at his first touch vanished replaced by a need for his full attention.

When he moved lower, sliding his tongue down between her breasts until he reached her belly button, she arched her back, wanting to give him all he wanted, all he would take.

As he moved even lower, she cried out with need. "Please," she begged.

He shifted, whispering against her mouth. "Please what? Tell me what you want."

"Please love me," she answered, struggling to free her hand. "Please love me."

He let her go and leaned up. In the darkness she felt a longing for him even though she could still hear his breathing. She waited, the need for him so strong she thought she'd die if he didn't touch her soon.

His fingers slid feather light along her sides, then gripped her legs and tugged them apart. Slowly, he moved into her, letting his body settle over hers. A perfect match.

She arched wanting more of him, wanting him to move faster.

The rough whiskers of his week-old beard brushed her cheek as he whispered her name so softly she couldn't be sure she wasn't reading his mind. Then, slowly at first, he began to move, taking her with him on a journey to heaven.

She wrapped her arms around him and held to him as their bodies became one. All the world drifted away and they floated among the stars riding wave after wave of gentle delight until he shoved deep inside her and the stars exploded into a thousand tiny points of pleasure that rained over her.

Closing her eyes, she let the sensations float over her, then she drifted down still holding tightly to him. She felt as if she'd been waiting for this, for him all her life so that she could finally be complete. Even his breathing matched her own and though she was fully satisfied, she still reached to touch him.

When finally he rolled to his side, pulling her with him, she noticed tears drifting across her cheeks.

His thumb wiped a few warm tears away and he whispered, "Are you all right, Libby? I didn't hurt you, did I?"

"No." She couldn't help but smile. "Sometimes the happiness that I feel just leaks out."

He hugged her against him, pulled the blanket over them both and kissed her head. "I know how you feel."

"Good night," she whispered as she wiggled against him.

"I'll wake you in an hour if you're interested in a little more happiness."

She laughed softly. "All right."

And he did.

CHAPTER 28

Tobin woke with the first light and realized he'd slept without dreaming for the first time in years. Rain still tapped on the roof of the barn, blocking out all other sounds.

Libby slept soundly in his arms. She looked so beautiful he had trouble believing that he wasn't dreaming. He'd made love to her three times during the night. The second had been slow and sweet, the third time had been her idea. She'd advanced, wanting to touch him the way he'd touched her and he'd been defenseless to stop her.

Tobin smiled. This much lovemaking would probably kill him, but after years of celibacy he had some catching up to do. He moved his hand over her bare hip loving the fullness of it, the softness of it, and the way her flesh gave to his touch. She was a wonder he'd never get tired of exploring.

She didn't wake, so he slipped his fingers slowly up until he cupped her breast letting the nipple press against his palm. He'd touched her all night; even when they were both asleep, their bodies caressed each other. Her mouth looked puffy, a little swollen from his hundred kisses. Her throat had red marks on it where his beard had scratched her. Her thigh bore a slight bruise from where he'd pulled her to him wildly.

He wanted her again.

But he'd not wake her. They'd hardly slept at all and they had a long day ahead of them. If the rain kept up it might be wise to move on, but riding in the storm would be cold and she didn't have a coat or shoes. If they went into the fort, they would be spotted. If they ran, they might have to sleep out in the weather tonight with no fire or shelter.

He thought about how she didn't complain. She'd go if he said it was time. He knew she would. But riding double they couldn't move as fast. Once the rain stopped they'd be easy targets. If Captain Buchanan was smart, he probably had scouts out searching everywhere. The land would be muddy once the sun came out, and it would be almost impossible to travel without leaving sign.

Tobin leaned back and put his arm over his eyes, blocking out the sight of Libby's beautiful body beside him so he could think. Maybe they should stay here another day. Wait to see if the rain stopped. Wait to travel at night. He could probably go into the fort alone and blend in well enough with the trappers and farmers to collect food.

He drifted back to sleep to the sound of the rain.

It seemed only minutes when he felt Libby poking his side. "Tobin," she whispered. "Wake up. We've got company."

The rain still rattled and plopped from the roof, but Tobin heard the jingle of a rig beneath them. He tugged on his clothes and slid to the edge. Below him, halfway between the ladder and the door were an empty wagon and six mules. Tobin couldn't believe he'd slept through their entrance.

He smelled the mule skinner before he saw the man. A barrel-chested fellow with layers of animal skins pieced together for a coat. The skinner hadn't bothered to unhitch his rig before climbing in the wagon bed atop a crumpled tarp. With hair sticking out from all directions beneath his hat, it was impossible to guess his age, but there was no doubt the wagon driver had already drunk his limit for the night. He mumbled to himself as he downed the last of one bottle and looked for another.

Judging from the few words he used that were not obscenities, it appeared he'd unloaded his goods and been told that if he didn't take a bath he couldn't stay within the walls of the fort. After he'd bought his whisky, he'd told them all to go to hell and they'd apparently shoved him out the door.

Tobin watched as the man downed half the second bottle before drifting off to sleep. Once Tobin felt sure the skinner was out cold, he slipped down the ladder and checked the mules. They were strong and hardy but needed water and hay.

When he returned to the loft Libby, still cuddled in the blanket, whispered, "What are you doing?"

"Feeding the stock," he answered. "Get dressed."

He grinned when she made a face at him but followed directions.

By the time she climbed down the ladder, the animals were ready and the drunk had been tied in the back of the wagon so he wouldn't roll out in his sleep. Tobin loaded hay on both sides, making the wagon look full. He then covered the hay, his saddle, and the drunk with a tarp and laced it to the sides of the wagon. "He'll sleep for hours," Tobin whispered as he lifted Libby to the seat. "By then we'll be miles away."

"Do we have to bring him?"

"If we don't, we'd be stealing his wagon and mules. This way, we're just watching over him while he sleeps it off. Once he's awake, I'll offer him money to take us further. If he doesn't agree, we'll make it on one horse."

Libby frowned as if she saw a few holes in his plan, but she didn't say anything. He covered her with the blanket and then his oil slicker and drove the wagon out into the rain.

With the storm still active it was impossible to tell the time of day. He'd guess midmorning, but the sky bubbled in turmoil. The mules balked at the pace even if the wagon was nearly empty.

"Libby," he yelled so she could hear over the storm. "Slip beneath the tarp until we get out of sight of the fort."

"But he's back there."

Tobin laughed. "Trust me, with the amount he's had to drink, he won't be moving for hours. Plus, I put the saddle between you and him."

She held to his shoulder for balance and stepped over the seat. He felt the chill of her absence from his side immediately. Concentrating on keeping the mules moving, Tobin tried not to think of how much he'd miss her when she went back to her father. She'd needed him last night, she'd even begged him to make love to her, but she hadn't said a word about loving him and neither had mentioned believing they might have a future.

Shaking his head, he tried to tell himself it didn't matter. If she fell in love with him, she'd only end up with a broken heart. It was better this way. She'd never stay with him and he swore he'd never leave Whispering Mountain.

But he had, he thought. For once in his life he'd ridden across the hills without looking back at the ranch. He'd left to find her and she'd known he would. Even when she'd written for him not to follow, she'd known he'd come for her. When he had, she'd gone with him without asking a single question.

He could tell himself all they shared was a physical attraction. Two people who were well mated for one another in a basic way. He could tell himself that all day and night, but deep down Tobin knew it was more. Only he'd never ask and she'd never offer. What they had was enough. It had to be.

He waved at the guard in the corner tower as he rattled onto the main road. The guard waved back. In this rain it was impossible to see faces, and Tobin had forced himself to shove on the freighter's hat.

The wet leather reins cut into his hands as Tobin controlled the team, but he'd forgotten his gloves in his haste to find Libby a week ago. The cold rain kept the cuts numb.

The mules were poorly trained and the front two didn't seem to have any idea how to lead. Tobin trained teams of horses to respond with a nudge or tug on the reins; these animals needed a whip to keep moving. He worked with them more from reflex than any desire to train the team. By the time the rain had stopped and the fort had passed from sight, Tobin had managed to control the lead pair with just the sound of the whip.

He lifted the tarp to tell Libby that it was safe to climb back up in the seat, but she was curled up in a ball fast asleep. Tobin could hear the freighter snoring near the back of the wagon. Replacing the tarp so it covered Libby, he slowed the animals and decided to let her sleep a while. It was probably for the best anyway. If a scout saw the wagon with one driver, he'd ask fewer questions than if a woman rode on the seat.

It was almost dark when she woke up. Tobin stopped the wagon as soon as he heard her. While the team rested, Tobin broke into the drunk's stash of food. He must have picked up bread and cheese, along with boiled eggs at the fort. Libby ate as if she were starving.

"We're not stopping for the night," Tobin said as he handed her the last egg. "The land is flat for miles. We need to put as much distance between us and the fort as we can while the drunk sleeps. When he's awake and probably angry, he's likely to threaten to turn us in. I don't want to make it easy on him to find someone to tell."

"What about the mules?" Libby asked.

"They're used to it and the wagon isn't loaded down. I'll let them rest an hour, then we'll travel another four or five hours before we stop."

She agreed. "The first thing I plan to do when I get back is commandeer the mud room and take a two-hour bath."

"I might join you." He laughed. "But we'll have to tie up Martha first. I'm afraid she wouldn't consider it proper."

Libby laughed. "What could she do?"

"She'd tell Mrs. Dickerson on us." Then he told her all about the old schoolteacher's stopping the mob from town.

Libby had never heard him say so many words at once. She couldn't stop smiling.

When they climbed back on the wagon, he slipped his arm behind her almost shyly. After the night they'd spent together, she'd thought he'd be more comfortable with her. Then she realized how new all this must be to him.

Cuddling into his side, she talked of her life in Washington, wanting him to know all about her. Slowly, with description and brutal honesty, she introduced him to all her friends . . . people he'd never meet for real. The Martin sisters with cheeks as round as green apples and a mother who told everyone within three sentences of meeting that both girls were single. The Hoppers who never walked anywhere for fear someone would think they were strapped for money. Old man Davis who'd been her father's friend for fifty years and still couldn't remember her name when he came to dinner. She talked telling of all the others, wishing he could meet them.

When he didn't say anything, she told him of the places she liked to go. She described in detail how it felt to sit in the balcony and listen to Congress and how on the Fourth of July the entire town had a party. People danced in the streets and music seemed to come from everywhere. She told him of her morning walks where she stopped in at a little bakery for tea and scones just like the English have.

Finally, they fell into a comfortable silence, each lost in thought.

About the time the moon came out, Liberty whispered, "If I asked you to come—"

He stopped her with "If I asked you to stay?"

Neither answered the other's question.

An hour after midnight, the drunk in the back yelled, "When do we get to the hospital? I'm dying back here!"

Liberty laughed and Tobin stopped the wagon.

He walked around to the back and untied the drunk. "You're not dying," he said calmly.

Libby heard the drunk tumble out of the wagon and run for the trees. "What's he doing?" she whispered.

"Don't ask," Tobin answered.

"Oh." She was thankful Tobin couldn't see her blush. "Do you think he's coming back?"

"I'm afraid so."

Before Tobin could say more, the drunk stumbled out of the trees. "Water," he yelled. "I'm dying for a drink."

"He's got more lives than a cat," Tobin mumbled to Libby as he fished an old canteen out from under the seat.

The freighter downed it all and burped. "What the hell is going on?"

Before Tobin could tell the truth, Libby lied. "We're saving your life, and I'll thank you not to swear around me."

The drunk looked confused. "What happened?"

He scratched his head and Libby swore she could see fleas jumping free even in the moonlight.

"Whatever it was, I ain't responsible. When I get a little too much, I sometimes do things. It ain't nobody's fault but the bottle."

Libby played along. "That's what I told the captain, but he said you could cool off in the stockade for a month. Lucky for you we were leaving and offered to drive your team out or you'd be in jail right now."

"I don't remember nothing," he challenged.

"Do you usually?"

"Nope," he finally admitted and turned to Tobin. "I guess I owe you folks a debt."

"You're welcome." Tobin glanced at Libby, obviously not as comfortable with lying as she was. "If you'll let us ride along with you for a spell, we'll call it even."

The drunk nodded.

"I'll take care of the mules if you'll start a fire," Tobin said to the man as he helped Libby down.

The drunk remembered his manners and made a slight bow to Liberty. "Nice to meet you, missus. I'm Hoot Brown. How long you and your man been married?"

"A month," Libby lied again as quickly as she had the first time. "He kind of rode in and swept me off my feet."

Hoot grinned, but no teeth showed in the moonlight. "I did that once, but the gal didn't take to the idea for marriage when I got her home."

Libby had no trouble guessing why. She reminded herself to stay upwind from the man.

The damp grass was cold as she walked in her stocking feet, but she didn't mention her lack of boots and Hoot didn't seem to notice. When Tobin came back he'd refilled both canteens. She reached for Tobin's, knowing she'd die of thirst before she'd drink from Hoot's.

Hoot built a fire and offered them the wagon, claiming he preferred the ground to sleep on. He didn't ask about his food, just finished off the bottom few inches of his whisky bottle and curled up near the fire.

Tobin didn't say anything until they heard him snore. He helped her in the wagon, then slid in beside her. With the hay stacked up, they had a small amount of privacy.

"I'd like to make love to you," he whispered. "But . . ."

"I know," she answered. The idea that Hoot might wander around the wagon and see them made her shiver. "Maybe we'd better just sleep tonight."

She lay her hand on his chest and he covered her fingers with his.

Just after dawn when Hoot awoke, his mood was dark. He mumbled, swearing at the mules and claiming Tobin had fed them far too much. "They'll be fat and lazy for a week."

As he kicked out the fire, he complained about the cold and the mud and the blasted hay someone had put in his wagon. Though he admitted to being a mean drunk, sober he seemed little improved.

Libby made a point of staying close to Tobin and wasn't surprised when he saddled his horse and bid the drunk goodbye.

Hoot seemed surprised but was obviously a man who enjoyed being alone. He waved them off, claiming they'd taken him a day out of his way.

Tobin lifted Libby up on the horse. "We'd better be miles away before he figures out we ate most of his food."

"What will he do?" she whispered afraid Hoot might turn around and decide to follow them.

"Eat one of his fat mules," Tobin answered.

Tobin turned into the trees following no path that she could see.

"Where are we headed?"

"We'll cross into the hills and come out north of Elmo's Trading Post. We can make better time this way, and the soldiers never ride through here."

"Why not?"

"Because it's my grandfather's hunting grounds."

CHAPTER 29

Libby wasn't sure what she expected. She knew she'd be safe with Tobin, but having him tell her he was half Indian and seeing him ride into an Apache camp like an old friend was something else. A few people turned to watch, or gathered closer in curiosity, but for the most part they simply raised a hand in welcome and went on about their work.

"Stay on the horse," he whispered against her ear a moment before he slid down. She watched him move into a group of people casually surveying her.

Liberty had been around foreign diplomats most of her life. She'd been able to speak French and Italian before ten. Listening to people talk in languages she didn't understand was nothing new to her, but Tobin crossed into another culture without hesitation. And, more surprising, they accepted him.

He talked with a brave who looked about his age, then nodded and returned to her.

"My grandfather is north of here hunting." Tobin touched her leg as he spoke calmly. If he'd done so on the streets of Washington, people would have stared and frowned their disapproval. Here, no one seemed to notice.

"Will your grandfather come back to camp to see you?" Libby saw women whisper as they pointed at Libby's bare feet.

"No." Tobin turned his horse. "He'll expect us to come to him."

A girl of about twelve stepped forward and offered them each an apple. Tobin thanked her with a slight bow. When Libby said thank you, the girl laughed and ran away.

Liberty leaned closer to him and whispered though she doubted anyone could understand her words. "Do you know all these people?"

"No." He laughed. "Only a few. Grandfather sends young braves to check on us now and then. And while he's at his winter camp, we're welcome to visit, but never for the night." Tobin winked at her. "The old chief thinks we might steal his granddaughters the way our father stole his daughter. He sees us as white, and though we're also of his blood, he looks over us more like he's watching an experiment than a relative."

Tobin swung up behind her. "Over the years I've figured out that Grandfather knows most of what goes on around these parts. He'd never help us fight, but he might send his braves to make sure the fight was fair."

"You love him, don't you?"

Tobin shook his head. "I respect him. He sent his daughter to the mission all those years ago because he knew the world was changing. There was a time, after my mother died, that he could have come onto Whispering Mountain and brought us here. He was our only relative. We might have gone with him too, but while we were still boys he let us stand as men."

Tobin waved and turned his horse toward the hills.

Libby asked questions filling in the details of Tobin's life. She couldn't believe, when she'd first met him, she'd thought his life must be boring, staying on a lonely ranch raising horses.

They even talked of the day he'd been shot when he was six. The bullet must have brushed past his heart. One hair closer and he would have been dead.

Finally, he asked, "Does it bother you that I'm a—"

"A half-breed?" she finished his sentence.

"Yeah, a half-breed."

Libby smiled and twisted so that he could see her eyes when she said, "I don't like that word. It seems to me you should be a double-breed, because you are a little of both."

A slow smile spread across his face as he leaned and kissed her. His lips were gentle as if he were promising something.

Libby twisted trying to get closer, wanting more.

Tobin laughed and led the horse up a hill several yards to where trees grew thicker. "We'd better rest here for a while," he murmured as he pulled her off the saddle and into his arms. "The horse looks tired."

Laughing, Libby wrapped her arms around his neck as he carried her beneath the shadow of a willow. He set her on her feet in the yellowed winter grass and walked back to the horse.

A moment later, he tossed her his bedroll. "Get undressed," he ordered. "I'll stake the horse so he can graze."

Liberty stood, holding the bedroll under one arm. She wanted nothing more than a chance to make love to Tobin, but she'd not disrobe on command.

After a few minutes, he glanced back and noticed her standing exactly where he'd left her.

At first he looked confused; then he straightened and started toward her. "I said, get undressed. We don't have much time."

She folded her arms. "I don't remember joining your army."

He crossed to within two feet of her and tugged the blanket from beneath her arm. "I plan to make love to you, Libby," he said as he spread the blanket over the dried grass. "And you want it too, so why the hesitation?"

"Maybe I want it," she admitted. "Maybe not. Maybe I've grown bored with you."

His hand rose slowly and slid beneath her jacket. Warm fingers brushed over her blouse feeling the fullness of her breasts through the thin layer of cotton and silk. She couldn't help but close her eyes and enjoy his touch.

"You want it too," he voiced the fact. "You've been brushing against me and cuddling into me since we rode away from old Hoot this morning. You could never lie to me about how you feel."

Refusing to acknowledge his comment, she took a deep breath as he removed her jacket. His hands caressed her so gently she ached for more. When she didn't say anything, he began unbuttoning her blouse. "I want to see you. I love making love at night, but I need to see what I touch. I need to see you."

She'd thought to hesitate, to play a game of being courted, but her body already longed for his so strongly she couldn't think.

He opened her blouse, letting his hand cover her breast as he whispered, "Come to me, Libby, with no games or teasing. Come to me and I promise I'll give you what you want."

He knelt and unbuttoned her skirt. When he captured one breast in his mouth, her knees buckled and she tumbled into his arms. She knew there would be no games, no promises to later break. There would only be him and her, and the endless attraction that had drawn them together from that first night.

He spread her out on the blanket and studied her while he stripped off his clothes. When he knelt over her, she could see the hunger in his eyes and knew it reflected in her own.

When his gaze moved down her body, she opened her legs. He spread his hand over her most private place to make sure she was ready, then entered her. They stared into each other's eyes as he pushed deeper and deeper. She could see passion and need building in the depths of his blue gaze. He was allowing her to see openly what she did to him . . . how much he wanted her . . . how dearly he needed her. The knowledge took her breath away more than any kiss or touch could have.

Finally, she moaned and leaned her head back as pleasure rocked her body. He lowered over her, covering her, warming her as he made love. The afternoon light, the birds, the wind in the trees, all drifted away as she came alive beneath his warm body. Slowly, she realized he wasn't taking his pleasure, but pleasing her. He stoked a fire deep inside her that spread along her body making every part of her warm and vibrant.

She let him set the pace rising to meet him, but not pulling him to her. As their dance continued, she rose higher in the flames that consumed her.

This time when the stars exploded and she rocked with pure joy, she cried out his name. He slowed his movements letting her circle in the fire a moment longer. Then, as she knew he would, he held her as she drifted back to earth.

"Thank you," she whispered as he wiped a tear from her cheek. "That was . . . that was unbelievable."

He kissed her softly. "Oh, we're not finished yet, my Libby. We're not near finished."

She felt like clay in his hands, unable to move on her own yet responding to his every touch. At first he held her tightly to him, moving his hands down her back until his fingers gripped her hips, then he gently shoved her back atop the blanket.

He moved down her body, kissing, holding, tasting her flesh still warm from his lovemaking. She stretched, letting him take his pleasure. She drifted with him enjoying the way he knew her body and the way he loved touching her. When his kiss returned to her mouth, she opened, letting him taste deeply while he slowly entered her.

About the time she smiled at the knowledge that she was pleasing him, a flame started once more in her belly, burning wild over nerves already alive and raw with feeling. The blaze grew hot, driving her toward heaven once more when she hadn't caught her breath from the last journey. He shoved so hard and fast into her that she pulled her mouth from his kiss, gulping for air as a passion unlike she'd ever known consumed her.

This time he was taking his pleasure and she gave willingly.

When she dug her nails into his back, pulling him to her, Tobin covered her mouth with his hand and pushed deep one last time.

Vaguely, she felt him climax as lava ran through her veins. She jerked with the pleasure, once, twice, three times, and then he pulled her to him and held her as she rocked with ecstasy unable to stop her body from trembling.

Drifting back down from the stars, he kissed her long and tenderly as his hands moved over her, branding every part of her forever.

She was his now, she thought, completely. She'd given all that was hers to him and taken all of him in return. Whatever he wanted of her was his for the taking and she knew he'd never deny her.

When he finally broke the kiss, she cuddled against him and cried.

"Libby," he whispered, moving her damp hair away from her face. "Are you all right?"

She nodded against his chest.

He tugged her face up so he could see her.

"I never thought it could be like that." She shoved a tear away. "So completely consuming."

He pulled her close. "Neither did I."

They were silent as their hearts calmed back to a normal beat, then he whispered, "Watching you go will be the hardest thing I'll ever do in my life."

Libby felt his words ice across her heart, but she didn't move. They'd made no promises. He'd said from the first that he'd never marry or leave Whispering Mountain. She'd told him a hundred times how she couldn't wait to get back to Washington and her life. What they'd done had been out of need and wanting, not love. Neither had ever mentioned love, not once.

Libby's heart cried silently. Then why did his words hurt so much?

CHAPTER 30

TOBIN WATCHED LIBBY DRESS AND WISHED HE KNEW the right words to say. How does a man tell a woman that he'd rather make love to her than breathe? He'd told her she was beautiful. He'd said he wanted her, he needed her, but somehow his words were not enough for his Libby.

His Libby. Tobin laughed. She would be mad if she knew he even thought of her that way. Each day since she left her father's house, she'd grown more independent. She'd made plans to set up her own house in the capital city. She'd even spent an hour one afternoon telling him all the things a lady could attend alone or with a group of friends. Plays, concerts, even parties. All of which Tobin knew nothing about.

He spent most of his time when near her doing what he'd done today. He thought of how it would be when he had her alone long enough to make love to her. Their time beneath the willow had been perfect. At first, she'd reacted like he knew she would, hungry and passionate, but somewhere something had changed. What they'd done was far more than satisfying a need for each other.

What they'd done was a mating, not only of bodies, but

of souls. He would remember every detail of their time together, from the first sight of her until the moment his heart stopped beating when she finally left. He knew that no matter how many lovers she took in Washington, it would be his name she called when she reached her satisfaction. And every night, when he fell asleep, it would be her body he reached for, if only in his dreams.

"I'm ready," she said as she folded the blanket and handed it to him as politely as if they'd been on a picnic.

Their eyes met and stared as if each were looking at the other for the first time.

"Did you have something you wanted to tell me?"

He thought of a hundred things he needed to say to her, but they'd set the rules between them that first night when they had shared a cup of coffee and her blanket. Neither spoke of what was between them. Neither mentioned a future that couldn't be.

"No," he said, wishing he could break the rule.

He couldn't help but think that her smile looked somehow sad. Maybe she didn't want this time to end anymore than he did. Each time they touched, each day that passed made one less they'd have together. Or maybe she was afraid he'd mess everything up between them by wanting more.

They walked to the horse without touching, but their steps matched as if they'd walked hundreds of miles side by side. He helped her up, then moved his hand slowly down her hip and leg allowing the feel of her to seep into his senses one more time.

She didn't respond. In fact, she looked away. Maybe she was embarrassed at his boldness now no shadows covered them? Their love seemed bordered by darkness and secrecy.

He wished they had days to talk so that he could understand this woman who changed so quickly, but it would be dark in an hour and he had to reach his grandfather's hunting camp before then. Visitors were not greeted warmly once the sun set.

He told himself he'd talk to her tonight when the moon was full and she lay in his arms. Only he knew he probably wouldn't. Tobin had spent his life not talking. He lived in a world where action, not feelings mattered.

He smiled. Maybe he'd show her tonight that he was willing to give it a try. He could change. He might even agree to meet her in Austin when she visited. If she were willing?

When he swung up in the saddle, he pulled her close against his chest and, as she always did, she molded into him. A perfect fit.

They rode in silence as he watched the signs his grandfather had taught him. No other settler would find the hunting camp, but to Tobin the direction was clear.

As the sun touched the horizon he rode into the Apache's winter camp. Only a few deer hides tanned by the fires told Tobin it was early in the hunt. Several women moved about tending cooking pots and preparing strips of meat that would feed the tribe all winter. The women who traveled with the hunting party were usually young, hard workers. Older women and those with children stayed at the main camp.

At this site all the men stepped out to watch him. This was not a place for visitors, even the chief's blue-eyed grandson.

Tobin knew one of the boys in the lower camp had probably ridden up to let them know he was coming. When his grandfather walked out of one of the tepees, Tobin saw no surprise in the old man's eyes.

"Is that him?" Libby whispered.

Tobin tried to see his grandfather through her eyes. The chief was tall and still built straight and strong even though his hair was completely white. His face was weathered into a thousand wrinkles by the wind and sun, and his eyes were black and alert, always reminding Tobin of a wolf.

Tobin slipped from the horse and walked up to his grandfather without speaking or even looking at the men standing around. It would have been an insult to his grandfather if he spoke to one of the men before he greeted their chief.

The old man smiled and spoke in his native tongue. "I knew you would come, grandson. Our winter camp is the shortest way back to your land."

Tobin answered him in kind not bothering to ask how his grandfather knew he was traveling. "You are wise. I thank you for the guards you sent to watch our bridge. Thanks to them no one will cross onto our land without warning."

"No white man," his grandfather corrected.

Tobin agreed. The Apache rarely visited, but they knew the back trail through the hills. He remembered once he asked his grandfather how the Apache knew his father's secret path and the old man asked him how he thought Andrew McMurray first learned the way.

When Grandfather lifted his head and looked at Liberty, Tobin knew introductions were in order.

"Libby," he said calmly. "Will you come meet my grandfather?" He hoped she wouldn't refuse. It would have looked bad for him to help her down or carry her. She might think she needed shoes to walk, but those around her wouldn't.

"All right." She slipped off the horse and followed his lead by walking past the men without looking at them until she raised her head to greet the chief.

As if she were at a formal ceremony, she bowed. "Will you tell him I am honored to meet him?"

Tobin hesitated. He knew his grandfather had understood every word, but the old man stood staring at Libby and waiting. Tobin translated her words.

Grandfather answered in Apache. "Is this the woman you kidnapped away from her people? Couldn't you find one a little fatter to warm your tepee?"

Tobin frowned. He never knew if his grandfather was teasing or serious.

Grandfather smiled. "Tell her she is welcome here."

Tobin translated.

Libby returned the chief's smile. "Thank you."

Grandfather then asked Tobin. "Why didn't you take one who had mocassins? Are white women so hard to find that are fully dressed?"

Tobin grinned. "I'll try to think of that next time, but she's not an easy woman to keep shoes on."

"Do you plan to keep her as your woman?" The chief's eyes studied them both and Tobin knew he missed little.

"No," Tobin answered, glad Libby couldn't understand what they were saying. One blush from her, and Grandfather would change his direction in questioning.

"Why not? Is something wrong with her besides having no shoes and being too thin? Is she damaged?" His black eyes looked from her feet to her head as if looking for broken bones.

"No," Tobin answered. "She does not wish to marry."

"Oh." Grandfather nodded and looked back at her. "She chooses to walk alone. She's crazy, I think."

Tobin wasn't sure what his grandfather meant, but he didn't want to go into more detail.

"What did he say?" Libby asked when the old man turned to one of the women by his side.

"He says you're a very fine woman." Tobin didn't miss the slight lift of his grandfather's eyebrow at the lie, but the chief did not correct his grandson's translation.

Tobin took a few minutes to introduce Libby to all the men he knew. For the most part, the braves weren't very interested in meeting her. Libby would probably be hurt if she knew just how plain and washed out most Apache thought white women were.

He wasn't surprised when a girl a few years younger than Libby invited her to sit with the women for the evening meal.

Libby didn't look too sure about going, but Tobin promised her it would be all right. "The women sit close to the cooking fires," he encouraged. "You'll be warmer. It gets really cold this high up after dark."

Though he joined the men, Tobin sat so that he could see Libby. As they ate and talked he found himself feeling a great deal of pride for her. Libby might not be able to speak a word, but she managed to help with the meal and show her appreciation for everything passed for her to eat. He also guessed she had no idea what she was eating and he decided that was probably best.

The women touched her clothes and one even rebraided her hair. By the end of the meal he heard her laughter blend with the other women's and knew that somehow she'd won them over.

His grandfather talked of the hunting and how the white man was slowly changing the land. As the night aged, he talked of Tobin's mother. She'd been his oldest daughter and he'd loved her dearly. He said that when she married Andrew McMurray he rode for three days and three nights without sleep to kill this man who claimed his daughter. But when he saw them together, he saw the way Andrew looked at her and the way she looked at him. And he knew it was too late. If he had killed Andrew, he would have snuffed out the light in his daughter's eyes.

Tobin had heard the story many times but he never tired of it. Somehow it took away a little of the pain of his mother's dying young. It helped to know that she was loved.

When he stood to go collect Libby, a wrinkled hand stopped him.

"We must go," Tobin said, knowing his grandfather never asked any of the McMurrays to stay the night. "We'll camp farther down the hill tonight and be riding toward the ranch by dawn."

"No Shoes stays with the women tonight." There was no room for argument in his grandfather's tone.

"I'll go tell her. Thank you for the offer." Tobin didn't want to stay. He wanted to sleep with Libby alone beneath the stars. But he also didn't want to offend his grandfather.

"I will tell her." Grandfather grinned to himself. "It is time she knows I understand her." As he walked off toward the women, he whispered just loud enough for Tobin to hear, "Can't trust translators."

With that he left Tobin with the men and walked to the campfire of the women.

Tobin could do nothing but watch as the chief took Libby by the hand.

She stood.

He couldn't hear what his grandfather said, but Libby

nodded, glanced in Tobin's direction, then turned and left with the women.

Tobin had never spent a more miserable night. He'd been offered a bed in the tent, but he chose to sleep outside, wanting to keep an eye on where Libby had gone. For about an hour after the men settled down, he heard the women talking and once he thought he heard Libby's laugh.

It was almost dawn by the time he dozed off. He awoke to find everyone in camp moving around him as if he were a snoring rock that had fallen in their way overnight. He looked around and caught no sight of Libby, so he stumbled off to a nearby stream to clean up.

Stripping off his shirt, he dunked his head in the cold water, then splashed water on his chest. The shock woke him but didn't improve his mood.

Scrubbing at his beard and wishing he had a razor, he turned and saw three women staring at him, giggling. One was Libby.

"What are they saying, Tobin?" she demanded.

He groaned but decided not to lie. "They're saying it's no wonder you won't have me, I'm hairy as a bear."

Libby laughed and nodded her agreement to both women.

They all three bumped heads in another round of giggling. One of the women reached out and almost touched him, then jumped back laughing.

"Glad you're having fun," he snapped.

"Oh, great fun. I slept on a warm, soft bed and I've already learned a dozen words. And look." She lifted the hem of her split riding skirt.

"Moccasins," he shouted. "Don't tell me the princess of Washington, D.C., is wearing moccasins."

She pouted. "They're very comfortable and warm all the way to my knees."

"Let me see," he teased.

She lowered her skirt. "I don't think that would be proper. I'll have to ask your grandfather first. He said he'd watch over me as if he were my father since mine is not around. We've already had a long talk this morning."

"What does my grandfather have to do with us?" Tobin decided coming here had been a mistake. She was safe, but away from him.

Libby wiggled her eyebrows. "He said he's heard my father is a great chief and I should be treated with proper kindness, so he's made arrangements for men to accompany us back to within sight of Whispering Mountain."

"That's not necessary." She'd been away from his arms for one night and he already ached for her. The idea of having braves with them for the next three or four days didn't work into his plan.

"I insist." His grandfather stepped into the clearing. "You can't keep up with her shoes, grandson. What if next time you lose the whole woman?"

Tobin swore he saw the old man smile a second before he drew himself up to his full height and announced. "I will send men."

There was no argument. Before the sun was high enough to offer any warmth, they were riding out of the hunting camp with three braves. And worse, Tobin decided, Libby had been given her own horse for the journey.

He tried to tell himself his grandfather had only been thinking of her safety, but a tiny part of him decided the old man was simply meddling.

Tobin took a look at Libby. She looked rested and happy and more beautiful than ever, even though she did look thinner, which worried him. He, on the other hand, felt like he might very well be turning into the bear the women accused him of looking like. Seeing her and not being able to be close enough to touch her was pure hell.

His mood didn't lighten that night when he realized one of the guards planned to stay awake all night to watch over the camp. Tobin managed to sleep, but when he did he dreamed of making love to Libby and awoke feeling lonelier than ever.

On the fourth night, they camped within five hours' ride of his land. He wanted to push on through the night, but Libby looked tired and the food they'd eaten on the trail hadn't agreed with her. She never complained, but she wasn't used to living off the land and it was starting to show in the paleness of her skin and the dark circles beneath her eyes. Every morning he insisted she eat something and before they'd gone a mile she had to stop to throw up.

Tobin decided to send one of the braves to Whispering Mountain to let his brothers and Sage know they were near. He also knew either Travis or Teagen would ride through the hidden pass and meet them at dawn. Once he had Libby home, he'd know she was safe and maybe she'd rest. She looked like she needed a warm bed and a few hot meals. With each day on the trail she'd grown quieter, showing less and less interest in her surroundings or in him for that matter. He'd tried to talk to her a few times and she'd simply told him she was tired.

He wasn't surprised at dawn when both Teagen and Travis rode into their campsite.

"Is she all right?" Travis asked the minute he saw Libby.

Tobin resented his brother's comment. "Of course she's all right, but she's a lady who's been through a lot these past weeks. We need to get her home."

"No," Teagen interrupted. "We're taking her straight to town. Her father's there taking up every room finished in the hotel. He figured you'd be back with her."

Libby smiled. "My father is safe."

"Safe and wanting to see his daughter. He's wearing the grass out to the bridge by sending a man every few hours to see if you're back."

"Is he still in danger?"

Travis shook his head. "Right now I'd say whoever tried to ambush him that night between his place and town is the one who is in trouble. The senator never looked better and half the lawmen in Texas are trying to track down the band of outlaws." Travis turned to Tobin. "I got word from Wes. He said thanks to a marking he found near the road that looked a lot like something I would have left, they found where the outlaws camped."

A bit of color came into her face as she smiled. "It's

over." She combed her fingers through her hair and tied it back with a scrap of string. "I'm ready, gentlemen. We must not keep the senator waiting."

Tobin helped her up on her horse, but her thank you was formal, not personal. The princess was back. For a moment he thought maybe it was hard on her to see him and not touch him. It was hell on him not to touch her. But if his distance bothered her, she was doing a great job of concealing the fact.

The Apache took their leave and the brothers surrounded her as they rode toward town. Tobin had a sickening feeling that his world was about to come to an end. All he wanted to do was hold Libby, maybe spend one more night with her so he would have another memory to carry for the rest of his life. The closer they got to town, the more unlikely that possibility seemed.

The senator rushed out the hotel door before Tobin could help Libby down from her horse. He must have been watching from the window upstairs.

"Liberty," he yelled as he stormed down the steps and held out his arms to his little girl.

Libby screamed and jumped into his embrace, crying and laughing at the same time.

The senator held her close as he also laughed and cried, not caring that he stood in front of a dozen men.

Tobin felt like his heart was being pulled out of his chest. She didn't look at him as her father almost carried her into the hotel.

At the door he turned to the McMurrays. "Come in and have some dinner, boys. I'll get my little girl up to her room so she can rest and clean up, then I want to know everything that's happened." He looked directly at Tobin. "I'll want a report."

Tobin wanted to yell that the senator's little girl was a woman—his woman—but he didn't have the right. He'd never told her she was his. He'd never told her how he felt. And now. Now it was too late.

CHAPTER 31

LIBERTY ALLOWED THE HOTEL MAID TO HELP HER undress, then lay on the bed curled up in her own warm robe until the maid, a girl of about fifteen, said her bath was ready. The room smelled of fresh-cut wood and looked plain and newborn. Her father had brought her trunk filled with all her things. Her soaps and silks and shoes. All of which she realized she should have missed, but somehow hadn't.

"You've got some mighty fine things," the girl said as she poured bath oil into steaming water. "Those combs for your hair are the prettiest I've ever seen."

"Thank you," Liberty whispered, thinking she'd wear the ribbon Tobin gave her instead if she could, and none of the shoes were as comfortable as the moccasins.

She relaxed in the bath, washing every inch of her body several times. Her father had insisted on the best for her, even in this primitive town. She leaned back in the water and let the girl wash her hair. When the bath grew cold, Liberty slipped into fresh undergarments and wrapped back into her robe. She sat by the tiny fire, letting her hair dry and thinking of her weeks with Tobin.

The maid was either too shy or too kind to talk. She moved around Liberty, making sure everything was just right. Without asking, she poured tea and left it next to a plate of biscuits and jam.

Liberty closed her eyes, and when she opened them she was alone. Truly alone for the first time in over a month. Drinking her tea, she thought of all she'd learned, about this part of the country and about herself. It seemed more a dream than real. She felt she'd lived an adventure like a heroine in a book and now it was time to go back to the real world.

Tobin had been her lover. He'd taught her to be a woman. And he'd demanded nothing of her. She thought of how little they'd talked and how completely they'd loved. In a few days she'd return to her world where everyone talked and talked yet it seemed no one loved.

A tap sounded at her door. Liberty made sure her robe was completely closed before saying, "Come in."

She'd expected her father, but a pale old gentlemen with a square bag entered. He seemed to lead with his good leg and almost drag the other behind him, but he had a warm smile and kind eyes behind glasses that set low across his nose.

"I'm Dr. Nevad," he said politely. "I've been taking care of your father's injury."

"My father was injured? When? How?" Liberty had been so anxious to get to a bath and clean clothes she'd missed the fact that her father may have been hurt.

"The night you were kidnapped, miss. He didn't want anyone to know. Thought it might make him seem weak. He took a bullet in the muscle of his left arm. It bled a might, but I kept it clean and wrapped tight." The doctor set his bag down on the table that held her tea. "He asked me to travel with him and I agreed." The doctor laughed. "We've been on a merry chase, first looking for outlaws and then riding to find you."

Liberty thought of telling the doctor her father only had two speeds, asleep and full gallop. Even in Washington, when he was dealing with nothing but budget cuts, he stormed and raged through his days. "How is he now?" she asked, needing an answer.

The kind doctor seemed to understand and sobered immediately. "He really hasn't needed me for days, but when he said he was coming this way and would be bringing a carriage for you, I came along. I wanted to see how the place was growing. Haven't been here for a few years. Used to make my rounds this far north."

Liberty straightened, only hearing part of what he said. "How is the senator's wound?"

"Good, miss. The bleeding stopped within twenty-four hours and I've seen no sign of infection. He's right as rain now that you are safe. He was truly worried about you, miss, what with men out to kill him."

"I wasn't kidnapped." Liberty swore she would stop this lie once and for all.

"I know." The doctor winked. "All of us with the senator knew just from the way he talked about Tobin. He never said much. We knew you were in danger but not from a McMurray. Some even think you might have eloped that night you ran. From what I've heard he's a fine man."

She ignored his prying remark, having learned years ago to make no comment where gossip was concerned. "I'm glad my father is better. Thank you for taking such good care of him." She looked at the man guessing there was more or he would have picked up his bag. "What else, Dr. Nevad?"

"The senator wishes me to check with you, miss, to see that you have no injuries." He opened his bag. "I brought an examining gown."

Liberty smiled. She'd always thought the boxy gowns were ridiculous. It wasn't considered proper for a lady to reveal too much of her skin even to a doctor, so she was expected to put on a gown that covered her from head to toe and only allow him to open a tiny spot at a time.

"How long have you been a doctor?"

"Thirty years, miss. Until my wife died five years ago, I had a practice in New Orleans. After she was gone, I took mostly traveling jobs, not wanting anyplace to go home alone to."

He has such kind eyes, she thought. The kind of eyes that see both too much joy and sadness.

"Will you please have a seat, Doctor?" She poured him a cup as he pulled up a chair. "I'd like it very much if you'd have tea with me before we begin."

His knowing eyes agreed even before he spoke.

For a few minutes they drank their tea in silence. Finally, he leaned forward. "Miss Liberty, what you say to me will go no further than this room. If you were hurt in any way and do not want your father to know, I will respect your privacy." He frowned. "Do you understand?"

Liberty nodded. The doctor probably thought she'd been mistreated and guessed quite rightly that her father would go into a rage if he knew anyone had laid a hand on her.

"Now, Miss Liberty, did you suffer any injury during your ordeal?"

She shook her head. "The night Tobin McMurray rescued me, Captain Buchanan slapped me almost senseless, then he claimed I grew clumsy and fell. Though I can't prove it, he shoved me twice. Once into a chair and once almost knocking me down the stairs."

The doctor nodded. "Were you hurt or bruised in the attack?"

She undid her robe and lifted her camisole a few inches so he could see her ribs. The dark blue bruise had faded to brown and almost disappeared.

"May I?" he asked as he leaned closer.

Liberty's cheeks heated, but she nodded.

"Tobin wrapped my ribs for me the first few days and slowly the ache went away." She laughed suddenly. "We were riding so hard the pain may have just blended with all the other aches."

The doctor nodded and leaned back in his chair. "Any other injuries?"

She shook her head.

"Now, dear, tell me how you feel over all." It seemed it was his turn to grow red. "Is everything timely with you? Sometimes when a woman is under great fear or stress, her body suffers. I can give you something to ease your nerves if you feel you need it."

Liberty understood. "I hadn't thought about it, but my monthly time hasn't come and I'm usually quite regular." She decided to add her other complaint of late. "I've had trouble keeping food down."

The doctor raised an eyebrow. "Is there another attack you wish to tell me about, my dear?"

"No," she said, confused that he'd think her trouble with food would have anything to do with an attack.

He looked even more uncomfortable. "Are you tender here?" He touched his chest.

Liberty couldn't believe he'd asked, or guessed, but she didn't lie. "Yes, I am."

He looked at his hands. "May I be frank, Miss Liberty?"

"Please," she encouraged.

"Have you been with a man? If not through an attack, then of your own will."

Liberty straightened. For a moment she almost lied. After all it was no one's business but hers and Tobin's. But she couldn't bring herself to be ashamed of what they'd done. She couldn't lie. "Yes. But it was not an attack."

The doctor nodded as if he finally understood. "I'll not tell your father," he promised, "but you must sometime in the near future. Young lady, unless I'm very wrong, you are with child. It's very early yet so you have time to think of what you wish to do."

Liberty stared at him. She'd known, in the back of her mind, that it might be possible, but it had taken her mother four years to conceive. She didn't think pregnancy could come so quickly. Growing up, she'd had no one to ask such questions, so she'd just assumed.

They sat in silence for a while. He finished his tea then walked to the window allowing her time to think.

Finally, Liberty lifted her head. "Doctor, do you know where my father is?"

"When I came up he was sitting on the porch with the McMurrays and a few rangers. Now that you are safe, he plans to get the bottom of who tried to kill him that night in the carriage. Since a ranger was killed, every lawman in the state wants to help him. Word came in two days ago that one of the outlaws who fired on the carriage has been caught. He'd been injured when they attacked, and apparently the others left him behind. Unless I miss my guess, I bet your father will want to head to Austin as soon as he knows you're well enough to travel."

"I can leave tomorrow morning."

"But—"

"Pregnancy is not an illness, I believe. Please tell my father I'll be ready before dawn. I know the senator. He'll want to watch the sun rise while traveling."

"But, miss. You cannot ignore your dilemma for long."

"I assure you I won't." Liberty straightened. "I've been galloping over this entire country for a month. I believe I can make the trip to Austin without any problem. My father will want no delay."

Liberty wasn't surprised that her father had moved on to another battle. He was good at planning strategies. Now that she had returned safe and he'd hugged her to him, he'd probably forget to invite her to dinner.

"Would you do me a favor, Doctor?"

"If I can, miss." Nevad looked worried.

"Without anyone noticing, would you ask Tobin McMurray to come up in an hour?"

The doctor shook his head. "I'm not sure that would be proper."

Liberty almost laughed. "I'll dress while you go downstairs and since I've no sitting room, this will have to do. Tobin has cuts on his hands that I worry may not heal without infection. I'd like you to take a look at them."

The doctor nodded and stood. "I'll bring him back with me." He left his bag and walked to the door. With his hand on the knob, he turned, "Miss, if you don't mind me saying, it's been my experience that a great many first children born in this world come early."

Liberty understood but found little comfort in his words. She stared at him and said simply, "I'll hold you to your word to tell no one."

He nodded, his eyes looking even sadder. Without another word, the doctor closed the door behind him.

She sat perfectly still. One of the things that had helped her make it through the trials of the past weeks had been her planning for the future. She'd thought of every detail right down to the way she would decorate her house in Washington. Nowhere in that plan had been a child. Until now.

She spread her hand over her still flat abdomen. A life grew inside her. A life no one would want, or welcome . . . except her.

The training she'd had watching her father helped her now. She must act fast and she had to do the right thing. If her father found out she was pregnant, he'd kill Tobin. He might even disown her or try to make her marry someone. He prided himself in living above scandal. If he thought the baby were Samuel's, he'd probably be hell-bent to marry her to the captain no matter how much his opinion of the man had dropped.

Liberty tried to think.

If her father turned her away, she'd have enough money to live, but there would be no social life for her in Washington. She'd be one of those invisible people who rode alone in carriages in the park and never got invited to anything.

Only she wouldn't be alone. She'd have a child. A fatherless child.

Liberty stood. Suddenly it didn't matter what happened to her. She would not bring a child into the world to have people whisper about him behind his back. Or, if she had a girl, she'd never be accepted. She'd have no chance of marrying well.

Liberty walked to the window and looked in the direction of Whispering Mountain. Because of her father's pride, Tobin might be killed if the truth got out, but he wouldn't go down without a fight. If her father went after him, the senator might die, or worse he might have to kill all the McMurrays if he killed one. And why? Not because Tobin had attacked her, or hurt her, but because he'd loved her.

A tear drifted down her cheek. If the truth were known,

she'd been the one who attacked him. She'd begged him to love her and now she had to beg him to help her. He'd have to save her one more time before he went back to his mountain to live forever.

If he'd do this one last thing for her, she would go away and never bother him again. She wanted to remember all the wonder they'd shared and dream of him on his mountain taking care of his horses and remembering her. And most of all she didn't want him to regret what happened between them.

Liberty closed her eyes. How many times had she heard Tobin say he wanted no wife and children? This last favor might be too much, even for her hero.

Pulling on the first dress from her trunk, Liberty dressed as she pieced together the only plan that might work. This time she had to save Tobin and herself.

As she buttoned her cuff, a tap came again on her door. She glanced at the small clock beside her bed. It hadn't been ten minutes since the doctor had left.

Before she could say anything, Tobin stormed through without waiting. The doctor followed him in and closed the door.

"I told Nevad I didn't need any doctoring, but he's insisting you say I do." Tobin paced. He looked exactly as he did when they rode in—dusty, unshaven, and handsome. "Then he told me to wait an hour, which made even less sense. Travis and Teagen are ready to ride for home and you need sleep. I'll ride back in tomorrow and we can talk, but I've no need for a doctor."

Tobin spread his hands out. "The cuts weren't deep. They've already healed."

His gaze finally met Liberty's and he froze. "What's wrong. Are you all right?"

Libby saw the fear for her in his eyes and knew he'd give his life for her. And that was exactly what she planned to ask.

"I need you to do one more thing for me before you go."

"All right," he said without asking what.

Liberty lined her argument up carefully. "I think we both have made it plain that neither of us wishes to marry."

He didn't move.

"I know you plan to go back to your ranch and spend the rest of your life there. I plan to live on the money left me by my mother's parents and never take a husband." She noticed the doctor standing by the door looking uncomfortable. Ignoring him, she turned back to Tobin. "Now that I'm back with my father, I realize I have a problem. He wants to see me married and settled. In fact, he seems almost obsessed about it. He wants it so badly he'll push the wrong man at me again as soon as he gets the chance. I seem to lack the knowledge to be a good judge. I almost married a man who would have turned my life to hell and I've no confidence that I'd be more careful next time."

In Tobin's usual lack of tolerance for conversation, he asked, "Is this going somewhere?"

She frowned at him. "Yes," she snapped, then forced herself to breathe. "I'm getting to the point. Would you like to sit down?"

"Is that the point?" he asked.

"No."

"Then no, I'll stand."

Liberty took another breath. No wonder they never talked; if they had, they'd probably never have gotten close enough to make love. "The point is, Mr. McMurray, that my father will hound me to marry now more than ever I fear and I see but one solution."

"And that is?" he said looking like he had no clue what was about to hit him.

"I marry you. Tonight. Then we go our separate ways." Now she held her breath.

The doctor at the door shook his head, but again Liberty ignored him. She couldn't tell Tobin the real reason she had to marry and she couldn't leave this place without a ring on her finger. If he agreed, it would cost him nothing. It wasn't as if he planned to marry someone else.

"Look at it this way," she said softly when Tobin didn't move. "I'm helping you keep your promise. You never want to leave a wife and children. Now I'll leave you. You can go on living your life without fearing your bloody dream will destroy others. When we've left Texas I'll inform my father we married, and it will be too late for him to change anything."

Liberty hadn't thought through the reaction she'd expected of him, but she wasn't prepared for no reaction. Tobin just stood in the center of her bedroom, his feet wide apart, his fists at his side, his eyes watching her almost as if he didn't know she was talking.

Liberty couldn't endure his stare. She turned and began to pace. "I'll be a married lady and go back to Washington to live a very respectable life. For the first few years I'll tell everyone you're planning to join me. Soon they'll stop asking and maybe even whisper that I'm a widow unable to face the truth. Either way, I'll be living the life I'm accustomed to. I'll serve as my father's hostess at parties and attend gatherings with friends. I'll—"

"All right."

He said the words so calmly, she wasn't sure she'd heard them. She almost continued her verbal portrait of her life. "What did you say?" she asked as she turned to face him.

"I said, all right. We marry. On one condition."

Liberty squared her shoulders preparing for the worst. Whatever he asked in payment, even half her inheritance, she'd give. She must. "Name your price."

Tobin took a step toward her. "One more night."

Liberty tried to hide her shock. "What?"

Tobin faced her, his features hard and unreadable. "I'll do whatever you want, but we'll have one more night together before you go."

"Agreed."

He nodded once and shoved his hat on low. "I'll be back at dusk."

"I'll make the arrangements," Libby whispered, feeling more like she had to plan an execution instead of a wedding.

Tobin turned toward the door. "Doc, will you act as a witness?"

"And keep our agreement secret," Libby added. It seemed she and Tobin were destined to make silent pacts together.

The old doctor shook his head but said, "I will."

Tobin walked out of the room leaving Liberty to face the doctor.

"You're making a mistake," Nevad whispered.

"I'm doing the only thing I can do."

"He's got a right to know he's going to be a father."

"Why? He doesn't want children, and if I told him his honor would demand him to give up all he loved and follow me, or worse he'd try to tie me to this wilderness. I'd wither in this country and he'd suffocate in Washington. I'm doing the only thing I can to do."

The doctor sighed. "But he loves you."

"He doesn't love me. He's never said the words."

"Yes, he has," the doctor argued. "He asked for one more night."

CHAPTER 32

T obin had to fight to keep from running from
Libby's room. He'd been miserable for hours waiting downstairs. Liberty's father had asked a few questions about her
well-being, then went on to talk, in detail, about his campaign
and how much time he'd lost in Texas.

Tobin spent the hours thinking of a hundred ways to tell
her not to leave. Then when he finally got up to her room, she
hadn't given him a chance to say anything. All she'd wanted
was his name.

The afternoon had turned cloudy with a storm threatening by the time he walked back downstairs. He'd delayed
earlier because he thought he had to see her. Now he'd seen
her and couldn't leave because he was about to be married.
His brothers would never understand the mess he was in.
Travis did everything for the love of Rainey, and Teagen
swore he didn't believe in love. Neither would think a marriage, based on saving Libby from having to get married to
someone else, would make sense.

Tobin had to face this problem alone.

Travis met him at the bottom of the stairs. "How's our Miss Liberty doing?"

Tobin thought of saying that she wasn't theirs and never would be, but instead he said, "I think you and Teagen should head for home before the storm hits. I'll stay around here for a while."

Travis raised an eyebrow, but he wasn't in the habit of questioning his brother. "All right," he said. "We'll saddle up."

Tobin knew they'd probably talk about him all the way home. He'd never stayed in town a minute longer than necessary.

He walked to the porch and raised his hand as he watched his brothers leave. Part of him wanted to ride with them, to get back to his land and his horses and never leave again, but he'd said he would do this one last thing for her. For Libby. He'd marry her. Even if she'd made it plain she didn't want him, she only wanted his name.

As Teagen and Travis rode away, Tobin felt more alone than ever. He realized his planned offer for her to stay for a visit at the ranch, or even stay in town with Mrs. Dickerson, would never do. She was back under her father's wing. She'd returned to being pampered and spoiled. She didn't need him anymore. Even his idea of meeting her once in a while in Austin seemed nothing but a fool's plan.

He closed his eyes thinking that tonight would be the last night he'd ever see or hold Libby. She'd said several times over the past weeks that if she ever got back to Washington she would never leave again. He couldn't see himself making a trip to her. After tonight, all he'd have left of Libby were memories and all she'd have was his name.

The old doctor stepped out on the porch and lit a pipe. "Storm's coming. Big one from the sound of that thunder rolling over those hills. Seems like we've had one storm after another this fall."

"Looks that way," Tobin responded.

"Air's so cold I wouldn't be surprised if we get hail."

Tobin didn't want to make small talk with the doctor. He didn't want to talk at all.

But the doctor didn't seem to feel the same. He leaned against the railing and crossed his arms. "I got a room upstairs if you need a place to clean up."

Tobin hesitated, then accepted the key. "I'll go over to Elmo's and buy a change of clothes. I don't have time before dark to ride home and back."

The doc agreed. "I'll be downstairs when you're finished with the room. I've already told the senator Miss Liberty has asked to have her supper sent up and plans to retire early. I told her I'd get the local preacher and meet you in her room at just after dark."

Tobin felt like he was being swept along in a flood. He didn't care about the marriage. It wouldn't be real anyway. She'd never be his wife.

Except for tonight. Tonight would have to be enough for a lifetime.

Dr. Nevad sat down on one of the porch's ladder-back chairs. "Funny thing about the senator, he was all wild and determined to get to his little girl, but once he knew she was safe, he hasn't bothered to check on her."

Tobin looked at the doc. "What are you saying?"

The old man shrugged. "I'm saying that he loves his only child, but she's a thing to him. Something he'll fight to keep safe. Something he'll spoil, but not something he wants to include in his life." The doctor's eyes narrowed.

Tobin tried again. "Say what you mean to say."

"I guess I'm asking if she's more than a thing to you."

Tobin stared out into the cloudy sky. He remembered telling her once that she was just a job to him, just a promise he had to keep.

Without another word to the doctor, Tobin stepped off the porch and walked to Elmo's Trading Post. He barely noticed the rain starting.

For once he went in the front door. The drunks who usually sat on the porch would not want to cross him tonight.

No one but Elmo was there closing up his place for the night. Anyone with any sense would stay out of the rain.

"How can I help you, McMurray?" Elmo asked as he leaned his broom against the doorframe.

"I need a few things." Tobin began collecting clothes.

Elmo reached for his tally sheet. "You staying in town tonight? I hear there's a new girl over at the saloon that opened last week. Folks say she can sing."

Tobin didn't answer.

Elmo shrugged as if he didn't expect conversation from a McMurray.

"I'd like a yard of this." Tobin tossed a spool of thin blue ribbon toward the counter.

Elmo pulled the length, measuring it by the gashes on the table. "Sage usually likes the green."

Again Tobin didn't answer. He grabbed a new black hat and tossed it with the clothes on the counter.

While Elmo totaled, Tobin looked around. He noticed a case of snuff boxes and another of rings. Lifting the lid to the rings, he examined several.

Elmo laughed. "You thinking of needing a wedding band, Tobin? You know you'd have to talk to a girl before you marry one."

"I'll take this one," Tobin said as he held up a ring.

Elmo raised one bushy eyebrow. "That's the most expensive one in the case. It'll set you back twelve dollars."

"Add it to the bill."

Elmo shook his head. "You might want to find the girl first, son. That's a lot of money to put out."

Tobin dropped the ring in his pocket and picked up the clothes. "Good night," he managed before walking out the door with Elmo shouting questions.

Once in the doctor's room, Tobin wasn't surprised to find a bath waiting. The doc seemed determined to help. Tobin thought of riding down to the stream to wash up, but with the lightning popping around, and his luck lately, he'd probably take a direct hit.

He laughed and murmured, "Like marrying Libby wouldn't be." If her father found out before they were a hundred miles away, he'd probably ride back to shoot the groom. Mayfield was a man who wanted everything one way. His. Libby was right about how he'd never stop trying to marry her off. She was twenty, and before long the senator would find an old-maid daughter an embarrassment.

Scrubbing a week's worth of trail off him, Tobin tried not to think of the future. He and Libby both knew they could never live in one another's world. The last thing either of them wanted was a husband or wife. Now, by bonding themselves on paper, they both would be free. She may have asked for the favor, but she was doing him one as well.

He dressed and went downstairs suddenly wanting to get this night over. Loving Libby one more time while knowing it would be the last time might be harder than simply walking away. But he couldn't walk away. He knew he'd take the pain of knowing it was the last time as long as he could hold her once more.

The doctor sat in the front parlor with a nervous young man, who couldn't have been more than twenty, across from him. If he hadn't held a Bible in his hand, Tobin never would have believed him a preacher.

When Tobin walked in, the young man jumped up from his seat and offered his hand. "I'm Brother Steven, Mr. Mc-Murray. I've only be here a few weeks, but I've heard about your family and how you saved the senator's daughter."

Tobin glanced at the doc guessing who the town crier would be. The doctor didn't meet his stare.

"Brother Steven came in with the lumber delivered for the new church," Nevad mumbled as he cleaned out his pipe. "He brought the proper papers, and I've told him he's to tell no one of the ceremony."

Tobin nodded and turned, leading the way to Libby's room. "Where's the senator?" he asked as they climbed the stairs.

"He left for a poker game with some of the rangers. I told him I'd check on Miss Liberty before I turned in." The doctor paused. "Are you sure you want to do this? I know she asked you for this favor, but—"

"I'm ready," Tobin cut in.

Dr. Nevad tapped on Liberty's door.

Tobin braced himself for Libby's beauty, but it was Mrs. Dickerson who opened the door. "Come in, gentlemen. The bride is ready." The old schoolteacher smiled at Tobin. "Thank you for asking me to be the other witness, Tobin. That was kind of you. I consider myself a dear friend to your family."

Tobin nodded, afraid if he opened his mouth he might tell the truth. He stepped past Mrs. Dickerson, his eyes hungry for the sight of Libby.

She stood by the windows, her back to him. Her hair had been curled and hung down her back to her waist. She wore a simple high-necked dress as violet as a stormy evening sunset. When she turned, he swore his heart stopped. She was the most beautiful woman he'd ever seen. Her eyes were wide, a little frightened and as uncertain as the weather outside.

He took her hand. "We can call this off," he whispered.

She shook her head, holding on to his fingers tightly. "If you're still willing?"

He smiled. "I'm still willing."

"So am I."

Without another word, Tobin faced the preacher.

CHAPTER 33

LIBERTY HUGGED MRS. DICKERSON WHILE TOBIN shook the doctor's hand. The preacher unfolded a paper he'd already penned the date and names to. They all signed.

Relying on years of practice, Liberty stood at the door and thanked them as they all left swearing to tell no one of the marriage. Tobin stood at her side without a word.

When she closed the door, she was alone with Tobin for the first time in days. He walked to the window and pulled open the curtain. He watched the storm now in full rage outside.

"Would you like something to eat?" Liberty had never felt so nervous around him. "I had a tray brought up."

For a moment, she didn't think he heard her, then he faced her. "No," he said as he took a step toward her. "I'm not hungry."

She nodded. "Are you cold? Your hair doesn't look quite dry." It was obvious he'd bathed and shaved.

He took another step, running his fingers through the damp mass.

Liberty smiled as a lock fell over his forehead. She remembered thinking that first night she'd seen him in her father's barn that his hair was far too long to be fashionable. Now she considered the fashion too short.

He stood in front of her, broad shouldered, lean and silent. Hers, she thought. If only on paper. If only for tonight. Hers.

Without a word he leaned and brushed a kiss so soft across her lips that she almost cried out. His big hand moved to her waist and tugged her gently to him. The second kiss lingered, tasting.

Liberty thought they'd talk for a while, but if this was how Tobin wanted it she'd go along. She closed her eyes memorizing every touch, every smell, every taste. She opened her mouth slightly, inviting him in. From the beginning they'd done most of their communicating through touch. It seemed only right that their last good-bye be the same.

Leaning against him, she stretched, fitting her body to his. A perfect fit, as always.

Tobin kissed her again, then gently pulled away, but not before she saw the hunger in his eyes.

"I forgot to give this to you." He drew a ring from his pocket. "I know you don't want to wear it now, so I thought you might put it around your neck on this ribbon." He looped the ribbon about her neck and tied it so that the ring hung between her breasts.

She stared at the gold band. "You didn't have to buy me this."

"I know. I wanted to." He toyed with the ring. "I like the idea of something of mine going with you, Libby."

She swallowed hard. Something of him was going with her.

"As soon as we set sail from Galveston, I'll tell father we married. He'll be angry that we didn't tell him, but I think he respects your family so he'll adjust to the idea."

"You're going with the lie that I'll be joining you."

She nodded. "Then he'll understand why I must set up my own house. By the time he realizes you're never coming, it will be too late for me to move back into his home."

Tobin looked like he knew nothing of such things so Libby changed the subject. "If you'll excuse me for a few minutes, I'll get ready for bed."

Tobin leaned and kissed her again, then smiled. "Where am I supposed to go?"

She laughed nervously. "Over by the windows and keep your back turned until I tell you I'm ready."

"I've seen you before," he commented as she pushed him away.

"But we've never slept in a bed before. I want to do this right."

When Tobin turned back to the window, she tugged off her dress and slipped into a silk nightgown she'd ordered from Paris months ago. It was straight and plain in line, but showed off her every curve.

When Libby moved to the fire, she whispered, "All right, I'm ready."

He turned slowly and stared at her as she warmed in front of the fire.

"I can see right through that gown, Libby."

Libby didn't move. He could look all he wanted to. She had no modesty where he was concerned. In fact, she liked the hunger she saw in his gaze.

He moved to her, but when he bent down he didn't kiss her. He lifted her up in his arms and carried her to the bed. She wanted to tell him how much she needed him. How starved for him she'd felt this past week on the trail with others always around. She wanted to beg him to love her as she had the first time they'd shared a blanket.

But she remained silent, loving the feel of his arms around her.

He pushed her hair aside with his chin and tasted her neck, then kissed his way to her ear. "You're so beautiful."

He placed her gently on top of the covers and stood. "I know I bargained for this night in exchange for the favor, but if you don't want it tell me now. The marriage stands just as you asked."

Libby rose to her knees and spread her hands over his shirt. "I want it too." She began unbuttoning, exposing his chest a few inches at a time. "If you hadn't suggested it, I would have."

He let her undress him, smiling when her fingers moved over his bare skin. When he knelt to untie his moccasins she crawled between the covers of the feather bed and smiled as she waited.

Before she was warm, she felt him slide in behind her and pull her body to him. For a while he just held her as their bodies warmed and grew accustomed to the feel of one another.

He spread his hands over her hips. "Libby," he whispered. "Can we get rid of this gown?"

She laughed. "But it's from Paris."

He tugged at the hem. "It can go back there for all I care. I want to feel my Libby."

She wiggled while he pulled it over her head and then his hands were on her, and she didn't care what happened to the gown. As always his kisses grew ravenous, but he took his time moving down her body taking his fill of her. She welcomed his touch, his kiss, and his exploration of her senses. When he finally came to her, he entered slowly as if wanting each moment to last longer.

She cried his name over and over as he made love to her. Mating with him was bone and blood to her and she ached for the future even before she let go of the present.

The stars exploded at the same time for each and they held tight as they drifted back down together. He rolled an inch away as they let their breathing slow to normal.

Finally, he rose to one elbow and stared at her in the light from the window.

"If I asked you if you'd stay . . ." he whispered.

"If I asked you if you'd go . . ." she answered.

The room hushed except for their breathing.

Finally, he lifted the ring. "Promise me you'll always wear this, on your finger or around your neck, I don't care. Just promise me."

He kissed her wedding band.

She couldn't see his eyes. "Love me again," she whispered, breaking her promise not to beg him. "Please love me again."

His palm slid down the center of her body. "How could I

not? If lightning strikes this hotel and starts a fire, we probably won't notice."

He kissed her then so gently her heart ached.

The second time they made love, she turned wild in his arms, demanding a hard and fast mating, needing to lose control. He made no protest but handled her desire just the way she knew he would.

When they finished, he held her as she cried, this time not for joy, but for longing, already missing him. As she drifted near sleep, he began touching her again, bringing her to climax once more just because he knew he could. This time when she floated back from heaven, she drifted into her dreams without a tear.

She slept for a while but awoke to the thunder of the storm outside. Feeling his warmth even before time registered, she rolled against him noticing how soundly he slept. Even in his sleep he pulled her to him and she lay wrapped in his arms.

"I'm not leaving you," she whispered. "A part of you will go with me."

Then, with one final kiss, she returned to sleep.

CHAPTER 34

TOBIN AWOKE SLOWLY FROM A DEEP SLEEP. HIS FIRST thought was that he hadn't dreamed. No nightmares distorted the night.

The second thought was that Libby was not by his side. He sat up searching for her, expecting to find her by the fire or making tea. But she was nowhere in the room.

Regret that he'd slept even a few hours of their last night together hit him full and hard.

He shoved the covers aside and reached for his clothes trying to decide where she would be. Glancing at the window, he noticed it was long past dawn, and still cloudy.

Maybe she went down for breakfast with her father? No, she wouldn't leave without waking him. The last thing she'd probably want was for him to go looking for her. He'd planned to leave before dawn to avoid any questions, but that plan was now impossible.

Dread settled into the pit of his stomach by the time he laced his moccasins.

The tray of food she'd had waiting for him last night sat

untouched by the window. Her gown lay on the floor. Nothing else of hers remained. Tobin tried to think back, but he'd only had eyes for her last night. He couldn't remember seeing her trunk in any corner or even a comb on the dresser. Could she have already been packed and ready to leave when she'd married him and spent the night making love?

No, he thought, if she were leaving she would have told him. He thought back to last night when she'd lain in his arms, curled up and safe. They'd both been awake part of the time. He remembered thinking of all the things he could say to her and wondered if she'd been thinking the same thing.

But he hadn't broken the silence. He'd told himself he'd wait until morning.

Only now, morning may have been too late.

He opened the bedroom door quietly, expecting one of the rangers who always guarded the senator to be sitting at the end of the hall. The chair was empty. Mayfield must already be downstairs.

Tobin moved silently to the landing. No one, not even the desk clerk, was there.

He took the steps slowly, listening for conversations coming from the dining area to the left or the small parlor to the right. Nothing.

At the bottom of the stairs, Tobin noticed the desk clerk sweeping the front porch. "Where is everyone?" Tobin said, trying not to sound as if his world were shattering apart.

The clerk looked up in surprise. "You mean the senator and his party? They left about an hour before dawn. He had everything packed up yesterday afternoon but wanted to wait out the rain."

Tobin couldn't believe Libby had known last night that she'd be leaving today and hadn't told him.

"You Tobin McMurray?"

Tobin nodded.

The clerk reached in his back pocket and pulled out a letter. "The doc told me to give you this."

Tobin took the note frowning. He thanked the man and

walked to the end of the porch. When he opened the envelope, he found one page. Three lines from Libby.

Thank you for the memory I'll cherish.
I'll always think of you on your mountain.
Please remember me. Love, your Libby.

She must have written it in haste and asked the doctor to
see that someone get it to him. She hadn't even said good-
bye to him.

He was halfway home before he slowed his horse to a
walk. There didn't seem enough air left in the world. He
couldn't breathe. All the things he'd thought he was going to
say to her over breakfast log-piled in his brain.

If he went home, his brothers and Sage would have a
dozen questions. He didn't want to talk about her. He couldn't
share his pain. They'd probably think he was a mad man for
even thinking a princess like her could be interested in
someone like him. Hell, she spoke five languages. He didn't
even speak one most of the time.

Frustrated, Tobin turned his horse toward Whispering
Mountain. For the first time in his life he wouldn't be afraid
to dream his future. Without Libby he wasn't sure he had a
life.

CHAPTER 35

Tobin TURNED HIS HORSE TO THE MOUNTAIN AND not toward the lights of home. He needed time to think. The rain started again, dribbling down in thoughtless tears. Wind whipped around him, slowing him as if not wanting him to go.

Halfway up the mountain he had to leave his horse and continue on foot. Tobin didn't even bother to take a bedroll. In minutes it would be as wet as the ground anyway.

He trudged through the mud, pulling at plants to climb in places and sliding backward on rocks in others until finally he reached the summit.

Thirty years ago his father had dreamed his death here. Andrew McMurray had still been in his teens when he'd married and brought his wife to Whispering Mountain. He'd set on this summit and known he was going to die.

Tobin dropped to one knee, understanding how his father must have felt for the first time in his life. Andrew had loved their mother, loved her enough to go against both his people and hers, loved her enough to stand alone in a land still wild. He must have been happy when he came to this place. He must have been looking forward to seeing into his future. Autumn had been pregnant. They'd just begun a life.

But on the summit that night, Andrew McMurray dreamed only of death.

Tobin crumbled onto the wet ground and let the rain hit him in the face. If his father loved his mother like he loved Libby, how had he found the strength to stand and return, knowing his days were numbered? Knowing that he'd be leaving her alone. Knowing he'd never see his sons grown.

The soft rain washed over him relaxing tired muscles and Tobin closed his eyes. But sleep didn't come, only Libby's face smiling at him.

Hours passed. The rain finally stopped and the clouds cleared enough for a few stars to twinkle through the fog. Tobin's last thought before he dozed off was that it must be near dawn.

When he dreamed, he dreamed of horses running across Whispering Mountain. Glory, Sage's old mare, led the pack. Only she was young and strong, not old and half broken down like now. Her offspring raced behind her and mixed with the generations of horses they'd bred on the ranch. Horses born of Glory and his father's horses. Horses bred from the best of the wild mustang blood.

Tobin could name them all. They'd all been a part of his world for as long as he could remember. He felt his heart racing as if he were with them running full out against the wind.

When he awoke, the first pale light of dawn shown on the horizon. Through the watery fog it looked violet, the same color Libby's dress had been that last night.

Every bone in his body felt stiff. His clothes were caked in mud. Knocking off the earth, he smiled. If Libby saw him now, she really would think him half wild animal. He probably looked worse than a coyote caught in a muddy creek. He'd slept out off and on all his life, but he usually had the sense to do it under a tree or cliff edge. This time he'd challenged the storm full out.

The dream of generations of horses running across the land

drifted through his mind. He knew what he had to do. It would take some time, some courage, but he was his father's son.

Tobin smiled, realizing he'd come to the same conclusion his father must have; otherwise, he wouldn't have left the letter his sons called "the rules." The number of years a man lives isn't nearly as important as how he lives them.

CHAPTER 36

THE BALLROOM FLOWED WITH THE COLORS OF A winter garden as the dancers whirled in icy blues and hunter greens. Liberty watched, smiling at the friendly faces. She'd been back in Austin for almost three weeks and tomorrow they'd leave for the Gulf of Mexico where they'd travel by ship back to Washington.

Her father had finished his investigation of his attempted murder. He'd found that the men who'd attacked his carriage that night had been paid by a small group of businessmen who lived along the border and strongly disagreed with his views on trade with Mexico. When the rangers finally rounded them up, the businessmen swore to the man that they hadn't planned to kill the senator, only scare him into having second thoughts. Only the outlaws they hired carried the plan a step further thinking there might be a bonus if they killed Senator Mayfield.

Liberty smiled to herself, glad her father finally seemed relaxed. Or as close as a warrior ever gets to relaxing. He'd find another battle in no time, he always did. It seemed to be what kept his blood pumping though his veins.

She studied the dancers. Here in Austin there were many men in uniform and whenever she noticed one her senses came alive with warning, but none were Captain Samuel Buchanan.

Libby wondered, if she did see him again, would he still look handsome. She somehow doubted it. On the way back, she'd told Dr. Nevad the details of her fight with Samuel and they'd both agreed to not tell her father. The senator had already decided the captain was incompetent before all the trouble started. That was why he'd turned to Tobin to keep his daughter safe.

Samuel had never wanted her, only her money and a slice of her father's power. At least Tobin had wanted her, if only for a few days.

Dr. Nevad walked up beside her and offered her a champagne glass.

"Cider," he said with a smile. "And you should sit as much as possible."

Liberty laughed. He'd been lecturing her since they'd met.

They both turned to watch her father leave the ballroom. He was surrounded by men jockeying for his attention. It seemed as soon as her father knew she was safe, he moved on to more important matters.

Dr. Nevad drew her attention back. "Your father told me this morning that Samuel Buchanan had sent him a letter asking if you were sure you wouldn't reconsider. Apparently, he managed to show up at Elmo's Trading Post about a week after you left."

Liberty grinned. The doctor always seemed to make her smile. "And what did my father say?" The senator's favorite rant of late was about how the bungling captain had almost got him killed. Any other man would have known there were outlaws on his property.

"He said not only no, but hell no." Nevad laughed.

"You don't think Samuel will show up here?" Tomorrow they'd be traveling and she'd know that she was safe from ever seeing him again.

Nevad shook his head. "One of the rangers said he saw Buchanan traveling to his new assignment on the front line.

He said he had a redhead with him who never seemed to stop talking."

Liberty shrugged. "He'll never find a more loyal companion than Stella."

Dr. Nevad accepted her glass and moved aside as one of the Austin officers in full dress uniform asked Liberty to dance, pulling her back to the party. She didn't want to dance, but she couldn't be impolite. In another week, while they sailed, she could tell her father she was married. He'd be aggravated that something happened out of his control, but he'd settle into the idea by the time they reached Washington. She'd let another month pass and then tell him he was going to be a grandfather. She smiled, thinking he'd probably like that idea.

Liberty followed the officer's lead and nodded at his comments as if giving him her full attention, but in the back of her mind she planned all that would need to be done as soon as she was home. Thanks to her friends marrying of late, Liberty knew of a few houses available. One sat in a wooded area a few miles from town and would do perfectly. She'd decorate it while she waited for the baby. If she remembered correctly, it was small enough to be run by only a few staff and had a rather nice barn and grounds. Liberty had already decided to ask Anna and Dermot to come with her. Between the three of them and a few hired day staff, she should be able to have the place ready for the baby.

With each passing day, the parties and theater seemed less important. She wanted the baby growing inside more with every heartbeat. Her baby. Tobin's baby.

Thankfully, most of the people in Austin knew little of her adventure. Her father had told everyone that he'd sent her to stay at a friend's ranch and invented the kidnapping to to keep her safe while he helped solve the plot against his life. Most were polite enough to believe him. The few who weren't were not brave enough to ask questions.

The music ended and the officer returned her to her place at the edge of the dance floor. She thanked him and wondered how he'd react if he knew she wore moccasins beneath her gown. Everyone would be shocked, but she just thought how comfortable she'd been all evening.

Liberty glanced at the huge grandfather clock in the foyer just beyond the ballroom door. She'd been watching it all night, counting the hours until it would be acceptable to leave. She hadn't wanted the party in the first place. If it had been her choice, she would have stayed in the carriage all the way to Galveston and boarded the ship immediately.

Sleep would have been her choice tonight. It seemed she'd been sleeping a great deal of late.

She tried not to think that she was getting farther and farther away from Tobin. She was keeping her word. She'd be building a new life. Inside her grew someone who would need her . . . someone who would love her. She could build her world on that, only that.

The wind brushed a strand of her hair across her cheek and Liberty turned to see the front door open.

Her first thought was that it was far too late for anyone to be arriving at the ball. Her second thought was that the man coming through the door looked familiar.

The way he moved, leading a little with one broad shoulder, walking softly as if he never left tracks.

A cry caught in her throat as the man turned. Chestnut brown hair cut perfectly, a strong jaw set by a frown, and dark blue eyes as stormy as a hurricane.

"Tobin." She'd only whispered his name, but he heard her.

He faced her, taking in the look of her like a man starved for the sight of her. Without warning, he walked straight toward her.

Several people turned to look.

When he reached her, he bowed as politely as any gentleman. "Libby," he said. "I've come to take you home."

Before she could think to answer, he swept her up in his arms and headed for the door.

The music stopped. Everyone in the room stared. Several of the officers present moved to help her.

The man she'd danced with blocked Tobin's path. "Now

just a minute. What's going on here? Does the senator know about this?"

Liberty felt Tobin's muscles tense. "I'm taking my wife home."

In the moment of confusion that followed, he stepped around the officer and reached the door.

She looked over his shoulder and saw several officers rushing to follow. One buckskin-clad ranger closed the exit with his body and held up his hand.

Liberty didn't know whether to scream or laugh. Though Tobin had surprised her, she felt no fear of him. She had no idea what he wanted, but he'd solved the problem of when to tell her father. Within minutes, a hundred people would probably repeat Tobin's words.

The thought that he'd learned of the baby, and somehow came because of it, frightened her. What would he do—hold her prisoner until she delivered? He'd consider the child a McMurray whether he wanted it or not.

He tossed her up on his horse and swung up behind her. "Hold tight, Libby," he ordered.

"Where do you think you're taking me?"

She wasn't surprised he didn't answer. He only kicked the horse into a full gallop and raced through the streets.

"This is kidnapping this time, Tobin." She tried to keep her hair from blowing wildly as hairpins and combs flew in the wind. "My father won't stand for it. We're due to leave tomorrow, and he thinks I've already delayed him long enough."

He slowed to make sure he wasn't being followed. When he turned onto a narrow street, she twisted to face him. "You can't just come into a ball and grab me."

His mouth came down on hers hard as his arm pulled her so tightly to him she couldn't breathe.

When he broke the kiss, she gulped for air as he turned down a dark alleyway.

"Where are we going?" she demanded.

"Be quiet, Libby," he whispered. His words were an order, but his nuzzle against her neck could only be a caress.

The horse slowed at the side door to a home Libby recognized as being very close to the state capitol. Tobin gently lifted her down and carried her along a path to an open door. The house was dark, but he seemed to know his way. After two turns, she saw the light of a fireplace.

"If you've kidnapped me to ravish me, Tobin McMurray, I swear I'll—"

He laughed as he dropped her into an overstuffed chair by the fire. "Since when have I ravished *you*, Libby?"

She got to her feet as gracefully as possible. "Then why did you bring me here?"

"Get undressed."

She straightened as excitement blended with fear. "I will not."

He jerked off the formal coat he wore and tossed it along with his tie. "Get undressed, Libby."

"No." She faced him. "Not until you talk to me. Why did you kidnap me tonight?"

He pulled off a black shoe and threw it across the room.

"Tobin, talk to me."

After removing his other shoe, he took a deep breath and nodded once. "I can't sleep without you."

Libby stared. Of all the reasons she'd thought he might say, that had not even been in the running. She waited him out.

He paced back and forth for a while then added, "With you gone I figured I was dead already, so what difference did fearing the future make?" He stared at her, hunger and need in his eyes. "I dozed off once and saw generations of horses running . . . But after that . . . I sat on that damn mountain for three days trying everything to fall asleep. When I closed my eyes, all I saw was you."

Anger boiled in Liberty. "You embarrassed me in front of half of Austin because you can't sleep."

He moved closer. "I can't sleep without you, but I didn't want to embarrass you. I got dressed up, had a real haircut and shave. I even wore shoes, though they hurt like hell."

She turned her head when he leaned to kiss her. "You'll have to do better than that."

He caught the ribbon at her neck and tugged his ring from between her breasts. "You belong to me. You signed your note 'your Libby.' Not Liberty, but Libby. And not just Libby, but my Libby."

She wouldn't settle. "I don't belong to you or anyone. I'm on my own." Pushing past him she headed for the door. "I suggest you take drugs to sleep and I'm sure you can return the clothes and shoes no longer than you wore them."

With her hand on the knob, she turned back. "I don't want to be just needed or wanted. I'll not be handled like a thing, not even by my husband."

He looked so handsome standing by the fire she almost ran back to him. For a shy man it must have taken a great deal to rush into the ball and take her. But that wasn't what she wanted in a man. In a strange way he'd given her the strength to walk away.

As she opened the door, she heard him say, "I came because I know you love me."

"I never said I did." Her pride wouldn't let her run to him.

"Yes, you did." He pulled the tattered note from his pocket. "You signed it."

"You came all this way because of a note?" Each word caught in her throat as hope grew in her heart.

"No, Libby, I came all this way because I love you. I don't know how long I'm going to live but, however long it is, I want it to be by your side. If you're set on going to Washington, then I'll go. If you want me to get all dressed up, I'll do that. Just promise me that you'll sleep beside me."

Libby smiled amazed he could say so many words all at once. "You'd really go?"

She took a step toward him.

He nodded once, looking very much like a man agreeing to take poison.

She moved closer. "And you'd wear proper clothes and shoes?"

He stared at her as she neared, his dark eyes almost burning her skin.

"Tobin answer me."

He smiled. "I can't think when you're smiling at me, but whatever the question was the answer is yes."

His stare met hers. "If I agreed to go . . ."

She smiled. "If I agreed to stay . . ."

She was so close she felt the warmth of his body, but she didn't touch him. "What do you want?"

"I want you," he whispered, "to get undressed and come to bed."

She began unbuttoning her dress. His gaze followed her every movement. "Not before you say it again, Tobin."

"Say what again." His tone left no doubt that he thought he'd done enough talking for a while.

"Say you love me."

He stopped her hands and pulled her to him. Looking into her eyes, he said, "I love you, Libby. I think I have since the moment I saw you. I'll love you every day for the rest of our lives."

"Good." She smiled. "Get undressed and come to bed."

He kissed her gently then lifted her up and carried her to the bed. As she watched him pull off his clothes, he said, "I won't mind living in Washington or wherever you want to during the days as long as I'm beside you at night."

She loved seeing every part of him. He was a man who looked grand in formal attire and even better without it. "Good." She laughed. "Then you won't mind living at the ranch for a while first."

He frowned as if not believing her.

She grinned. "I really think the next McMurray should be born at Whispering Mountain, don't you, Papa?"

He froze, his shirt open, his trousers half unbuttoned. He stared at her so hard she could almost believe he could see through her. He showed no emotion at her sudden announcement.

No playfulness remained in her voice as she whispered, "I know you planned no family, but I'm going to have a baby." Lifting her chin, she added, "I want it. In fact, I already love it. If you want me, you'll have to want our child."

He knelt beside the bed and slowly finished unbuttoning her dress.

Liberty watched him, her heart shattering. If he walked away now, it would be a hundred times harder for her to leave, knowing that he loved her but wanted no family.

He pushed her undergarments aside and spread his hand over her belly. When he raised his head, she saw tears floating in his eyes.

"The next generation." He smiled. "After you left I climbed Whispering Mountain and dreamed of horses running across our land. I dreamed of generations of McMurrays."

Libby put her hand over his. "I love you, Tobin, and I love your child already. It doesn't matter where we live. If I'm with you, I'm home."

He spread out beside her and pulled the covers over them both. Then he pulled her close and whispered, "Go to sleep, Libby. You'll need your rest for the ride home."

She cuddled against him. "And?"

He was silent for a moment, then he added, "And I love you." His hand moved across her middle. "I love you both."

When she woke him a few hours later to make love he was so gentle she almost cried with joy. This time the room was silent as they communicated all they felt without saying a word.

Turn the page for a special preview of
Jodi Thomas's new novel . . .

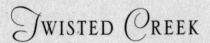

TWISTED CREEK

Coming soon from Berkley!

IF ROTTEN LUCK WAS A MAN, I'D HAVE A STALKER. IN college I used to wait for just one of those "many blessings" my grandmother promised would fall down on me. All I got was a string of loser boyfriends and part-time jobs going nowhere. But that didn't stop me from rounding every corner, hoping luck would be waiting with open arms.

About the time I thought my goal of teaching art might come true, my grandfather died during my junior year pulling any hope of finishing college out from under me. Since then, I've been tap dancing on the bones of dreams thinking I could make it rain.

Autumn in Memphis made me believe nothing would ever change. It had been almost five years since I'd left school and moved back in with Nana. We were no better off than we'd been that day we'd returned home after my grandfather's funeral to find the eviction notice. But, we were together and for Nana that was enough. She was a solid in my life, always there, always caring.

On the outside I felt young. But inside—the part of me who believed in fairies and danced down the yellow-brick road—was slowly petrifying into a cynic. I was aging on the inside, giving up on dreams.

Today felt like one more nail in my coffin. I could almost smell the lilies.

Pulling my van into the front yard of the duplex I shared with my grandmother, I concentrated on guessing what color they meant to paint the place and tried not to think about my boss at the greenhouse. He'd threatened to fire me for the third time. I'd been the low employee on the totem pole before and knew last-hired would be first to go when business turned bad. With winter coming on, the plant business was bound to turn bad.

I might have consoled myself that the nursery job wasn't where I wanted to be anyway. It wasn't where I belonged. But if I admitted that, I'd have to ask the next question. Where should I be? Most of my life I'd felt like the last guest at a dinner party. I kept circling the table looking for my seat as all the food disappeared.

Nana, my grandmother, opened the door of our place as I grabbed the mail out of the box. "How was work, dear?" As always, Nana reminded me of a hundred pounds of bottled sunshine.

I forced a smile. "Well, I didn't kill any patients today." I rubbed the tag on my uniform smock that read "Allie Daniels, Plant Doctor." "But it was touch and go with an ivy determined to commit suicide."

Nana grinned and followed me through the tiny living area, where I slept, and into the kitchen. "I'm sure you do the best you can."

Flipping through the mail, I mumbled, "It may not be good enough. There's talk of layoffs." I paused, noticing a letter from Texas amid the bills. I stared at the fat envelope with interest. Though Nana had grown up there, she'd been gone too long for any relative or friend to be writing. I balanced the envelope on my palm, weighing it.

"You've got to open it, Allie, if you plan to read it," my grandmother said as she prepared our dinner, a can of pork and beans over toast.

I twisted a strand of my sun-bleached hair behind my ear and shrugged. "It can't be bad news, Nana. Surely nothing terrible can travel three states to get us." We'd been on the move for almost five years, first Kansas, then Arkansas, and now Tennessee. I'd hear about jobs opening somewhere with better pay and Nana would pack. We'd learned our lesson when Grandpa died. It didn't pay to get too attached to a place or to people. The duplex was only ours while we paid the rent, and people tend to forget they know you when times get hard.

Nana called us corner peepers, always thinking something better lay just around the bend. Every time we moved I'd notify the post office in Clinton, Oklahoma, where I'd grown up, just in case someone was looking for us. No one ever had. Until now.

"What's it say, child?" Nana's voice had taken eighty years to mature into pure twang.

At twenty-six, I no longer considered myself a child, but I knew I'd always be one to her. "It's from a lawyer in Lubbock." I raised an eyebrow as I unfolded the papers. Nana loved for me to read the mail, even flyers addressed to occupant. I read the first paragraph, then frowned.

Nana leaned over my shoulder as if she could see the type without her glasses.

I straightened. "It seems this is the fourth address he's tried."

Nana dried her hands on her apron. "Well, whoever it's from is persistent. What could he want with us?" I could hear the unsaid words in her deep breath that followed. We'd had bills find us before and somehow we'd managed to pay them.

I read the entire first page before I whispered, "I've inherited Uncle Jefferson's lake property out on Twisted Creek."

Nana looked up at me, her light-blue eyes as clear with reason as ever. "You don't have an Uncle Jefferson, Allie. Your mother was my only child."

Twenty-four hours later, after driving all day and spending the night in a Motel 6, I was ready to meet the lawyer and inherit my property. I held my foam coffee cup in one hand as I drove toward the office of Garrison D. Walker, attorney-at-law.

"Maybe you knew Uncle Jefferson, Nana? Maybe he was a friend of your family from way back?" We'd played this game for a hundred miles with no luck.

Nana shook her head. She'd been a tenant-farmer's wife all her married life, and once my grandfather died, she'd lived with me. She could count the number of people she called friend on her fingers. And as for Nana having a rich secret lover hidden away somewhere, that was about as likely as magnolias in Alaska.

"I knew a Jeff once, but he went by the name of Red 'cause he had hair as red as an apple," she mumbled around a doughnut. "He took me to a dance that summer I spent time in Texas. My mom sent me to stay with my brother, Frank's wife who was expecting. She'd taken a summer house for one week when Dallas was burning up 'cause being big pregnant is hot on a body even in the winter. She drove up to Oklahoma and picked me up, then we wondered around the most nothing land until we found the place she rented."

Nana smiled as the wind tickled through her short gray hair. "All the boys had been called up after Pearl Harbor. My mom wanted me to stay with Mary until school started. She weren't but a year older than me."

I remembered the story and didn't want to hear the retelling of how Frank was killed in the war and his wife died in childbirth. "Tell me about this Red you met," I encouraged.

Nana licked doughnut icing off her fingers. "He was real nice. We talked almost all night, every night that week. He was turning eighteen in the fall and couldn't wait to join up."

"Why didn't you marry him?" I winked at her.

She laughed. "I was already engaged to your grandpa. My folks had promised we could marry as soon as I finished my eleventh year of school. They said your grandpa was solid on account of him being older then me and already a farmer." She popped another doughnut and turned to look out her side window. "Some folks didn't think so, but those men who stayed to farm did their part in the war too."

I frowned. If Nana didn't have anyone in her past, it had to be me. But who?

I'd had my share of boyfriends in college, but most had wanted to borrow money from me, not keep in touch because they planned to name me in a will. Once I moved back home, I hadn't known a single man in the county I wanted to have a cup of coffee with, much less get involved with romantically. When the few single guys my age did come around, they lost all interest as soon as they discovered Nana was part of the package.

Glancing at Nana, I smiled. She'd been a real help and didn't even know it. A man who couldn't love Nana too wasn't worth having.

Nana refolded the map she'd been trying to get back in its original shape since Oklahoma City. She stuck it over the visor where I'd put the lawyer's letter. Nana had read it aloud so many times during the trip; we could quote almost every line. She hummed as we passed through the streets of Lubbock.

This morning, we'd had our motel showers and hot coffee. It was time to meet with Garrison D. Walker and solve the mystery. I tried not to hope for anything. If the inheritance was nothing, we'd already had an adventure, and I could look for a job here as easy as I could have in Memphis.

I turned off of Avenue Q onto a tree-lined street named Broadway. Finding the lawyer had been no problem, thanks to the directions he'd left on the back of his letter. When I called to tell him we were coming, he sounded excited. Maybe he was glad to be rid of his responsibility with the will.

A very proper secretary welcomed us. She offered us a seat and disappeared through one of the mahogany doors behind her desk.

"Don't say anything about not knowing Jefferson Platt," I whispered to Nana, who was busy pulling the tag off the suit I'd bought her at a Wal-Mart last night. I thought if I was going to inherit something we should look like we didn't really need whatever it was. We'd found dresses for both of us, for under a hundred dollars. Nana's was navy, made to look like a suit, with a white collar. Mine, a shift that buttoned down the front, was the pale blue of a summer day. Like everything I bought, it seemed a few inches too long, but we hadn't had time to hem it.

"I won't say a word," Nana mumbled. "It's not right to talk about the dead, dear." She'd managed to pull the tag off, but the plastic string still dangled from her sleeve.

I think the world of my Nana, but she is a woman far more comfortable in a housecoat than a suit. "All dressed up" to her meant taking off her apron. She helped me through those first two years of college cooking at the elementary school a mile down from the farm my grandfather worked. She'd walked the distance every morning and cooked, then returned home to a full day's work of a farmer's wife without one word of complaining.

I covered her hand with mine, wishing for the millionth time that I could make things better for her. When you've only got one person who loves you, you have to wish extra hard.

"Miss Allison Daniels?" a man about fifty asked as he neared.

I stood and shook his hand. "My friends call me Allie," I said. "And this is my grandmother, Edna Daniels."

"Garrison D. Walker, at your service."

The lawyer smiled and waited for her to offer her hand. But Nana wasn't about to let him see her plastic string, and he was too much a southern gentlemen to offer his hand first to a lady.

Walker turned back to me. "We've had a hell of a time finding you, Miss Daniels."

"I wasn't aware I was lost." I smiled, thinking Garrison Walker had too many teeth. "I didn't know Uncle Jefferson was dead." I knew I should be concentrating, but the man made me nervous. His grin looked like it belonged on a mouth one size larger.

"Your mother didn't tell you Jefferson died?" Walker asked as he stopped grinning—thank goodness. "We sent her a registered letter the day of his graveside service. He'd listed her phone number and address as the only person to be notified." Walker paused as if expecting me to fill in a blank. When I didn't, he added, "Quite frankly, I was surprised when Mr. Platt named you his only heir. I told your mother to let you know of his passing since we had no address on you."

"Maybe my mother had trouble reaching me. She's out of the country a great deal," I managed to mumble as I remembered the string of men who always stood beside her in pictures. She'd send us snapshots from all over the world with little notes on the back like, "Walter and I in Rome," or "Me and Charles—Paris." I'd decided years ago that in her odd way she thought she was sharing with us by sending photos. No gifts or calls, just pictures of her and strangers.

"How long ago did he die?" I'd made a point that every time we moved I called and left a message on my mother's machine. She could have found me, but I didn't feel like going into family problems with Garrison Walker.

"Almost two months." Walker lowered his head and sighed. "He had a long life though, dying at the age of eighty-three."

I couldn't shake the feeling that Walker was pretending to care. But the information was helpful. His age eliminated any possibility of Jefferson being my father, unless he played football in high school during his fifties.

Walker continued, "Your mother said to send all the information to her and she'd forward it to you, but I've been in family law long enough to know to deal directly with the source. Since you are not a minor, I had to locate you."

Nana found her voice. "Did you hire a PI to find Allie?" She loved detective shows. She even told me once that she'd leave my grandpa if McGyver ever came by the farm.

Walker smiled as if talking to a child. "No. When I realized weeks had passed, I went online. I had your legal name and the county in which you were born. Within fifteen minutes, I'd located your current place of employment."

"Former employment," I corrected without explanation. The man could probably piece together my whole life from what he'd learned on the Internet. Places of employment, changes in addresses. Going-nowhere jobs.

To my surprise, Walker looked embarrassed. "Oh, sorry. I didn't mean to leave you standing. If you'll step into my office, I'll need you to sign a few papers, and then the keys are yours. I'm afraid the only money he left was to cover our fees and for your traveling expenses."

He paused as if expecting me to question him.

I shrugged. I hadn't expected anything, so Walker's news wasn't disappointing. The idea that I had the keys to something I owned, other than my van, was a foreign concept to me.

The lawyer glanced around the empty waiting area as if wishing for clients to appear. "Would you like me to drive you out? I could work it into my schedule."

"No, thanks. I've got a map." Something in the way Walker stared at me gave me the creeps. Mixed signals were bouncing off him. I found myself thinking a little less of Uncle Jefferson for picking him to handle the will. If it's possible to think less of someone you don't know.

Walking to the van a few minutes later, I tried to forget about the lawyer. I had the keys. I could leave his problems in his office. They weren't in my bag of worries.

"Did you notice?" Nana whispered. "That lawyer had wobble eyes."

Laughing, I had to ask, "What are wobble eyes?" Nana thought she could tell anything from a person's eyes and most of the time she was right. She told me once that she had Gypsy blood on her mother's side and Gypsies are all born with a gift for something.

"The lawyer's eyes wobbled between caring and disliking, maybe even hating. I've seen it before a few times in salesmen who used to come around. They'd do their talking; swearing they had one hand on the Bible, but the other would be trying to get into your pocket." She sat back and crossed her arms. "I don't like him."

And that was it, I knew. Nana wouldn't be changing her

mind. "Well," I consoled, "we'll probably never see him
again." Cross my heart, I almost added out loud. "We've got
the keys."

We drove out of Lubbock, Texas, giggling. Keys! I had
keys to my very own place. Some man I never knew, in a
place where I'd never been, had left me a house I never even
knew existed. Maybe he got my name mixed up with someone else. Maybe he met my mother and figured I was over-
due for a break. Maybe he picked me out of the phone book.

It didn't matter. I didn't care. If the place was rundown
and in need of paint, we could fix it up, and what was left of
the five thousand would keep us going until I found a job. I
had half a degree and a ton of experience doing everything
from retail to bookkeeping. I'd find something to keep food
on the table. After all, we already had a roof.

We changed into our comfortable clothes at a truck stop
on the edge of town. I found a county map plastered to the
wall and studied it as I braided my hair. A pinpoint dot
marked the forgotten lake community where my place was
located. The middle of nowhere, I thought.

When I got back to the van, Nana was staring out at the
dry, flat land with an acre of topsoil blowing across our hood.
She whispered, "You sure there's a lake in this county?"

"The man inside said it was about thirty miles from here
in a little canyon. He said he thinks it's an old private community made up of mostly rich folks who want to get out of
the city."

Nana stared at the skyline of Lubbock. "I can see why,"
she said. "I've been through here a few times when I was
young. Nice people, as I remember, but you'd have to have
roots growing out your toes to want to live in this wind."

Before I could leave the city limits, Nana saw a dollar
store and yelled, "Stop."

I pulled into the parking lot without argument. I had long
ago given up trying to understand her fascination with stores
where everything cost a buck, but twenty-seven dollars lighter
we were back in the car with enough snacks to last a week.
Nana still had pioneer blood in her. She believed that wher-

ever we traveled, there might not be food and she needed to be prepared.

Almost an hour later, after two wrong turns, we pulled past a broken-down main entrance to Twisted Creek Community. The gate had been propped up by the side of the road so long ago that morning-glory vines almost covered it. From the entrance, the road wound down into a canyon, twisting between brown sagebrush and foot-high spikes of faded buffalo grass.

"Walker said the road makes a circle, so it really doesn't matter much which way we turn at the gate." I looked for any sign of life. The place reminded me of a forgotten movie set left to decay in the sun and wind. Everything in the canyon seemed to have turned brown with the fall. The monochromatic landscape might have seemed dull to most people, but I found it a grand study in hues. The wonder of a world painted in browns reminded me of the Civil War photographs by George S. Cook. Dark, haunting, and beautiful.

Nana watched as views of the water flashed between the weeds. "Look. I see the creek."

I slowed, noticing a winding, muddy stream of water with reddish-brown banks on either side. At the base of the canyon, the creek pooled into a lake.

"I remember living near a creek when I was a kid." Nana rolled down her window. "We used to carry our laundry down beside it every Monday morning. My momma would have my two brothers build a fire while my sister and I filled the wash pot with water and lye soap so strong I could smell it in my nose until Wednesday. Then, while we all played in the stream, she'd wash the clothes and hang them on branches to dry."

I looked for a mailbox with 6112 on it as I asked the same question I'd asked every time I heard this story. "Why didn't your mother make all you kids help?"

Nana smiled and repeated what she always said, "Your grandmother liked to do laundry."

I didn't correct her that the story was about my great-grandmother. I just nodded knowing she'd confirmed that craziness runs in the women of my family. The men, it appears, just run, for not one of Nana's stories ever mentioned her father.

My grandfather, Nana's Henry, had stayed around. If you can call staying around working from dawn till dusk. Every night he'd stomp in and fall asleep as soon as he ate supper. Same routine every day, seven days a week, until a heart attack took him in the middle of a half-plowed field. He would have hated that.

It seemed strange, but the only memory I have of Henry is him in his recliner with his eyes closed. Maybe that's why he looked so natural at the funeral. Nana always said he was a good man, but I remembered no good, or bad about the man. Except maybe how he liked order in his world. He wanted the same seven meals served at the same time and on the same night of the week. Growing up I always knew what day it was by the smell of supper. I never saw him hit Nana, or kiss her. Their life was vanilla.

"I'm glad we had those days by the creek," Nana interrupted my thoughts. Her short white hair blew in the wind. "With Frank and Charlie dying in the war, they didn't have much time for fun in this life. We used to laugh so hard when we swam that Momma would make us get out and rest. There's no better sleeping than lying in damp clothes on a hot day by the creek. I'd feel so relaxed and lazy I wouldn't even bother to swat at flies buzzing by."

Nana stretched, as if feeling her memory, before continuing, "We were always careful though with Poor Flo. I thought she'd grow out of being frail, but she didn't even live long enough to marry." Nana leaned back in her seat. "She had the flu back when she was little, and it left scars on her heart."

I felt sorry for Poor Flo even though I never met her. She'd been dead over sixty years, and Nana still mourned her. Nana told me once that some memories stick to your soul. I think Flo was like that with my grandmother.

As we moved around the circle of homes and barns huddled close to the water, I noticed how every house looked overgrown with weeds, and all were in need of paint. This may have been where the rich folks lived fifty years ago, but now the neighborhood had fallen on hard times. I saw a few gardens, a few fishing boats, and a few signs of life.

We passed a junkyard of broken down boats and old, rusty butane tanks with worthless cars parked in-between. The mess made me think of those wild salads at fancy restaurants where it looked like they mowed the alley and washed it up to serve.

Nana patted my knee three times as she always did. Three pats for three words she used to say.

She didn't say the words now, she didn't have to.

"I know," I said as the van rattled across a bridge. "I love you too."

Jodi Thomas

TEXAS RAIN

The First Whispering Mountain Novel

Honest, straightforward, and ruggedly handsome, Travis McMurray is also more than a little bit busted, the result of an ambush during his service as a Texas Ranger. Beautiful Rainey Adams is in a fix of her own: On the run from an arranged marriage, she'll do just about anything to keep her freedom. The first time they meet, she steals a kiss—and his horse. The second time, she's an angel of mercy who eases him through a terrible fever…and then disappears.

When Travis recovers, he's determined to track down this intriguing woman and bring her back to the Whispering Mountain Ranch as his bride. But this renegade may be too much for even the toughest Ranger to handle….

LOOK FOR THE NEXT BOOK FROM
NEW YORK TIMES BESTSELLING AUTHOR

Jodi Thomas

TWISTED
CREEK

COMING IN SPRING 2008